CITY OF
LIGHT

CITY OF LIGHT

THE TRAVELER'S GATE TRILOGY | BOOK THREE

WILL WIGHT

HIDDEN GNOME PUBLISHING

*To Dad, who doesn't read fantasy
novels…but he read these.*

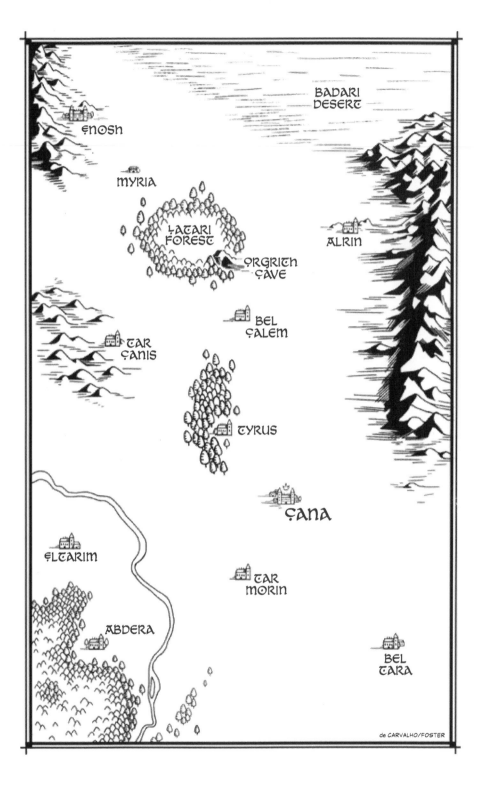

ENOSH

BADARI
DESERT

MYRIA

LATARI
FOREST

ALRIN

ORGRITH
CAVE

BEL
CALEM

TAR
CANIS

TYRUS

CANA

ELTARIM

TAR
MORIN

ABDERA

BEL
TARA

de CARVALHO/FOSTER

CONTENTS

Chapter 1
GATHERING WEAPONS

As the sun sank below the horizon, the Eldest Nye moved from shadow to shadow across the battlefield.

He felt weak, here in the outside world, and he would feel weaker the longer he stayed exposed. Sheltering in the shadows made him feel a little better, a little stronger, a little closer to his powers in the House. He still moved with the stealth and grace that were his birthright—none of the soldiers in red-and-gold caught so much as a glimpse of him as he glided in and around their camp. Or what was left of it. The field had once been an orderly tribute to Damascan military discipline: row upon row of white tents arranged according to some plan that the humans had no doubt thought wise at the time.

The order was broken now. The grass was slick with blood and littered with bodies. The tents lay in ruins, shattered and broken. Some of the camp had shifted, transformed and rearranged by the Valinhall Incarnation's presence: here a barrel whose warped planks had turned into an armchair, there a patch of grass curled into a thin layer of green carpet, over there a pile of firewood grown into a rough-carved table. In the presence of his master, this world strove to imitate Valinhall.

In the Eldest's opinion, it was a huge improvement. Valin should have spent more time here.

The survivors hobbled around, using sheathed swords and broken spears as makeshift crutches, hauling corpses from one place to another. They made a mockery of propriety, and the Eldest couldn't see why they bothered. There were far too many dead to deal with each of them appropriately, so the survivors simply threw them in pits and covered them with dirt.

He approved of their attempts to clean up the mess, but why bury the bodies at all? Why mark the grave? In only a century or two, no one would remember anyone who died here today. A rock with a dead man's name on it would not change that.

There was such a room in Valinhall, meant for honoring the memory of those who had died. His master had placed it there. Even the Wanderer was human, and the Eldest honored his human frailties, even when he didn't understand them.

The Eldest corrected himself: the Wanderer had *once* been human. Then he had become something more.

And now he was something less.

The Nye slid around a patched-up tent, inside of which a young man was grieving over a discarded helmet. His back was to the tent entrance, and the Eldest's hands itched to pull out his chain. This boy had left himself completely defenseless, which was a bad habit that would someday get him killed. Bad habits should be corrected.

But he restrained himself and kept moving, passing through the part of the camp where Travelers had come to blows. Here the devastation was more exotic, but no less total. Human corpses mingled with the inhuman: three-tailed orange lizards with smoke still drifting from their bodies, tall white-furred beast-men lying in inch-deep puddles of chill water, a flock of sparrows lying on top of one another in a bloody pile.

He didn't spare a thought for the violence. He had seen far worse. He had *caused* worse.

The Eldest scanned the carnage, looking for one specific corpse among all the others. After only a few minutes of searching, he found it.

Something that looked like a man lay on a patch of bare grass, naked from the waist up. His skin was almost totally covered in tattoos like black chains. His head was bare, the chains covering him in place of hair.

His blank, staring eyes were black, with circles of silver in their center. Other humans had different colors there, and for some reason found the metallic gleam of these eyes especially disturbing. The Eldest wasn't quite sure why. To him, the eyes were the color of steel and shadows. Beautiful.

Even though this body had taken many wounds when it was alive, only one showed now: a single ragged hole through the left side of the chest. Veins of red spidered out from the stab wound itself, worming their way through the corpse's skin.

The poison of Ragnarus leaves its mark, the Eldest thought. He tried to summon up the old resentment toward Ragnarus, but he felt nothing. It had been a long time since his last encounter with the Crimson Vault, and most of his hatred he had acquired secondhand from Valin.

He had settled his own debts with Ragnarus long ago.

The anger didn't come. Instead, he felt a sort of eagerness for the weapon that had struck this blow. A hunger for something that could make his Territory that much stronger.

The sword lay nearby, unsheathed, its blade blood red and gleaming. No one had looted it, despite its obvious value. Perhaps even humans could sense something of the nature of this body and this weapon, and they wanted nothing to do with it.

No, it was probably something else. In the Eldest's experience, humans were rarely that wise.

The Eldest scooped up the sword, tucking it away inside his robe. Perhaps the humans Caius Agnos and Olissa Agnos could make something useful out of it. If not, well, he could surely find another use for an unbound Ragnarus weapon.

When the blade was secure, the Eldest stood looking down upon his master's body.

"You made promises to me," the Eldest said, in his raspy voice. Here he was, speaking to a corpse, just like an emotional human. But the dead body wasn't his only audience. "You did not keep them. You have given me much, my friend, but in the end, you too failed to uphold our bargain."

He leaned down, letting a bit of his essence flow out like a shaft of light from this world's moon. The shadows grew soft, a rent in the world, and Valin sank down deep, running along his connection to Valinhall like a cart in a rut.

He would arrive soon, and the other Nye would take care of him as he deserved. He had insisted on adding a graveyard to the House of Blades, and now the room would be his new home.

The Eldest straightened, and the only remnant of the Wanderer's presence was a patch of slightly bloody grass.

Simon, son of Kalman, had promised to bring the Ragnarus blade to Valinhall, and technically he had not done so. But he had created the circumstances that allowed the Eldest to retrieve it, so the Nye decided to give the boy some credit. He had great hopes for Simon.

"Do not worry, my old friend. We have another to fulfill our purposes now, and he will not slip away so easily."

The Eldest Nye turned his hood to the second sword lying on the grass: an unusually long weapon, six feet from end to end, its blade slightly curved and sharp along only one edge. A long, smooth line of gold ran up the middle of the blade, beginning at the hilt and ending at its tip.

"Isn't that right, Mithra?"

The Wanderer's blade glimmered in answer.

CHAPTER 2
ARRIVALS AND DEPARTURES

Zakareth left the Crimson Vault to find his palace in ruins. The dungeon beneath the Blue Room, where the Ragnarus Incarnation was once sealed, had been broken from within. He stood on the chips of shattered floor tiles, looking down a ragged hole torn into the earth that had once been a carefully sculpted tunnel. The bottom was covered in a layer of ash and brown, dead branches: the only remnants of Cana's Hanging Tree.

His son Talos lay nearby, face blue and bulging. A bruise wrapped around his throat, as though he had been strangled.

Good. Talos was one of the loose threads that Zakareth had planned to snip. Someone else had done him the favor of removing his son, which meant he could proceed that much faster.

The Ragnarus Gate hung open behind him. He had never intended to close it, but it used to take him a significant effort of will and energy to hold the portal. Now, he sustained it with a thought.

Already, he could see the benefits of Incarnation.

Queen Cynara the First, the original Queen of Damasca, stayed in the Vault, lounging on a black wooden chair she had summoned from somewhere. "This city has grown since my time. There are a lot of raw materials here, if you put them to the right use."

Zakareth glanced at her. Her skin was made of gleaming red steel, her eyes crimson flame, her dress a waterfall of scarlet light. The original Ragnarus Incarnation. "I'm surprised at you, Queen Cynara. Was it not you who said, 'Never ask another to pay a price if you can pay it yourself?'"

Cynara's smile was shining white. "My stay underground has changed my mind on many things. But not my dedication to this country. Your first step will be to secure the city, so that you may have a throne from which to rule."

"If I sit here until Cana is restored, I will rule but one city amid a smoking wasteland." Zakareth met Cynara's burning eyes with his own new set. His glowing red stone, once set into the socket of his left eye, had been replaced by a rolling crimson flame. The vision wasn't at all the same—he couldn't see the connections between Territories, the influence of each Territory imprinted on this world—but in some ways it was better. He could see rivers of crimson flowing in the objects around him, pooling in some things, trickling straight through others.

Without asking, he knew what it was. Power. Potential power, energy, and ability that Ragnarus could harvest and use to fuel its armory of thirsty weapons.

Cynara, lounging on her chair with her legs crossed, kicked one bare foot. "The Incarnations will not destroy everything. Not unless encouraged to do so. When unbound, the Incarnations will act according to their nature. Naraka will judge and punish, Endross will fight, Asphodel will spread and grow and seek the wild energy of emotion. Some of this will result in destruction, but Ornheim, for instance, should simply find the mountains and wait. Lirial will likely find a library and start reading. You see? It's not all wanton death."

Zakareth doubted that his dying citizens would appreciate the distinction. "Many of them will kill, though. You know that better even than I. The death toll will be unspeakable."

"Indeed. Imagine the kind of power that will follow when you pay such a high price."

Zakareth saw nothing wrong with her logic. The higher the price you were willing to pay, the more power you could call. That was how Ragnarus worked.

"Be that as it may," he went on, "you said a first step. What is your plan?"

"What is *yours*, King of Damasca?"

His plan was simple enough, as these things went. He had no reason to complicate matters. "I had intended to reveal myself and take back the throne, then turn my intentions to crushing Enosh."

Cynara nodded along as he spoke. "And how do you think your Overlords will react to an Incarnation on the throne?"

"They will react as I order them to," King Zakareth said. "Or they will be replaced." He spoke with simple honesty. Their job was to govern in his name, not to question his motives.

"What about this new Territory? Valinhall, is it called?"

Zakareth considered that. He wanted Indirial on his side, but if the Overlord of Cana decided that he needed to oppose the Incarnations at all cost...well, Zakareth had little doubt that a team of Valinhall Travelers would be able to bring down an Incarnation. Even the Incarnation of Ragnarus.

"How do you know of Valinhall?" Zakareth asked, struck by a sudden thought. "You were imprisoned during its creation."

Queen Cynara examined her appearance in a mirror she must have called from deeper in the Vault. Reflected red light shone from its surface. "In a prison of my own creation," she reminded him. "The other Incarnations should have experienced something like a restless, painful sleep. Not me. I was awake, I was aware, and I was connected. I can assure you, it is not an experience you wish for yourself."

He believed her.

"Very well," he said. "I will secure the city for now, and then I will rebuild my country."

Cynara laughed, and the Vault rang like a bell along with her. "Do not let the loss of one eye limit your vision. I told you what the Incarnations would do of their own volition.

"Now, imagine what they could do if they were directed."

Zakareth imagined Lirial crystals hanging in the air above every city, giving him access to an unparalleled network of instant information. An army made up of burning Naraka creatures and ferocious flying wyrms from Endross, blasting apart any force in their way. A host of golems tearing down the walls of Enosh.

"I admit, the idea appeals to me," he said. "Enosh would not oppose me long."

Cynara laughed again, more cruelly. "Enosh? Enosh is nothing. You could wipe it from the memory of mortal man with only the power you now possess. Let us focus our attentions on the real threat."

Zakareth stroked his short beard, thinking back on the only Travelers who could match him in combat. "Valinhall," he said.

Queen Cynara waved one red hand airily. "Valinhall is a resource. You can bend it to your own purposes. There is only one opponent that can stand against us now." Her face crumpled like foil into a look of loathing. "Elysia."

The King thought back to his lone encounter with the one remaining Elysian Traveler. The boy did not seem like much of a threat. He would stack Indirial against four of Alin, son of Torin.

Then he remembered what he had done, back in his previous life. The weapon he had given to Alin.

The Seed of the Hanging Tree.

How could I be so foolish? he thought, but he knew the answer. His thoughts had been clouded, uncertain, back when he was no more than a man. Now, for the first time, they were clear.

"Yes," Zakareth said slowly. "We should begin with Elysia."

Cynara rose from her seat, and the black wooden chair vanished into the shadows at the corner of the Vault. "If there is any justice in the universe, let me be there when we tear down the walls of the City of Light."

Intense personal hatred for Elysia, Zakareth noted. He understood her feelings, given Cynara's history—she had lived during a time when the whole continent had almost been destroyed by the last of the Elysian Travelers, and according to legend had given her life fighting an Elysian Incarnation—but he filed the fact away. If the Queen was going to act irrationally based on personal bias, he would have to carefully filter her plans.

Once Alin was dead and the Seed was destroyed, all of Ragnarus' power would be back under his control. He would have no need to destroy the City of Light then. He knew of no other Elysian Travelers, and if it took three hundred years for the next one to show up, so much the better.

How best to defeat the boy, though? Alin would only have to retreat back into his Territory and hide behind his City's walls, and he would be protected. Zakareth did not like his chances of fighting an Elysian Traveler within the City of Light itself.

He would need Travelers who specialized in killing other Travelers. Those whose powers did not fade in foreign Territories, and who could follow the Elysian no matter where he went.

The solution was clear. He needed the House of Blades, whole and behind him. No more could they be allowed to stand fragmented and unsupervised. They had to stand for him, and him alone.

"We have many plans to make," King Zakareth said, and he felt his red eye flare with heat.

"Then let us get started," Queen Cynara responded. She gave him a slow smile. "But first, why don't you try out your new powers? We need to remake Cana in our image, and we wouldn't want to be…interrupted."

She was clearly implying something, but Zakareth didn't understand what. Not at first. Then he cast his mind back, into the part of him that was the Incarnation of Ragnarus, and knowledge flooded his mind like a sunrise. He knew every weapon in the Vault, knew its name and history, knew its price, felt its hunger like his own.

He held one hand out over the dungeon beneath the palace, where Cana's Hanging Tree once stood, and he called upon his Territory.

The Pillar of Sunset rose from the ground, a column of smoldering red and black stone. It rose steadily, foot by foot, rising past the King's hand. He let his fingers trail along the smooth stone as the pillar slid by, its black stone marbled with veins of shining red. Finally it cracked the ceiling, emerging out of the royal palace and towering above the entire city.

From the top of the pillar, a curtain of red light spread like a pool of blood over a glass dome, trickling down until the entire city of Cana was sealed in an inverted bowl of crimson light. No one would be able to walk past the light, not in this world or in any other.

Zakareth had never been taught that this artifact existed. He'd never even heard of it. But now he knew exactly how to activate it, knew precisely what price it would exact from the city's citizens over the coming weeks and months.

But some prices must be paid.

Alin landed on the walls of Enosh in a flare of orange light.

He stood with his back to the sun, golden armor gleaming, and the city buzzed beneath him. Guards on the walls pointed and murmured to one another, some running off to spread the word. The people below, going about their everyday business, pointed to him and dropped what they were doing. Laundry baskets fell unnoticed to the ground, street vendors boarded up their carts, and mothers dragged their children over to stand beneath him at the foot of the wall. They called up to him:

"Welcome back, Eliadel!"

"Where have you been?"

"Give us a speech!"

Alin smiled down on them, welling up with compassion.

These are innocent people, whispered the Rose Light of Elysia. The light was a part of him now, and he could feel its thoughts as easily as his own.

You can teach them, the Silver said. They had never known what their leaders were planning. Their only crime was to trust in the words of those in authority.

But he did not speak to them. He was waiting for someone, and patience was a part of him now. The Green Light approved.

A few in the crowd seemed to notice his eyes. They whispered to one another, hiding their gossip behind cupped hands, and pointing at him as subtly as they could. He knew what they were seeing, but he offered no explanation. His eyes shone with the light of Elysia now, with all its rainbow of colors. The lights would shift, angry red one moment and soft blue-green the next.

He remained silent, waiting. And soon the people grew silent with him.

Patience, the Green Light whispered. *You only need to wait.*

It did not take as long as he had imagined for the Grandmasters to come investigate. Grandmaster Helgard, by reputation and title the most skilled Helgard Traveler in the city, hurried across the courtyard. He was a shaggy bear of a man, with broad shoulders and a brown beard down almost to his chest. As a representative of his Territory, he wore a blue cloak lined with white fur: the standard Helgard uniform.

He marched toward the nearest guard tower as though he meant to walk through it, his shoulders set like he was heading into battle. It would take him a few minutes to climb the stairs of the guard tower all the way up to the top of the walls, where he would want a word with Alin in person.

Alin didn't mind the wait. He silently studied his people, searching their expressions.

In the eyes of many, he saw worship. They thought of him as an idol, as a messenger descended from the heavens. He would have to dissuade them of that. He was not an idol, but an ideal.

However, this group was still the closest to perfection. They would obey him, following his orders without question, and as a result their training would be the lightest and easiest. They had the shortest distance to travel.

On the faces of many others, he saw confusion. They looked upon him while trying to decide what they thought, wondering what he represented, asking themselves what he wanted. This group could be persuaded. He would have to prove himself to them, but he knew that they would see it, given time. He would show them that he was worthy, and that they could be too.

Their road would be hard, but not long. They, too, could find the way.

Then there was the third group: those who wore the uniforms of different Territories. There, an Avernus Traveler in a buckskin dress with feathers adorning her head. And over there, another man in the blue-and-white coat of Helgard. The Travelers had the longest and most difficult path to perfection.

They had been aware of their leaders' goals. They knew what the Grandmasters meant to do. These lesser Travelers were not beyond redemption, but their transformation would be filled with pain.

He turned his smile on them. The Travelers didn't know it now, but they would be better off for the pain.

It will be a long, hard job, the Red Light said. *But it will be worth doing.*

Grandmaster Helgard clapped a hand on Alin's armored shoulder, and Alin realized that he had been watching the crowd for several minutes.

Helgard frowned through his beard. "What is this, Eliadel? What have you done to the wall?"

That was not the first question Alin had expected.

To the wall? He looked at his feet.

Where he stood, the bricks that made up the wall had turned to gold. He was standing in a perfect golden circle, about two feet across, that had once been made of stone.

Your presence as an Incarnation, the Violet Light told him. *You're not human anymore.*

"And where have you been?" Helgard continued, anger creeping into his voice. "There's much work to be done. We can't have you running off at a time like this. No one has seen you or Naraka all day, and some of us are getting worried."

That name acted like a spark on the dry timber of Alin's spirit. His patience evaporated in a cloud of smoke, and he found that one of his gauntleted hands was holding Grandmaster Helgard around the throat.

Fascinating. Did anger still have that much of a hold over him? He would have to work on that.

The man struggled, and yesterday he would have been able to overpower Alin in a purely physical contest. Today, Alin called Red Light from Elysia. Shining ropes of red twisted up his limbs, feeding him strength, and Helgard might as well have tried to wrestle a statue.

The crowd below noticed, and their murmuring swelled to a worried roar.

Alin reached out to his Territory, summoning a creature that he sensed deep within the Silver District. It appeared in midair almost instantly, like a single steel eye hovering on fluttering insect wings. It buzzed around his head, bobbing up and down in excitement.

"My people," Alin began, and the fluttering eye repeated his words at a much louder volume. Alin's voice boomed throughout the streets of Enosh. He would have been surprised if anyone in the city failed to hear him.

"I have discovered a disturbing truth. As many of you know, I have executed the King of Damasca for his crimes against life and humanity."

Somewhere among the people, a cheer was born, but Alin drowned it out. "Imagine my disappointment when I found that your Grandmasters were guilty of even greater crimes."

The remnants of the cheer faded to uneasy silence.

"While the royal line of Damasca has based its three-century reign on the sacrifice of their citizens, they have done so for a cause. They believed that they were protecting the world from a more violent fate. Even if their actions were detestable, their intentions, at least, were pure.

"The Grandmasters of Enosh, by contrast, sought to release that deadly fate upon the world." Alin turned to the thrashing man steadily turning purple in his grip. "Isn't that right, Grandmaster Helgard?"

Alin's hand opened, releasing the Grandmaster. He fell to his knees, coughing and retching, trying to get a full breath.

Alin waited, Green Light whispering patience into his mind.

"What Damasca is doing is an abomination," Helgard finally gasped out. "We were trying to restore the Territories to their natural state." The silver eye carried the man's words to the citizens below.

"By releasing the most powerful monsters in all the Territories onto an unsuspecting world," Alin announced. "By letting the Incarnations slaughter as they please. I have visited the village of Myria, which is now little more than a pile of ashes. When the Naraka Incarnation was released—as a direct result of your actions, Grandmaster—it tore Bel Calem to pieces. Then it moved on to an innocent village."

Grandmaster Helgard looked like he was trying to focus on getting his breath back, more than his next turn to speak. The crowd muttered, confused.

"Who cares?" someone called out. "That's a Damascan village."

"I was born in Myria," Alin said softly. The people fell silent once again. "The people there knew nothing of Damascan royalty or human sacrifice."

Except for Leah, he thought, though the idea didn't inspire the anger it once had. She would have to be held accountable for her dishonesty, but it was nothing to upset him. Not anymore.

Beneath him, the circle of gold had widened. A spot on the wall, about three feet across, had transformed from rough stone to shining gold. Even the texture had changed, smoothing out to a polished gleam.

Like the walls of Elysia.

"Here is my question to you, Grandmaster, to be answered in front of all your people. Why? Why release the Incarnations? What have you to gain from this?"

Grandmaster Helgard had risen to his feet, and there was a dangerous gleam in his eyes. "Why? Because the reign of Ragnarus over all other Territories is unnatural and unjust. Because, despite what they would tell you, Damasca has no divine right to control the Territories. And because the Incarnations will not go wild, as those *royals* claim. They will *join us* in destroying Damasca! Why would they not? We have some of the most powerful Travelers in the world, and we alone oppose those who have imprisoned them for three centuries."

"So," Alin said, and the word echoed through all of Enosh. "You think you can control the Incarnations." He filled one hand with shining golden light. "Why don't we put that to the test?"

In his mind, the Gold Light laughed.

Alin's last words were almost drowned out as the howling wind of Helgard blasted him from empty space. Only a flare of Orange Light kept him from being blown over by the sheer force of the wind, and he was all but blinded by a rush of snow. Something roared over even the wind, and he sensed more than saw a flare of silver behind him.

Alin spun around, hurling Gold Light as he turned.

The light slammed into a white-furred, horned creature almost twice Alin's height. It did nothing more than scorch the beast's fur. The creature drew itself up on its hind legs like a man and growled, reaching one paw out to fill its hand with an icicle longer than Alin's leg.

Grandmaster Helgard knelt behind his Gate, chanting and contorting his fingers into twisted shapes. As he did, his Gate grew wider, as though he were preparing to call something much bigger.

In the back of his mind, Alin reached for the Violet Light of honesty. He summoned sheets of shimmering violet, like fabric made entirely of light, into his hands and cast them like a net toward the huge, furred beast. The light wrapped around the summoned monster like a layer of bandages on a body prepared for burial. The creature roared once more from within its purple wrappings, and then the whole package imploded into a pin-prick of vivid violet.

The Violet Light corrected the balance of the world, banishing any-thing that didn't belong back to its home Territory. It was also, Alin sensed, one of the most difficult to summon. One strip of the paper-thin light would cost him more effort than a dozen orbs of golden force.

At least, it would have yesterday.

Another strip of violet twisted up from the ground like an unspool-ing bandage, wrapping itself around the Grandmaster's Helgard Gate. It shivered for a moment, as though resisting, and then blinked shut.

Grandmaster Helgard staggered back as though he had been slapped, and Alin stepped forward to meet him.

"If you are so weak, how can you protect your citizens?" Alin asked, and the hovering silver eye caught his words and cast them out to the crowd. "I will do a better job protecting Enosh. Protecting my people."

The silence from the crowd lasted a moment longer, and then they burst into applause. With a simple mental effort, Alin banished the silver eye. He didn't need it anymore.

The Grandmaster didn't bother with a rebuttal. He was muttering in his strange language again, making signs with his hands.

Red Light swirled around Alin's arm as he reached out and slapped Helgard's hands apart. "I only have one question for you, Helgard. Where is Grandmaster Naraka?"

Helgard's face filled with stubborn fury. "Is this what you wanted all along? A city to call your own?"

"I have a city," Alin said calmly. "It's much nicer than this one, so I'm thinking about bringing it here. Now, I will ask one more time. Where is Grandmaster Naraka?"

"With *you,* Eliadel. If you don't have her, then I can only be pleased that she escaped. If anyone will be able to flog your rebellious hide, it will be her." Then he spat at Alin's feet.

Such gestures did not bother him now. He simply summoned his sword—its blade formed from interlocking planes of golden light—and ran Helgard through.

There was no road to perfection for this Grandmaster. He had knowingly endangered his people and the world. It was only right that he should suffer the consequences. The Blue Light begged for mercy, the Gold cheered his decisive action, and the Rose asked him to stop. But in this, his mind was made up.

The Grandmasters would have to die.

The golden circle had engulfed most of the wall near Alin, and he thought the gleaming gold looked much better than the irregular, dirty stone. The gold was clean, smooth, and even. He would have to make sure to rebuild the entire wall of Enosh in the image of Elysia.

Alin looked out over the city, and he realized that there was much work to be done before he could oppose the other Incarnations. Months of work, at least. He accepted that fact, letting green patience rule him. He would do as much as he could for this city. As much as needed to be done.

He would start by finding the other Grandmasters and introducing them to their fate.

No matter how long it took.

Simon leaned on the crutch the Nye had made for him, hobbling down the hallway. He wasn't supposed to be out of bed except to use the pool—Olissa's orders—but this was his responsibility.

"Where are you going to go?" he asked.

Ilana stopped at the entry hall. Her hair was bound up behind her, and she carried a pack of supplies on her back. "I'm going after my brother. Somebody has to keep him from making an even worse mess of things."

"Alin's an Incarnation now," Simon said hesitantly. "Are you sure he'll even want to see you?"

She leaned over and ruffled Simon's hair, which she'd done to Alin when he was a little boy. Simon had always thought it looked embarrassing and uncomfortable. Now, he discovered that he was absolutely right.

"I don't understand all this Traveler stuff," she said, hitching her pack up onto one shoulder. "But you don't need to worry about me. I'll figure something out."

This wasn't the first time they'd had this conversation, and Ilana had clearly made up her mind. So, even though the strain felt like it would kill him, Simon called steel. Then he reached up and pulled Azura down from the wall.

After Ilana passed through the Gate and into the outside world, he stood in the entry hall for a few long minutes, thinking. Back in Myria, he'd never known Ilana particularly well, but he found himself wishing she would succeed. He hoped she found Alin and talked him back to sanity.

Because if she failed, and Alin went on a rampage, Simon would have to kill him.

CHAPTER 3
GATES IN THE SNOW

Six months later, Simon gathered his black cloak around him. For once, he was glad of its warmth. The color stuck out even more than usual against the snow, painting him like a single blot of ink on a sheet of parchment. He was higher up in the mountains than he had ever been, nestled in a tiny valley surrounded by rock walls.

The whole scene was covered in three feet of snow—more than Simon had ever seen in one place except through a Helgard Gate. He had seen mountains, where snow would gather on the very tops, and they experienced the occasional flurry in Myria, but the flakes usually melted the moment they hit the ground. Before he left the village, he'd never seen more than wet patches of slush.

He had only imagined an endless white blanket like this. It was even colder than he would have expected.

Oh my, the wind is so violent up here! Gloria exclaimed. Simon pulled the doll out of his coat pocket, partially to look at her, partially to see if she would react to the cold. He wasn't sure if the dolls could or could not sense temperature, but he always savored the opportunity to learn new things about them.

Gloria in particular had a wide smile on her painted wooden face, and her white hair was done up into an ornate bun, tied with fine golden chains. More gold ornaments adorned her fluffy pink dress.

Aren't you cold, sweet one? It has to be freezing in this snow, but you're not saying a word! Like all of Simon's dolls, Gloria's mental voice sounded like it was coming through a long tunnel filled with whispering wind.

I feel like if I open my mouth, my tongue will freeze off, Simon sent.

Don't complain, now. It's unbecoming of a sweet young man like you. No one likes a boy who complains too much.

You asked me! Simon had only taken Gloria because she had irritated him for months about favoring Caela and Otoku over the others. He had only been out here waiting for an hour or two, but he was already regretting his choice. *Please tell me there's a Valinhall power that keeps you warm. I'll go challenge that room right now.*

Hmmmmm, let me think, Gloria sent, in tones of exaggerated thoughtfulness. *The winter garden has an ice dagger that will help you ignore pain and discomfort. I don't think it does quite as much for temperature, though. As a matter of fact, I bet it makes you even colder!*

Simon let Gloria chatter on, because she seemed to be most happy that way. He wished he had taken Caela or Otoku, even if that did mean he played favorites. Not only would they be better company, they both understood Leah better than he did. Maybe they could help him feel better about his role in her plan.

"Stay where I tell you and wait," Leah had told him. She was wearing a fancy red-and-gold dress and her crown, so it was more of an order. "When I need you, I'll give you a signal."

"What signal?" he had asked, in the foolish and naïve hope that someone would, for once, explain a plan before requiring him to follow it.

"I assure you, you won't miss it," she'd said, and then practically shoved him through a Gate. And now he had been standing around in the cold for the better part of two hours. He had come here to fight an Incarnation, not freeze his toes off when his boots soaked through.

Gloria was still babbling, and Simon began to wonder if the dolls could run out of breath when they didn't have any lungs. *...and you know about the white flame, though that's more the illusion of warmth than real heat. It burns poisons out, but you know that, it's not intended for comfort, and look out!*

Simon almost didn't hear the warning buried in Gloria's chatter, but a shadow loomed over him and he hurled himself to the right. As he collapsed into a snowdrift, he called steel.

His muscles chilled and tightened, as though they had been banded with ice-cold metal. Chains crawled up his arms, beginning with one black link on the backs of his hands and snaking slowly up his wrists. They looked like ink, but they felt like rough iron on his skin.

All in all, the sensations did nothing to make him more comfortable. The shadow swelled for a moment before something huge and white slammed into the spot where he had been standing, sending puffs of snow blasting into the air. The sound echoed off the nearby rocks in an endless crash.

Before Simon could get a good look at the thing that had just landed—it looked like a ball of dirty white fur embedded in the snow—a shining crystal came rocketing through the sky, flashing like a shooting star. It was a chunk of grey-white stone about the size of his fist, and it flew at him as though it were going to slam into his teeth.

It finally settled into an orbit around his head, shouting at him in Leah's voice.

"Simon!" Leah called, through the Lirial crystal. "There's something headed your way."

"You're a little late," Simon responded. He held his hand out to the side and summoned Azura. The sword shimmered as it vanished from its rack in Valinhall and appeared in his hand, seven feet of mirror-bright and slightly curving metal.

Without the power of steel running through him, he would have a hard time lifting the sword, much less using it in combat. With the strength of Valinhall, though, he flicked the blade through the air like a switch.

The white-furred creature rose from the crater it had driven into the snow, unfolding into its full ten feet of height. It looked almost like one of the *mirka*, humanoid monsters from Helgard that Leah had told him to expect, with its thick, shaggy pelt and curling goat horns on the top of its head. But as it shook snow from its fur and turned to snarl at Simon, he got a better look.

Its back was swollen into a hump, as though it were concealing a turtle shell beneath its hide. It lurched forward on all its limbs...of which it had six, not the *mirka's* four. Its extra set of arms nested underneath the top set, and it seemed to use them for balance, pushing against the walls of the small canyon. Instead of summoning a jagged spear of ice into its hand, as Leah had told him to anticipate from a *mirka*, this thing lunged toward him on all six limbs, jaws snapping like a wolf's.

Simon inhaled, calling upon the Nye essence as he did. He felt the familiar chill in his lungs—which was not much of a comfort when he was actually breathing freezing air—and the world slowed to cool honey. Clouds of snow hung above the ground, still settling from where the whatever-it-was made impact. Wind slowly ruffled the creature's fur.

Gloria made a disgusted noise. *That thing is absolutely hideous! Why can't you Travelers call something lovely from your Territories, for once?*

I called you, didn't I? Predictably, that sent Gloria into a few seconds of flattered murmurs and false humility.

Simon tried to adjust his stance, twisting to the side and bringing Azura forward in the hopes that the monster would impale itself on its own momentum, but his feet wouldn't budge. It took him a few seconds of struggling before he figured out why: his feet were encased in ice.

Didn't I tell you? That monster froze your feet to the ground. I imagine it likes to lock its prey down. How horrible!

Simon drew a bit more steel and kicked his way free of the ice, but even the agility of the Nye couldn't redeem his graceless stumble as he finally came free. He had to stagger forward, almost planting his nose into the snow, to avoid the creature's final rush.

"What is this thing?" Simon called, as the beast caught itself with its upper four arms against the canyon's far wall.

"I'm not a Helgard Traveler, Simon," Leah said, her voice stressed. "Take care of it. Quickly. You might have much worse incoming. Give me a—"

Leah cut off when something streaked through the air, shattering the crystal into a puff of shining dust.

"Lirial," a woman's voice said in disgust. "They always think of themselves as preserving knowledge, but where are the libraries in Lirial? The Daniri didn't leave any of *those* behind, did they? Nothing but dusty crystals. Helgard, by contrast, has a library on every other floor. If you lived to be as old as I am, you still wouldn't have the time to read all the books in the Tower."

While keeping his sword pointed at the snarling monster against the canyon wall, Simon spared a quick glance for the speaking woman. She stood above him, looking down on the shallow valley in which he stood.

She had a pair of tightly curling ram's horns on the sides of her head, just above her ears. She looked only a few years older than Simon, but the curly hair that ran down her back was pure white. She wore a suit of long white fur, and where her skin showed through, it was a pale blue, like early morning sky. Strangest were her eyes, which ran through all the glacial colors, from ice-white at the center, to a shifting gradient of green, purple, and blue at the edges.

Simon had met too many Incarnations by now not to recognize this one. He tightened his grip on the Nye essence, ready to call more at once.

"I am Helgard," the woman said simply. Around her, the snow on the ground rose and drifted in a soft, powdery veil. "What is your name?"

Under ordinary circumstances, Simon would have attacked by now. People let their guards down while they were speaking, even Incarnations. But he had allies to consider, so his mission was to buy time.

He would have rather attacked.

"Simon, son of Kalman," he answered. "I don't mean to offend, but you seem different than the other Incarnations I've met."

She sniffed dismissively. "I should hope so."

"You're a lot more...chatty than Endross was."

He had wondered if she would take that as an insult, but she didn't seem bothered. "Endross is an unsophisticated beast. Like sha'da'narile, there. Good for nothing but pointing at a target and setting loose."

Simon hoped he wasn't supposed to remember the creature's name.

"And you're not?" Simon asked. He had been instructed quite clearly to keep the Incarnation engaged for as long as he could, if he was unlucky enough to stumble across its path. The longer he could do that without fighting, the better, and he hadn't met an Incarnation this willing to talk since Valin.

The Helgard Incarnation held a clawed hand to her chest as though he had wounded her. "I? I am the most refined, erudite, and articulate being that you are ever likely to meet. Incarnation did not change that much about me."

It's a good thing she didn't say 'humble,' Gloria sent.

The Incarnation's eyes shifted, becoming even colder. "You, however, have much in common with Endross."

"Do I?" Simon tried to keep one eye on the hunchback creature, but it didn't seem to be doing anything other than making threatening noises, and the Incarnation was by far the greater threat. Even though she was chatting pleasantly enough.

She chuckled. "You're a Valinhall, aren't you? I've learned much about your kind since I was released. A Territory that exists only to kill other Travelers."

"I haven't seen Helgard Travelers do much else but fight."

"Ah, but where have you met them, except on the battlefield?" She waved a hand through the air. "Nonetheless, I digress. I'm going to have to insist that you come with me."

That wasn't in the plan. "Where would we go?" Simon asked warily. He still had to buy time.

The Incarnation smiled, revealing pointed teeth. "You have my word, I would not harm you. I was instructed to retrieve a Valinhall Traveler, and at last I have found you. Will you come with me peacefully, or must I resort to the barbaric approach?"

The six-armed monster snarled next to him, and Simon recognized that his diplomatic strategy had failed.

Come to think of it, when have I ever managed to talk an enemy down?

Rebekkah tells me that your foray into Endross was quite successful, Gloria sent. *You didn't even have to kill anyone, did you?*

I doubt it's going to work out that well this time, Simon said. He turned on the balls of his feet, sweeping Azura up and around, slicing a line through the snow. He happened to pass through the hunchback creature's neck on the way.

Sky-blue blood splattered the snow like paint as the summoned beast fell into two pieces.

The Incarnation's eyes closed, and a look of grief crossed her face. She whispered a word, too quietly for Simon to hear over the wind. Then a snout, like that of a blue-skinned, hairless bear, peaked over the canyon wall beside her. It growled softly down at Simon. Beside the bear stood a four-eyed goat, and then something like a long, white-furred snake with a head like a dog's. A whole menagerie of creatures crawled, slithered, and ran to join their Incarnation, looking down at Simon as though at the last scrap of food in the bottom of the bucket.

The Helgard Incarnation walked from one animal to another, placing her hand on their pelts and speaking a single word to each of them. It took Simon a moment to realize that she was naming each individual, one by one. When she finished, she turned from the crowd of impatient beasts to regard Simon once again with her glacial eyes.

"I would like a chance to know you better, Simon, son of Kalman." She waved a hand forward, looking to her summoned army. "Retrieve him."

A blue hand burst from the snow at Simon's feet, big enough to grab a horse around the middle. Gloria shouted a warning, and only the Nye essence kept Simon from being seized. He leapt to one side, catching himself against the canyon wall.

A giant hauled itself from the snow, its skin as blue as a drowned body. It was at least ten feet tall, and Simon didn't see how it could have concealed itself in such a thin layer of snow. It must have come through a Helgard Gate somehow, though he wasn't sure if it was possible to open a Gate that way. Incarnations seemed to be the exceptions to all sorts of rules.

Simon was lifting his blade to confront the giant when the furred snake crept up to his side. It didn't slither, but instead ran on fifty pairs of dog's legs. It sank its teeth into his leg, sending pain shooting up past his hip. He smacked Azura's hilt into the monster's skull, making it release its jaws, but the pain had made his leg all but useless.

Above you! Gloria called, and Simon swung Azura up in an arc, meeting the giant's blue hand in midair.

He expected the blade to slice straight through the summoned creature's flesh, as it normally did, his imagination providing the image of thick fingers scattered across the snow. But Azura hit the first finger, drew dark blue blood, and stopped as soon as it hit bone.

The giant had a face like a nightmare, with a huge nose, black eyes, and a disproportionately wide mouth filled with needle-sharp teeth. Its forehead wrinkled and it howled in pain, thrashing out at Simon. Shards of ice whirled in the air, seemingly called by the creature's pain. They flew around the giant, drifting on the wind, drawing a dozen tiny cuts on Simon's skin. The cloak stopped many of the shards from penetrating, but it was still like being pelted with handfuls of broken glass.

Worse, the pain in his leg had not yet subsided. It seemed to be getting worse, burning more than it should, and Simon was starting to feel light-headed. Surely he hadn't lost that much blood.

Oh, dear, Gloria sent. *It seems that long dog was venomous. What do you know? I wouldn't have expected it, that's for sure.*

It's poisonous?

Venomous, dear, let's try to be correct. You didn't eat it, after all.

Simon cast his mind out to the Valinhall forge, which he had first conquered long ago. He had returned to challenge the room's new guardian only a few weeks before, since his first visit hadn't left him with a new power.

His second visit had gone much better.

A single white candle-flame filled Simon's mind, flooding his body with a clean, pleasant heat. The warmth focused on his wound, growing uncomfortably hot, burning the bitten area almost like a brand pressed against his leg. Then, all at once, the heat vanished. Simon tested his leg and found that, while it was still painful, he could at least stand. More importantly, the lightness in his head had subsided.

The Helgard Incarnation noticed that something had happened. She smiled slightly. "Give in, son of Kalman. Let yourself slide into sleep. No harm will come to you now."

She expected the poison to be enough for him. *Maker knows, if you hadn't noticed it, she probably would have gotten me.*

No need to thank me, Gloria responded, her mental voice bursting with pride. *That's what I'm here for.*

Simon pulled as much steel and essence as he could and kicked off with his good leg. He hurtled toward the giant's head, leading with Azura's point, and buried his sword into the enormous eye socket. The Dragon's Fang scraped on the back of the creature's skull without penetrating, but the giant's body spasmed and started to fall. Within the world of the Nye essence, it seemed as though the monster was drifting underwater.

When they hit the ground, the Incarnation was waiting for him.

She was surrounded by her snarling, white-furred guardians, so Simon first swept Azura in a single swipe from left to right. He left a few heads and limbs tumbling to the ground, along with a bucketful of blue blood. Most of the monsters were still standing, but Simon hadn't intended to kill them all. He only meant to distract them.

He dashed through while the animals still reacted to the pain, bringing Azura down in a two-handed strike aimed at the top of the Incarnation's head, in between her curling horns.

The edge of the Dragon's Fang met a surface of solid ice.

A bar of black ice, thick as a tree trunk, hovered over the Incarnation's head. She didn't seem surprised, or startled, or afraid. She simply watched him from the other end of his sword, her icy eyes calculating.

Simon pulled Azura back, elbowing the barking blue-skinned bear when it tried to rush him from behind. His steel-fueled strike sent the beast stumbling awkwardly backwards on all fours.

The first time Simon had met an Incarnation—Valin, the creator of Valinhall—he had only held two useful powers: Nye essence and Benson's steel. While those were still the most useful weapons in his arsenal, he had wished for more at the time. Once the Hanging Trees had failed and the other Incarnations were released one by one, he had been faced by a simple truth: he was not prepared.

He had spent most of the next two seasons in Valinhall, emerging only when Leah called him to help with one mission or another. As a result, the past six months had given him, from his perspective, more than a year's worth of experience.

He had used that year well.

Simon reached out to the armory, where every weapon except the thirteen Dragon's Fangs were kept. In his mind, he focused on the ornate bronze key, which had been his reward from the room after he had finally solved its puzzles.

As he called the power of the key, the Valinhall armory opened its doors.

Simon swung Azura one-handed at the Incarnation's side. As expected, the length of dark ice whirled in the air, spinning itself around to intercept the Dragon's Fang. His blade's edge bit into the frozen surface.

In the same instant, Simon brought his left hand forward, a spear in his fist. He had initially tried to use a second sword in his left hand, but the Dragon's Fang was so long that it made wielding any other weapon difficult. A spear was one of the few weapons that Simon could use at the same distance as Azura.

The spearhead sliced through the Incarnation's pale-furred chest, driving into her ribs. The blade scraped on bone, and dark blue blood oozed down the front of her stomach.

Simon pulled his spear out and hopped back, landing on his good leg. He was forced to use Azura like a club, knocking enraged Helgard creatures away as they tried desperately to reach the one who had wounded their Incarnation. He hurled the spear as an albino wolf-man tried to charge him. The weapon pierced the creature's belly and sent it tumbling to the ground.

He turned, clutching Azura in both hands, to keep the Incarnation in view.

The wound would have been fatal in a human: there was a ragged hole torn in her chest, its edges dark and weeping. But Helgard didn't act injured. She hardly seemed to notice that he had stabbed her. She simply stood staring at him, puzzled.

When she spoke, there was blue blood in her mouth, staining her teeth, but her words were perfectly clear. "Who are you, Simon, son of Kalman? What do you feel? Why do you fight? Where do you come from? Your leg must pain you. It should be agonizing. What keeps you standing on it? Tell me *everything*."

Leah hadn't mentioned this when she briefed him on the nature of Helgard. She had emphasized the ice and wind and the vicious creatures native to the Territory, but she hadn't talked about how curious the Incarnation would be.

"Why do you care?" Simon asked, because he was supposed to stall for time. He had hoped that he would be able to stall by inflicting a crippling injury on the Incarnation, but that seemed out of the question. Now he was back to talking.

The black bar of ice hung over the Incarnation's head like a doorframe.

Helgard's icy eyes flashed with an internal blue-green light. "I want to know who you are. When I understand you, I will save that information. I will savor it. Even when you are long dead, Helgard will remember, and to me, you will live on."

"Why don't we sit down and talk about it?" Simon suggested.

The Incarnation remained motionless, but the black bar of ice spun over her head like a staff in invisible hands. "I know you have allies here, and you clearly want to wait for them. I do not blame you, but that would be an unforgiveable delay. Step into my Territory, and we can talk for years. After your purpose has been served."

"What purpose?" Simon asked, keeping a wary eye on the Helgard creatures surrounding him.

Below you! Gloria called desperately, and Simon jumped.

Not high enough. Normally he would have been able to clear ten feet from a flat jump, with Benson's steel flowing through him, but he made the mistake of pushing off from the ground on his injured leg. He made it three feet into the air before a column of solid ice reached up from the snow beneath his feet and snagged him around the ankles.

Simon struck at the ice with Azura, but more flowed up, steadily covering his hips, his ribs. The cold seeped into him, sharp and biting, leaving a complete absence of feeling behind.

"You were fighting my partners before," the Helgard Incarnation said, gesturing to the pack of white, furry creatures around her. "You have not faced me yet."

Simon raised one arm to try and throw Azura at her, as a last-ditch effort, but the ice grew to cover his right arm.

It did not, however, cover his left. He was able to slip that hand into his cloak, searching through the internal pocket. His fingers, trembling from the cold, brushed past Gloria's soft hair until they finally found something broad, smooth, and flat.

The object felt like a shallow, metal bowl, almost as cold as the ice now surrounding him. With an unsteady hand, he managed to pull it out.

It was a mask.

The left half of the mask was made of rough, black iron, and the right half of mirror-bright Tartarus steel. The two halves were joined in the middle by a jagged line where the two pieces had been welded together by Caius and Olissa Agnos. The eye slits were simple lines that didn't seem wide enough to offer a full range of vision, and there was no hole for the mouth. Nor were there any straps or clasps to hold the mask onto the wearer's head, though Simon knew from experience that the mask would bind itself to him even without any visible means of support.

He fumbled with cold, clumsy hands at the mask, trying to press it onto his face. Even confronted with imminent capture by an Incarnation, Simon couldn't ignore his fear. The last time he had used this mask, he had almost Incarnated himself. Even after using it successfully, once he had removed it, he had collapsed. It had taken him a full day to be able to walk again, and over a week until he could call any powers from Valinhall safely.

He had promised himself that he wouldn't use this mask unless he absolutely had to. But surely this counted as an emergency, didn't it?

Gloria gasped in Simon's head. *Simon! Put that back!*

You want me to let the Incarnation take me? Simon snapped. Why wouldn't his fingers work? His left elbow was frozen, and he strained his neck trying to push his face against the back of the mask.

It would be better if you died, Gloria said quietly.

Better for who? Simon wondered, but he stopped grasping at the mask. In theory, he would choose death over Incarnation. At least if he died, he wouldn't hurt anyone else.

But that was much harder to remember when it looked like he would soon freeze to death. Or, if Helgard lived up to her promise, he would die as a captive to a mad Incarnation. He would rather end his life here, in battle.

The Helgard Incarnation ran a hand over one of her horns, watching him. A patch of cloudy ice had formed over her wound, and Simon could see hints of her blood within. "Don't worry so much," she said softly. "I'll take care of everything."

A black form streaked over the snow behind her, like a flash of dark lightning, and Simon's icy prison shattered.

It's about time, Gloria complained. *You have no idea the trouble I went through trying to keep him from doing something crazy.*

"Sorry," Indirial said out loud. He pushed back his hood and flashed Simon a bright grin. "Looks like I made it in time."

Simon was barely able to move through the cold. His body seemed to do nothing but shiver, no matter what he wanted. Still, he managed to give Indirial a weak smile.

The Helgard Incarnation didn't look shocked; she raised white eyebrows curiously. "I didn't feel you. Why is that?"

Indirial turned his smile on her, raising his hood. He let out one breath that shimmered with the colors of the moon.

Nye essence.

He seemed to vanish, then he was standing behind the Incarnation, raising his sword—Vasha, a Dragon's Fang almost as long as Azura, but chipped and cracked along the entire blade, as though he had slammed the sword repeatedly against the side of a mountain. He brought it down against the side of her blue-skinned neck.

The blade met black ice. Helgard glanced from side to side in evident confusion before spinning around to look Indirial in the eye. "Remarkable," she breathed. "I didn't feel you there at all."

"Amazing, isn't it? And I look great in black, too."

Helgard cocked her head, confused, but Indirial didn't explain. He just reversed Vasha so that the blade pointed behind his back. The Overlord thrust backwards, impaling the serpentine dog that had tried to rush him while he was distracted. The creature swallowed cracked steel and choked on its own blue blood.

Simon pulled his own hood up, still shivering from the cold, and called Nye essence again. He was running out, but he had enough to help him escape.

The Incarnation turned to Simon, and her icy eyes widened. "Where did he go?"

This was a trick Simon had learned from Indirial, and it had certainly come in handy through a whole autumn and winter hunting Incarnations. While you wore a Nye cloak and called their essence, you were all but invisible to all supernatural detection. Leah couldn't stand it—she couldn't monitor his and Indirial's status while they were fighting in their cloaks, because she could only catch glimpses of them through her Lirial lens.

The power had several drawbacks. Travelers could see them with their eyes, and the cloaks only activated when the hood was up. Simon pre-ferred to fight without wearing the hood, because it had a tendency to flop down and cover his eyes. He had learned to deal with it for the sake of partial invisibility, but it still irritated him. How were you supposed to fight with a black cloth falling down and cutting off your vision every thirty seconds?

When the Nye essence wore out, he would be perfectly visible again, but until then Simon had a few moments. One of the things they had learned, that even Indirial hadn't known, was that the cloaks gave Incarna-tions no end of trouble. The Incarnation would be almost blind to their movements. As long as the essence lasted.

Simon rolled out of the way and watched Indirial fight the Helgard Incarnation while he waited for the feeling to come back into his limbs.

Vasha struck at Helgard's side, then when that was blocked by her floating black ice, Indirial used the opportunity to step in closer, sweeping a leg underneath the Incarnation's. A blast of snowy wind literally picked Indirial up and tossed him backwards, but he twisted in midair and caught himself against the canyon wall with his feet, leaping back down at Helgard, his Dragon's Fang clutched in both hands.

The silver blade flashed again, and a chip of ice flew into the air.

You poor thing, Gloria murmured sympathetically. *You don't need to worry. Indirial will take care of her, so you lie back and rest.*

That was all Simon needed to climb back to his feet. There was no way he would lie back and let Indirial do all the work.

His left leg still felt like it was being stabbed, his skin stung all over from contact with the ice, and he couldn't seem to stop shivering. More importantly, his Nye essence was fading: he could only see Indirial's movements as a blur, as he tried to slip a thrust or slash past the Incarnation's whirling frozen bar.

But he had a few seconds left, and he intended to use them.

Indirial landed in a crouch, his blade falling down at the Incarnation's head. It sunk into the ice and stuck there for an instant.

Simon had managed to make it a few feet closer to Helgard, but for once he was glad of Azura's awkward length. He summoned it into his hand, lunging on his good leg and stabbing straight into the Incarnation's unguarded back.

The black bar swung behind her, knocking Azura away, but not before he managed to score a blue slice across Helgard's skin.

The snow erupted underneath him, tossing him backwards, but he had enough Nye grace left to land on his feet and catch a glimpse of Indirial throwing a summoned hatchet and hitting Helgard in the shoulder.

Three whirling razors, like snowflakes the size of wagon wheels, buzzed out of nowhere and converged on Indirial. He slipped underneath them, and they flew past one another, each skirting the other by mere inches.

Helgard gestured, and snow fell by the ton toward Indirial. At the same time, another blue-skinned bear roared and sprung at Simon, and it was all he could do to hold it off with his steel-enhanced strength. Azura fell to the snow.

Then a second blue bear crashed into the first. Both of them roared, slashing one another with their claws and rolling around in the snow. The air seemed to grow even colder as they scratched and cut and bit with animal ferocity.

Simon looked up to see Leah, in a crimson coat and the long red dress she always wore when she was acting as Queen of Damasca, directing half a dozen Travelers in the white-and-blue coats of Helgard. They twisted their fingers into nimble shapes, muttering inaudibly as they opposed the will of their Territory's Incarnation.

Leah looked down at Simon, her dark hair caught up in a red, fur-lined hood. Her blue eyes were sharp. She mouthed something to him, and Gloria translated.

She says, 'Get on with it,' the doll related. She chuckled. *Oh, she is cheeky. What a wonderful young lady.*

Simon scanned the white landscape, looking for Indirial. It had looked like he was on the verge of getting buried by a summoned avalanche, but if anyone could have escaped, it was the Overlord of Cana.

And there he was, his hood up, bursting out of the snow with Vasha flashing against the Incarnation's bar of dark ice.

The Helgard Incarnation didn't seem like she was inclined to pay attention, though. A shadow crossed her face as she saw Leah. "Ragnarus," she said, her voice grating audibly. The wind howled, and the snow seemed to shift and hiss around Simon in tune with the Incarnation's anger. "This is not the opportunity I had hoped." She turned back to Simon. "We will speak again, Simon, son of Kalman."

Then something appeared in her hand. It looked like a sheet of paper, as though someone had torn a single page out of a book and written a single character on it in bright red ink. She pressed the paper against the air, where it stuck as if it had been glued to a wall. The Helgard Incarnation tore open a Gate in a flash of swirling red light.

Helgard didn't look like Simon had imagined. He would have expected more ice.

The Gate opened onto a rough-hewn cavern dominated by silver doors, carved with an ornately detailed portrait of a one-eyed, bearded old man. On the rock walls around the doors, a pair of torches burned an unnatural crimson.

He had seen a few glimpses of Helgard, but only the parts most occupied by Damasca. Supposedly there were dozens of floors in the Tower of Winter that Simon had never seen, but he couldn't imagine this place among them. Then again, if it wasn't Helgard, where else could it be? There was no way a Helgard Incarnation could open a Gate to another Territory.

The Incarnation reached up and grabbed the end of the dark, frozen bar in one hand, plucking it out of the air. She swung it like a club, striking with supernatural speed and strength against Indirial's blade. The Overlord caught the blow with both hands, but the force still knocked him a few paces backwards.

Helgard stepped through the red-lined circular portal, turning to watch Simon as the Gate closed around her.

"Don't let her leave!" Leah shouted, loud enough to be heard over the wind and the sounds of battle. The Helgard Travelers cast giant, razor-sharp snowflakes, clusters of snow, and summoned beasts at the portal. Leah held both hands out as if she were straining, but the Gate didn't slow as far as Simon could tell. In seconds, it imploded into a brief flash of red light.

"Did she trap herself?" Simon called.

Leah shook her head, eyes burning with anger.

"That wasn't Helgard," Indirial said. Somehow, during the fight, he had found the time to push his shirtsleeves up past his elbows, baring forearms marked with shadowy chains.

Simon didn't bother asking which Territory it had been. They would tell him eventually. He looked up to Leah.

After a moment, she reluctantly spoke. "Ragnarus," she said. "That was the door to the Crimson Vault."

Gloria sighed. *Oh, dear.*

CHAPTER 4
A DEAD MAN
IN THE GRAVEYARD

When Leah tried to tear the Ragnarus Gate back open, nothing happened.

It shocked her, at first. A shiver passed through her that had nothing to do with the sharp wind or the ankle-deep snow. Opening the Crimson Vault was her birthright, guaranteed by her blood, the proof of her connection to her ancestors…and now she couldn't forge a Gate to her own Territory. Had the power abandoned her?

She summoned and banished the Lightning Spear three or four times before she was satisfied that she could still count on herself as a Traveler of Ragnarus. But now, a more troubling problem remained.

Indirial's left hand was covered by the Valinhall gatecrawler: a spiked black gauntlet. He'd grabbed the spot where the Gate had vanished, trying to tear it open, but red light flared and he couldn't get a grip.

They tried for almost an hour before they returned through Helgard to their camp, only a mile or so outside the shining red city of Cana. The others had all left her—the Helgard Travelers to their assignments, Indirial to his work, and Simon to the House—abandoning her to consider the most troubling question of all.

Who had let the Helgard Incarnation into Ragnarus?

She was one of the few people alive who could open a Ragnarus Gate at all. Only she and her two sisters—one insane, the other imprisoned in Lirial—could enter the Crimson Vault, according to Queen Cynara's ancient pact. So how had the Helgard Incarnation done it?

Leah could come up with a few theories. Helgard collected and stored information, and it wasn't beyond reason that the Incarnation of that Territory would have been able to find an old artifact of Ragnarus, pay its price, and figure out how to activate it. Several Ragnarus weapons had been lost over the years, and it was entirely possible that one of them had the ability to open the Vault. It could be that simple.

Less likely, there was the possibility that the Helgard Incarnation was some ancestor of Leah's. Perhaps she had inherited the right to enter

Ragnarus like every member of the Damascan royal family. That was an uncomfortable idea for several reasons, and Leah couldn't bring herself to believe it. For one thing, she doubted that the transformation process left much human inside the Incarnations. Would she still be able to open a Gate to Ragnarus after becoming the embodiment of a different Territory? Leah wasn't sure, but she didn't think so.

That left the final possibility, the most likely, and the one that Leah least wanted to consider.

Another Ragnarus Traveler had let the Incarnation in.

For the past six months, the Damascan capital of Cana had been sealed within a barrier of crimson power. All travel in and out, both physically and via Territory, had completely halted. If Helgard and Ragnarus were working together now, that was bad enough—two Incarnations united would be almost impossible to defeat in open battle. And if there was an ordinary Ragnarus Traveler involved...

Leah leaned an elbow against her desk, which wobbled and almost pitched over, and rested her head in her hand. They had returned to camp via Helgard after their battle with the Incarnation, then Simon and Indirial had gone back to their House to heal up. Leah had been forced to explain to Overlord Yaleina that the mission to stop the Helgard Incarnation had been a failure. She had even endured a lecture from the Overlord on the dangers of Helgard. An Overlord, lecturing a royal! The reigning Queen, no less!

That confrontation had done nothing to add to Leah's mood, though she was most disturbed by the implications of an Incarnation entering Ragnarus. It brought to mind suspicions that she had pushed to the back of her mind for months.

On a whim, Leah tore open a Gate to Ragnarus there in her tent. The red-edged portal swirled open, a circular entry to the cave outside the Vault itself. One edge of the portal brushed against her camp cot, and the top scraped the tent fabric overhead, but she had enough space to make it work.

She surveyed the familiar sights: the silver double doors carved with the one-eyed king, the two crimson torches to either side. If she wanted to enter, she would have to press a drop of her blood against the doors, but she left the Vault shut. She couldn't even bring herself to walk through the Gate.

A vague sensation had bothered her for two seasons, ever since her father's death. She couldn't quite pin it down, but something had changed in Ragnarus. Leah held a Traveler's bond with two different Territories—the Crystal Fields of Lirial and Ragnarus, the Crimson Vault—and their powers felt very different from one another. Drawing on Lirial felt dusty and cool, like a draft of air blowing from a crypt or a library. Ragnarus, on the other hand, was warm and hungry, as though it begged to be used.

Seizing Ragnarus for the past six months had felt like clenching a fist around a still-beating heart. It throbbed and moved, as though the entire Territory was dancing to a will other than hers. More tangibly, something was wrong in the Territory itself, physically. She had never seen a living creature native to Ragnarus, but she could hear them often. In the cavern behind her Gate, outside the silver doors of the Vault, one could always hear the sounds: shuffling, hissing, distant growling, occasionally even screams.

Now? Perfect silence. The one-eyed old man stared at her from his silver doors, and Leah thought she saw the beginnings of a smirk on his frozen lips.

She had never been comfortable here, but this Territory was *hers*, in a personal way that Lirial couldn't match. She was one of only a few others who had ever been able to Travel here, and she would never have to worry about being interrupted by someone outside her family. Now, Leah didn't even walk inside. She was too afraid to open the doors. Nothing had ever happened to her in there—she never saw anything unusual—but she sensed something. A quiet amusement, as though the Crimson Vault was laughing at her.

And now the Helgard Incarnation had escaped into Ragnarus. That suggested that matters were about to get worse. Worse even than six months of hunting down Incarnations that had killed thousands of her people.

Leah closed her eyes and pressed her hand harder against her forehead. She felt another headache coming on.

"Knock knock," a woman's voice came from the tent entrance.

Seven stones, there's my headache now, Leah thought. *Right on time.*

She opened her eyes and summoned a polite smile. "Overlord Feiora, I apologize. I was lost in thought. Please, come in."

Overlord Feiora Torannus was a strong-looking woman with a heavy jaw, very short hair, and piercing dark eyes. She walked into the tent as though she meant to fight someone within, and sat in one of Leah's folding camp chairs as though it had personally offended her and she meant to crush it in retaliation.

Feiora didn't wear the typical buckskin and feathers of her Territory. Leah had never seen her do so. Instead, she wore black pants and shirt, plain and unadorned, with a single bronze-and-pearl pin on her breast to mark her as an Avernus Traveler. Unlike her brother, Lysander, she rarely spent time with other Avernus Travelers. However, that didn't mean she had broken all ties to her Territory: a large raven perched on her shoulder. It made no noise, staring Leah straight in the eyes and remaining completely silent.

Feiora found Travelers too unpredictable to make valuable allies. She preferred to cultivate contacts among the royal family, other Overlords, and influential citizens. As a result, she was well-liked in certain circles high up in Damascan society. Circles that Leah could not afford to offend.

Therefore, Leah had no choice but to maintain her alliance with this woman, no matter how much she would rather appoint someone else as an Overlord of Eltarim. The position was typically taken by an Endross Traveler, anyway; Feiora had won the seat through her political connections and sheer determination. No matter Leah's personal feelings about her, Overlord Feiora was an impressive woman. And Leah had sealed her little brother in a coffin of Lirial crystal.

Leah regretted that more and more each day. She should have killed the man.

"I hear the mission to neutralize the Helgard Incarnation was a dismal failure," Feiora said, her tone polite, and her words anything but.

"I wouldn't say that," Leah said casually, as though she had overlooked Feiora's complete lack of respect. And basic manners. "We retrieved some critical information, and the Helgard Incarnation is certainly not in play, at least for a short time. We have a reprieve."

Feiora's eyebrows raised. "A reprieve? Maybe. I have good news: the second Endross Incarnation has gone quiet."

The Overlord certainly didn't sound as if she were delivering good news, and Leah understood why. Sealing Endross back in its Territory would have been cause for celebration, and killing it would still be good news. But this Incarnation had vanished. If it wasn't causing chaos any-more, where had it gone?

Simon, Indirial, and a contingent of other Travelers led by Leah had taken down the first Endross Incarnation months ago. It had been re-placed almost immediately by a second Endross Traveler, almost all of whom were crazy enough to make wonderful Incarnations.

"How many does that make now?" Leah asked quietly.

"That depends. If you only consider the ones we saw firsthand, and then vanished afterwards, then at least five."

"And if you count all the Incarnations whose whereabouts are currently unknown?"

"Including Helgard? Eight."

Leah's head pounded. She had spent the past six months trying to take care of the Incarnations, and matters had moved much more quickly since she recruited Simon and the other Valinhall Travelers. However, in all that time, she had only successfully sealed the Avernus Incarnation back into its Territory. They had killed the Endross Incarnation, but it was quickly replaced, and they had defeated the Tartarus Incarnation in battle, but it had escaped. No one had heard from it in two months.

Several others had vanished as Leah was preparing to attack them. The Helgard Incarnation, for instance, had seemed to expect an attack. The Asphodel Incarnation had simply not been there when Leah and her Travelers had arrived. The citizens were highly encouraged by her apparent success rate—they seemed to think that she had driven the Incarnations off singlehandedly. The truth was much worse.

She had no idea where the Incarnations were.

Evidence suggested that the Naraka Incarnation had burned much of Bel Calem and Myria, as well as most of the land in between. When the Damascan Travelers had arrived in Myria, the Naraka Incarnation was gone. Several villagers had stories of strange monsters and gold-armored warriors, but their accounts were confused. They seemed to have witnessed a battle between the Naraka Incarnation and dozens of Travelers, but Leah had certainly authorized no such battle. And Enosh would never have mobilized to oppose the Incarnations; it was their fault that the crea-tures were released in the first place.

The fact remained, however, that the Naraka Incarnation had been the first to vanish. Then the others, one by one. The Ragnarus Incarnation was presumably still in Cana, since the city was isolated by a barrier of crimson light, but Leah had never seen the creature.

So all the Incarnations that had been sealed underneath the Hanging Trees, with the sole exception of Avernus, were now missing in action. And Helgard was last seen opening a Gate to Ragnarus.

Leah didn't like what that suggested.

"Thank you for the information, Overlord," Leah said at last. "Return to Eltarim and do what you can to rebuild. I will let you know when we have found a way to return to Cana."

Feiora glanced at the black bird on her shoulder. "I think I would be more useful here."

Leah rubbed her head, the old frustration rising. Did the woman think she was making a suggestion? "Return to your post, Overlord Feiora," Leah said firmly.

"We're already shorthanded here," Feiora responded. "We have to find those Incarnations. You don't have anyone else to unify the Avernus Travelers, so I'll have to take that role myself."

"Yes, if only we had another loyal Avernus Overlord here. In his absence, I suppose I will allow you to stay here and perform his duties." Leah kept her expression clear, but inside she was seething. At least she had managed to remind Feiora about what had happened to her brother.

The Overlord barely seemed to hear Leah. She was staring at her raven, occasionally muttering something as if in conversation.

Leah waved to the tent flap. "If that will be all, Overlord, feel free to show yourself out." She didn't have time to listen to a Traveler hold a private conversation with her bonded creature.

Feiora squared her jaw and turned back to Leah. The raven turned at the same time, meeting Leah's eyes again. "Eugan asks me to express his concerns about Alin, son of Torin."

Where had that come from? "Alin? As far as I know, he's still in Enosh."

And Simon thinks he's an Incarnation, Leah thought. She had never seen any indication of it—she hadn't seen Alin flying around blasting people to pieces, in other words—but that would explain why they had heard nothing from Enosh since the Incarnations had been released.

For the first time, the raven opened its beak and gave a *caw*. Feiora chuckled. "Eugan says you're holding something back. He's a perceptive one, but even I figured that one out."

"The Overlords know everything about Alin that I do," Leah said coolly. *Not everything I suspect, but everything I know.*

Feiora frowned, still looking at her raven. "I...Eugan made me promise to tell you something. These are his words, not mine, you understand. He says that you're adrift and sadly lacking in allies. 'You're lost on the wind and your flock is too small,' is actually how he said it. He has suggested that you need an advisor."

The Overlord shrugged the shoulder without a bird on it, seemingly as lost as Leah felt. "You should visit the Corvinus tribe in Avernus. I suspect you'd find it worthwhile. That's all he said, and may Naraka take me if I know why."

Was that a trap? Leah couldn't draw on her powers fully in a foreign Territory; did Feiora want Leah in Avernus so that she would be weaker, and the Overlord could make some kind of a hostile move? Even if the suggestion was made in good faith, how could Leah justify the time it would take to Travel through Avernus?

Leah was still considering how to respond when the tent flap opened and one of her Tartarus guards poked his head inside.

"I'm sorry to bother you, Your Majesty, Overlord. But there's a woman there who says she knows you. She claims to have information regarding the current situation in Enosh."

Leah shared a glance with Overlord Feiora, and they rose to their feet at the same time. Eugan squawked, and Feiora nodded.

"He says to be careful with this woman," she translated. "She's old and dangerous."

Then, at Leah's gestured command, the visitor entered the tent. She was a shriveled old woman with straggly white hair and a pair of cracked red spectacles. She wore a patched, stained robe that might once have been red, and a ragged pink scar wrapped her one remaining wrist like a scarred bracelet. Her right arm ended in a smooth stump. Leah couldn't see from her perspective, but she knew that on this woman's palm lay a Naraka Traveler's brand. The guards had known to check, which was why they had tied her arms behind her with a short length of ragged rope.

"State your name and business, woman," Feiora said.

Leah held up a hand. "That won't be necessary, Overlord Feiora. Please, allow me to introduce Grandmaster Naraka."

Feiora's eyes narrowed, and she rubbed her jaw thoughtfully. On her shoulder, Eugan squawked.

The Grandmaster grinned, revealing gaps in her teeth. "So you're the Queen of Damasca? I never would have thought. Grandmaster Lirial thought you were nothing more than a scared natural Traveler from the villages, but I had my suspicions that you were a spy for one of the Overlords. Looks like we were both wrong, eh?"

In Enosh, Grandmaster Naraka had always scared Leah. She could admit that now, if only to herself. But here, in Leah's tent, wearing clothes that looked like they had been stolen from a beggar, the Grandmaster was anything but intimidating.

"The past few months have clearly not been kind to you, Grandmaster," Leah said. "But things can always get worse."

"As I said, I bring you news of the current state of affairs in Enosh," Grandmaster Naraka said, seemingly unfazed. "We have been occupied by an invading force."

Leah rubbed one temple. She would rather send a Grandmaster to the executioner's block than suffer unfounded accusations from her. "I am afraid you're mistaken. We have sent no force to Enosh."

Naraka chuckled humorlessly. "Not you. We're occupied by the Elysian Incarnation."

Overlord Feiora turned to look at Leah, and her raven began to chuckle.

Alin, Leah thought. Her head hurt worse than ever.

Simon swept Azura in an arc, stepping forward as he did. The blade sank into a standing column of thick stone, creating a single crack in the rock.

A distant chuckle filled the courtyard of Valinhall.

"Not there..." Makko taunted. "Almost..."

The courtyard was a vast plain of smooth square tiles in a uniform gray.

The columns stood in rigid, even rows all throughout the room, made of the same gray stone as the floor. The whole room, like a handful of others in Valinhall, served no purpose that Simon could tell. You could march an army through this room, but how would you get them here? Most of the House's other rooms had small, tight corridors. What did all this empty space accomplish?

This room produced nothing, it did nothing, and it seemed like a complete waste. Why was he spending his time doing this?

Don't whine, Caela said. *It doesn't suit you. I told you, patience is the way through the courtyard.*

The light in this room was provided by small, yellow-white candle flames that whirled around the low ceiling like lost fireflies. As a result, shadows were his constant companions in this test. They danced and shifted all around the room, cast by columns and guttering flames.

Simon thought he saw a flicker of movement to his left, and drew a weighted hatchet he had brought from the armory. He hurled it left-handed and ran after it, on the chance that he had actually struck the room's guardian.

Nothing. The hatchet's blade rang against plain stone.

"Not there..." Makko's voice drifted over to him. "Behind you..."

Simon spun around, Azura held at the ready. He saw nothing.

The other way! Caela shouted in his mind. Another lance of pain shot up his half-healed leg as Makko sank her teeth into his thigh.

The miraculous healing powers of the Valinhall pool had restored the wound enough so that he felt no pain walking on the leg, only a little tightness. But he still needed time before he was fully healed, and now this guardian insisted on tearing open his old wounds. Thanks to her and her useless room, he would take even longer to recover.

Simon kicked back, his heel connecting with something that felt like kicking a down-stuffed pillow. He turned to see Makko rising into the air: a wolf, but a wolf knitted out of a dozen different colors of yarn. Her eyes were smooth black pebbles, her snout a twisting nest of red, green, blue, yellow, and purple threads. Her teeth, now stained with his blood, looked like knitting needles made of smooth bone.

He rarely caught a glimpse of Makko, so he had to take this opportunity. He raised Azura, preparing to bring it down on the guardian's back.

His steel ran out.

His muscles sagged, feeling indescribably weak when restored to their natural strength. Azura suddenly weighed five times as much, and sagged in his hand. He managed to lower the sword without dropping it.

Makko vanished behind a column with a flash of her multi-colored tail, still chuckling. "A hunt takes patience...Next time, remember..."

Then she was silent.

Simon kicked his blade in sheer frustration, sending it clattering across the tiles.

You shouldn't do that, Caela sent, in the smug tones of an older child lording her knowledge over a younger. *She won't like it.*

Who? Makko?

Caela let out an exasperated sigh. *Not Makko. Azura.*

Simon pulled the doll out of his cloak pocket, looking her in the eye. Her curling blond hair rested beneath a powder blue bonnet, and she wore a frilly dress in a matching shade. She had the same self-satisfied expression as always. "The sword can't talk," he said. "It's only a sword. It would have said something by now."

You're speaking out loud again, Caela reminded him.

Simon gave a mental sigh. *Fine. But I've used Azura for a long time now. If it could talk, I would know.*

Just because someone doesn't talk doesn't mean she doesn't listen.

Simon eyed his sword, shining in the yellow candlelight. The dolls had lied to him before, as part of a series of pranks, and they didn't know everything. They could be wrong as easily as he could. But this seemed like something they would know.

A shadow detached itself from the pools of darkness behind one of the columns. The Eldest Nye stepped into view, his black outer cloak faded to a dark gray. Unlike most of the Nye, who stood hood-and-shoulders taller than Simon, the Eldest only reached Simon's shoulder. He was hunched with age, as though he should be bent over a cane, but he glided over the tiles like he moved on wheels instead of legs. If he had hands—Simon had never seen them—they were well hidden in voluminous sleeves that draped down almost to the ground.

The Eldest lifted his black hood to stare at Simon. Within, Simon saw only darkness.

"It seems that you are frustrated, son of Kalman," the Eldest said, in his scratchy whisper.

"I'm sorry, Eldest," Simon said, bowing a little. The Nye seemed to greet one another with bows, so Simon had started adopting the habit. "I didn't mean to disturb you. I've been working on this one room for so long, it's starting to grate on my nerves."

Simon had stayed deep in debt to the Eldest practically since he first came to Valinhall, but the Nye had rarely mentioned it. Somehow, his silence made it worse. Whenever the Eldest decided to call in his marker, Simon wasn't sure he had the leverage to refuse.

The Eldest shook his hood from side to side. "There is no reason to let this room anger you. Many of the Dragon Army tried for months or years to pass the test of one specific room, only to never succeed. Not every reward is meant for every Traveler."

Simon pictured himself in a few years, having rushed at this room hundreds of time and failed to catch Makko. He would go as crazy as Kai. "But I almost got her!"

The Eldest made a thoughtful sound that had a lot in common with the sound of a rasping saw. "In any case, perhaps it is time for you to attempt a different room. There is nothing that says you must try this one again and again."

"I'm not sure where else to go," Simon said. He had gone back over every room that he was allowed to enter, earning the powers of the forge, library, and armory, but this was the only new door he had seen.

"Wait," he said, as a thought occurred to him. "Will you tell me where Kai is?"

Not bothering us, that's all I need to know, Caela sent, her voice whispering along their mental connection. *These have been the most wonderful months I've ever had.*

In the fight against the Valinhall Incarnation, Kai had suffered a wound from a Ragnarus blade. After that, he had retreated deep into the House, and Simon hadn't seen him since. Knowing Kai, he was probably lurking somewhere in one of the deeper rooms, and wouldn't emerge until he felt like it. Or until he missed the dolls.

It had been months, though, and Simon was actually starting to worry.

The Eldest stared at him for a long moment, the shadows beneath his hood writhing and shifting. "You would be wise to try the graveyard, son of Kalman."

"Is Kai there? Can I open the door? Wait. We have a graveyard?"

The Eldest started to glide back toward the door, and it seemed that Simon had no choice but to follow him. He scooped up Azura—which felt unnaturally heavy when he wasn't full of Benson's steel—and followed the Nye out of the room, limping on his wounded leg.

"We have a graveyard," the Eldest said at last, "because the Wanderer insisted upon it. It is not part of Nye traditions to honor the dead. This is the place where you may earn ghost armor, which will protect you from the powers of other Travelers."

Phantom pain throbbed through Simon's right side, and he unconsciously rolled his shoulder. He had been badly burned by Endross lightning when he hunted down that Territory's Incarnation, and the pool had taken weeks to heal the wound. That had been one of the most painful injuries Simon could remember. And, living in Valinhall for as long as he had, he could remember a lot.

The Eldest placed one draping sleeve over the doorknob leading back into the rain garden. "As for whether Kai will be there...who knows? Even I could never predict Kai's actions."

He twisted the knob and pushed the door open.

The rain garden was not on the other side.

Stormclouds rolled about twenty feet overhead, grumbling with surprisingly quiet thunder, and twisting with a thousand bolts of constant, bright green lightning. The room filled with a constant, flashing emerald light, though it remained surprisingly dim.

The whole room was about the same size around as Malachi's great hall in Bel Calem, and was supported around the outer perimeter by a series of stone columns and arches that looked like they had once belonged to an ancient coliseum. Ivy and cracks snaked up the columns, giving the impression of great age.

In the center of the room, within the circle of columns, lay a park's worth of dark soil and grass. The smell of grass and earth hung in the room, combined with something unpleasant and somewhat sweet that Simon couldn't quite place.

Headstones rose from the ground. They were mostly carved out of some gray stone, with names etched into them in a rough, blocky hand. Only eight headstones filled the ground for now, but there was room for dozens more.

Simon glanced behind him, into the shadowy column-filled forest of the Valinhall courtyard. "How did we get here? I came through the rain garden. This was never here before."

"What a coincidence," the Eldest rasped, his sleeves pressed together in front of him. He seemed very proud of himself.

A man stood with his back to Simon, facing the opposite side of the room. He wore a simple white shirt and gray pants that looked as though they had lived through a battle or two without being washed, stitched, or replace. He held a lightly curved silver sword, almost as long as Azura, in one hand, its point held carefully up so that it didn't drag in the grass. A line of gold ran up the center of the blade.

The man cocked his head of shaggy white hair to one side, like a curious bird.

Simon took a breath to call out to Kai, but Caela shushed him.

Wait! she called. *There's someone else!*

Another man dashed out from behind the stone columns, a gleaming Damascan infantry sword in each hand. He moved so fast that Simon couldn't keep track of him, which could only mean he was holding the Nye essence. But it clearly wasn't Indirial; his skin was too pale, and there was no gold medallion around his neck. More importantly, Indirial would never allow his chains to cover so much of his body. This man's black chains marked not only his arms, but also his bare chest, his neck...even his bald head was capped in black chains.

Simon's breath froze. It was impossible. He had only met one bald Valinhall Traveler with chains covering his whole body. Unless Denner had taken up a radical change in fashion, there was only one man this could possibly be.

And he was dead.

Simon himself had driven the sword through Valin's heart.

CHAPTER 5

DISTURBING EXPLANATIONS

Leah placed a recording crystal on the table in front of her. Not a camp table this time, but a real, solid piece of sturdy furniture. She sat in one of Overlord Malachi's offices in his home back in Bel Calem, a well-appointed room with bookshelves covering the walls. Most of them were philosophical studies on the nature of the Territories, but she spotted a few mythologies, a handful of plays, and even a popular historical romance. She sat in a plush, comfortable chair across the desk from the room's other occupant: Grandmaster Naraka.

On Leah's orders, the Grandmaster had enjoyed a bath, donned new robes in the burnt red of Naraka, and even found an unbroken pair of crimson spectacles. Now she sat opposite Leah, with manacles binding her forearms together. A trio of guards stood inside the doors, one Naraka and two Tartarus, in case Leah needed the backup.

The recording crystal glimmered in the sunlight streaming in from the west window. The device was from Lirial, a clear teardrop of stone that looked more like a diamond than a crystal formation.

"This will keep a visual record of everything that you say here today," Leah said, keeping her voice brisk and businesslike. "Afterwards, I will review the record, and will decide how to act based on your information and whether or not I find it credible."

The Grandmaster cackled. "Whatever makes you feel better, girl." Her red spectacles blazed with reflected afternoon light.

Leah was in no mood to play games with a Grandmaster. Either this woman had useful information, or she was on her way to a noose. "Now. What is the current situation behind the walls of Enosh?"

"The walls, hm? When was the last time you had a look at the city's walls?"

Leah gave Naraka a precise smile. "I would prefer it if you told your story and left the questions to me."

The older woman smiled and massaged the stump of her missing hand. The gesture looked awkward, with the manacles clanking and banging together, but Leah watched her hand motions closely. At the slightest hint that she was calling Naraka, Leah would summon crystal and bind the Grandmaster in her chair. Then the guards would go to work on her.

But Grandmaster Naraka simply kept talking. "If you'd kept an eye on those walls, as is your duty as a Lirial Traveler, you would notice a startling change. They're taller, for one thing."

"Why have you been building up the walls, Grandmaster?" Leah asked.

Naraka made a 'tsk' sound. "You want me to tell this story, girl, then don't interrupt. They're five feet taller, and they're solid gold. You could probably see them gleaming all the way from that village, Myria. Gold's not a practical metal for building a wall, if you ask my opinion, but these walls seem solid enough. Maybe it only *looks* like gold."

Leah let the woman ramble, digesting the information. The walls of Enosh had grown higher, and Naraka claimed the Grandmasters weren't responsible. That seemed reasonable; if the Grandmasters wanted to raise their city's walls, they would have had a team of Ornheim Travelers and golems add bricks on top. They wouldn't have torn the old walls down and built new ones out of gold.

"In the city itself, it's much worse," Grandmaster Naraka went on, and for once she didn't sound smug. She sounded haunted instead, as though she was staring into a nightmarish memory. "The first thing the Elysian Incarnation did, when he took over the city, was publicly execute Grandmaster Helgard. The people cheered him for it. I suppose that's not much of a surprise. With all the spit and polish we gave that boy, the people would cheer him if he burned down their homes in front of them."

They had finally come to the point that Leah most wanted to clarify, but she had to pretend to be casual. "Let's be clear, Grandmaster. When you talk about the Elysian Incarnation, you mean Alin, son of Torin?"

Grandmaster Naraka shot her a scornful look behind her gleaming red spectacles. "How many other Travelers of Elysia do you know, girl? Of course it's Alin."

Leah nodded like she had cleared up a minor point of procedure, but inside her stomach churned. Alin was an Incarnation. Would she even recognize him? Some of the Incarnations she'd seen had seemed human enough, but others looked like the monsters they were. You would never be able to tell that they had once been men and women.

Even then, while she tried to imagine what the Incarnation of Elysia might look like, another part of her mind was hard at work. Alin was born as a Traveler of one of the most powerful Territories. If he had Incarnated, he must be all but unstoppable. How could she use that to her advantage? Could he, perhaps, be lured into getting rid of the other eight Incarnations?

Worse, she had *known* Alin. Was there anything left of the young man he'd been, or was he nothing more than a monster?

"He hunted through the city for the remaining Grandmasters," Naraka went on. "He said we tricked him into releasing killer monsters on the world, and that we deserved to die for our crimes."

"You did," Leah said. "And you do."

Grandmaster Naraka twisted her lips into a smirk. "How sad you must be, that the Incarnations are exacting just retribution upon your nation for your family's crimes. Nature will achieve balance once again, though the process might be painful. The longer the balance goes without redress, the greater the pain."

Leah nodded as if that made sense. "I see. Then for what crimes is the Elysian Incarnation punishing you?"

The Grandmaster stretched the fingers on her left hand. It looked like a nervous gesture, and she wasn't meeting Leah's eyes anymore, but Leah still tapped gently into her Lirial Source. She didn't trust any enemy Naraka Traveler moving their hands for any reason.

"He hunted through the city for us," Naraka said, ignoring Leah's question. "And in the meantime, he changed the city. His very presence there turned the walls to gold. It made the trees taller, healthier. It turned shops into towers and homes into palaces. The people loved him for it even more. Then he started changing the people…"

Grandmaster Naraka's voice trailed off, and she stared into space, seemingly lost in memory. "You should see it for yourself, girl. I wanted the Elysian Travelers in charge. They are the pinnacle of human virtue, unhindered by the petty greed and factionalism of other Territories. But the Elysian Incarnation…he is morality without sympathy or conscience, a king with no opponents and no self-restraint. You have to see it for yourself. I can't describe it."

Leah agreed: she would have to see Alin's effect on the city. She had already begun weaving a plan, but the Grandmaster didn't need to know that.

So she pushed the recording crystal across the desk, toward Grandmaster Naraka.

"Try," she ordered.

Simon nearly choked, and his heart went from a casual rest to a full sprint. His steel was still empty, which meant that he was about to die, but he had some essence left. He heaved Nye essence into his lungs, drawing as deeply as he could on the wisps of cool power that remained, straining to hold Azura in front of him with one hand. With his other hand he felt around in the pocket of his cloak, trying to grab the mask before Valin noticed him, crossed the distance, and killed him.

One dark gray sleeve rested on Simon's arm. It used no force now, but Simon knew from personal experience that the Eldest was more than capable of stopping him physically when he had no steel to draw upon.

"You act when you should watch," the Eldest whispered.

Acting on faith, Simon drove Azura into the soft earth at an angle, its mirror-bright steel reflecting the bright flashes of green overhead. Caela wasn't shouting a warning, and the Eldest didn't think he was any danger, so he supposed he could let his guard down a bit. Besides, he could hardly carry the sword without the steel. He was about to drop the thing in the dirt, which would have been more than a little embarrassing.

He did hold on to a wisp of Nye essence, and he kept his trembling fingers brushing the mask in his pocket. Just in case.

The gold-lined Dragon's Fang, Mithra, outmatched the other man's swords by three feet of reach, and Kai attacked in broad sweeps, drawing shimmering sheets of silver and gold in the air. Valin—if it was Valin; Simon still couldn't bring himself to believe it—ducked underneath the blade, almost impossibly limber. He drove the blade in his right hand up into Kai's stomach.

But it seemed that Kai had anticipated the move, dropping Mithra at the end of his slash and punching down with a dagger he had drawn from his waistband. At the same time, he twisted to his right, avoiding Valin's slash.

Mithra spun as it flew through the air, hurled away by Kai's attack. It rang like a bell when it crashed into one of the columns, falling with a thud to the grassy earth.

Kai and Valin remained frozen. Simon's mentor was bleeding from a long slash down one side, where Valin had scraped him with the edge of his sword. Not that Valin had escaped unscathed: a sheet of blood ran down the side of his cheek, from the line that Kai had drawn across his cheekbone with his dagger.

Acid-green light flickered overhead.

Valin levered himself to his feet, and he gave Kai a grin that stood out from his chain-masked face. "Not bad, Kai. That's where we'll have to stop, unless you want a trip to the pool, but not bad at all. You're getting faster." Casually, the Incarnation leaned the blades of both his swords back against his shoulders, which made Simon almost painfully uncomfortable. He would never have put a blade so close to his neck unless he meant to shave.

The Wanderer's eyes flicked to Simon, and his grin broadened. "Hey! We've got an audience today! Your name was Simon, right?"

I never thought I would see him again, Caela sent. She sounded awed. *What has the Eldest done?*

Simon remained silent. The last he had seen Valin, Simon had been driving a blade into his heart.

He had never expected a reunion.

Valin's grin faded to an understanding smile. "Don't worry, I get it. I didn't think I would see myself back here either." He looked around fondly, and Simon realized what was different about him: his eyes. They had been his most noticeable feature: all black around the edges, where the whites should be, and mirror-bright silver in his irises. Now, his eyes were a completely human shade of gray.

It was almost more alarming seeing him that way. What had happened?

Kai finally seemed to notice Simon. He, too, gave a soft smile. "Simon," he said fondly. "Which of my little ones have you brought me today?"

Of course.

Wordlessly, Simon held out Caela, who stammered a protest before Kai scooped her up and began drawing a tiny brush through her curly blond hair.

"I killed you," Simon said at last. "Didn't I?"

Valin chuckled, tapping the point of one of his short swords against his bare chest. "Seems like it."

"Then what happened? Incarnations don't come back when they're killed. They leave the way free for someone else to Incarnate." That was what Leah had told him, at any rate, and it certainly seemed true. But what if Valinhall was different?

The Wanderer pointed straight at the Eldest Nye with one of his swords. "Ask him."

The Eldest bowed to Valin over his crossed arms. "It was a simple matter, though it took some time to ensure his…stability. As an Incarnation, he was still bound to Valinhall. I simply returned his body back here, and restored him to his proper place as a part of the natural order in this world. He is not what he was, merely an extension of the Territory."

Valin raised one leg, and it took Simon a second or two to see something around his bare ankle, beneath his tattered pants: a coil of smoke wrapped around his leg like a manacle on a prisoner.

Not a manacle. A chain.

A chain of shadow or smoke rose from the ground beneath the graveyard, wrapping in coils around each of Valin's ankles.

"I'm stuck here, now," the Wanderer said. "And I am no longer an Incarnation, thank you very much. That fades away, with time. I'm nothing more than a room guardian, like Makko or Kortali."

The Eldest cleared his throat. "Kortali was destroyed almost twenty years gone."

A look of grief flashed across Valin's face. "The forge?"

The Nye dipped his hood.

Valin sighed. "Well, I hope she deserved it."

Simon couldn't think of anything else to say to the founder of Valinhall, so he turned to the Eldest instead. "Why?"

The Nye remained motionless, staring at Simon from his empty black hood. "I still have a task for him. Even death could not erase his debt."

A shudder ran through Simon, though he tried to hide it. Surely, even Valin didn't owe the Eldest as much as Simon did.

"What task?" Simon asked.

"You will see," the Eldest responded. Then he turned back to Valin and bowed over his crossed arms. "The son of Kalman wishes to challenge the graveyard, Master."

Valin grinned like a boy on a holiday. "Is that so? Don't worry, Simon. I'll go easy." He tossed both of his swords to the ground and stood, arms spread, waiting for Simon to attack.

Simon had to stop himself from reaching for his mask.

CHAPTER 6

A Test and a Ghost

359th Year of the Damascan Calendar
1st Year in the Reign of Queen Leah I
Spring's Birth

When he fought, Valin never stopped smiling. Simon couldn't stand it.

Over the past two days, the older man had begun to remind him of Indirial: he grinned a lot, made jokes, and taught Simon with much more patience than Kai had ever shown. But Valin, unlike Indirial, frightened him.

It wasn't the fact that Simon had initially met the Wanderer as a crazed, bloodthirsty Incarnation, though that played its part. When Valin cut Simon, he cut deep. When he kicked Simon into a pillar, he was there a second later, swinging his blade at Simon's neck. In every fight, he acted as if he wanted it to be Simon's last.

He always stopped at the last second, helped Simon up, and told him what he had done wrong.

But that didn't help the fear.

I wonder why Indirial would take after him? Otoku said sarcastically. *It's not like Valin raised him like a son. Now, if you would kindly* help me, *then maybe I could stop Valin from knocking you around the graveyard like a child's brand-new ball.*

Otoku lay twenty paces away in Kai's lap, as the white-haired man crooned to her and stroked her dark hair with his little brush. Every once in a while, he smoothed out her red flower-print dress.

You seem to be doing fine on your own, Simon sent back. It was petty revenge for her refusal to help him, but it wasn't like he could stop Kai from doing whatever he wanted. They shouldn't hold it against him.

Beneath a sky of green lightning, Simon leaped over a granite headstone, bringing his blade down two-handed onto Valin's head. The Wanderer caught Azura's edge on one of his own gleaming infantry swords, dropping the second one to the grass. With his empty left hand, he hooked Simon's legs and pulled them into the air, sending Simon flipping over. He slammed into the soft earth with his chin, knocking the air from his lungs and earning a mouthful of mud and grass.

After Simon's panicked choking fit subsided, he managed to look up at Valin. The older man was still grinning, the chains on his bare chest crawling. He didn't say anything, but Simon knew what he was thinking.

"I know," Simon said.

"You shouldn't go leaping around like that."

"I know."

"Keep your feet on the ground. You're not a frog."

"I know." Simon couldn't help but feel a little disappointed about this last match. His hopes had been high today.

Valin reached out and ruffled his hair. "You'll get it eventually, even if I have to beat it into you. Though I never did manage to teach Denner to stop jumping around. And plenty of the Dragon Army never earned ghost armor. I remember Janesh..."

His voice trailed off, and his grin died a horrible death. Kai's white head came up, and he stared at his old master. As usual, his eyes were hidden behind shaggy bangs, and what little Simon could see of his expression was completely blank.

Simon followed Valin's gaze to a gravestone a pace or two to Simon's right. It was a squared-off block of granite with a few words carved into its face.

Here lies Janesh, son of Yaman.

All the members of the Dragon Army, except the surviving four, had encountered the same fate. They had fallen to the Wanderer in combat. He glanced around at the headstones surrounding him. Eight graves, eight dead Valinhall Travelers.

Everyone here had died at the end of Valin's blade.

Valin's hand tightened around the sword in his right hand, and he lowered his head.

Behind his head, lightning flared in a constant green mesh.

Simon rose to his feet and carefully, quietly, crept over to Kai. "Should I come back later?"

Kai cocked his head to one side like a bird, and his mouth quirked up in a smile. "Why, little mouse, who taught you such patience? No need to worry about him. You should continue."

Simon shot a glance over at Valin, who was still frozen, staring at Janesh's grave. "You don't think he needs some time?"

"Why should he? The monster who killed my brothers and sisters lies dead. This is no more than a ghost. And where better to find a ghost than a graveyard, hm?"

Kai hummed to himself and raised Otoku in both hands, holding her up to the sky like a father with a new baby. In Simon's head, she shrieked at the indignity.

Valin glared at Kai, his smile a distant memory.

Simon had never been good in situations like these. His instincts told him to shut his mouth and leave before one of the men tried to kill the other. Or at least before the conversation got even more awkward.

In fact, he had taken a step toward the exit before Kai surprised him by rising to his feet, cradling Otoku carefully in the crook of one arm. He held Mithra out to one side, and the sword shimmered and vanished.

"Do not worry, little mouse. I have finished my business for today. Why don't you escort me out?"

Confused, Simon followed Kai, leaving Valin glaring after them. As they pushed through the graveyard to the courtyard, where yellow firefly-lights danced above a forest of columns, something occurred to Simon that he had never thought of before.

"Master, you banished Mithra."

Kai stared in mock surprise at his empty hand. "Why yes, I believe I did. Truly, your observation skills have grown to epic heights."

"I mean, you banished it within the House." Now that he thought about it, Simon had seen Kai do so on other occasions as well, back when he was using Azura instead of his apprentice. "How? I can't do that."

Kai clapped Simon on the shoulder in a fatherly gesture. He leaned in, as though about to tell Simon a secret. "There are things I know," he whispered, "that you don't."

He seemed to consider that enough of a lesson. Simon probably shouldn't have expected anything more.

So he asked the other question that had been bothering him ever since he had seen Kai in the graveyard. "Is this where you've been for so long? I haven't seen you in months."

"I have spent a good deal of time here, among my brothers and sisters, with the shade of my old master. I have wandered into the depths of the House, where the Nye dare not go. And I have often whiled my days away in our lovely pool."

"The pool?" Simon repeated. The bathroom was close to the entrance of Valinhall. If he had made it that far, surely he should have been able to greet Simon every once in a while. "Then why didn't you ever say anything?"

"What was there to say?"

"We've been fighting Incarnations, Master. We could have used you." Simon knew what Kai was like. The man had an incurable tendency to wander off at the worst possible moment. Simon knew he shouldn't be offended, but he couldn't help himself. Whatever the reason, Kai had effectively abandoned him for almost a year, as time passed in Valinhall. No matter how crazy Kai was, that still felt like a betrayal.

Kai cocked his head to the side. "Did no one tell you about me?"

Simon stared at him blankly, not sure what to say.

Kai shook his head. "Oh, little mouse…" He turned his back to Simon, as though he meant to head back into the graveyard. Then he pulled up his shirt a few inches, exposing his back.

A hideous red wound gaped in his lower back, almost glowing with a bright, unnatural red, as though it had been painted on. Beneath the surface, veins of the same red crept through his skin, like his blood itself had become infected. Layers of scar tissue bordered the wound like layers of rock in a canyon, ranging from pale white to a fresh pink, as though it had been healed and torn open again a dozen times in short succession.

Heir Talos, the son of King Zakareth, had struck this blow with a Ragnarus weapon. Simon had been sure that it would take Kai's life. Then, when Kai had survived, Simon had been equally sure that the danger was past.

"It hasn't healed?" Simon found himself asking. "Even in the pool?"

Kai let his shirt drop back into place, turning to face Simon. He wore a strange little half-smile. "The pool is the only reason I'm still alive. That, and the fact the power of the Crimson Vault is weaker in a foreign Territory."

So if Kai left the House…

"You can't go outside anymore?"

Kai shook his shaggy head. "Never again can I leave Valinhall. I have spent most of my life here, you see, so at first I did not think it such a burden. I am comfortable here. I did not realize that my occasional trips into the Latari Forest were all that kept me sane. That, and my dear little ones."

He ran the back of his hand down Otoku's long, black hair, and Simon somehow heard her shudder.

"Now I am deprived of them both," Kai said with a sigh. "I must find other pursuits to distract me."

Simon imagined how that must feel. He had grown used to staying in the House, but he left at least once every few days. He knew he *could* leave, and that made the confines of Valinhall bearable. If he were trapped here by something not of his own choice, how long would it be before he went even crazier than Kai?

"I'm sorry." That was all he could think of to say.

"Ah, well. Years of my own poor choices catching up to me." He started to walk away, back through the courtyard, to the front of the House. "And now, I seek the sweet release of the healing pool once more. Maybe, if I'm lucky, I'll drown."

Kai's sense of humor had always had a grim edge to it. At least, Simon hoped that was all it was.

No, wait! Otoku cried. *Don't let him take me! My hair can't take anymore!*

The courtyard door slammed shut.

The yellow firefly lights danced against the low ceiling, making the shadowed columns flicker. Kai had almost died. Now he was trapped, here in a Territory, for the rest of his life. Somehow, it made Simon think about himself. He was risking the same fate as Kai, or worse, and for what? He could stop Incarnations from hurting ordinary people, but any Traveler could do that. Indirial and Leah said they needed his help, but they would get along fine without him.

Slowly, Simon made his way back into the graveyard. He didn't have anywhere else to be.

Valin was seated on a gravestone, waiting for Simon. He had driven his short swords into the ground to either side of him.

The former Incarnation didn't say anything, so Simon didn't either. For a long moment, the Wanderer stared at him, his fingers laced together thoughtfully.

"Let's get back to it then," Simon said, trying to force some enthusiasm into his voice.

Valin continued lounging on his tombstone. "Why?"

Because I've got nothing better to do, Simon thought sarcastically, but there was no doll around to appreciate it. "Because I need the ghost armor," he said.

The Wanderer leaned forward. "For what?"

For a moment, that simple question kept Simon stumped.

"It will be a great help against the Incarnations," he said at last.

"Against the Incarnations..." Valin mused. "That's a big task for a man your age. I hope you won't mind a few questions, then."

"Well, I—"

"Glad to hear it." Valin pulled one short sword out of the soil beside him and pointed it at Simon. "You want to stop the Incarnations. Why? More specifically, for whom?"

Simon felt like he was being backed into a corner by a superior duelist. "I've been working with the Damascan army, but..." He trailed off as he realized how Valin would feel about him working alongside Leah.

The Wanderer's hand tightened on his sword, and his eyes flashed from gray to an almost metallic silver so quickly that Simon might have imagined it. "For *Damasca?* Do you think they deserve your protection? Will the Ragnarus Travelers be grateful to you, do you think, or do they see you as another weapon that they've bought and paid for?"

For this one, Simon had an answer. "It doesn't matter," he said firmly. "You, above anyone else, know what kind of destruction the Incarnations are capable of. If I can spare anyone from that, no matter who they are, I should. And, if you remember, I *can* fight Incarnations."

There. At last, he felt like he had gotten off the back foot and launched a solid attack.

Except Valin waved that remark away with a casual flick of his blade. "Let's say you're right. When does it end? Even if you seal all nine Incarnations in their Territories, nice and tidy, you've only bought yourself some breathing room. In a few weeks, maybe months—years, if you're impossibly lucky—another one will pop up. Will you seal that one, too? And the one after that? What about if you can't seal it, and you have to kill one, then another Incarnation can pop up *right away.* You won't have any respite at all. When will it end?"

Simon tried to answer, even though he wasn't perfectly sure himself, but Valin rode over him.

"And what about the times in between Incarnations? You stay in the House, going deeper and deeper, getting more and more powerful...and all the while getting closer and closer to Incarnation yourself."

His voice was heavy with weight, and Simon didn't have to remind himself that he was speaking from personal experience.

"For what?" Valin went on. "Will that be your whole life? Will you stay in the House forever, effectively ceasing to exist until the *King* or *Queen* calls you out to clean up an Incarnation?"

Simon thought about it. He tried to picture himself, weary from finally beating the Incarnations that were loose now, but knowing that the threat was over. He would go back to Valinhall, seeking more and more power, until the next Incarnation showed up and Leah called him back out.

Over and over.

For the rest of his life.

But there was one person who had offered him...not a purpose, but at least something to break up the monotony.

"The Eldest has tasks for me," Simon said. "He wants me to work for him in the outside world."

Valin threw his one-handed sword to the ground and launched to his feet, pacing between the graves as though he had too much energy to keep still any longer. "Ka'nie'ka is selfish and afraid. He—"

"Who?" Simon blurted.

The Wanderer froze for a moment, then kept walking. "That was the Eldest Nye's name once, before his title. Forget it. I knew him long ago."

Simon would have no trouble forgetting the name, since he wasn't sure he could pronounce it even now.

"I confess to you, Simon, that I don't know how the Eldest brought me here. Do you understand the implications of that? I am the founder of this Territory, it was bound together by my will and shaped to my intent, and *I don't know how he did that.*"

Valin began pacing in a circle around Simon, reminding him uneasily of a vulture circling a carcass. He tried to keep an eye on his teacher while at the same time following the man's words.

It didn't sound good.

"What does that mean?"

"It means that the Nye have more power than I ever thought they did," Valin said grimly. "That frightens me. The one thing I know the Eldest fears is *losing* that power, as they once almost faded away to nothing. Ka'nie'ka would have you restore Valinhall's power because that's what *he* wants, because *he* fears fading back to the state in which I once found him."

Valin finally stopped stalking around Simon in circle after circle, and faced him head-on. "What do you want, Simon? Is it your own desire to make Valinhall more powerful? What drives *you?*"

Simon's first thought was, *I wish I had a doll.* Otoku or Caela could have provided him with a clever response, Angeline would have worked the Wanderer's problem with him, Lilia would have said something incomprehensible about dreams that may have at least lightened the mood.

But he put aside those thoughts and tried to seriously consider the Wanderer's questions.

What did he want to happen? When he eventually defeated the Incarnations, left Leah securely on her throne, and—somehow—figured out something to do with Alin, what did he want to do for himself?

What was he fighting for?

Simon tried to picture himself in the best possible outcome, if everything went according to plan, and he drew a blank. He couldn't do it. The best he could imagine was a continuation of the days the way they were now, as Valin had described: training constantly in Valinhall until he was summoned to deal with an Incarnation. And what kind of life was that?

Simon opened his mouth to say he didn't know, but no sound came out.

Valin nodded, as though he had figured something out, and clapped his hands together.

"How would you like to take the test for the ghost armor, Simon?" he asked cheerfully.

The transition felt like a slap, and Simon tried to force his mind to shift direction. "That's what I've been doing for days now."

Valin chuckled. "No, no. That wasn't the graveyard test, that was a fight. You don't think every single room requires you to duel its guardian, do you?"

Did that mean he had wasted the past day and a half? He expected Leah to need him today, so he had spent all of his time in Valinhall, hoping to achieve something in the two days worth of time he could squeeze out of one real day. But Leah was sure to call for him any time now, and he had spent almost two full days playing around with Valin?

The thought sapped any enthusiasm he might have felt for challenging the room. He looked at Azura lying on the grass where he had dropped it, and felt no desire to pick it up.

Valin reached back, behind one of the nearest ivy-wrapped stone columns. He pulled out a tall, silvery bow, strung with what looked like a cable made of steel wire. "It's an interesting test," Valin said, his tone thoughtful. "The details change with time, but the essence of it remains the same. To show you're ready for the ghost armor, you have to prove that you don't need it. Almost a paradox, in a way."

Simon had never heard the word 'paradox' before, but he could figure out what the man meant.

Once again, Valin reached behind a column, this time pulling out a two-foot-tall, heavy-looking hourglass. He placed it on top of the head-stone next to him. "The different guardians execute the trial in different ways, but essentially it's simple: you have to dodge my attacks until time runs out. In this case, until the hourglass is empty. It's supposed to keep you from relying too much on the ghost armor, so you don't run out in the middle of a battle." He tugged gently on his bowstring, testing its draw. "Do you know what the ghost armor does?"

Simon picked Azura up, his wariness returning. Valin could, and probably would, attack him without warning at any time. This was Valinhall, where constant vigilance was the highest virtue. "It seems to block attacks from other Travelers."

Valin pointed at him with one end of his metal bow. "You got it! Most of my students didn't realize that the armor won't protect them from mundane attacks. Spears, swords, arrows...we've got other powers for those. You use ghost armor when you're attacked directly by a Traveler. It'll stop a lightning bolt, a fireball, things like that."

Simon realized that Valin had actually set the hourglass with the sand up. He hadn't noticed before, because he couldn't see the sand draining down. It was the barest trickle, practically one grain of sand at a time, and the glass was huge. How long would it take to drain? Longer than one hour, surely. Simon didn't have any powers that would last more than a few minutes.

Valin ran a hand lovingly along the curve of the bow. "I found this in

Tartarus myself, you know. Deeper in the Labyrinth than most real Tarta-rus Travelers go. You wouldn't believe me if I told you the trouble I went through in bringing it back here." He sighed. "Ah, well. One of the perks of guarding this room is that I get to shoot at you until time runs out. If you're hit...well, unless you're exceedingly lucky, you won't even make it back to the pool."

He stood, pulling the string back in one smooth motion. The bow was as tall as he was, and the string a metal cord almost as thick as a finger, so that Simon wasn't sure if he would be able to draw it even with Benson's steel in him. But the Wanderer bent the weapon with relative ease.

As he pulled back the string, an arrow shimmered and appeared, nocked in the bow. It looked like the rough outline of an arrow sketched in the air, made of pure white light.

From experience, Simon knew that arrows like that could scorch stone and blast holes through trees. There would be no such thing as a non-lethal wound from that weapon. Even if he got hit in the leg or the shoulder, it would tear enough flesh from his body that he would bleed out in seconds.

Fear and the thrill of battle sang through him, and he inhaled a deep breath of Nye essence. Steel and icy power flowed through him, and his breaths carried the faint color of moonlight.

He bent his knees, balanced on the balls of his feet, turned slightly to the side. He held Azura in both hands, elbows bent, the sword point-ing back over his head. He would be able to attack quickly from this stance. No matter what Valin said, he didn't like his odds dodging. His best chance of surviving was to get inside the bow's range, attacking Valin, knocking the weapon away from him or preventing him from using it in some way.

Valin smiled again; his smiles seemed most genuine when he was about to fight. "I'm glad I got a chance to know you, Simon. And I'm glad we're in a graveyard."

"Why is that?" Simon asked. The other man seemed to expect him to say something.

Darkness bled into the whites of Valin's eyes like a cloud of ink spread-ing through water. His gray irises brightened until they were almost white, and then gleaming, metallic silver. Soon, his eyes were two silver circles sitting on pools of solid black.

An Incarnation's eyes.

The dark chains on his skin shifted and writhed like a nest of hungry snakes. His smile never faltered; if anything, it grew brighter, warmer. That made his expression all the more horrible.

"Because you killed me, Simon, son of Kalman. Now, I have a chance to return the favor."

By the end of his sentence, his voice rang with the unnatural sound of steel-on-steel. His arrow loosed, a white bolt of light that shrieked as it blasted through the air.

Simon ducked to the side. The arrow scorched him as it flew past, tearing a chunk out of one of the columns with a deafening crack.

Terror shocked Simon's limbs and clenched at his heart. He had thought this fight was over. Why, in the Maker's name, did he have to fight the Valinhall Incarnation again?

Simon fumbled at the pocket of his cloak, trying to pull out the mask. He had no chance against Valin without the mask, that was why he brought it every time he challenged the graveyard, even though the dolls and Valin himself assured him that he didn't have to be worried. He had been afraid that something exactly like this would happen.

There was nothing in his pocket.

He scrambled at one pocket, then the other, then at the pockets of his pants. Nothing. Had he forgotten the mask? Had he dropped it?

He managed to dodge a blinding arrow, and the tides of panic began to rise.

But some part of him was still focused, still calm, still ready to fight. His first plan had been a good one, he knew: attacking instead of dodging, staying on the offensive instead of on the back foot.

If he ran, the Incarnation would only shoot him down. If he fought, he at least had a chance. As he ran at Valin, Azura clasped in both hands, he couldn't shake a single thought.

He *really* wished he hadn't let Kai take his doll.

Kai snuck a peak through the cracked door and into the graveyard, where Simon had charged the Wanderer. This was for the best, all things considered. Simon needed to be strong, especially now that Kai himself was trapped and utterly useless. He would be the first of a new generation, and Valin would teach the boy better than Kai ever could.

He's not teaching Simon, he's trying to kill him, Otoku sent. *And remove your hand!*

Kai reluctantly pulled his fingers away from the doll's silky black hair. *All the better to leave them alone. If Simon lives, he will have learned a valuable lesson. I don't know what it will be, but I'm sure it will be valuable. If he dies here, I will focus my attention on the other one, the girl. Alissa, was it?*

Otoku's mouth actually twisted into a frown, which was such a rare display that Kai felt his eyes welling with tears. *You don't even pay attention, do you? Olissa is the mother, Andra is her daughter. They've been living here long enough for you to know that.*

Alas, I have had other things on my mind, Kai said. Inside the graveyard, steel rang on steel as Azura made contact with the metal bow. The boy moved in an endless dance, managing to stay ahead of each new white arrow.

Kai lifted the object in his right hand and stared at it. Half black iron, half mirrored steel, with two narrow slits for the eyes. This mask looked like it had been designed for a man who intended to beat his foes to death with his face.

At least he will win or lose this fight as himself, Kai thought.

Well, maybe he will survive. And maybe *he'll learn to appreciate our advice more,* Otoku replied, in tones of self-satisfaction that reminded Kai painfully of Caela. *He relies on us too much and listens to us too little. Lately, he's far too quick to put on that mask. Perhaps this will be good for him.*

I'll make sure he understands the message before I give this back, Kai sent, tucking the mask back into his belt. *In the meantime, how about we go visit your sisters? It's been so long since I've seen you all...*

I'll give you fair warning, Otoku said evenly. *Rebekkah's going to punch you.*

Kai smiled fondly.

The arrow blasted past Simon's shoulder, so close that he could feel the scorching air on his neck. He put it out of his mind, swinging Azura with both hands to knock the bow from Valin's hands.

The Incarnation spun the bow like a staff, knocking Azura's blade aside with one end, while the other whipped around and cracked Simon across the temple.

He felt only a little pain through the reinforcement of Benson's steel, but his vision still flashed white with the impact. He reacted the way he was trained, by long practice in the House: a controlled retreat, stepping backwards evenly, his long blade warding his opponent away.

It bought him another split second for his vision to clear, but the first thing he saw was the Incarnation drawing back another arrow.

The last time Simon had faced this weapon, he had dodged and run, thinking of nothing beyond his desire to *get away*. Indirial had saved him then, so stalling had turned out to be a valid tactic.

Indirial wasn't here now. He would have to try something else.

Instead of backing off, Simon stepped forward, ducking as low as he could. The arrow streaked by, leaving a fiery line on Simon's shoulder that must have burned *through* the cloak, but he didn't have time to take stock of his own wounds. He was still five feet away from Valin, but Azura made that distance trivial.

He brought his blade diagonally up, cutting across the Incarnation's body.

As he had done before, Valin spun the bow around, knocking the sword aside. This time, Simon let it go.

He completely released the hilt of the sword, letting it fly out of his hands. And with his newly freed hands, he pulled his hood down over his forehead.

Nye essence flowed through him like a cold breath. It was waning already; he estimated he had, at best, half a minute left of increased speed and grace. But right now he wasn't looking to enhance his reaction time.

Valin's eyes flicked from side to side and his brow furrowed in confusion. His fingers began to draw back the string, but he didn't know where to aim his arrow.

Simon stopped in front of him and thrust upward, putting all the force he could call behind a two-handed strike to Valin's stomach. As he had suspected, the Wanderer had returned to being another Incarnation: relying on his eyes was the same as relying on the supernatural vision of his Territory. He must see Simon as little more than a shadow…which meant that he couldn't react in time.

Valin's body shuddered under the blow, and the force of it actually lifted his feet from the grass. He flew up and back, and Simon ran to follow, his Nye essence leaving him a little more with every breath.

The Valinhall Incarnation twisted in midair, his bowstring pulling back, a shining arrow sprouting to point in Simon's general direction. Simon ducked, not only to dodge the arrow, but to scoop up one of the short swords that Valin had dropped. An arrow scorched the grass behind him, singeing the edge of his cloak, but he kept moving with a sword in hand. The last thing he wanted was Valin landing with a distance advantage.

As soon as Valin did hit the ground—perfectly balanced and on both feet, of course—Simon was already there, slipping to his side, driving the Incarnation's own short sword up into his ribs.

He scored a hit. The blade bit flesh and, though it scraped along the ribs and Valin twisted, he had done some damage. If he could keep this up, he would not only escape with his life, he would have killed the Valinhall Incarnation a second time.

And then he could address the other questions that plagued him, such as: how could Valin have come back to life in the first place? Could it happen again? Had the Eldest not *noticed* that Valin could still call on his power as an Incarnation, or had he chosen not to say anything?

As the Wanderer's blood sprinkled the grass, Simon shoved all the questions out of his mind. They could wait until later.

Simon drew back the blade and drove it in at another angle, trying to impale the Incarnation through his bare, chain-shrouded stomach. He exhaled as he struck, sending another puff of white mist from his lungs. The world moved noticeably faster, and he wasn't quite agile enough to land his blow before Valin got his bow between his stomach and Simon's sword. Simon still drew blood, but not nearly enough to drop the man permanently.

Simon didn't glance back at the hourglass. He didn't need to; only a few seconds had passed. He would either kill the Incarnation and pass, or die. In that light, failing to earn the ghost armor didn't seem like such a problem.

Valin struck at Simon with the butt of his bow, forcing Simon to back off a step. He didn't want to—his only hope lay in continuous attack—but if he had remained close, the Incarnation would have simply bludgeoned him to death and accepted his stomach wound in return.

But the Wanderer was pursuing *him* now, rushing at him and swinging the bow two-handed like a hammer, and now he was on the back foot again, forced to swing wildly and turn each of Valin's attacks. If he had been using Azura, the Incarnation would have been too close, inside Simon's reach. But maybe if he could find a way to back up and into Azura, he could scoop the longer blade up and use it to create exactly the right distance...

There was a sharp, burning pain on the backs of his thighs, and he stumbled and landed flat on his back. The rest of the Nye essence flooded out of his lungs in a starlight cloud, the world lurching back to normal speed.

Above him, the Incarnation's black-and-silver eyes stared pitilessly into his own. One chain-shrouded arm drew back the steel cable, and a white arrow traced itself in midair, pointed straight at Simon's chest.

"What do you want, Simon?" Valin asked.

Simon almost didn't hear the question. He scrabbled backwards on his elbows, pushing his heels against the grass, trying instinctively to get away. Maybe if he could reach Azura, he could launch another attack, or even slip out of the room until his Nye essence recovered...

Valin drew the string of his bow back farther, and Simon froze. "*What do you want?*"

"I want to live!" Simon blurted, trying to stay as still as possible even though he was propped up on trembling hands.

The Wanderer leaned over his bow, the mirrored circles of his eyes gleaming. "Why?"

Simon hesitated. Did Valin want an answer from him? What did he want to hear? How was Simon supposed to get out of this without a doll or the mask?

Valin made a disgusted sound and kicked Simon hard in the ribs, leaving a flash of pain that flooded Simon's gut even through the steel. His body flipped over with the impact, landing face-down in the grass, and Simon curled up around his stomach.

He heard the creaking of a steel cord bending, and then something was burning his neck. It was actually burning, as though Valin had pressed a red-hot poker against the base of his skull. Simon squirmed, pressing his cheek into the soil to escape that horrible pain, but the Wanderer rested a heavy foot on Simon's back. He simply couldn't move enough.

He smelled char and smoke, and realized with horror that they must be coming from the burning hairs on his neck.

Simon couldn't help but keep thinking of a way out. That was what he had made of himself. He'd spent almost two years of relative time inside Valinhall, and in all that time he had embedded in himself a core belief: death was everywhere, all the time, but there was always a way out.

He didn't give up. But somewhere, deep in a place that he didn't like to think about, he realized that this was the end. He couldn't help but picture the arrow, burning through the base of his skull, leaving a mutilated corpse for the Nye to find. The Agnos family would eventually realize he had died. They might put up a headstone for him here…it had never occurred to him before, but he wouldn't be buried next to his family. He would be here, in a Territory with only a handful of Travelers, and no one to remember him.

Would Leah care? Would Alin even notice? What about Kai?

Still, part of him kept thinking of tactics—*maybe I could summon a little Nye essence, maybe I could call the mask to me, maybe Azura will fly into my hands*—even as he squeezed his eyes shut and waited for the end.

Until an emerald light began to shine, like a green sun coming up, bright even through Simon's clenched eyelids. The rolling light of the storm overhead was nothing compared to this, and he felt something like a cool wind against his head.

He looked up, turning his face up toward the source that radiated cold like a coal radiates heat, and saw a floating suit of luminous green armor. It drifted in midair, like a spirit all its own, and Simon could see the far columns *through* the breastplate.

The pressure on his back vanished, and Valin let out a huge breath. "Wow, that hurt more than I thought," he said casually.

Then there came a heavy thud of a body collapsing.

CHAPTER 7
ELYSIAN RULE

359TH YEAR OF THE DAMASCAN CALENDAR

1ST YEAR IN THE REIGN OF QUEEN LEAH I

1 DAY SINCE SPRING'S BIRTH

Leah tapped her pen against the edge of her map, leaving a spot of ink. She had assigned a pair of artists to draw this map according to Grandmaster Naraka's descriptions, and it was now their best information on the new layout of Enosh.

To say she had little faith in the map would be an understatement. She felt that they might have better luck navigating Enosh by flipping a coin at every intersection and hoping for the best.

Enosh had originally been divided into four quarters with the Grandmasters' palace at the center. Each of the quarters was then subdivided into smaller blocks, for a city that was remarkably simple to navigate.

According to Grandmaster Naraka, Elysia was built in nine districts. Not evenly distributed, equal districts, like nine wedges of a pie. That would have been too simple. Some districts were long, others wide, some large, others small. And Alin had ordered reconstruction to try and replicate this layout in Enosh.

That, in itself, wouldn't be so bad, but his very presence as an Incarnation had begun to reshape the world around him. They were forced to rely on a secondhand map of an ancient city, which was itself being rebuilt in the image of a *second* city that none of them understood…all while the city re-formed itself around the construction crews. Not to mention that they were sketching all this based on the eyewitness testimony of a hundred-year-old woman that Leah was still half-convinced was blind.

The map of the city looked like a pile of sticks dropped randomly inside a lumpy circle. There were a number of notes on the map, none of which made her feel better.

One annotation, at the end of a main thoroughfare, said: *Watch out for bats.* Another note, outside what had once been the city armory: *Whole building may be an illusion.*

Another: *At noon, bridge dissolves into sugar.*

He can see you from here. Travel through tunnels instead. Are there tunnels? This could be the School for the Disobedient, or possibly a fish warehouse. Street ends in turtle?

It was all a confusing, nightmarish mess, and that didn't even count the numerous parts of the map shaded in gray, accompanied by the words "Unknown Area." Those took up far too much of the city for her tastes.

Assuming any of this was accurate at all, there were a few constants even in a half-finished city like this. For one thing, the Naraka waystation couldn't have moved in relation to Naraka, or it wouldn't function. That put it inside the city walls on the north side.

"You understand that we'll have to go in through Naraka," Leah said with a sigh.

"Who says?" Indirial responded. He stood across the table from her, both of them underneath a canopy high overhead to keep off the sun. While she was bent over her map, Indirial had his long, cracked sword resting on the other half of the table. He carefully ran a rag down first one side of the blade, then the other, his sleeves rolled up to reveal tanned forearms marked to the wrist with black chains.

"It's the only route that makes sense." Leah tapped the waystation with the end of her pen. "We come in through here, and we know exactly where we're going to end up. We've also heard that Alin spends most of his time in the southeast quarter of the city, personally overseeing the construction there. So this puts us about as far from him as we're going to get. We'll have plenty of time to show up, take a look around, and retreat."

Indirial wiped the blade one more time, then turned his attention to the thread wrapping its hilt. "I could list all the things wrong with this plan, but I'm not sure you have the time."

Leah sighed. "We're taking the word of an avowed enemy…"

"Whose map *happens* to suggest that her own Territory is the best way into the city," Indirial pointed out.

"…and we're planning on heading into a hostile city controlled by the Incarnation of a Territory about which we know almost nothing," Leah finished. "We don't know anything about his motivations or goals, we have no reasonable expectation of his capabilities, and our map looks like it was scribbled by a blind child with the shakes. How am I doing so far?"

Indirial began reaching into his pockets, behind his back, into his boots, under his belt, even inside his cloak—which looked comfortable in this biting wind. Each time he reached in, he pulled out a knife or another small weapon, more exotic, that Leah didn't recognize. One was a hatchet small enough to hold in one hand. Was he supposed to throw that?

The Overlord began oiling and wiping down each weapon, still talking. "There's one thing that bothers me more than any of that, though."

Leah raised an eyebrow.

"You keep saying 'we.' Do you think you're going?"

She ticked off points on her fingers as she spoke. "Well, let's see. I'm a Lirial Traveler, and as such best-suited for surveying and mapping the area. I have a personal connection with the Incarnation, as I spent most of two years observing him as a trusted friend. I lived for several weeks inside the city, and thereby familiarized myself with its original layout. Finally, I am your Queen, and I will accompany you if I wish."

Leah was quite proud of that speech. For all of five seconds, until Indirial raised his head from his weapons and met her eyes. He didn't speak sternly or angrily—he was still Indirial—but he wasn't smiling.

"Your father always encouraged his children to operate independently. As Ragnarus Travelers, they were well equipped to deal with danger, and independent action fosters self-reliance and creative thinking. So he said. What happened to your brothers and sisters, Leah?"

She saw where he was going, and tried to head him off, but he simply kept talking.

"Your brothers are dead. One of your sisters was exiled for treason, and the other isolated to treat her incurable insanity. You are the last child of Ragnarus we have left, and risking yourself on a fact-finding mission is not only absurd and unnecessary, it is irresponsible."

Coming from someone else, those words might have put Leah's back up even more, *forcing* her to go into Enosh or else lose face. But coming from Indirial...

She felt a blush creeping up into her cheeks, but she refused to allow it. "The fact remains that I am the best individual for this assignment, if you set my rank and responsibilities aside."

Indirial smiled a little. "I'm not sure I'm willing to do that. But I figured you'd say something like that, so I sent four Travelers through to Enosh last night."

"You did *what?*"

"Two Naraka, two Avernus. They scouted the trail between the closest Naraka waystation and the one in Enosh, removing a couple of the traps that Grandmaster Naraka 'forgot' to tell us about. They didn't notice them all. One of our Travelers will walk with a limp for the rest of her life."

Leah showed nothing on the outside, but inside, she winced. That could easily have been her.

Indirial had returned to maintaining his weapons, but he kept speaking. "They reached the city and managed to dispatch the *scout* that was waiting for them by the waystation. He almost escaped and raised the alarms."

That was no surprise—Leah had expected Alin to set guardians on the waystation. It was one of the few permanent, predictable ways in and out of the city.

"One of the Corvinus ravens managed to modify his memory, and they mapped the quarter around the waystation without incident. I have their report here."

He reached out with a single finger and tapped a pile of papers on the table next to his knives. "I stacked it on top of the other reports I received from the six other teams I sent out at the same time—"

"Indirial!" Sending out a single team was one thing, but seven? Without telling her? That was too much.

"—to check if there were any other routes through any other viable Territories. There were none. We lost no men, but the guardians in Helgard, Asphodel, and Endross were formidable. It seems that, indeed, Naraka is our best option. Perhaps he has fewer Naraka Travelers to defend it after the Grandmaster's defection, or maybe he wants us to show up at the predictable waystation. I can't be sure."

"Overlord Indirial," Leah said, letting her anger seep into her voice. "That was *much* too large an action for you to authorize without my approval. You have risked dozens of our finest Travelers on a fact-finding mission that we could have done ourselves! Not to mention that you may have alerted the Incarnation to our intentions."

Indirial poured some oil onto his rag and kept working, seemingly unfazed. "As opposed to risking one of our last Lirial Travelers, our *last*

Ragnarus Traveler, and our *ruler?*"

Well, when he put it like that…

"Your father hired me to guard the ruling monarch," Indirial went on, still talking in his usual calm voice. "The best defense is preemptive action. I have now determined that, in fact, it *is* safe for you to accompany the team to Enosh, as long as you swear not to leave the Naraka Gate. I will make sure to send enough Naraka Travelers that they will be able to hold it open for the duration of your stay, which will be no more than half an hour."

Leah didn't enjoy following orders. She never had, even as a child, even from her father. Come to think of it, she had never seen her father fighting with Indirial. Why was that?

After a moment, she realized: she had never seen them disagree because her father hadn't ever argued with Indirial. He simply accepted the protection. And her father was much more capable of defending himself than she was. It irritated her to admit that, though the feeling wasn't logical.

"Thank you for your care, Indirial," she said carefully. "I would be glad to accept your precautions."

Indirial smiled broadly, as though she had made a joke, but he bowed in her direction without saying a word.

Leah glanced at the sun, wishing for a clock. It was a little before noon, but she would have liked a more accurate estimate. "How long will the trip take?"

"Three hours," Indirial said. "I can have a team ready to leave in twenty minutes."

Leah stared at the map, considering. It was the perfect time to leave. The Grandmaster claimed that Alin practically locked down the city at night, and no one without official authorization was allowed out of their home. She had initially believed that those restrictions would make it easier to move around after dark, until Grandmaster Naraka told her exactly what patrolled the streets from sundown to sunup. If they tried to sneak into the city at night, they were far more likely to run into a patrol of gold-armored troops or a floating tentacled creature.

It would be much easier, the Grandmaster believed, to slip in during the middle of the day and blend in with the crowd.

If they left now, they would have plenty of time to arrive, take a look around, and even return before sunset.

But were there any pitfalls? Was there anything she was missing? What could she do now to make the plan more likely to succeed?

As always when she thought like this, she fished around in her pocket until she found a small, square, wooden box with rounded edges. It was the right size to hold a ring or a pendant.

But she could feel the contents of this jewelry box radiating frustration through the thin layer of wood, pressing against her fingers, wanting release.

It hardly felt like an eye at all. Maybe some sort of horrible, still-beating heart.

Indirial didn't look up from his weapons when he spoke. "You should use it."

Leah sighed quietly. Did he ever miss anything? She pulled the jewelry box out of her pocket and, with only a moment's hesitation, opened it.

A smooth, round stone of pure red gleamed on a velvet cushion inside the box. The stone was dark now, and until she turned it to catch the light it looked almost black. "We've talked about this, Indirial."

"You need as much power as you can get," he said simply, scraping a stone down the edge of one knife. He tested the edge with his thumb. "I risked my life more than once for a power I thought I needed."

"A moment ago, you were more concerned for my safety than I was."

He shrugged. "Your father survived. I doubt it's any more dangerous for you than for him."

Carefully, Leah placed the box on the table. "I don't know anything about this, Indirial. There's no shelf for it in the Vault, so I'm not sure where it came from. I don't know what its price is, or even what it does."

The Overlord spoke over the steady *rasp, rasp, rasp* of a whetstone against one of his knives. "Whatever it does, your father thought it was necessary to fight the Valinhall Incarnation. I understand he went through a great deal of trouble to get it. He even lost his eye in the battle." He made a thoughtful sound in his throat. "Now that I think about it, that worked out pretty well for him."

Leah thought Indirial had his priorities exactly backwards. Going into Enosh wouldn't be *nearly* as dangerous to her as using the crimson eye. She had an even chance of winning or escaping any given fight. But placing something *in her body* that had an unknown effect and a mysterious price? She would rather fight an Elysian Incarnation alone.

Then again, her father had used the eye for as long as she'd been alive. It hadn't hurt him much.

Had it?

Leah rolled the stone in her fingers, ignoring its pulsing warmth. She would have to get used to handling it if she meant to have it surgically inserted into her skull. She couldn't help but imagining it, then: a long-handled metal spoon descending toward her left eye socket, ready to scoop out her eyeball...

She shuddered. It wasn't realistic—they would certainly give her something for the pain, and any Asphodel Traveler could hold her unconscious until the operation had ended—but she couldn't shake her instant revulsion. No matter how it happened, she would still have to give up an eye. And she had to wonder: was that the final price? Only an eye was a small cost, compared to what else Ragnarus might demand of her.

She shivered again, and almost jumped when a raven croaked behind her. She managed to move smoothly, placing the Ragnarus eye back into its case and turning to face Feiora Torannus.

The Overlord wore black trousers and a black shirt again, as usual, with Eugan the raven perched on her left shoulder. She stood with her arms crossed and jaw clenched, as though she anticipated having to physically knock someone down.

"Enosh?" she demanded. "What idiocy is this?"

There were *seven* other Overlords that hardly ever bothered Leah. Where were they? *Seven stones, why is it always Feiora?*

Briefly it occurred to Leah that she might pretend to know nothing. *Enosh? What are you talking about?* But that would be a fool's move; obviously the Overlord knew enough to be certain, or she wouldn't have barged into the conversation in the first place.

"Who told you?" she asked instead.

Feiora jerked her head at Eugan, who let out a loud caw. "The Overlord of Cana over there had to borrow some of my personnel. A few of them were Avernus Travelers. They didn't tell me where they were going, but the Corvinus tribe likes to keep tabs on one another."

The raven croaked again, and somehow managed to radiate self-satisfaction.

Indirial didn't look up from the weapons on the table. He had put down his whetstone and was now giving each blade a few strokes of an oiled rag. "I apologize for using your Travelers without permission. What else can I do for you?"

Feiora's jaw tightened so much that Leah imagined she could hear teeth grinding and muscles straining with tension. "When do you leave, Indirial?"

Indirial swept his blade across a stone with a steady *whisk, whisk, whisk*. Maybe he hadn't finished sharpening after all.

Or maybe he was doing it to be annoying.

Leah spoke into the silence. "I thought you were headed back to Eltarim, Overlord." There was no need for Indirial to antagonize the woman like that, just because Leah always wanted to.

"I delegated," Feiora said. "You should try it some time. Your Majesty, I formally request that I be assigned to the Enosh team."

Leah mulled it over for a second, mostly for show. "Why?"

"It's a scouting mission, isn't it? I'm the best Avernus you have. I don't have any contracts with the Sarin tribe, which would be even better for gathering intelligence."

Lysander had been the premier Sarin-tribe Avernus Traveler in the nation. Did she have to bring up her little brother every time they spoke? The man was imprisoned for an attempted *coup;* she wasn't going to release him for nothing more than a few extra eyes. She had frozen or killed most of his sparrows anyway, so he wouldn't be much good.

"I'll keep that in mind," Leah said at last. Meanwhile, she tried to figure out exactly what Feiora stood to gain—or thought she might gain—from going on this mission. On the surface, it was a loss for her: she had begged a favor from Leah. If Leah granted it, that would put the Overlord slightly in her debt.

On the other hand, Feiora needed a high card to trump her brother's treachery. If she wanted to persuade Leah to release him anytime soon, she would have to provide the throne with some great service. Like, perhaps, taking down an Incarnation.

That would work for Leah. It was in Feiora's best interests to further the Queen's goals right now, so she could be trusted. Marginally. If they encountered any enemy troops, the plan called for them to retreat in any case.

And she *was* the best Avernus they had.

Leah nodded once and turned back to her map, as though the decision had been an easy one. "You may come with us," she said. "We leave within the hour, as soon as Indirial gathers the proper personnel."

Indirial grinned and drew his long, cracked sword off the table. He swept Leah a bow and raised his blade, starting to cut open a Valinhall Gate.

Overlord Feiora's thick eyebrows raised. "Us? Surely, Your Majesty, you don't think you're coming too."

The white marble had grown on its own, in batches next to what had ended up as Enosh's Green District. It came in perfect, square blocks, stacked one on top of the other, leading Alin to believe that they must have once been crates. Like so much else in the city, the blocks had been transformed by his radiant presence into their new form.

One of the blocks drifted up on a cushion of Orange Light, sliding over to slam on top of its fellows in a neat stack. Dutifully, the workers applauded to show their gratitude. Then they got back to work.

Diligence. He approved of that.

The sight of the wall going up—block after block of pure white marble, cemented together by his human workforce—satisfied something in him. This wall represented order, purity, cleanliness…and, he supposed, self-sacrifice. He wasn't sure. Why didn't he know the exact nature of Elysia's White Light? He was trying to put up a White District, as there was in his Territory, but how could he do that if he couldn't even call the White?

The thought put a wrinkle in his previously unmarred peace of mind, and he frowned.

"Rhalia, what does the White Light represent?"

The Gate swirled beside him, its edges shining like pure sunlight. Rhalia hung motionless in the air behind the Gate, her white dress and gold sash blowing in the light breeze that ruffled Elysia's grass. Her golden eyes were sad as they touched on the workers, but he couldn't figure out why.

She heard him and started to respond, but he held up a hand. "No, that's not the right question. It doesn't matter what the White represents."

"I would say it matters very much," Rhalia said softly.

Alin rubbed his chin with one gauntleted hand, trying to phrase his thoughts clearly. "I mean, what matters is that I *don't know* what the White Light means. Why does it elude me, even now?"

Rhalia brushed a strand of blond hair out of her face, still watching the workers. "The White Light is selflessness. It's pure devotion to the service of another at your own expense—even its power can only be used on behalf of someone else. That part of Elysia is beyond you." She didn't meet Alin's gaze.

Alin stepped fully in front of the Gate, forcing her to look him in the eye. "I am Elysia," he said. "There is no door in the city barred to me."

A small smile tugged at the corner of Rhalia's mouth, and she gestured behind her. The walls of the City of Light rose in the distance, bright gold in the light of Elysia's eternal sunrise. They had been worked with silver and set with precious metals, gleaming a dozen different colors, and the tops of the nine Districts rose high above the city streets.

"You want to open the White Door?" Rhalia asked. "Feel free." She kept her hand held out like a native giving a tour. Which she was, now that Alin thought about it.

Alin tapped into the Green Light. He didn't form it into a shield, he just held the light, flooding him with patience and soothing away his irritation at Rhalia's jokes. He couldn't see himself, but he knew that his eyes would have turned a bright emerald green.

He managed a sad smile. "Why don't you approve?" he asked, turning back to the workers building their wall. "I have given them order. Nobody starves here, not anymore. No man cheats another."

The Violet Light whispered the answer: *Because you gave up your humanity to do it. What are you now?*

He ignored it. He was finding it easier and easier to ignore the Violet, these days.

"You think I'm sad for them?" Rhalia asked. "Alin, my heart breaks for *you.* I've failed you as badly as I failed my own people. I only pray that you don't pay the price they did."

Alin couldn't stand hearing her like this. Rhalia was usually brighter than the sun; she was supposed to be cheery even in the shadow of death.

What had gotten to her?

Find out what's wrong, the Rose Light pleaded. *You have to fix her.*

You owe it to her, said the Orange Light.

It's your fault, added the Silver. *There's only one way to—*

Alin quieted the Silver Light. The colors didn't talk to him in audible voices, but they clearly reminded him what *he* would think if he were drawing on their Light. He was starting to avoid calling the Silver Light, even staying as far away from the Silver District inhabitants as he could.

Wisdom, he decided, wasn't everything.

He thought compassion held the answer now, so he tapped into the Rose Light. Soft pink warmth bloomed in his mind, suffusing him with empathy. One of the workers, down by the half-formed wall, had slumped down with his back half-propped against the white marble. How had he not noticed that before?

"Don't be too hard on yourself, Rhalia," he said. "You kept me safe. You gave me great advice. If I strayed, it was my fault, not yours."

Before he had finished the sentence, he stepped off of the fifty-foot wall, and the street rushed up to greet him. A flare of Orange Light caught him before he slammed into the cobblestones and he landed lightly, knees bent. Rhalia's Gate fell with him, exactly parallel to his right shoulder, as though it was tied to him.

"When I was a girl," Rhalia said, "potential Elysian Travelers were given months of ethics and morality training before they would be allowed to take the compatibility tests. I was only offered the option after I saved a man's life. But you...I taught you nothing. I only set you loose."

"I'm sure you had a good reason," Alin said, as he strode past the citizens of Enosh. They all bowed to him as he passed, each at exactly the correct angle. The boots of his golden armor rang out against the cobblestones, echoing in the silence.

Rhalia sat, cross-legged, in midair. Alin sensed her calling on the Orange Light, but he couldn't see it, which he suspected was more impressive than he realized. How many little tricks did she know that she hadn't shared?

"I trusted your blood more than I trusted the old teachings," she said bitterly. "You were prophesied to be the first natural Elysian Traveler in three hundred years, so I was *sure* you could handle yourself. And we can both use Violet, so let's be honest: I didn't trust myself. I was sure that anything I taught you would be poisoned by my past, that everything I said would lead you down my path."

Alin said nothing, he simply kept walking and let her speak. Perhaps this would be good for her, talking about her problems.

She knows far more than you do, the Violet Light said. *Maybe if you'd listened to her, you wouldn't be a tyrant and a monster.*

Alin crushed that voice. Maybe Violet and Silver were in this together.

"It looks like my path was wider than I'd thought," Rhalia whispered, almost to herself.

It occurred to Alin that he had never asked Rhalia about her past. That had been foolish of him. Who knew what wisdom she might have to share?

Are you brave enough to face it? the Gold Light asked.

That was odd. Usually the Gold Light was on *his* side.

Alin reached the injured man, who still lay slumped against the half-built wall of the White District. His clothes were ragged and dirty, his beard spilled across his chest.

Another worker, a younger man, hovered nearby, seemingly torn between helping Alin and going back to work. He was little more than a child.

The child was probably Alin's age, now that he thought of it, but the comparison was hardly fair.

Children these days, standing around like that, the Red Light muttered. *Pure laziness!*

Alin raised one gold-gauntleted hand and crooked a finger. All the color ran out of the young man's face, and he hurried over, giving a precise bow as he arrived. "How may I serve you, Eliadel?" he whispered.

"Don't be afraid," Alin said, full of Rose Light. "What happened to this man?" He knew his eyes would be bright pink, which couldn't be comforting, but if he released the Rose Light, his eyes would go back to their natural state. He didn't think this young man would appreciate staring into two circles of a thousand swirling colors, so he kept holding the Rose.

"I…I don't know," the boy choked out. "He fell over, and we tried to get him up, but he told us that he needed a rest. That's two hours ago, sir."

Alin placed one hand against the bearded man's neck. He could feel very little through his gauntlets, certainly not enough to check a pulse. He only needed to call a quick flash of Silver Light, and he'd know everything that was wrong with this man in an instant. Every cut, scrape, tumor, and lesion in the body would practically shine, and he could direct the Rose Light as needed. In a severe case that stretched beyond his abilities, he could even summon a more experienced or powerful healer from the Rose District.

But he hesitated. Calling the Silver Light would mean hearing what the Silver Light had to say, and he wasn't sure he could handle that at the moment. Perhaps later.

You're afraid to look into the Silver, the Violet Light said, *because it will show you as you truly are.*

Coward, spat the Gold Light.

"Can you help him, Eliadel?" the boy asked.

Alin cupped an empty hand, and it filled with a perfect flower blossom sculpted of bright pink light. He cast it out over the man's body, and glowing rose petals drifted down, sinking into the bearded man's flesh like pebbles into a pond.

"What are you doing, Alin?" Rhalia asked, her voice alarmed. The boy was making a point to look away from the Gate, as though he thought he wasn't allowed to look upon Elysia directly.

Alin didn't answer. The flower in his hand split into a flurry of pink petals, each sinking into an area of the body that needed healing.

"You didn't search him first," Rhalia said. "You have to use the Silver Light, Alin! Call the Silver!" She was straining to lean out of the Gate now, trying to get a closer look at his work, and it looked as though she was pushing on an invisible screen. She pressed with both hands, but the Gate's invisible barrier wouldn't let her pass.

She wasn't panicking, but she looked close to it.

The bearded man coughed once, and then his eyes opened wide. He took one huge, rattling breath so deep that he sounded like a corpse trying to breathe after a week in the ground.

Finally, he collapsed back down, panting, his eyes very much alert.

Alin smiled at Rhalia and stood, brushing off his armor. "Don't worry so much, Rhalia. You have to learn to accept these things as they come."

Rhalia looked like she was about to respond, but the bearded man coughed one more time, stealing both of their gazes back. He pulled a palm away from his mouth and held it out to Alin. His hand was spattered with blood.

"What is..." he began, but he stopped as he coughed again, falling to his knees. He kept coughing as he almost spasmed inward, curling up on the street.

"Search him!" Rhalia commanded. "Call the Silver!"

Red, Gold, Violet, and Rose all agreed, adding their voices to Rhalia's, and even Alin couldn't think of any other reason to hesitate.

Reaching out to Elysia, he tapped into the Silver Light. Instantly, he put together details that he hadn't thought were significant. The way the boy shuffled his feet, how he kept back far enough but never too far away to help, the concerned glances he kept shooting the bearded man...he was a relative, maybe even the older man's son. But he hadn't reacted much when it looked like the man was going to cough himself to death, so not a son. A nephew, maybe?

Once, Alin had enjoyed calling the Silver Light. It made him feel astute and intelligent, as he noticed trivial details and spun them together into the truth. The problem was, he couldn't turn it off.

If you had searched him first, you could have saved him, the Silver Light said. *Rhalia told you to, but in your fear, you didn't listen. Are you afraid you'll see what you're doing to these people? Can't you look yourself in the eye?*

According to Elysian legend and tradition, the Silver Light was the power of wisdom, given only to those who possessed extraordinary insight. He had never found that to be true; to him, it only ever sounded like the voice of accusation and guilt.

Alin spun a cloud of tiny lights into the man's body. To him, the Silver looked like a handful of glittering metal dust, shining as it flowed in a solid river into the man's veins, along his muscles, tracing the outline of bone and nerve. No one else could see what he saw, but in his vision, the human body became translucent under the effects of Silver Light. He could see straight through the skin, into the marrow.

The Silver flashed a warning, and it didn't take Alin long to see why: there was a dark mass around the worker's heart, twisting down until it even lay one tendril into a lung. Alin had never learned much anatomy, but he had heard of tumors, and he had spent his share of time around animals suffering from parasites. Whichever this was, it was killing him.

You killed him, the Silver Light said. *A growth like this feeds on the heal-*

ing you gave this man. If you had simply looked before injecting the Rose, he might have made it home tonight. As it is...

Rhalia let out a soft sigh. "He has maybe three, four hours left. It's best to get him some water and make him comfortable."

Alin kept kneeling. The man coughed once more, splattering blood on his gold breastplate, but Alin ignored it.

The Rose Light in him ached along with the bearded man, sympathizing with his pain, agonizing in sympathy over his terrible fate. *If only we had searched him first,* the Rose cried.

The Red and the Gold told him to get over this man's death. It was tragic, sure. But Alin hadn't meant any harm. In fact, he had tried to help. It was only natural that he should fail every once in a while, so long as he didn't let that slow him down.

The Green and Orange Lights were slower to judge. *He was a stranger to you,* the Orange pointed out.

Have peace, said the Green Light. *Everything will work out in the end.*

The Silver and Violet were more accusing. *This is your fault,* they said. *You could have fixed this.*

Alin didn't know what to think. His thoughts, his emotions, his very nature were all pulling him in very different directions, threatening to tear him apart.

Then the Blue Light shone, soft and cool, in his mind.

Mercy, it suggested.

That sounded like a good idea.

"Step back," Alin said to the boy. The young man took two or three steps backwards. "On second thought...take the day off. Go home. You don't need to witness this."

With tears in his eyes, the boy shook his head.

The Orange Light of loyalty couldn't help but approve.

Without another word, Alin called the Blue. Translucent tendrils of blue light, like tendrils made of sapphire, reached up out of the ground all around the bearded man. He continued hacking and coughing, but his eyes were glazed over again. They had none of the life in them that Alin had seen from him a moment before.

The ropes of blue light lay limp on the man's flesh. And then they began to draw his life away. Bright sparks of light, little chunks of the man's heat and life force, traveled down the tentacles, draining into Elysia. If Alin chose, he could take that power and use it to fuel his own summoning...but he hardly needed that, now. He let the energy go directly to his Territory instead.

As the Blue Light slowly killed this boy's relative—father, uncle, adoptive guardian, it didn't matter at this point—Alin decided it would be better for him to say a few words to honor this man he hardly knew. He opened his mouth to speak.

Only to find that, for perhaps the first time in his life, he had absolutely no idea what to say.

"May he find his way into the Maker's arms," Rhalia said softly. "May his life be remembered, his deeds honored, his family comforted. He will not be forgotten."

The boy was crying now, and the spectacle had attracted a smaller crowd that Alin had not noticed. Some of their overseers—a handful of squat gnomes with bright red caps—scratched at their beards, obviously wondering why their employees hadn't come back to work. Alin had summoned these from the Red District in Elysia, and constant diligence was all they knew. They would stay on a job until it was finished or they died of exhaustion, and they simply couldn't understand why humans weren't the same way.

Rhalia said something else that Alin didn't catch, and the crowd murmured in response. The boy was weeping openly now, but he nodded to Rhalia. She bowed back, her blond hair falling around her eyes so that Alin couldn't see what expression she was making.

The Blue Light retreated, leaving one lifeless corpse on the streets of Enosh.

At last, Alin figured out something he could say that might make a difference to a grieving family member. "He is gone, but I will take his body with me. He will lie in a grave in the City of Light, and Elysia will remember him forever." He would have to ask someone the dead man's name, at some point, but he was proud of the gesture.

The young man glanced at another worker, who patted him reassuringly on the back. The boy turned back and met Alin squarely in the eyes. "I'm honored, sir. More than I can say. But we'd rather have him back, if... you know, if it's okay with you. All our family is buried in the same plot, you see, and..."

He shrugged helplessly, unable to finish the sentence.

Alin felt a flash of irritation. He had offered to bury the boy's uncle in a rare and beautiful Territory, there to be remembered forever. How many people got a chance like that? But the Rose Light told him what he should say: "Of course, I completely understand. Take him with my blessing."

The boy and several of the other workers gathered up the man's body and carried him away. Alin had to command the gnomes twice to let them through; they would rather shave their beards than let workers go before the task was complete.

After that, the other workers simply milled around, shooting him and Rhalia nervous looks. He no longer felt like levitating marble blocks, so he simply told them to go home to their families. They all bowed to him and retreated, leaving only a few horrified-looking gnomes standing in an empty corner of the street next to a pile of shoulder-high marble blocks.

You did everything you could, the Rose Light said.

That was a tough job well done, said the Red.

You spared him worse pain, said the Blue.

He stood there for long minutes, long after the red gnomes had departed, letting the encouragement soothe him. Naturally, he had done the right thing. He was Elysia. He never did anything except the right thing.

Alin meditated on his own virtue until his smile returned and the world seemed right again. Only then did he fly back over the city, where more work awaited him.

He hardly noticed that the Silver Light had said nothing.

And neither had Rhalia.

CHAPTER 8

THE GALLERY

"So you lied to me," Simon said.

"I'd say I verbally misled you for the purposes of deception," Valin responded.

The Wanderer lounged in the grass, his back propped up against a tombstone. He held a three-foot Damascan infantry sword in his left hand, and was using the point to clean dirt out from under his right fingernails.

He couldn't move any more than his arms. He had exhausted himself so much, calling on his powers as an Incarnation, that he had stayed completely unconscious for two or three hours.

"I *think* that's exactly what a lie is," Simon said.

You'd know, you liar! Otoku sent. *You promised to protect us, and you abandoned me to my fate!*

I don't remember promising that. Simon hated having two conversations at once, especially when all he wanted to do was look for his mask. He couldn't even understand how he could have lost the mask in the first place, but the fact remained that it was missing.

"Do you want to know what the *real* graveyard test is?" Valin asked.

"Yes, please." Simon bent over and looked behind a tombstone, searching for the glint of mirror-bright steel. No good.

"You have to genuinely think you're going to die," the Wanderer responded. "That was why I went with the whole Incarnation act. Then, when you're sure you're dead, you have to reach out to Valinhall for power. The ghost armor will answer."

If you leave me with Kai again, even the ghost armor won't protect you, Otoku put in.

"So, when you said all that about having to dodge arrows…"

"That was a lie," Valin said.

Well, at least Simon had passed the test. That was worth something. He hadn't had a chance to call ghost armor yet, but he could think of at least three or four times when its powers would have come in handy.

Otoku didn't seem like she was in a celebrating mood. Her voice continued to beat at Simon from the inside of his skull.

You had *to leave me with him. I asked! I begged! No, I* pleaded *for you to come and help me, but you had to go play in the graveyard!*

I'm truly sorry, Otoku, Simon sent.

Are you? she demanded. *Are you, Simon? You would be if you'd seen what he did to me!*

His fight with Valin had torn holes in the soft soil of the graveyard, leaving slashes and furrows in the grass big enough to slip the mask inside. Maybe it had simply fallen in one of those?

What did he do? Simon asked, because it seemed like the right thing to say.

He gave me a bath!

Simon tried to imagine Kai fighting off imps in the giant, soapy pool that Valinhall had for a bath, just so he could scrub a wooden doll clean. He could picture it all too easily.

Surely he's done that before, though, right? Kai had been living with the dolls for decades, he had to have cleaned them at some point.

Meanwhile, Simon slipped his hands into the pockets of his cloak for at least the tenth time. He knew he wouldn't find the mask there, but where was it? The green light of the flashing lightning overhead made it hard to pick out any contrast with the grass, but the illumination was bright enough. He should have been able to see the mask gleaming from anywhere in the room.

The floating white crystal, hovering behind Simon's head, screamed, "SIMON, SON OF KALMAN, REPORT TO THE QUEEN FOR ASSIGNMENT. SIMON, SON OF KALMAN, REPORT TO THE QUEEN FOR ASSIGNMENT."

It had done that every sixty seconds for the past ten minutes, straight into Simon's ear. At least it was slightly quieter than a bellowing ox.

You think we can't keep ourselves clean, is that it? Otoku asked, outraged. *You think we sit there on our shelf, collecting dust and wallowing in our own filth?*

He'd thought the Nye cleaned them, actually, but he wasn't sure if he should tell her that.

"You know," Valin said, "I knew a few of this Queen Leah's ancestors. Some of them I quite liked. If you're not making any progress on the mask, you should invite her back here. I'm sure she'd enjoy a little chat. About her family, you understand."

The Wanderer looked very casual, scraping dirt out of his nails with the point of a sword. You would hardly believe that he was plotting an assassination.

"You can't murder her in the state you're in, you know that," Simon said wearily. The offer would have been more convincing if Valin hadn't made the same one five times since the flying Lirial crystal had shown up. He'd begged Simon a favor for the honor of seeing a Queen in person, then insisted that he had a secret for fighting the Incarnations, then threatened Simon with banishment from Valinhall if he didn't bring the Queen here.

Valin flashed a disarming smile. "See? I want a conversation. No threat here." Valin had angled his blade up, and appeared to be shaving his throat with its edge. Did room guardians even grow facial hair?

He removed my dress! Otoku railed, having taken Simon's silence as an invitation to keep listing Kai's sins. *Oh, sure, why not? Go right ahead! It's not like I have any dignity!*

Simon peeked behind a column for the third time. He distinctly remembered having the mask when he entered the graveyard, but maybe he'd been mistaken. Or maybe one of the Nye had taken it. Either way, he should check his bedroom soon.

You're made of wood, Simon pointed out. *Why do you care if you're naked?*

All of the dolls' voices sounded like they were being whispered down a long, windy tunnel, but Otoku did her best to make her scream of frustration heard. *It's like you don't even listen!*

She squirmed in his hand—actually, physically fighting his grip—and he was so surprised that he didn't react for a second. Not until he felt a tiny wooden hand slap his cheek.

Otoku stood in his palm, her arm outstretched, her red silk dress rumpled, and her black hair falling behind her. The doll's face was frozen in an unusual scowl.

You moved! Simon said in surprise. She hardly ever did that. Some of the other dolls often moved a little at a time, changing their expression or shifting their position, but Otoku almost never did. She hated spending so much energy, she said.

And that should show you how important this is! she sent. She looked like any other doll now, completely still, but Simon carefully raised her up to eye level.

"Otoku, I am—"

"SIMON, SON OF KALMAN, REPORT TO THE QUEEN FOR ASSIGNMENT. SIMON, SON OF KALMAN, REPORT TO THE QUEEN FOR ASSIGNMENT."

At the bellowing voice, Simon stumbled, and Otoku spilled from his palm. He snatched her out of the air in time, before she landed in the graveyard grass. The last time he had placed her on the ground, she had complained for days about the grass stains in her dress.

The loud rock will die, Otoku promised. *I'll see to it. Simon, kill that crystal for me.*

I don't think Leah would like that very much, he sent. But he was already tempted. If this kept up for another ten minutes, the communications crystal would likely end up as nothing more than shattered glass.

Otoku, would you mind helping me look for this mask? It would go a lot faster if—

Oh, I see! the doll sent. *When you want something, it's 'Otoku, would you mind? Otoku, please help! Otoku, I'm worthless without you!' But when I abase myself and beg, do you save me from the hideous white-haired beast? You do not!*

Simon raised Otoku up to eye level again. She was sitting now, as usual, but she hadn't lost the scowl. "Otoku," he said aloud, "would you mind? Please help. I'm worthless without you."

Well, she said, *when you put it like* that...

"It's good to hear you finally admit it, Simon," Indirial said, walking up behind Simon and clapping him on the back. "Humility is good for the soul, they say."

Simon blushed, and he couldn't think of a clever response.

"I'm here to pick you up," the Overlord said. He nodded to the floating silvery-white crystal. "I told Leah that I'd go myself, but she insisted on sending that thing in first. I followed as soon as I could, but you know how time works here."

Indirial put his hands on his hips and looked around the graveyard, smiling broadly. "Maker, it's been a long time since I've seen this place. Who's the guardian now? I thought the Eldest—"

Simon, stop him!

He should have seen it coming. But only with Otoku's warning did Simon have the time to call essence and throw himself at Indirial. Indirial was still faster. Simon avoided snatching the edge of the older man's trailing black cloak as he shot like a dark comet toward the master who had betrayed him.

The master he had, twice now, seen die.

Valin's expression didn't change. He held the infantry sword out casually in front of him, but he didn't have the strength to move. Indirial didn't have Vasha with him, but he had produced a knife from his cloak almost big enough to double as a sword. If the Overlord slit Valin's throat, would Valin die? Would he fade away? Would he regenerate?

Simon had no idea, and he wasn't sure whether or not he wanted to stop it from happening. What did it matter to him if the Wanderer was destroyed again? In the end, that might make his life easier.

A blast of dark smoke exploded at one end of the room, like someone had slammed a hammer into a pile of ash. Simon had a hard time following the smoke's path, even with the Nye essence in his lungs, but it flowed from the edge of the room over to the Wanderer, then exploded again in another burst of black smoke.

And Kai was there, standing *inside* the smoke, his own short sword raised to catch Indirial's blow. With a heave of his whole body, Kai turned the strike aside.

"We need him now, so let him go," Kai sang. Valin put his own sword down, his expression amused.

The two students of the Dragon Army stood there for a long moment. Indirial was dark and black-cloaked, crouched on the ground, staring at Kai as though trying to decide whether to spring up and bury his dagger in the other man's throat. Kai stood straight, by all appearances relaxed, an infantry sword held reversed in his left hand. Clumps of white hair hung down into his eyes, preventing Simon from reading his expression. The air burned with tension, and Simon was afraid that, one way or another, he was about to see a good man die.

"SIMON, SON OF KALMAN, REPORT TO THE QUEEN FOR ASSIGNMENT. SIMON, SON OF KALMAN, REPORT TO THE QUEEN FOR ASSIGNMENT."

Indirial staggered forward a step, and Kai cocked his head toward the crystal. Simon raised his hand on instinct, almost ready to smash the Lirial stone out of sheer reaction, but Leah had impressed upon him, more than once, exactly how rare and expensive communication crystals were. Granted, they normally didn't *shout in his ear* every minute.

But this one had distracted Kai and Indirial long enough to keep them from killing one another, so he could hardly complain.

Valin waved his hand in front of his face, dispelling the cloud of black smoke. He wore an expression of distaste, like he had bitten deep into a rotten fruit. "You called the smoke, Kai? Really?"

"I never was a friend of the Nye," Kai replied smoothly. "Even if the Eldest won't share his toys with me, I still need something for speed. Don't you think? Now that I have it, I can't believe how I went so long without it."

"The smoke makes things too easy," Valin said. "It's like cheating. How are you ever supposed to have an even match with anyone when you're appearing and disappearing like that?"

Kai wagged a finger at his former master. "Tsk, tsk, tsk. It's thinking like that kept you from killing the Damascan King. You had to wait for an Elysian Traveler to do your work for you."

"What are you doing here?" Indirial cut in roughly, staring at Valin.

Valin gave him an ironic smile. "It looks like the Eldest had further plans for me, and dying at the end of a Ragnarus blade was not in them."

Indirial said something low and harsh in a language Simon didn't understand, but he would have bet Azura that it was a curse. "What has he done now? I should have ended him years ago."

Indirial wore such a dark look, as though he could hardly hold himself back from tearing out Valin's throat, that it made Simon uncomfortable. Indirial wasn't supposed to be vengeful or cruel, he was supposed to stay calm and humorous even in front of an enemy.

Yes, because everyone stays the same, all the time, Otoku sent. *Indirial and Valin have a long and painful history. He's only human. He would need the patience of a doll to be able to smile right now.*

The patience...of a doll.

That's right.

You mean you.

Otoku made a shocked sound. *I can't believe you haven't noticed. My sisters and I are the very avatars of patience and humility.*

Sometimes, he couldn't tell when she was joking.

Kai nodded to Simon. "It seems that the little mouse has misplaced his cheese."

Indirial squeezed his eyes shut. "What are you talking about, Kai?"

"My mask," Simon put in. "I had it when I came into the room, I know I did, but it's gone now."

"You didn't give it to Olissa, did you?" Indirial asked. He opened his eyes and looked at Simon, deliberately turning away from Valin and Kai. "She's been working on the new versions, and she's mentioned more than once that she could use the prototype."

Simon imagined thirteen Valinhall Travelers with masks like his, and his stomach twisted. "She's making copies? And you're okay with it?"

"I decided not to fight it," Indirial said. "It looks like Valinhall will soon have a mask among its weapons, no matter what I do. And who am I to stand in front of progress?" He shot a glance over at Valin, and his face darkened again. "This isn't the first time I've failed to stop one of the Eldest Nye's plans."

Simon didn't see how Olissa could have possibly taken the mask from him while he was here in the graveyard, but he had nothing else to try. "Is she in the workshop, then?"

Indirial shook his head. "New room. Kai, will you show him the way?"

"I dash, I run, I positively *leap* to obey." Kai swept the other man a mocking bow. "But where, dare I ask, will you be?"

The Overlord looked down on the Wanderer, who met his gaze with an amused smile. "I have a few questions to ask our founder. And then Simon and I have business with the Queen."

"Please, leave him in one piece," Kai said, as he walked over to Simon. "The graveyard has never known a better training dummy."

The door to the graveyard swung shut behind Simon and Kai, cutting off Valin's mocking laughter.

Wordlessly, Kai held out one hand.

Let him touch me, Otoku said, *and you will beg the Nye to choke you in your sleep.*

They arrived in the workshop a few minutes later, Simon carrying Otoku in both hands, and Kai looking like he was on the verge of tears. The communication crystal floated after them like a lonely bird, having shouted out its message two or three times on the trip through the House. Twice now, Kai had threatened to force-feed the stone to Simon if he didn't release Otoku. To which Otoku had responded that she would rather be carried off by a swarm of cockroaches, leading Kai into bouts of dramatic wailing.

The sight of the workshop's cast-iron door was an indescribable relief.

Caius Agnos stood inside the workshop, carrying a box overflowing with odds and ends: gears, springs, metal wire, rolls of cloth, and tiny wooden cups practically spilled over the top. Caius, Olissa's husband, was a friendly-looking balding man who permanently wore a blacksmith's leather apron. His bulging gut and warm smile made him look like an innkeeper, but his arms were corded with muscle.

"Good to see you both. It's been a while since I've seen you, Simon. Is the Queen keeping you busy?"

"She called me now, actually," Simon said, only a second before:

"SIMON, SON OF KALMAN, REPORT TO THE QUEEN FOR ASSIGNMENT..."

Caius almost dropped his box. While Simon waited for the crystal to finish shouting, he took a look around the workshop. It had changed since he had last seen it, when it had been filled with cluttered boxes and dusty tables. Now, workbenches rested against each of the walls, covered neatly with an array of tools and half-finished projects. One rack on the wall held an array of hammers, arranged by size, and a tray on one of the workbenches showed a variety of gold ingots.

The copper shelves were a recent addition, nailed to the walls slightly above head-height, and they held a number of labeled boxes—the labels advertised everything from 'Metal Scraps' to 'Blood Jars' to simply 'Exciting!'

All in all, it looked like a professional craftsman's organized shop, now, rather than an enthusiastic collector's old woodshed.

The floating crystal finally stopped yelling.

"I guess the Queen doesn't like waiting on you, does she?" Caius asked, chuckling nervously.

"No, it keeps doing that," Simon said. "You get used to it. Almost."

Kai moved toward one wall, placing his hand against the bare stone in between two benches. "I'm entranced by your witty repartee, but we're not here to chat. Open the gallery, would you please?"

"Oh, yes, of course." Caius bustled over to a table, deposited his box of raw materials, then moved to the wall beside Kai. There was an iron rod sticking out of the wall at an odd angle; it had blended in so well with the tools a few inches away that Simon had hardly noticed it.

"This is one of my wife's favorite innovations," Caius said, smiling proudly. "Are you ready?"

Caius heaved the lever down, and the bare wall swung away from Kai's hand.

The next room was largely bare, and looked half-finished. He was looking down a long rectangle, like a hallway, with a chest-high counter running down both of the side walls. It looked almost like a tavern bar: the counters were smooth and polished, made of dark fine-grained wood, and there was a three-legged wooden stool every few feet. The walls looked like they were made of white plaster, and a long rug softened the stone floor stretching from the workshop door to the far wall.

Instead of drinks, the bars were covered in some of the same debris that Caius had been carrying in his boxes. Ingots of iron, plates of steel, tiny hammers, and huge tongs lay strewn on the polished wood surfaces.

On the walls, above the counters, hung a series of copper racks. They looked like elaborate hooks, designed to suspend paintings, and there were six racks on these walls. Since there were twelve of them, Simon would have thought the racks were backup storage for the wooden sword racks in the entry hall, designed to hold the Dragon's Fangs. But not only were these mounts far too small to hold a sword, four of the slots were occupied.

On his left, running down the wall, four masks hung on the wall in a row. It was easy to see the similarities between these masks and his: one half was dark, the other light, with two squared-off eye slits and no opening for the mouth. However, no one would mistake his mask for one of these. The light side wasn't quite the same mirror-bright polished steel of a Dragon's Fang, and the dark half didn't look like the rough, solid black of the wrought iron in Simon's. Now that he was looking at them more carefully, he noticed that the join in the middle, where the two halves met, was smooth and straight, unlike his own, which showed a jagged, uneven, sinuous line where two metals had been melted and joined together.

The steel half of these masks was almost pale, like it had been whitened somehow, and the iron half looked more dark gray than black. While Simon's mask looked like a rough-forged weapon, like it could itself be used to kill someone, these seemed like the delicate products of a craftsman.

He had no doubt that they were much deadlier than they looked.

Two of the stools in the room were occupied. Andra Agnos, the youngest Valinhall Traveler and the daughter of Olissa and Caius, brightened when Simon entered the room. She was fourteen—she had passed her latest birthday in the House—and she had been born with the same naturally tan skin and blond hair that marked Alin as part villager and part Damascan. She sat at a stool with a device in front of her: like a small hammer with a squared off tip, only the hammer was welded into some sort of metal frame. There was a half-finished mask sitting underneath the hammer's head, clamped into place by a vice at the bottom. The hammer's sharpened head was poised over the mask, leading Simon to believe that the machine was designed to punch eye slits in the metal.

Andra's brother, Lycus, sat at the stool next to her. He had turned eleven in the House, and unlike his older sister, he stared at his machine with focused intensity. He had to stand up and lean all of his body weight on the handle in order to push the machine down, pushing a hole into the metal with a sharp *thunk*.

Unlike Andra, who usually seemed happy to see Simon, Lycus wouldn't look Simon in the eye.

Simon couldn't blame the boy for that. Lycus had seen Simon kill people that the Agnos family considered friends. Maybe he would grow to understand. Maybe not.

Olissa Agnos had her auburn hair pulled back and tied behind her neck. She had pushed a pair of leather-banded goggles up her forehead, and she wore a thick pair of work gloves. Since the opening of the workshop, which sometimes felt like an age ago, Olissa had perpetual smudges of ash on her face.

At the moment, she was rubbing an eyeless mask down with a rag. Then she looked up and saw Simon and Kai enter. Olissa smiled and dipped into a mocking curtsy.

"Simon, Master Kai, allow me to introduce the gallery."

Simon had expected her to be making more masks, so the sight of them shouldn't have hit him as hard as it did. He already had enough trouble trying to decide when to use the mask and when to hold back. The feeling of it was addictive, overpowering. So far he had managed to restrain himself except in open combat with an Incarnation, but it was a struggle each time. The more masks, and the more people who had them, the greater the chance that someone would hold on a little too long. Then there would be another Valinhall Incarnation running around, one that he would have to stop. Again.

"Four faces hung on a wall," Kai said softly. "I wonder which of them is me?"

Olissa looked at Simon, who shook his head. "It's best not to question him. Mistress Agnos, could you tell me about the masks?"

Olissa held the incomplete, eyeless mask up to the light for inspection. "Happy to explain," she began.

"SIMON, SON OF KALMAN, REPORT TO—"

With a tinkling sound like a breaking bottle, the crystal shattered.

Simon wasn't holding the Nye essence, so he didn't see Andra move. One second she was sitting on a stool, trying to punch holes in a metal mask, and the next instant she was beside him, her Dragon's Fang drawn, standing in a falling cloud of crystal dust.

She looked at him, eyes wide. "What *was* that thing?"

"That was the Queen's expensive communications crystal," Simon replied. "Nice job. Now I can tell her honestly that I wasn't the one who broke it."

Otoku let out a sigh of pure relief. *Someone finally shut that thing up. When you die, try to make sure that she picks up Azura. I could work with her.*

She's already got a Dragon's Fang, Simon sent. *And who says I'm going to die?*

It's not a risky bet.

Andra's eyes widened even further, and she stared at the glittering shards on the ground. "She's not going to make me pay for it, is she?"

"You shouldn't swing your sword around like that," Lycus said. "That's why you keep breaking things."

Simon waved a hand at Andra. "Don't worry, Leah can afford it. More importantly, Mistress Agnos, can you tell me about the mask?"

Olissa straightened, wearing a proud smile. "Why, yes I can. I learned a lot when I put together your mask, you know, but I found all *sorts* of fascinating things trying to make one from scratch. Valinhall has its own source of power, you know. Its own energy. It's like..."

She searched around the gallery before she spied a small glass vial, and she snatched it off the counter and held it up. It was full of thick, yellow-gold oil.

"It's like this bottle of olive oil," she announced.

Andra giggled, but Lycus shushed her.

"In its natural state, the power of Valinhall is inaccessible," Olissa went on. "It's there, but it can't help us. Like a bunch of olives before they're pressed."

"You can eat olives," Andra pointed out. Her mother ignored her.

"Now, the power needs three things so that we can use it: it needs to be re-forged into a new shape, it needs a room, and it needs a guardian. It's basically the same process as making olive oil."

"Those fearsome olive oil guardians," Andra whispered.

"Olives need to be pressed, that is, formed into a new shape. That's what happens when we make a new tool, like this mask." She held up her unfinished mask, holding it next to the bottle of oil. "We're giving it a purpose by processing the power into a state in which it can be used."

She paused and looked at Andra, as if waiting for a comment.

Andra held up empty hands, so Olissa went on. "Now, what would happen if we didn't have a bottle around this oil?"

"It would escape?" Andra suggested.

"It would spill everywhere," Simon said, feeling like an idiot for answering such an obvious question.

Olissa pointed to Simon with the bottle's corked tip. "Exactly! So this power needs something to hold it. You see where I'm going with this? It needs a room to contain it. And the room needs to be separate from other rooms, so that the two different powers don't start mixing together."

"So the oil is like the mask," Simon said, "and the room is like the bottle. How about the guardian?"

With a self-satisfied smile, Olissa tapped the bottle's cork. "You need a way to get to the olive oil. Defeating a guardian is like pulling out the cork. But you've got to do it in the right way. You can't fight them all. It's got to be something that resonates with the nature of the shape and the nature of the room."

"You can't just *duel* your cork," Andra added, in mock seriousness. "Don't you see? It makes complete sense…" She dissolved into laughter as Lycus shook his head wearily.

"I see," said Simon. It was mostly true. "So who's the room guardian for your…gallery?"

Olissa slapped the mask and the bottle down on the counter, a little harder than necessary. "We don't have one. Not yet. The Eldest said there were 'more pressing vacancies to be filled.' So we're stuck here with a room nobody can use and a power nobody can call." She waved up at the wall, where the four complete masks hung in a row. "I even tried to get Erastes to do it, but he turned me down."

"Can you believe that?" Andra said. "It's like he doesn't want his skin to turn to leather and his bones to steel."

Simon had never thought about that before. Were all the guardians fated to end up like Chaka or Benson? Did they turn from ordinary humans into artificial constructs? Would that happen to Valin?

He almost asked Otoku, but he had more urgent concerns at the moment. "So, are you done with the original? I'm going to work for the Queen, and I need it."

Olissa frowned. "You never gave us the original. I've been working from my notes, but I still haven't quite managed to recreate what yours can do. I suspect yours can draw more power from Valinhall, but it doesn't have the safety measures in place that mine do. But I'd be able to know that for sure, if you would let us borrow yours…"

Simon chuckled awkwardly. "Sorry, it seems to have run off. You don't know where it is, then?"

Olissa looked like she couldn't decide whether Simon was making fun of her or not. "Isn't that it, right there?"

She pointed at Kai.

Kai stood with his hands at his sides, staring up at the four masks with his head cocked. He didn't seem to be listening.

"Where?" Simon asked.

Lycus slid off his stool and marched up to Kai. "He's got it right here," he announced. Then he pulled the mask from Kai's belt.

Kai had been carrying it the entire time. He had made sure to stand where Simon couldn't see it.

Simon let out a heavy breath and took the mask from Lycus. "Why, Master?" He tried to keep a lid on his frustration.

Kai shrugged, still staring up at the masks. "My little ones asked me to keep it from you. Maybe if they would speak to me, I would hold their secrets longer." His head slid from one side to the other, slowly, until it flopped onto his left shoulder. "They were right to try, I think, but they were too late. Is there a worse date than too late?"

Why didn't you tell me Kai had the mask? Simon demanded silently.

Oh, sure, let your dolls solve all your problems for you, Otoku responded. *I was going to tell you before, but that noisy rock interrupted.*

You could have told me at any point since then. 'Hey, Simon, I found the mask.' But that would have made your life so easy. How boring is that?

CHAPTER 9
INSIDE ENOSH

It had been over a half an hour, and Indirial still hadn't returned with Simon. That meant that he had spent better than an hour inside Valinhall. What was he doing in there? Thanks to him, Leah had been forced to spend most of the last half-hour explaining to a group of seven Travelers why her urgent mission wasn't departing immediately.

Overlord Feiora was dressed in what, for her, must have passed for armor: she wore a dark leather breastplate, and hardened leather of a matching shade shielded her shins and forearms. Beneath that she wore a chainmail shirt that came down to mid-thigh, and an iron-and-leather cap that must have served in place of a helmet. Eugan rested on one of her padded shoulders.

The clothes underneath Feiora's chain mail and leather armor were, of course, black.

Leah had never seen an Avernus Traveler prepared so practically for combat. It wasn't a full suit of armor; any foot soldier in the Overlord's service would have been better equipped. But the fact that she had *any-thing* on to defend her from a knife or a random sword blow suggested that she didn't suffer from the same affliction that got most Travelers killed: arrogant reliance on their powers.

I'm not wearing any armor, Leah thought. *I'm sure I'll be fine. My powers have protected me for a long time, why should they stop now?*

Leah paused, considering that thought for a moment. Silently, she resolved to bring some armor on the next mission.

Grandmaster Naraka was looking much more herself now, after a change of clothes and a series of baths. She wore the traditional dark red robes of Naraka, with sleeves that left her scarred wrist bare, and a pair of specially ordered scarlet spectacles perched on her nose. Leah had ordered the woman's arms bound together with a double knot of rope. That should allow her enough freedom that she wouldn't hinder the group as they marched through Naraka, but would still keep her from performing any of the complex hand gestures that summoning her Territory required.

Just in case that wasn't enough, she had recruited five loyal Travelers with the sole purpose of keeping an eye on the Grandmaster through the whole mission. There was a team of three Tartarus Travelers—all women, which was a rarity; usually Tartarus Travelers mixed genders in their teams—and two Naraka Travelers. Those two had paled when she had explained that they were supposed to guard *the* Grandmaster Naraka. They hadn't taken their eyes from the old woman since they first entered the tent, and their branded hands twitched every time she so much as yawned.

In Leah's mind, the two of them had already earned a reward.

The team of Tartarus Travelers was there as a contingency plan, in case it came to a combat situation. It was intended to be a routine mission, she had explained, but if things went wrong she would be more comfortable with three Tartarus Travelers to back her up.

And in the absence of any other orders, the three of them were to take Grandmaster Naraka's remaining hand off if she so much as snapped her fingers. Leah's father had never believed that you could have too many security measures in place, and she intended to take that lesson to heart.

Of course, she still needed the pair of Valinhall Travelers. Their preparations would go for nothing if the daylight burned away while Indirial and Simon wasted their time in the House. Where *were* they?

So she stood in awkward silence with an old lady, her five prison guards, and an impatient Overlord who insisted on asking every five minutes why they even needed Indirial for routine intelligence gathering, why they couldn't go without him. And better yet, she implied, if they could go without Leah.

She would have a headache before they made it into Naraka, she could feel it.

Leah had exchanged her red dress for something she would have been more likely to wear as a villager in Myria: a brown skirt and off-white blouse. The fabric likely cost less than a good meal in Cana, and the outfit made her look like a milkmaid, but she had forgotten how comfortable it was.

It wasn't a disguise, though. The weapons she carried with her made certain of that. She held the Lightning Spear in her right hand like a walking staff, and wore her crown on her head. Not for the symbol of status, but so that she could call on its power without having to summon it in a foreign Territory, which would take far too long.

If Indirial takes too much longer, I will leave without him. We've got a schedule to keep.

As if that thought had summoned the Overlord from Valinhall, a sword blade appeared in midair. It began to slice down slowly, tearing open a Gate in the exact same place that Indirial had opened one in the first place.

Simon and Indirial stepped through the Gate, both of them in their black cloaks. Indirial released his blade, letting it vanish, and Leah actually *saw* it shimmer and appear on a wooden rack in Valinhall's entry room.

The Gate zipped back up in reverse, bottom to top, and vanished as if it had never been.

"Welcome back," Leah said, instead of 'What kept you?'

Simon nodded to her. "Your crystal's broken."

It would take her six weeks of work to carve another one of those. "How exactly did that happen, Simon?"

Simon raised his eyebrows. "I can honestly say that I didn't do it." As usual, she could read nothing else of his expression.

There was that headache again.

Overlord Feiora made a disgusted sound. "What were you doing in there, Indirial? We could have left without you an hour ago."

It was an exaggeration, but Leah agreed with the sentiment.

Indirial did not smile, or smirk, or sigh, or make a joke. He turned and looked Feiora in the eye. "I met someone I didn't expect," he said, in a flat voice.

Something terrible had happened, she could see it in him. He hadn't reacted that badly when he'd found her father's corpse.

She looked at Simon in a silent question. He shook his head. What did that mean? Did that mean she shouldn't ask questions about it, or that it was too terrible to discuss? Or even that nothing significant had happened, and Indirial was just in a bad mood?

"I'll expect a full report from you later, Indirial," Leah said, keeping her tone businesslike. "But now we have a schedule to keep."

The Overlord remained expressionless, but he snapped an order at the Naraka Travelers. "Traveler Mikael, we need a Naraka Gate. Lead the way."

One of the Travelers, a young man, saluted and marched out of the tent, gently steering Grandmaster Naraka in front of him. His partner followed, as did the three Tartarus Travelers. Overlord Feiora strode out afterwards, shooting a glance back at Leah, but she was rushed out by Overlord Indirial. His cloak streamed behind him like a dark flag, and for once it seemed to suit him.

Simon started to follow, and Leah walked along with him.

"What happened in there?" she whispered. "I can't remember the last time I've seen him like that."

Simon opened his mouth as though he meant to explain, but after a moment he closed it. "I'm not sure I should tell you," he said at last.

Leah arched an eyebrow at him, and he sighed.

"Valin's back," he said, and a shiver of alarm ran through her. Valin, the deadly Incarnation that had been bent on killing her and her entire family? The man that they had only managed to defeat when Simon and Indirial had both risked their lives, and she had managed to catch him in a Ragnarus binding? That Valin?

"Turns out he wasn't dead," Simon said. "Or maybe he was dead, and the Eldest brought him back. I don't know. But he's in the House now."

Given the fact that Simon wasn't inside Valinhall right now, fighting the Incarnation, that meant that they had either already defeated Valin, or else determined that he wasn't a threat. Indirial looked far too upset to have won a recent victory, which meant that Valin must be safely contained.

And *that* opened up a whole new world of possibilities.

"Is he...himself?" Leah asked.

Simon shrugged. "I don't know. By the time I met him, he had spent twenty-five years as an Incarnation. But Indirial and Kai are treating him like he's the same guy, and he hasn't snapped and tried to kill us all. Not yet, anyway."

As they walked, Leah turned her eyes to the east. A dome of red light covered the city of Cana, her home and birthplace. It shone like a smoldering crimson sun rising from the horizon.

As always, she wondered about the Ragnarus Incarnation. Who was it? Why were they keeping the city imprisoned?

Was it the ancient Incarnation, as had been sealed beneath the Hanging Tree for over three centuries? Could it be her brother, Talos? Or was it her father?

Before, she had seen only two ways to deal with Incarnations: seal them, if possible, and earn a grace period during which no one else could successfully Incarnate. If that wasn't possible, they could be killed, usually with great difficulty, though it would open up space for a new Incarnation.

If Incarnations could be killed and *then* returned to their Territory, even as the shadows of the people they once were, might that be a third option?

Maybe they could not only stop the Incarnations, but save them.

The thought haunted her all the way to the nearest Naraka waypoint, until they stepped through into the Caverns of Flame.

At that point, she forced herself to stop considering the question over and over. The other members of the team didn't need her distracted, they needed her focused and alert.

She would work on the problem when she got back.

Simon had only Traveled through Naraka a handful of times, but he always left with burning eyes and a piercing cough. As he stumbled out of the orange Gate, he wiped the back of his hand across his eyes, trying to clear them. There was no way to escape the smoke in that Territory; it stung, it stunk, and now the acrid stench gripped his clothes in a tight fist.

Never let me go back there, Simon sent to his doll.

Oh, get yourself together, Rebekkah said. *Whining never helped anything.*

Simon let out one more deep, wracking cough. *I'm serious. We can walk if we have to, I can't handle Naraka.*

Rebekkah glared up at him from his left hand, but that was her usual expression. Her long red hair was tied back in a single braid, and she wore a brown shirt and brown pants, belted with a length of rope. She was dressed like one of the poorer villagers...in clothes much like the ones Simon himself had worn, in fact, before he came to the House.

Will Alin be in this city? Rebekkah asked. She had never met Alin, but she devoured Simon's stories about him. He was afraid he knew why.

Probably, Simon allowed. *But we won't see him. If we run into Alin, that means the plan went horribly wrong.*

So when everything goes wrong, then you'll get to fight him?

Simon tucked Rebekkah into a pocket of his cloak. *Why do you want me to fight him so much? I don't want to.*

He deserves it, Rebekkah said, no room for doubt in her voice. *I can't wait to see you punch him right in his face.*

Simon didn't want to imagine that the plan might fail so badly that they would run into Alin *and* have to fight him, but he tried to picture it. What would he do? Simon had once promised that he would personally put a stop to Alin, if he let the Elysian Incarnation take too much control.

He had never much liked Alin, and he was more than willing to oppose the Incarnations. But it felt like he had made that promise a long time ago.

Did he even want to fight Alin?

The Wanderer's words echoed in his mind: *What do you want, Simon?*

He wasn't sure. But at least this trip would let him know if Alin deserved to die. Maybe that would help him decide.

"Eyes up, Simon," Indirial said, in a softer voice than normal. Simon took a deep breath and shelved his thoughts, looking around at the Naraka waystation.

Like always, the way in and out of the Territory was marked by a fifteen-foot-tall obelisk of black stone, marked with twisting golden runes. This room, built around the obelisk, had once been made of ordinary stone. Simon could still see the rough pattern of the rock in the metal of the wall.

The whole building had been turned to gold. Gold walls led to an arched ceiling, supported by crossing beams that were also made of gold. The only feature in the room not turned to gold were the high windows, and those were now blue.

The Incarnation of Elysia had lived here for a long time.

Overlord Feiora's raven circled the room, searching for hidden watchers. Indirial, as the plan required, had rushed out of the Gate and subdued the guards. He had done so before Simon had even staggered out of Naraka: one human guard lay bound and gagged on the stone, tied with strips of cloth. The other, an inhuman thing that looked like a cross between a dog and a blue-skinned lizard, lay sprawled on its back, apparently unconscious. Tentacles twitched as it drew a shallow breath.

Indirial knelt down and pulled the wadded cloth out of the man's mouth. The guard started to scream, but the Overlord punched him in the throat.

It didn't look like he used much force. It was more of a tap than a punch, little more than poking him in the neck with a couple of knuckles. The man choked on his scream, struggling to draw a breath.

"Don't try that again," Indirial advised, giving the guard a friendly smile.

You see? Rebekkah sent. *At least* someone *knows how to handle his problems the right way.*

"I'm not going to help you," the man whispered through a hoarse throat, once he caught his breath. "I can't."

"Yes, he can," Overlord Feiora said. She was peeking out the door, not looking at the prisoner, but her raven fluttered down to land on Indirial's shoulder. "I can't quite see it clearly, but he knows what we need to know." The raven stared into the guard's eyes and let out one soft, subtly threatening sound, like a mewling growl.

Indirial nodded to Feiora. "You heard the lady," he said pleasantly. "Let me ask you a few questions, and you can decide whether to answer, okay?"

The guard nodded, eyeing the raven.

"How many guards are outside?"

"None," said Feiora and the guard at the same time. The man jerked as if she had slapped him, and he strained against his bonds to look at her.

"Can she...I mean, can she see into my..." he swallowed.

Indirial chuckled. "Now, don't scare yourself. She probably looked outside. I would recommend that you don't pay any attention to her or to the bird, okay? Just focus on me."

The guard nodded weakly.

The raven lowered its beak so that its eyes were as wide as possible. The captive visibly struggled with himself, trying to keep his head turned to the side, before he looked the raven in the eyes.

The bird let out a very slow, very deliberate *caw.*

The guard shivered, and Simon didn't blame him. He was growing a little scared of the bird, and its gaze wasn't even directed his way. He could only imagine how much worse it would be to meet head-on.

"That's a little unusual, isn't it?" Indirial asked. "Only two guards. It was my understanding that the Grandmasters assigned two inner guards and four outer guards, all Travelers. Am I wrong?"

The guard hesitated.

"Reassure him," Feiora said, staring out of a window.

The man jerked against his bonds again, and Indirial placed a hand on his shoulder. "Hey, don't worry. I'm working with the Grandmasters. Isn't that right, Grandmaster Naraka?"

Simon stepped aside, revealing the still-open Naraka Gate behind him. The two Naraka Travelers stood on either side of the Gate with their hands outstretched, holding it open and steady. A foul wind blew from within, carrying the scent of woodsmoke, sulfur, and distantly burning hair, but it was much more pleasant than actually being in the Territory.

Grandmaster Naraka stood directly in front of the Gate, her three Tartarus guards arrayed behind her. Even the Naraka Travelers holding the Gate didn't take their eyes from the Grandmaster for more than the time it took them to blink.

She smiled like a kindly grandmother. "That's right, son. It's okay, you can answer them."

The guard's forehead furrowed. "Why is her hand tied?"

"That's for her own safety," Indirial said smoothly, drawing the man's attention back to him. "Don't worry about that. Now, go ahead and tell me."

Simon noticed that he didn't explain how having a one-handed woman bound by ropes could possibly be for her own safety, but the guard seemed soothed. Simon stepped back in front of the Gate, to prevent the man from noticing that the Grandmaster was under heavy guard.

"Eliadel said the Travelers were needed elsewhere," the guard practically whispered. "Most of the Territories are guarded on the other side, but he doesn't think we're in danger. He tells us we're secure. He says that a lot."

"He's afraid," Feiora murmured. "He's very afraid of speaking, but he's even more afraid of keeping silent."

Their captive didn't seem surprised at her statement this time, but his shoulders slumped.

Indirial nodded, bringing the guard's attention back to him. "When you say Eliadel, you mean Alin, son of Torin?"

The man glanced from side to side, fearfully. "Don't call him that. He's Elysia now. You have to call him that, or Eliadel, or the King. You can't call him…his name."

Simon couldn't help it; he had to ask. "Is that what Alin wants?"

The guard flinched at the name, but he answered. "Not Eliadel, exactly. He's never told us what to call him. But the ones in the gold armor… they'll fight you if they hear you being disrespectful. No one ever wins a fight with the gold ones. And the silver ones always hear, and they'll tell the gold ones…"

He seemed to realize what he'd said, and he forced a smile. "Not that I'm unhappy! Far from it. We have plenty of food, and we're safe. You understand? We're safe from the Damascans."

His smile slipped away, and a dawning horror crept into its place. "Wait a second…you're not…"

"Damascan?" Indrial asked with a laugh. "Nope, I'm afraid not. We were on a long mission with the Grandmaster, and now we're back. Imagine our surprise when we came back and found the city occupied by a new force. We assumed it was Damasca, but you're saying Eliadel himself took over? What happened to the other Grandmasters?"

Simon couldn't help but admire the way the Overlord maintained control of the conversation. He deflected attention, forcing the guard to respond to him instead of the other way around, and he smoothly distracted the man from thinking about the inconsistencies in his story. Indrial had actually struck *first* upon leaping out of the portal, and somehow he had gotten his victim to overlook that. Not to mention that, if they *had* been on a long-term mission in Naraka, this would be their first time coming into the real world. How would they know the city was occupied?

But the guard seemed to invent something in his own mind that satisfied him, because he kept talking. "You want my advice?" His voice lowered, as if he were afraid of spies and traitors even in a sealed room. "Take the Grandmaster and run! Go now. You'll have to take that…blue thing with you," he nodded to the twitching creature lying next to him, "because I can explain its disappearance better than I can its death. But you'll have to hurry, or she'll end up like all the other Grandmasters."

"What happened to *them?*" Naraka snapped.

"Their heads are spiked on the city gates," the guard said softly.

Grandmaster Naraka made a 'pfah' sound and waved his comment away. "Old news. I saw Helgard there months ago."

The captive shook his head. "Not just Helgard. All of them. Everybody except Asphodel, Avernus, and Endross, and I heard they were dead already. Grandmaster Tartarus tried to lead a rebellion a few months in, but he couldn't fight his way through the Red District. Eliadel dueled him personally, and he had his silver eyes show everyone in the city how it ended." The guard shuddered. "I don't even know why. I liked the city well enough the way it was."

He seemed to hear his own words, and put on another bright smile. "Not as much as I like it now, of course."

"He hates it," Feiora said, still watching the window.

"I could have told you that," Simon muttered.

"He doesn't let anyone leave, does he?" Indirial asked. Simon more or less knew the answer to that; Damasca hadn't heard from anyone in Enosh for six months, at least before Grandmaster Naraka showed up.

"We have everything we need here," the guard said without hesitation. "There's plenty of food in the Green District, he opened new wells all around town, and…something…takes all the trash at night. All you have to do is leave it outside. And we can't go out after sundown, because it's not safe. But the Damascans were planning on destroying the whole city! The Grandmasters told us so before Eliadel took over. They can't do it now that he's here, right?" The man sounded almost pleading. "He's the one who killed their king."

"That's right," Indirial said, as soft as a knife being drawn. "He is."

Indirial stood up and walked over to Overlord Feiora. "Well?" he asked.

Feiora shook her head. "Images, fragments, it's all jumbled up. I'll make sense of it, in time, but I say we go take a look for ourselves. I've been looking through this window the whole time, and I haven't seen another soul. He can't make things invisible, can he?"

Indirial glanced at Simon, who shrugged. "I don't think so. Everything I've seen from Elysia has glowed pretty brightly, but he can probably do a lot of stuff I don't know about."

Overlord Indirial strode over to the bound guard. "Thank you, you've been very helpful. If Eliadel asks you any questions, tell him that a Grandmaster made you talk."

The guard's eyes widened. "Wait, no! Don't—"

Indirial shoved the ball of cloth back into the man's mouth, then placed his hand on the man's forehead. His eyes rolled up into his skull, and he fell limply on the ground.

"How did you do that?" Simon demanded.

The Overlord grinned. "Unorthodox application of a lesser-known Valinhall power. It wasn't meant for this, but you won't go far in life without a little creativity." He turned to the Naraka Gate. "What do you think?" he called. Grandmaster Naraka started to reply. "No, not you. Our esteemed leader."

Leah stepped out from behind the edge of the Gate and walked into the room. She wasn't wearing her crown, but she did hold the tall Lightning Spear in one hand. "I think he's got a tighter grip on the city than we thought," she said.

"Worse than I had imagined," Grandmaster Naraka muttered.

"Given that information," Leah went on, "we need to make this even faster than we'd planned. We can always come back if we need to. Simon and Indirial, hoods up. When your…shadows run out, come back here immediately."

'Shadows?' It wasn't quite accurate, but Simon liked the way it sounded. He should use that.

"Feiora, you stay here. You can send Eugan out, but keep him absolutely safe."

"Of course!" The Overlord sounded offended at the suggestion that she might do anything else.

Leah turned back to the guards. "The two Naraka can stay here. Tartarus, take the Grandmaster into this room, but stay away from the windows and do not, under any circumstances, take her anywhere out of this room. If I see her heading anywhere else, I will kill her and anyone with her. Do you understand?"

The three Tartarus Travelers saluted.

"I will be—"

"…standing right there," Indirial finished for her. "Prepared to jump straight back into the Gate at the first sign of anything unusual."

Leah made an unpleasant face. "Yes, thank you, Overlord Indirial. You plucked my very words from me."

Indirial swept her a bow.

"I will, however, be using a scrying lens to follow your progress in the city," she went on. "It will be difficult, given what your shadows do to my scrying, but I'll manage. Perhaps I will see something you miss. If I notice anything urgent, I will send you a signal."

"What kind of signal?" Simon asked. He felt they should be as forewarned as possible, just in case.

"Depending on the circumstances," she said, "it will probably sound like my voice shouting, 'Oh, seven stones! Simon, run, there's a huge slobbering beast about to eat your face!' Would you prefer an explosion?"

Simon cleared his throat. "No, thanks. That'll be fine."

"Then if we're all done with questions?" She looked around the room, meeting the eyes of Indirial, Simon, Feiora, and Eugan. They all nodded at her gaze, even the raven.

"Go quickly, and return safely," Leah said. Simon flipped up his hood, and Indirial did the same.

The door swung open for a brief moment. From the outside, it might have looked like happenstance, maybe a gust of wind. Anyone who didn't look directly at it might have missed the motion entirely, at least until they heard the door shut.

During the half-second in which the door was open, two Valinhall Travelers, one raven, and a glassy Lirial crystal the size of a marble passed through without a sound. An observant watcher may have noticed a flicker of shadow, a wink of reflected light.

Then the door slid softly shut.

Chapter 10
Stories in the City

Alin wrenched open the violently purple door and glanced inside. One of the native inhabitants of the Violet District stood within, on top of a wooden table. It looked like a giant ball of fuzz, as though someone had rolled up a bundle of wool, dyed it violet, and given it stick-thin arms and legs. A pair of clear, comically large eyes bulged from its head.

The furry creature was holding a dinner plate over its head, its spindly arms stretched high. It looked like it had climbed up on top of its table for greatest height, so that it could smash the plate on the ground.

It gave Alin a wide, bright smile. "Traveler! It disturbs me to see you, but I will smile as though I am pleased! I hope you have a pleasant day, as long as I am not in it! Please, leave me to my own business!"

It said all that in a chipper voice with a pleasant smile. Alin cast a brief cloud of Silver Light inside, found that the purple fuzz-ball was the home's only occupant, and pulled the door shut. He wouldn't have understood before, but now the Violet was a part of him. Honesty at all times, that was the Violet way, even at the cost of compassion, mercy, or understanding.

Behind him, through the closed door, he heard something shatter. As though a plate had crashed to pieces on the ground.

Rhalia's Gate still drifted beside him, keeping pace with his shoulder. He could have let it close and open it again, but the nature of Elysia was such that it preferred to open only once a day. When he could respect the rules, he would.

"Are you sure it was in the Violet District?" Rhalia asked.

Alin shook his head, letting Violet honesty have the reins. "I can't be sure. It might even have been my imagination, but I thought I had glimpsed something with the Silver Light. Just for a second. It's either here or in the Blue District."

Rhalia hovered in Elysia, her legs crossed under her, sitting three feet above the ground. She swept a lock of golden hair behind her ear. "It's worth looking into, then, sure. But please, try not to antagonize the people."

She's right, said the Rose Light. *We don't want to scare anyone.*

"I'm not antagonizing them, I'm conducting an inspection. They will accept it, as they were ordered." While Alin walked, the Enosh citizens to either side of the street bowed at the waist when he passed. He paid that no more attention than to the stones at his feet, which transformed when he walked by. Each cobblestone on which he stepped turned from a shade of purple or violet to bright white, as if his footprints were soaking them in paint.

Both the respect of the people and the transformation of the city were not unusual, to be noted or commented upon. They were natural reactions to the Incarnation of Elysia, and he accepted them as such.

Rhalia sat cross-legged in the air above Elysia, her hands resting in her lap. Her gold eyes were far away. "Alin," she said distantly, "can I tell you a story?"

You would be wise to listen, the Silver Light told him.

We have the time, the Green said.

But I don't want to hear it, Alin thought. None of the powers of Elysia liked that very much, so he relented.

"Of course," he said. The Rose Light was not pleased with his tone.

Rhalia let out a slow, even breath. "When I was a girl, the Elysian Travelers were in charge. They supervised all the other Territories, and whenever an Incarnation broke through into our world, they were the ones to take care of it."

Alin pulled open another violet door, revealing a woman sitting in a chair, holding a dripping shirt above a wooden tub. Her eyes went wide as she saw him, and her head jerked as though she were stopping herself from looking for a way out.

He shook his head at the foolish fears of humans, shut the door, and moved on.

"Back then, there were two ways to become a Traveler of Elysia," Rhalia continued. "You could be trained to do it, if you met the compatibility tests. Or, sometimes, you were born to it. That was very rare; I was the first in a hundred years to call power from Elysia without any training at all."

Only one hundred years? The Silver Light wondered. *Then why did it take over three centuries for the next natural Elysian Traveler to show up? Was it a bad run of luck, or did something change?*

Alin cast a flicker of silver light in through an open window, found no one inside the house, and kept walking.

"The Master Travelers trained me quickly. Too quickly, some said, but they agreed that my nature would bend me toward virtue and keep me from corruption." Sadly, she shook her head. "You'd think I would have done better, but it seems that some lessons you do have to learn twice."

She thinks you were a failure, the Violet Light whispered, but he managed to ignore it.

The next house he didn't have to check; he could sense two more Elysian creatures inside. Not only would they have warned him if any intruders had violated their home, they would probably ask him to leave if he stuck his head in. So he didn't bother.

"It was a time of great change," Rhalia said, still staring off into the distance. "Discord and dissent grew into a war. One by one, the other Elysian Travelers died. Until, at last, I was the only one left."

Rose-pink compassion swelled up in him, and he had to speak. "I can't even imagine how hard that must have been."

Rhalia twirled in place, gently, which was the first time Alin had seen her do so all day. Normally she spun and danced and whirled around in midair all the time, until it made him dizzy. Maybe she was focusing too much on her bitter memories.

"It...wasn't so bad," she said. "I had a sister, you see. Cynara."

At that, Alin had to shove down some bitter memories of his own. He had practically been raised by his three sisters.

And how did you repay them? the Orange Light asked. *You abandoned them, so two of them died. At least Ilana is safe.*

She's safe, but you're not doing your job, the Red Light barked. *You picked the lazy option, letting someone else take care of her. That should be your responsibility.*

You're afraid you can't do it, the Violet Light whispered.

And Alin shoved all of that down, floating on a cushion of pink comfort and green patience until he had his emotions under control once again.

"She wasn't a Traveler," Rhalia continued. "Not at first. She was a fighter, a mine-worker, and a leader. She had an amazing sense of justice." Rhalia shook her head. "It wasn't something I could appreciate until I had spent enough time in Elysia, but she never let a wrong pass when she could right it. She never saw someone hurting without trying to help them. She would have made a wonderful Naraka Traveler."

For the next two houses, Alin levitated their locks out of the way using Orange Light on the inside. He pushed Silver Light through the doors, frightening two human families, but finding no trace of anyone who didn't belong. Had he been mistaken after all?

The Green and the Red both told him to have patience, to keep working. He would know whether or not he was wrong after he finished searching.

Rhalia bobbed up and down in midair, sounding thoughtful. "I've often wondered if my sister would have done a better job in my place. She probably would have. I couldn't handle being the only Elysian Traveler, you see. It was my responsibility to lead the Travelers, to banish every Incarnation, to save everyone…and I couldn't do it. Often I failed, and the blame fell on me."

Her voice held the faint echo of pain, and once again the Rose Light begged him to make it better.

This is her wound, Alin and the Silver said at once. *I can't share it.*

"I drew more and more power," Rhalia said softly. "Even when I wasn't ready for it."

The remark stung. She had clearly directed that at him, and she wasn't being subtle about it. *She did try to warn you,* the Violet Light pointed out. *If only you had listened—*

Alin shut off its voice and shoved Silver Light in a broad sweep down the street. It wasn't nearly as accurate or detailed as if he had pinpointed a single house at a time, but he saw no silhouettes of a man holding a sword against a child's neck, felt no flares of pain or panic. It seemed, at first glance, that everything in the Violet District was as it should be.

"It finally occurred to me why I was having such problems," Rhalia said. She had stopped sitting in midair and started drifting back and forth, from one side of the Gate to the other, like a pacing ghost. "It was because no one was in charge! There was all this chaos…and I was sure it was up to me to impose order. I stopped banishing the Incarnations."

Now she had his full attention. He stopped walking, and mentally ordered the Gate to swing around so that he could face her head-on. "What did you do with them?" he asked.

She met his shifting eyes with her golden ones. "I bound them to serve me, each according to its nature."

Where did she get the power? Alin wondered.

The Silver and Violet Light both laughed. *You know the answer,* they said.

"You became an Incarnation," he said, and as soon as the words left his mouth he knew them for truth.

"My sister begged me not to," she said softly.

"But…" Alin struggled to form his thoughts into coherent words. "I am Elysia, now. I thought a Territory could have only one Incarnation at a time."

Rhalia smiled a little. "And so it does. With time back in my Territory, my status as Incarnation faded away. Now I am no longer Incarnation nor Traveler, but something…more limited."

Alin imagined himself in her position. Letting his power fade away, becoming a shadow of what he was now? He'd rather die.

"I see," he said, to keep the conversation on track. "What were you saying about your sister?"

"She tried to stop me with words, and even with force, but I was beyond her then. She gathered up others to oppose me, and they followed her. But I would not listen to reason." She took a deep breath. "When I was at last out of control, Cynara searched for darker weapons to bring a stop to my rampage."

"Did she?" Alin asked.

"After years of searching she found them in an old Territory. A place that we of Elysia had forbidden years before, on the grounds that it was too dangerous. The Crimson Vault."

Alin's hand automatically jerked toward his pants pocket, beneath his armor, where he kept the Seed of the Hanging Tree. Its power burned him, every day, begging to be used, pulsing in opposition to the light of Elysia, but he kept it with him. If someone stole it, they could use it as a weapon against him.

Especially if it made it into Leah's hands. Leah, or one of her family…

"Are you one of Leah's ancestors?" Alin asked.

Rhalia frowned. "Leah?"

Oh, right. She's never met Leah. "One of the Damascan royal family. She's a Ragnarus Traveler."

Rhalia spread her hands and shrugged. "As you would imagine, I haven't kept up with this world since I sealed myself in the City. But I do know that my sister made some sort of bargain with the Founder of her Territory."

Founder? Alin wondered, but Rhalia kept talking.

"One result of that bargain was the Hanging Trees, which can seal Incarnations at the cost of blood. But I heard rumors that Cynara may have also bound the Territory to her own bloodline. If that's true, then yes, I would be distantly related to Leah."

Alin stood at the center of the Violet District. The people in the streets hurried away from him, afraid of meeting his gaze, and the purple cobblestones steadily bleached themselves as he stood still. Thoughts whirled in his head; Rhalia's story blended with his own. She had made some mistakes, and he had to make sure he didn't repeat them.

"So your sister betrayed you," Alin said at last. The Orange Light agreed with him.

Rhalia smiled a little and drifted through a circle in midair. "She fought me in the streets of Cana. We were evenly matched for a while, but I knew she couldn't pay Ragnarus' costs forever. I was content to wait. And then she planted one of those Hanging Trees."

Alin almost shuddered, thinking of the bloody, carnivorous trees that had feasted on the sleeping Incarnations for centuries. He *would* have shuddered, except that he was beyond such petty reactions.

"I knew that the Trees meant living death," Rhalia continued. "So I opened a Gate to Elysia and bound myself inside."

His mind violently rejected the idea. Elysia called to him, it sang to him silently every day, begging him to step through a Gate and rejoin his Territory once and for all. But he knew what it would mean for him. He could feel it. Once he returned to the City of Light, he would become a part of its fabric, never to leave again.

Just like Rhalia.

"I thought I was getting the best of Cynara," Rhalia said. "She had given her life to her Ragnarus weapons, and all I'd sacrificed was my freedom. I had planned to wait until the next natural Elysian Traveler came along, and train them to take my place."

She sighed. "But it wasn't long at all before the fog in my mind lifted, and I realized what I had done. What I had become."

You're a monster, the Violet Light whispered.

Rhalia's eyes shone like gold coins. "I became a monster."

Don't walk the path she did, the Silver Light said.

"I don't want you to walk down the same path I did, Alin."

Think about what you've done to these people, the Rose Light begged. Alin glanced around, at the fear in the citizens of Enosh. They didn't love him. They cringed away from him.

"Think about what you could do to these people," Rhalia said. "Think about what you will do, when you lose control."

The Gold Light shone, comforting and powerful, in the back of his mind, like a new sun hanging out of sight. *Don't be afraid,* it said. *A truly brave man would face the truth.*

"You don't belong here," she said.

You don't belong here, the Light agreed.

Alin stared past Rhalia, through the Gate, at the shining silver-and-gold walls of Elysia. Behind those walls, the tops of the city rose: red brick towers, gold monuments, silver spires, gleaming amethysts the size of warehouses. A column of light rose from the peak of the city to pierce the sunset sky.

His heart ached for the City. It was where he belonged, he could feel it.

But if he took that one step inside, he would never leave.

Alin took in one deep, shuddering breath, and the spell was broken. He took a step back and turned his back on Rhalia, walking away. Silver Light spun at his command, flashing into every window, through every cracked door. It raced and flew through the entire city, spreading out, giving him a vague sense of everything in Enosh, tying him with tiny webs to every person in the city.

"Not yet," Alin said, his voice cold. "I still have work to do here." The very idea of Grandmaster Naraka blackened his thoughts, and the Incarnations were still loose. Leah was likely doing her best to keep them contained, but could she really handle it? Not as well as he could, he was sure.

No, he wouldn't make Rhalia's mistakes.

He would do *better.*

"There are nine virtues in Elysia," Rhalia said. "They're all important, but there is one which provides them all with context. Only one virtue that gives the others meaning. And you don't even understand it."

Alin marched toward the Blue District, his boots ringing on the stones. "I don't need to hear about the White Light, Rhalia. I think I'm done with stories for today."

"Then why is the Gate still open?" Rhalia asked softly. "Why do you carry me around with you every day, if you don't—"

He slashed a hand across empty air, and the Gate vanished.

Time to get back to work, the Red Light said.

He almost hoped he *did* find some intruders in the Blue District. In this mood, he would enjoy doing something clear-cut, something that was undoubtedly the right thing to do. Like protecting his city from invaders.

Before he made it to Enosh, Simon had wondered if they would find anything. What were they even looking for, aside from 'something wrong'? Unless they saw Alin actively dismembering a citizen, how were they supposed to know if he'd done anything?

It didn't take him long, running through the streets of Enosh, to figure it out.

The city looked completely different than when he'd last seen it, both because of Alin's presence and because of his reconstruction efforts. They were in the all-blue section of the city, which he had heard someone call the Blue District.

He clung to the side of a wall, fingers braced with Benson's steel, and watched a mother and her daughter cling to one another and shake as a shapeless blue mass, dangling six-foot tentacles, drifted down the street as though it were underwater.

He stood in the shadow of a doorway, his hood drawn and Nye essence running through him, watching one man beat another bloody with a shovel. A boneless blue lizard the size of a dog flowed up to him, hissing, but he dropped his shovel and held his hands up.

"Mercy," he said, in a lazy drawl.

The reptile sniffed him, flicked out a tongue, and then flowed away, leaving the bleeding victim on the street.

As soon as the blue creature of Elysia was out of sight, the man had picked up his shovel once more and continued his beating. None of the bystanders said a word; they went about their business.

Once Simon had shoved the attacker's unconscious body into a nearby shed, along with the scraps that had once been a bloody shovel, he moved on.

Under normal circumstances, he could hold his Nye essence for about two minutes. It seemed like longer, under the effects of the essence, and he could stretch that out if he used it less, or burn through it quicker. But he figured two minutes was a good deadline.

He saw his third crime before sixty seconds was up.

He was standing on top of a roof, eavesdropping—with Rebekkah's help—on the family speaking underneath him.

"I don't understand it," one woman whispered. "He was never...before..."

She says, 'he was never like this before he killed the king,' Rebekkah relayed. *She's talking about Alin, obviously. What more do you need?*

Keep listening, Simon instructed.

"Eliadel is a good man at heart," a man's voice said loudly. Then, more quietly, "Look, we've been through worse times. Alin is hardly the worst thing to ever happen to us. We'll get by."

Nearby, where they couldn't see it, a silver mirror on the wall began to flash. It was flashing brightly, but aimed up at the sky, so the only reason Simon could see it was because of his vantage point.

Less than a minute later, a winged figure landed. It had the head of a brown dog, bright blue eyes, and wore gold-and-white armor. Its wings were enormous, and looked to be made out of gleaming gold feathers.

It glanced around for a moment, sniffing the air, before its gaze settled on Simon. "You," it growled. "Why didn't I notice you?"

Simon shrugged.

The winged dog-man snarled, baring its teeth. "I should teach you fear, black robes."

Simon summoned Azura, which gleamed silver in the bright afternoon sunlight. He didn't attack, he didn't speak, and he didn't back down. He was sure the dog got the message.

It was amazing how much more used to lethal threats he had become since moving to Valinhall.

The dog-man looked at him for a moment, and then laughed, deep in its chest. It sounded like it was grinding rocks to gravel with nothing but its lungs.

"I like you, black robes. Come see us in the Gold District. You will do well there."

Folding his wings, the dog-man bowed, and then hopped off the flat roof. It landed on the street below and pushed the door open.

You should have attacked him, Rebekkah sent. *You're overdue for a fight.*

I'm not here to fight, Simon said.

How do you know?

A man's screams and a woman's echoed from downstairs.

"The Silver District has reported disrespect," the dog's growling voice said. "We will take this man with us to the Gold, where he will be taught better. If he does not resist, he will not be excessively harmed."

The man wept, but neither of them offered any words of resistance. Before Simon had figured out what to do, the dog-man had spread its wings and flown off, a small man tucked beneath one arm.

Rebekkah made a sound like she was clearing her throat. *Your Nye essence is running out. You should head back now, if you want to be able to fight any time in the next half an hour.*

I told you, I'm not fighting.

Uh-huh. Sure.

Simon started running back, but he couldn't help seeing the images of the victims in his head. The terrified woman in an alley, trying to protect her daughter with her arms. The bleeding man on the street, whom no one would lift a finger to save. The man, speaking not-quite-respectfully enough in his own home.

He had been angry at Alin in the past, but this made him a little sick. Was Alin really the one who'd turned the city into *this?*

Valin's questions were never far from Simon's thoughts, but they rang especially loudly now. *What do you want to do?*

He wanted to put a stop to this. He wasn't sure what the consequences would be, he knew that he should do it in the right way, and he still wanted to avoid fighting Alin, if at all possible.

But someone had to stop it. Simon knew that he could.

And, given half a chance, he would. The situation in the city was too bad to leave as it was.

Rebekkah mimicked Lilia's dreamy tones. *I sense a fight on your horizon…* she murmured.

Simon ignored her, running to the Naraka waystation.

The blue streets blurred, but nothing else noticed him, and he reached the building in a handful of seconds. He didn't see anything waiting for him outside, and Rebekkah didn't alert him, so he assumed he was safe as far as hidden watchers went. There wasn't even anyone out on the streets in this part of town, except…

Simon drew himself to a halt, and almost slipped and fell on the edge of his cloak. Thanks to the grace and agility of the Nye, he managed to turn it into a skipping step instead of a crushing tumble down two stories onto the cobblestones.

When he managed to pull himself to a complete stop, he crept back a few feet, trying to get a glimpse down the last alley. For a second, he thought he'd seen someone.

Over there, Rebekkah said, sounding eager. *Oooh, she's watching your building. You should punch her in the face.*

The doll was right. The girl down there might have been five years older than Simon, somewhat tall, with light brown hair and the clothes of a moderately wealthy villager: a long brown skirt, a tan shirt, a leather vest, and a pale linen cloak to shield against the cold. She would have fit in anywhere in Enosh, but for some reason Simon was reminded of Myria when he saw her.

I've still got a little bit of essence left. I might as well go check it out.

Make sure to save some for the fight, Rebekkah advised.

Glancing up and down the street for those floating, tentacled jellies— he saw none—Simon leaped down onto the stones and dashed across the street. He moved so quickly that he must have seemed to appear right next to the girl, because she gasped and backed up a step, pulling a dagger and pointing it at him with both hands.

Then her eyebrows climbed, and she lowered the knife.

"Simon?" she said wonderingly. "What are you doing in that cloak?"

He hadn't thought of her in, from his perspective, almost a year. The sheer surprise of seeing her here prevented him from even recognizing her for a second, but then his brain snapped to work.

"Ilana," he said. "Why are you here?"

He had wondered why anyone would be sneaking around in alleys, keeping an eye on the waystation building, but it was doubly strange if that person was Alin's sister.

I guess that means you're not going to hit her, Rebekkah said with a sigh. *Pity.*

"I've been keeping an eye on him for months," Ilana said, back in the waystation. Overlord Feiora had summoned a thick, comfortable chair and a blanket from her Territory. She set them out for Ilana, who sunk down gratefully into the cushions and began telling her story. She even had a footstool.

Why had it never occurred to Simon to call something as mundane as furniture? He had been freezing in the snow less than three days ago, and he could have dragged his comfortable bed and thick blankets out of Valinhall at any time! He couldn't summon them directly, but he could still walk through a Gate and pull them out.

The cold in the streets of Enosh hadn't been so bad, compared to the Helgard-summoned snow a few days past, but the wind was still piercing. He should have thought of that months ago.

Azura doesn't pick the smartest, Rebekkah said. *But she's a big fan of people who aren't afraid to start fights. She has good taste.*

"I wasn't here when Alin first came back," Ilana went on, sipping on a mug of hot tea that Feiora had *also* summoned. "I hear he wasn't so bad back then. But the longer he stayed in Enosh, the worse he got, and the more rules there were. There are some districts where there are rules for how many hours you're allowed to stay up per day. If you stay up longer, you get detained. Try to go to bed early? Detained."

She shook her head and took another sip of her tea. "I wouldn't have believed it was him if I hadn't seen him kill Grandmaster Tartarus myself. I tried to go up and talk to him, but…"

Ilana stared deep into her mug. "It was like looking at the Valinhall Incarnation. Scarier, even. You know, I've never worn a disguise in all the time I've been here. I've looked straight at him dozens of times without even trying to hide, and he's never noticed me. It's like he doesn't...look at people anymore."

She clutched her tea as though it held the answers. Simon didn't have any idea what to say.

Leah, standing over by the still-open Naraka Gate, wasn't so shy. "Where have you been staying, Ilana?"

Alin's sister glanced at the circlet on Leah's head, but she answered readily enough. "Here and there. There are plenty of people who are willing to give me a room for a night or two. I know a handful of Travelers who managed to avoid getting tangled up with the Grandmasters, so I've been helping them smuggle people out. A little at a time, you know."

Leah nodded thoughtfully.

Has anyone told Ilana that Leah's the Queen of Damasca? Simon wondered.

Who cares? Rebekkah responded. *Leah would have taken charge and started questioning Ilana anyway.*

That was a good point. Still, he reminded himself to clarify the situation for Ilana as soon as he got a chance.

"What were you doing waiting outside?" Leah asked. "How did you know we'd be here?"

Ilana shook her head. "I didn't. I check all the permanent waystations I can, every day, to see if anyone new shows up or if they post new guards. It's the only way to stay ahead."

She sounded firm, but he recognized the look of someone who had spent months under constant threat. Her eyes were shadowed, and she looked like she had lost ten or fifteen pounds since Simon had last seen her. It may not be Valinhall out here, but Simon got the impression that she would have been safer if she had stayed with him in the House of Blades.

Grandmaster Naraka stood beyond the Gate, amid her five guards on the red stones of Naraka. She looked totally confident, with a small smile and her hand folded peacefully in front of her. There was something wrong there, though he couldn't quite pin it down. She had seemed afraid of Alin and of the Elysian soldiers in Enosh, but now she didn't look frightened at all. Why not?

You should beat the answer out of her, Rebekkah suggested.

She's an old lady.

Good. You should be able to handle her, then.

The Grandmaster certainly wouldn't show him any mercy if their positions were reversed, and Simon knew it. But she was under guard, and not likely to be a threat anytime soon.

Overlord Feiora's raven rested on her forearm like a falcon called to its handler. She conversed with it in a low voice. Simon had seen the Overlord before, at a distance, but he had never spoken with her until today. Her jaw was tight, her shoulders squared, and she stood with feet evenly apart as though she thought she might have to fight. Did she know something the rest of them didn't, or was she always like that?

The door to the waystation blew gently open, and in a blur of black, Indirial flowed in. He straightened and released a heavy, moonlit breath.

Simon had known that the older swordsman's Nye essence would last much longer than his own, but seeing it was a nagging reminder of how far he had yet to go.

"He's got the city locked down tight," Indirial said, striding over to stand in front of Leah. He delivered his report right to her. "The citizens are on a strict curfew, and they're terrified of being reported for even minor infractions. I looked in on one of their sessions in the 'School for the Disobedient.' It was...not pleasant."

Then he gave an easy smile. "But hey, I've seen worse. Any city occupied by an invading army isn't going to be treated half this well. The village Valin destroyed, the one the Naraka Incarnation burned down, the mining outpost that Endross blew up, the schools that Asphodel infected...all of those would have paid to trade places with the people of Enosh right now. I don't see an urgent threat here."

Ilana remained silent, clutching at her mug, but Leah nodded. "I agree. There's no freedom here, but there is order. I see no threat to Damasca. Feiora?"

The Overlord muttered something else to her raven, and then turned to the Queen. "I'll get to that in a minute. First, did any of you notice any other Incarnations besides Elysia?"

Leah, Simon, and Indirial all shook their heads.

The raven cawed, and Feiora stroked his beak. "They're probably not here, then. So where are they?"

Silence reigned for a minute or so as everyone digested the question.

"There remains only one likely possibility," Leah said reluctantly.

Feiora nodded. "If someone is gathering the Incarnations in Cana, we need to stop wasting time here and get back to our capital. Who knows what they could do with us here?"

Indirial pushed his sleeves up, baring the chains on his forearms. "That does seem like the smart play," he said. "Alin's waited here for six months, so he can wait a little longer. He doesn't seem like he's in a hurry to go anywhere. Let's wait to sew this Incarnation up after we figure out what's going on with the other eight."

"We're not even going to try to help these people?" Simon said, without thinking about what he was saying. Everyone turned to look at him, Ilana hopeful, the rest surprised.

"Help them what, Simon?" Leah asked. "They're not dying. People in other places are. No matter how uncomfortable it is, they can hang on until we get back."

Simon struggled for a moment to find the right words. "Sure, but... this is *Alin* doing it. We might be able to talk to him, or even stop him!"

Or punch him in the face, Rebekkah added.

Leah looked at him sympathetically, and Indirial was smiling, but he doubted they would back him up.

"They're not our responsibility," she said simply. "We can't help everybody. If we get a chance, then we'll do what we can. But our people have to come first."

Our people.

Simon had never considered himself a Damascan. Then again, he wasn't from Enosh, either.

It *felt* like the wrong thing to do, leaving these people behind.

Leah reduced her scrying lens, a round crystal mirror, to about the size of a dinner plate. Then she banished it back to Lirial and started walking toward the Naraka Gate. The two Overlords were deep in conversation in the corner, with the raven croaking some input every once in a while.

"You're welcome to come with us, Ilana," Leah said, without turning and looking at the other woman. "You don't have to stay here."

Ilana's face twisted, as though she was having a painful internal fight. "I will come with you," she said at last. "But only for now. I need your promise that you will take me back here. My family caused this, and I can't run away."

At that, Leah did turn back and look at Ilana, but she didn't say anything. She simply nodded.

Indirial and Feiora finished their discussion, and Indirial clapped. "Well, now that's settled, let's get going. We're burning daylight. Come on, Simon."

Simon stood for a moment, torn. He felt like the heroic thing to do would be stay and try to talk to Alin. If he could talk and reason like a normal person, then he should be able to snap out of it, right?

On the other hand, he owed something to Indirial and Leah. What did he owe to Alin? He wasn't even doing anything *that* bad, compared to the walking natural disasters that were the rest of the Incarnations.

With a last, regretful look at the doors, Simon turned back to the Naraka Gate.

Rebekkah started to laugh.

Simon's spine crawled, and he summoned Azura before he was consciously aware of doing it. He almost gave Ilana an unwanted haircut, but she jerked back and avoided the point of the Dragon's Fang.

"I don't—" Feiora began, but then she staggered and grabbed the edge of Ilana's chair for support. Her raven gave one shrieking caw, much louder than any of the others Simon had heard from it, and took wing.

Indirial had summoned Vasha as well, making Simon feel significantly better, and he stared at the closed doors.

"What is it, Indirial?" Leah asked.

"Into Naraka," Indirial ordered, not turning from the door. "Into the Gate, Leah! Now!"

Then the doors opened, and Alin walked in.

CHAPTER 11
ELYSIA VS. VALINHALL

When Alin entered the waystation, he didn't blast his way inside, or order his army to do it for him. But he didn't touch the doors, either.

He wore the solid gold plate armor in which Simon had last seen him, though it seemed somehow more impressive now. The symbol of Elysia, a winged sword point-down in front of a rising sun, was etched into the chestplate. He wore no helmet, letting his bright hair shine in the reddening sunlight.

He stood with his hands on his hips, and his eyes...his eyes seemed to light up the stretching shadows in the waystation.

The Elysian Incarnation smiled like a boy expecting a present. "Simon! Leah! You should have told me you were coming, I thought I was going to have to clean up some intruders. And..."

He froze for a second when his gaze passed over Ilana, and Simon would have bet he was going to gasp in shock. But his smile returned almost immediately. "Ilana!" Alin spread his arms wide, taking a step forward.

Ilana scrambled out of the chair and walked away.

The Incarnation shook his head, showing an amused smile. "I understand your hesitation, Ilana. Believe me, I do. But I'm not like the other Incarnations. This *is* me."

Leah plastered on a smile and turned, smoothly executing a curtsy to cover the fact that she had taken a step closer to the Naraka Gate. "Pleased to see you again, Alin. I'm so glad you found us. Why don't you Travel with us back to Bel Calem, and we can talk there?"

Silently, Simon applauded Leah for trying to get Alin into a foreign Territory while, at the same time, not giving away where they were actually going.

Alin chuckled. "I'm sorry, I'm afraid I don't have the time to spare. Feel free to come visit anytime, though. I'll tell the guardians to let you through. Naraka, right?"

Leah nodded mutely.

"Well, then..." Alin looked directly into the Naraka Gate for the first time, and his face went blank. Not that he simply lost all expression, though that was true as well. His entire body froze with an inhuman stillness, as though he had briefly become nothing more than a statue of himself.

Grandmaster Naraka stared back, apparently in complete control of herself. The three women behind her, in the armor of Tartarus, drew their swords.

Alin pointed. "Did you bring her to me?"

"She came to me for sanctuary," Leah began, but Alin cut her off.

"I will give her sanctuary," he said, in a chill, terrible voice. "And then I will give her a fair trial, followed by a swift execution of the verdict. Which I suspect will end in, simply, a swift execution."

Leah hesitated for a moment, and then rubbed her chin in a display of thoughtfulness. "We could certainly discuss it," she said. "Her fate would be much the same in Damasca as well, so I don't see a problem with handing her over to you. Why don't we arrange a meeting for the first day of next week, say?"

"I will need her now," Alin said, with such absolute confidence that Simon shivered. The Incarnation spoke every sentence as though he were pronouncing a new natural law.

Valin's voice: *What do you want to do, Simon?*

For the first time, Simon spoke up. "I don't care about her," he said. "You can take her. It seems like she's earned it. But...what do you want to do afterwards? You know, after you're done punishing the Grandmasters?"

Alin looked startled, either at the question or at the fact that Simon had said anything. "Once the Grandmasters are dead, and the city is secure, I'll set out with all the Travelers who will join me. You are all welcome. I will find each Incarnation, and they will be given a choice: they can operate according to my instructions, or I will banish them back to their Territory."

He spoke with such complete openness and sincerity that Simon believed him. It would have been more comfortable to think he was exaggerating.

"What about Damasca?" Leah asked.

Alin smiled patiently. "It will need to be reorganized. No more sacrifices, that sort of thing, and I think the Overlord system is a relic of the past. But once I'm done, I'll have the whole nation ordered and peaceful."

"Like Enosh?" Simon asked.

"Exactly!" Alin seemed pleased that someone understood him.

"That sounds like a wonderful plan," Leah said. "It's definitely the kind of thing we can talk about next week."

Alin nodded toward the Naraka Gate. "You're free to leave as soon as Grandmaster Naraka is in my possession. And my sister, of course."

Ilana raised her eyebrows. "Since when am I your possession, little brother?" She said it mockingly, just as she would have back in the village, when she had been known for her sense of humor. Simon had the feeling it wouldn't do her much good now.

"Since our sisters died," Alin said simply. "You're the only one I have left, and I would not lose you."

"Where I go is my own business. Besides, *you* were the one who left me with Simon!"

Alin nodded. "I have since changed my position on that course of action. It's become clear to me that I am the only one who can keep you safe, and only if you stay close."

He stepped close and placed his hand companionably on her shoulder, smiling down at her. She tried to jerk away, used both hands to peel his hand away from her, but a red spark kindled within Alin's armor. She stayed where she was.

Simon's heart clenched. He couldn't get Valin's words out of his head. *What do you want to do, Simon?*

"Now, will you join me, Grandmaster Naraka?" Alin said, as if the matter with Ilana were settled.

"Let the girl go," Overlord Feiora commanded. The order landed with too much force, and Simon found himself looking for a girl so he could let her go. He almost pulled Rebekkah out of his cloak pocket before he realized this must be a mental attack from Avernus.

Alin didn't move, or even lose his small smile.

Some of Leah's authority as a queen bled into her voice. "Let's not rush into anything, Alin. We can meet next week, formally, as fellow leaders, and decide what needs to be done."

The Elysian Incarnation gave her a quizzical look. "But I have already decided."

Simon's grip tightened on Azura's hilt.

What do you want to do?

"Well, I haven't!" Ilana said. "Now let go of me!"

The gold gauntlet remained where it was.

"I have every advantage," Alin said calmly. "I don't like to put it this way, but you've backed me into the corner, so I must say it: you have no options remaining. I could kill every one of you and drag Grandmaster Naraka out of there before you could make it into the Gate. I have not done so because you're friends, and I'm trying to be polite."

The ruby in Leah's crown sparkled with red light. She reached out to the nearby wall, where Simon hadn't noticed the Lightning Spear resting against the stone. "Don't make this a fight, Alin," she warned.

"I wouldn't call it a fight," he said.

What do you want?

Simon wasn't sure about a lot of things. He had no driving ambition. He knew he wasn't looking for authority, or for lasting power. He couldn't quite put into words what he *did* want.

But this wasn't it.

Before he knew it, he had dropped Azura. The blade shimmered and vanished into Valinhall before it hit the ground. Benson's steel gripped his muscles and flowed like an icy river through his veins.

A second later, he stood face-to-face with the Elysian Incarnation.

For the first instant, Alin ignored him.

Then, with his right hand, Simon peeled Alin's gauntleted hand away from Ilana's shoulder.

Alin looked at his own hand curiously. "Valinhall, right? I should have paid more attention to you."

Red light wound up his arm like a snake, or like the chains currently crawling up Simon's own arms. Suddenly, Alin was just as strong as Simon. They struggled silently for a moment, both of them locked in the same position. Then Alin started to bend Simon's arm back.

By then, Simon had already done what he intended to do. For one thing, Alin had been forced away from his sister.

And Simon's left hand had made it into the pocket of his cloak.

He pulled out the mask and pressed it on. For a moment, his own breathing echoed against the metal of the mask, sounding hollow and tinny in his own ears. The slits in the front of the mask were so thin that they left him almost blind.

Then the eyes flared white, and the mask was all but transparent. His steel thundered through his veins, and the Nye essence—depleted to almost nothing an instant before—roared into his lungs like a freezing hurricane.

Time slowed almost to a stop. He could hear Indirial shouting, warning everyone to get back, before the world slowed so much that he could no longer understand speech.

Then he pulled his fist back and punched Alin in the face.

The air echoed with a crack like rock being split by a sledgehammer, and Alin flew backwards like a golden arrow launched from a bow. He smashed through the closed doors, which had been designed to only swing inward, landing in a tumble of gold limbs all the way across the street.

See? Rebekkah said, sounding as smug as Caela. *I knew you were going to get into a fight today.*

Above him, Cana's sky shone crimson.

Zakareth stood atop his palace and watched the people beneath him. They hurried from one place to another in clusters of five or ten, shepherded by hovering globes of Lirial crystal. The spheres didn't look threatening, more like floating balls of mirrored glass than anything, but a few statues adorned the streets here and there, men and women sealed into crystal. The others understood.

The King hated the waste. He could see the life, the blood, the energy of the living beings sealed into rock. He had to leave them there, to serve as object lessons for the others, but with the power sitting unused on his city streets in plain view, he could shatter the gates of Elysia.

"I know that look," Cynara said from beside him. She sat, as usual, on her carved wooden throne in the antechamber of Ragnarus. The Gate swirled in the air a few feet to his right. He left it open almost all the time now. The price wasn't worth mentioning, and he felt invigorated by the constant breath from his Territory.

"You have plenty of power," the Queen went on. "You're more than ready. We're only waiting for the right opportunity."

He glanced at her out of the corner of his eye, where she burned like one of the Vault's crimson torches. She had so much power, sadly limited to the borders of Ragnarus. If only he could find a way to break her out of there…

But no, she was blending into the fabric of the Territory too well. Already her skin had lost its sheen of metal. Her limbs were still red, but the dull shade of painted flesh instead of shining scarlet. And her advice had gotten increasingly difficult to comprehend.

Plenty of power?

He ground the butt of his ruby-studded staff against the tiled roof of his palace. The Rod of Harmony had never been his favorite weapon; it required him to wait for someone to attack *him,* and he had always been more comfortable on the offense. He would have preferred his Lightning Spear, but his daughter had kept it in her possession for weeks now without returning it to the Crimson Vault. He could summon it to himself, but doing so would alert her to his presence.

"Their energy is wasted," Zakareth said. "Power without purpose is wasted. It must be directed." And he should be the one to direct it, but that went without saying. He was the only one who could see the flow of scarlet potential within every living being. Who better to guide their combined force?

Cynara's glowing eyes had dimmed to little more than a pair of red sparks, but they grew troubled. "We have to consider the balance. Every cost fully paid, every reward fairly purchased. But they have paid a great price on our behalf. Where is their return?"

Zakareth turned to look straight at her, staff clenched in his hand. If she was going to be a problem, he intended to solve it now. "This is unlike you. We have set our course, and I, for one, intend to see it to the end."

Slowly, Cynara shook her head, her burning eyes far away. "No. This *is* like me, for the first time since my awakening. I think…"

She didn't finish her thought. Their attention had been captured by a thousand flashes of light, as though every mirror in the city had been turned to catch the sun at once. The floating Lirial globe flared, as did the prisons of crystal surrounding their frozen inmates.

The powers of Lirial welcomed their Incarnation.

Zakareth hefted the Rod of Harmony, preparing to pay its price. The Rod demanded emotions: it drained the user's feelings, eventually leaving them a cold shell.

During his first life, Zakareth had used the Rod three times. Not enough to effect him significantly, in his opinion; he had never been the most passionate of men. Now, he couldn't pay the Rod's price at all.

He had others to do that for him.

As he had expected, the Lirial Incarnation struck from behind while his attention was on her flashy display down in the streets. A blinding light flared behind him, and he felt his body grow slow and heavy as the will of Lirial sealed him into place.

The deep red gem on the end of his Rod flickered once, with a bloody light. He felt the well of emotions he had drawn from some of his citizens lessen, flowing out to pay the cost of the Ragnarus weapon.

He still couldn't turn his head to see his attacker. His neck was frozen in place overlooking the streets below.

The King heaved his arm into the air, raising the Rod high. The white light of Lirial touched the gem and was reflected, focused back on its source. Zakareth felt his limbs lighten at once, and turned to face the Incarnation.

She hardly looked human. She was like a featureless statue hewn from white crystal and wrapped in random loops of silver wire. The wire spiraled down her body, becoming a metallic tunic that flashed in the sun, and loosened again in lazy circles around her ankles.

Her eyes were globes of white so bright that they stood out even against her crystal skin. They shone with fear as she realized what had happened: her own efforts to bind him had been returned to her.

"Please..." she whispered, in a voice like the ring of silver. "Mercy..."

"Mercy is no part of what we are," Zakareth said. It was true; neither Ragnarus nor Lirial accounted mercy as a virtue. The merciful died as easily on the Crystal Fields as they did in the Crimson Vault. But Lirial Travelers were rare, and he couldn't afford to spend time waiting for another to Incarnate. Sometimes, the price wasn't worth the reward.

He cut off the binding.

"Be careful that you don't run up a debt you cannot pay," the King said, looking down upon his subject. The Lirial Incarnation sagged to her knees, begging his forgiveness, but she would already be calculating her next attempt to overthrow him. Of course she would be. She was Lirial.

"Report," he commanded.

"The Elysian Incarnation has all but total control over the city," she said, meeting his red eyes with her white. "He has already divided Enosh into nine Districts, in imitation of the City of Light itself." Her tone held admiration. She had once served the Elysian Travelers, including the last Incarnation of Elysia. He knew this, and monitored her behavior accordingly. "The few rebellious elements have been crushed, and he has recruited a large force of Travelers to his cause. He calls upon forty-two Asphodel, thirty Avernus, sixteen Endross, twenty-four Helgard, seven Lirial, eleven Naraka, twenty-eight Ornheim, and thirty-seven Tartarus."

"Almost two hundred Travelers," Zakareth murmured, turning the numbers over in his head. That was far more than he would have expected to survive the quiet fall of Enosh. Even Zakareth could not field so many Travelers with only Cana in his possession, though he held weapons far more potent than any human Travelers.

"One hundred ninety-five," the Lirial Incarnation corrected automatically.

Zakareth tapped the ruby at the end of his Rod against the roof tiles, thinking. He caught a glimpse of red lips pursed in careful thought and realized that Cynara had remained silent through Lirial's whole report.

He turned to her, Rod of Harmony held in his right fist. "I would have your counsel, Queen Cynara."

She was quiet for a handful of seconds, tapping crimson nails against the arm of her chair. "Let us hear the rest of Lirial's story before I render judgment," she said at last.

Lirial looked up, startled.

Zakareth kept an eye on the Incarnation, but addressed his words to Cynara. "She was ordered only to record the Travelers in the Elysian Incarnation's employ."

"Lirial watches," Cynara said, her voice gaining a rhythm as though she were quoting something. "Lirial listens. Lirial holds secrets tight, and never lets them go. None of us can fight our natures. Can we, Zakareth?"

The King ignored the question and turned back to Lirial. He held out his left hand, and a red stone hammer dropped into it. The weapon was carved out of one piece of stone, its head worked into the image of a snarling bear.

Hammer in his left hand and Rod in his right, King Zakareth walked forward until he stood over the trembling woman of silver-and-crystal. "Give me your secrets, Incarnation of Lirial," he said softly.

She trembled for a moment, and glimmering white dust fell from her skin like sweat. "Your Successor is in Enosh. She has the young Valinhall Traveler, two Overlords, an old woman, and five Travelers with her. The old one and the guards remained behind, in Naraka."

If she was in Enosh, that meant she was acting against the Elysian Incarnation. Then he could leave Leah unharmed, for now. As a Ragnarus Traveler, her blood was valuable, and he had no desire to hurt her. So long as she served his greater purpose.

"Two Overlords," he repeated. "Which?"

"The Avernus, Feiora Torannus," she said. "And the Valinhall Traveler, Indirial, son of Aleias."

Zakareth turned to Cynara, and red eyes met red eyes. She began to laugh, and even the King felt himself give a small smile.

Sometimes, when you paid the appropriate price, the universe rewarded you with an unexpected bonus.

"The time has come," he said, striding forward with a new sense of purpose. His heavy armor crushed tiles underneath his feet. "Send out the word, Lirial. It is time to release the Incarnations."

Lirial looked as though she would protest, but her white eyes dimmed, and she raised a hand. Once again, all across the city, silver-white light flared.

This time, there was an answer.

From the east quarter of the city, mist rose and rolled down the streets. A single yellow flower, tall enough to show even over three story buildings, spread petals each the size of a ship's sail.

From the south quarter, a roar shook all of Cana. A lightning bolt shot up from the streets and into stormclouds that gathered overhead.

In the west quarter, snowy winds swirled faster and faster as a blizzard gathered around an enslaved Incarnation of ice.

In the north, a gleaming giant of pure, mirror-bright steel leaped onto a house. He ran from building to building, shattering chimneys and churning tiles into dust as he hurried to heed his master's call.

They all hated King Zakareth, but their fear was greater, and their desire to serve their Territories greater still. As long as he allowed them to each express their unique natures, he could guide them to a greater purpose. His purpose.

Zakareth reached out one hand and placed it against the Pillar of Sunset. Its red-and-black marbled surface pulsed with living heat, and the scarlet dome over Cana's sky pulsed in time.

The King couldn't help but notice his own hand, pushed against the pillar. He wore a gauntlet of black and red, chased with gold, but he was seeing flashes of red and gold from between the armor's joints.

Was that his hand? He rejected the idea instinctively. That couldn't be *his* hand within the gauntlet. There was something inside made of metal, not flesh. For an instant, the thought disturbed him. But only for an instant.

He had paid his price. Now it was time to reap the rewards.

He tore his power from the Pillar, and it crumbled into ash and dust. The red veil in the sky tore itself to shreds and vanished, letting through the painfully bright sun and vivid blue sky for the first time in six months.

Counting himself, he had half a dozen Incarnations under his control. And now they were free.

From behind the Ragnarus Gate, Cynara kept her eyes fixed on the approaching Tartarus Incarnation, its steel armor gleaming under the newly revealed sun. "He will need a gatecrawler, and then the Spyglass to help him find the Gate. Perhaps something to help him once he's inside. That's quite a bill you're running up, for a single Territory."

"I assure you," King Zakareth said, "the prize is worth the cost."

Indirial would have left from Leah's camp, just outside Cana's walls. Which meant there would be the residue of an old Valinhall Gate somewhere down there.

They only had to find it.

Get up! the Gold Light screamed. *You have to fight!*

Alin didn't feel pain anymore. Not like he used to. He experienced the suffering of his body, but only in a distant way, like he was hearing about someone else's injuries rather than feeling his own.

His body was complaining quite loudly right now. His back ached, his armor pressed in on his chest, and he had scrapes all over his head and neck. If he were human, he would have been dead.

And the blow had come from *Simon,* of all people. Months ago, when he had seen the fight with the Valinhall Incarnation, Alin had wondered if Simon might actually pose a significant threat. But then he had Incarnated, and realized the truth: the Valinhall Incarnation must have simply been weak. No ordinary Traveler could oppose him.

Now Simon had made him look ridiculous.

Fury rose in Alin, and he levitated himself to his feet on a wave of Orange Light.

You're angry because you're embarrassed, the Violet Light said.

Don't let those emotions drive you, the Green Light agreed.

Alin called Rose, flooding his body, erasing his wounds in an instant. Then he summoned the Gold Light, filling his palms with destructive power, and the Gold Light became the loudest voice in his head.

Tear him apart! was all the Gold said.

Alin hadn't seen him move, but Simon was now standing on the top of the steps leading down from the Naraka waystation building. He stood amid the debris of the ruined doors, the silver-and-black mask glaring out from within his dark hood.

Combined with the seven-foot sword held in his right hand, the whole should have made Simon look ridiculous. Instead, he looked like an executioner, come to put an end to Alin.

The impression was completed by Simon's silence. He didn't say a word, only stared from behind his mask.

Filling his legs with Red Light, Alin dashed to the side. He didn't want to endanger the people inside the building; not while Grandmaster Naraka might escape in the confusion. When he had a clear shot at Simon without blowing the entire Naraka waystation to dust, he hurled both orbs of Gold Light.

They blasted through the air like balls of lightning, spiraling around one another and centering on Simon.

Well, where Simon *used* to be.

Then Simon wasn't over there anymore, he was *right here*, and his sword was gleaming silver as it struck for Alin's throat. He threw up a shield of Green Light in time, but the sword hit with such force that the Green Light actually cracked. Alin had a second to think, *That shield held under Overlord Malachi's best attack,* and then Simon had vanished again. Alin threw out a wave of Silver Light all around him in a panicked screen, trying to find him, and the Silver Light was screaming:

Where is he? Why can't we get a look at him, where is he? No! Up! He's above you!

Alin looked up, summoning Blue Light, the sapphire tendrils exploding from the ground around him to try and bind Simon, to trap him and drain his strength, using it against him. But Simon twisted in the air, somehow flowing *through* the tendrils of Blue Light, and only a last-second double-layered shield of Green kept Alin from being split down the middle by Simon's blade.

This was getting absurd. Simon was keeping him on the defensive in his own city. That shouldn't have been possible!

The Silver Light whispered to him, and Alin realized what was wrong. He was fighting out of shame, rushing the battle, trying to prove he was better. That was not Elysia. He was fighting as Alin, son of Torin, not as the Elysian Incarnation.

In a breath, Alin embraced the Green Light and covered himself in a shell of six-sided plates of shining green, interlocking to form a dome blocking Simon out. The Valinhall Traveler struck at the shield in pokes and probes, but he didn't assault it directly.

Alin used the time to hold the Green Light, letting its patience flow into him, washing away his recklessness.

He was not fighting to prove a point. He was not fighting for his pride.

He fought because he was *right*, and it was time he remembered that.

And what are you right about, exactly? the Violet Light asked, but Alin ignored it. He didn't have time for distractions.

Alin released the Green shield, whipping sheets of Violet at Simon, trying to banish his sword, his cloak, whatever he could get ahold of. Simon dodged with ease, as Alin had known he would, but at the same time Alin let his danger as an Incarnation flood out of him with invisible urgency, summoning all the Elysian natives in the city.

One by one, the fuzzy creatures in the Violet District dropped their meals, the red gnomes picked up their tools, and the Silver automatons stopped patrolling.

Elysia was in danger, and all of his sons and daughters came to answer.

Now Alin had to keep Simon from killing him before they got there.

For some reason, Simon had dropped his sword outside the Green Light. He was reaching out into midair as though to summon it again, but Alin couldn't figure out why he had banished the blade in the first place...

Then Simon drew out of nowhere a massive hammer, mirror-bright steel from its haft all the way up to its head, easily as tall as Simon himself. He hefted the hammer in both hands, swinging it against the plates of Green Light in a blow that Alin *knew* would break through the shield. That was a problem; when his Green armor broke, it gave him a piercing headache and enough painful mental feedback that it would disable him for a few seconds. More than enough time for Simon to take his head from his shoulders.

So, in the split-second before Simon's hammer made contact with the Green Light, Alin banished the shield.

Simon did an impressive job of controlling his momentum and not spinning around or staggering off his feet, but when his blow didn't hit the shield as anticipated, he did miss a step.

And Alin caught him in a trap.

A bubble of Orange Light rose from the ground where Alin was pointing, snaring Simon around the middle and raising him into the air. Simon struggled, trying to break free, but the Orange didn't bind him. It simply lifted him, quickly and easily, into the air.

Alin didn't have to win, not now. He had to stall out the fight until the legions of Elysia arrived. Then it would be an all-out fight between the City of Light and the House of Blades. In a contest like that, he liked his chances.

Besides, he doubted Valinhall had any powers that could deal with levitation. Simon would surely die from the fall.

I never took you for such an optimist, the Silver Light muttered.

Get down there! Rebekkah shouted. *He's going to get away!*

Simon had stopped struggling and was letting the orange cushion take him where it wanted. It was almost soothing, actually, once he had stopped panicking in sheer surprise at being lifted off the streets. He had never seen the world from this high up; the buildings looked like toys far below, Alin like a golden fly. From this vantage point, he could see that Alin had summoned help: brightly colored specks rushed toward him from every District in Enosh, all converging on Alin's position.

That was good to know. It meant he would have to focus on defeating Alin one-on-one, while Leah and Indirial and the rest took out Alin's army. He had no doubt they could do it, even though Elysia undoubtedly held some surprises.

He wondered if he could beat Alin in time.

He'd learned a few things about the mask, in the time since he had fought Valin. While the mask was active, he didn't run out of steel or essence. Not ever, as far as he could tell. Even the single-use powers like the frozen horn recovered much more quickly.

In exchange, his chains grew at an alarming rate. Since he had thrown the first punch, his chains had raced from his wrists to twisting around his back. Soon, they would be encasing his ribs like bands of iron.

So he couldn't fully release his powers without removing the mask, but he could slow the growth of the chains by drawing *less*. He pushed the steel out of his system as much as he could, until the chill flowing through his veins was negligible. Then he released Nye essence in a breath, so that the world returned to almost normal speed.

In this state, his chains would almost stop growing. It was a trick he had learned to extend the amount of time he could keep wearing the mask, which was critical: as far as he could tell, the mask crippled him after he used it, even if he had only worn it for a second.

So each time he put it on, he had to make it last as long as possible.

Simon twisted in the light's orange grip, looking up at the clouds. They were rushing toward him, and with a mix of excitement and alarm, he realized that he might actually reach a cloud. He had never thought of clouds as things that could be touched; they were always impossibly far away, like stars.

From this close, he could see wisps of mist coming off of the cloud. Was that all a cloud was? Was it nothing more than a bunch of fog floating up in the air?

Focus! Rebekkah sent. *There's a fight going on down there, and we're missing it! I'll tell you all about clouds later.*

I can't get there any faster by worrying about it, Simon pointed out. *I'm waiting until this light wears off.*

You should be more excited about this!

He sighed behind the mask and pointed himself back down at the ground, where the city now looked like a gameboard of nine colors. The white part was the smallest, and the Gold District the biggest. He had imagined that it would be laid out in nine equal wedges, but the size and locations of the different colors seemed almost random.

The Orange Light started to flicker, and Simon summoned Azura.

I can survive a fall from this height, right? Simon asked.

You need to, Rebekkah said. *Otherwise you won't get to see Alin's face when you beat him till he begs for mercy.*

The light had grown still more pale, and Simon called another trickle of steel.

The funny thing was, he still wasn't sure if he wanted to kill Alin. That was a crippling weakness in a fight, being unwilling to kill your opponent, he had learned that lesson long ago. Kai had never taught him, nor had Indirial; he had learned it from Valinhall. If he held back against the Nye, they would strangle him. If he had let the fiery snake in the forge live, it would have melted the flesh from his bones.

And if he didn't kill Alin, or find some way to force him back into Elysia, he had no doubt that Alin would kill him.

This has to be done, Rebekkah said, with uncharacteristic patience in her voice. *You know it does. Even if he's not completely evil now, he'll only get worse. You can put a stop to it.*

Simon clung to that advice, pushing the doubts out of his mind. Alin was an Incarnation, and Incarnations were both unstable and unbelievably powerful. He had to die, or he would become an even bigger danger than he already was.

He had to fight to kill. Anything else was unforgiveable.

On a whim, he spun around. A second before the Orange Light ran out, he swept Azura's blade through the belly of a cloud.

He felt no resistance, and the steel emerged trailing mist and patterned with dew.

Huh, he thought. *So that's a cloud.*

The Orange Light failed, and Simon began to fall.

Rebekkah made a sound like a growl. *Give me your killer instinct back! You almost had it!*

Sorry, Simon sent, as the ground rushed up to meet him. *I'll focus.*

He called steel and essence both, flooding through him in a rush of wind and ice. Then he pictured a stone amulet.

The stone was one of his newer powers, and he hated calling on it; steel protected him enough for most fights, and calling stone was distinctly uncomfortable. It felt as though his skin had become dry and solid, like he had to grind his skin to gravel every time he moved his joints. It didn't actually happen, but it felt like it should, and that unnerved him enough that he tried to avoid using the power.

But he had the feeling that he was about to need all the defense he could get.

Here we go! Rebekkah cheered.

He called stone.

CHAPTER 12

FIGHTING IN THE STREETS

When Simon knocked Alin through the doors of the waystation and out into the street, Leah didn't have time to react.

Indirial gave Ilana a hand up from the floor, where he had thrown her after snatching her out of the way of Simon's punch. Feiora had propped herself up against the wall, and was now struggling to stand on her feet again, Eugan squawking in panic.

Leah found that she had her spear raised, ready to throw, and nothing to target. She caught a glimpse, through the ruined doors, of Simon standing on the steps outside the waystation. Alin was levitating to his feet across the street, so Leah hurried over to the doors. She needed to get a clear shot; maybe if she hit Alin with the Lightning Spear, Simon could do the rest.

She found her way blocked by a black cloak.

Indirial gripped her arm and practically dragged her to the back of the room, toward the Naraka Gate. "Sorry, this is far too much of a risk," he said pleasantly. "You're pulling out."

"Release me!" Leah commanded. "I can kill him!" She struggled, but the man had a grip like an Ornheim golem.

Indirial nodded, but he didn't stop dragging her toward Naraka. "I'm sure you could, given the time. Legend says that's how the last fight between Ragnarus and Elysia went, after all. But this is *not* important enough to risk you. Do you understand?"

She did. As much as she would have preferred to win her way clear on the battlefield, it was a foolish risk. She was the only battle-capable Ragnarus Traveler they had, and gambling her life on a fight with an Incarnation in Enosh was not only sheer idiocy, it was selfishness.

She stopped fighting him, so Indirial released her arm. It was only then that she noticed something was wrong.

She couldn't see Grandmaster Naraka through the Gate.

Her two Naraka guards were clearly straining to hold the Gate, shouting something at one another. The three Tartarus Travelers had blades drawn, and one of them reached out to one side of the Gate, dragging Grandmaster Naraka back by the hem of her robes.

One lens of her red spectacles was gone, but she wore a mad smile. As a Tartarus pulled a length of rope out of her pack to tie the Grandmaster's arms, the old woman got one last gesture in with her branded palm.

Indirial rushed forward, his cracked blade drawn, but he wasn't fast enough. The Naraka Gate winked shut, Grandmaster Naraka's laughter drifting out.

From the look of things, the guards had restrained the Grandmaster before she shut the portal. If that was true, then they would be able to open a new Gate from their side at any moment.

Unless the Grandmaster knew a way to seal a Naraka Gate and keep it sealed. Unless she hadn't been tied securely as it had looked. Unless the Travelers took too long to open the Gate, and Leah's fight was already over.

Too many possibilities.

Indirial skidded to a halt where the Gate had once hung. "We need another way out," he said. "It takes too long to open a Valinhall Gate. What about Ragnarus?"

Leah hefted her spear, walking toward the broken doors. She could hear the fight between Simon and Alin in a series of deafening cracks and crashes, but she couldn't see much except a few flashes of colored light. "That's not an option. There may be enemies in the Crimson Vault."

Indirial didn't ask for any more details, moving on to the next possibility. "What about Lirial?"

With her Spear, she nudged one door open. It swung crazily from one hinge, dropping splinters like a tree dropping leaves, but she got a better look at the fight. Alin was standing in a dome of Green Light, and Simon had dropped his sword. What were they doing?

"Lirial's no good," Leah responded. "According to the scout reports, he's got a network of guards on the other side. We'd be detected and detained."

The Overlord's gaze snapped to Feiora.

Leah shook her head. "They've got guards on the other side of Avernus, too. That would be the same as Lirial."

Feiora hesitated. "Not quite," she said. "There are some other...complications."

Simon had produced a giant silver hammer from his Territory, and he swung at Alin's green dome. Leah silently cheered, waiting for him to break the barrier so that she could hurl her Spear.

The green shield vanished, and then Simon was wrapped in Orange Light. Before she could even think of interfering, he shot up to the sky.

She felt a moment of panic for Simon. How long would he rise like that, drifting toward the clouds? Would he ever come down? But she focused on what mattered most.

Alin was standing in the street, exposed and undefended.

She drew back the Lightning Spear, ready to throw...

And a blue tentacle wrapped around her right arm. A cold tingling, buzzing sensation ran up and down her arm, as though it was carried through her bones. The Spear clattered to the floor, and she collapsed to her knees, all but out of strength.

Then Indirial was there, and his blade passed through the blue tendril, severing it into two twitching pieces. The buzzing feeling passed quickly, but the weakness remained. She shook it off and looked up at the drifting jellyfish-creature that had managed to sneak up on her while she was focused on the Elysian Incarnation.

Its body was the size of a horse, its tentacles at least eight feet long. She wouldn't have thought it possible, but the thing spoke.

"Surrender and you will find mercy," the creature hummed, in a voice like a nest of hornets. "Resist and—"

Indirial's blade split it down the middle, and it collapsed into piles of shining blue goo.

Leah turned back to Alin. He was gone from his spot in the street, so she didn't waste time looking for him. She twisted her left wrist, until the crystal she always wore there caught the light.

Then she called Lirial.

A pair of white crystal spheres spun out of her Lirial sanctum and into this world, one flying up the street and one down.

Almost immediately, she heard a chime in her mind as one of the spheres spotted Alin. A silver-white light flared in her vision, invisible to anyone else, pointing at a spot hidden in a nearby alley.

Leah didn't wait until she got a clear shot. She didn't stop to think about the collateral damage. She had a chance, and she took it.

She threw the Lightning Spear.

As always, the Spear blasted from her hands with force dozens of times greater than her merely human throw. It streaked toward Alin in a blur of steel, ruby, gleaming gold, and black wood.

She didn't get to see it land, though, because she all but collapsed in pain. It felt like a thousand wasps stinging every inch of her skin, while at the same time a thousand hammers smashed each of her bones to splinters.

Leah had to cling to the stone wall to stop from falling over, and she bit her lip until she tasted blood to keep from screaming.

The Lightning Spear was not the most pleasant weapon in her arsenal.

There was a sound like a building collapsing, and Leah snapped her head up, worried that she actually had broken a building in which people lived. But the Spear hadn't needed to crash through a wall.

It had flipped into midair, after rebounding off Alin's shield of green light. Alin stood at the mouth of the alley, both hands out toward the spear as if he were trying to push it away with the force of his mind. A wall of green plates stood between him and the spear, and his face was twisted as if in pain.

With a thought, Leah summoned the Spear back. It flipped around in midair and started to hurtle toward her outstretched hand.

Upon further inspection, it looked as though there was a second layer of green light in the air around Alin, but this one had a hole in it big enough to drive a wagon through. It seemed that the Lightning Spear *had* been enough to punch through his green shield, but not enough to penetrate two layers.

The warm wooden haft of the Spear smacked into her palm, and she levered herself back to her feet.

Now that she knew she could break his defense, she would need to keep attacking until she drew blood.

Speaking of blood, something purple and sticky splattered the stairs in front of her, and she looked up in alarm to see a bird-man in the traditional wooden armor of Avernus shredding a fuzzy, purple Elysian creature with its twin blades.

The Gendo bird-man, which Feiora must have summoned from Avernus, turned its beak toward Leah. It dismissed her after a second, running off on taloned feet with leaps and bounds that ate up five paces at a time.

Indirial grabbed her shoulder and pushed her back into the building.

In the same motion, he turned around and put his back to the street.

A blast of gold almost blinded her, shattering against Indirial's back. The force from the gold light pushed the debris on the stairs back in an invisible ring, knocked one of the doors off its hinges, and set the other to smoldering.

Indirial offered her a smile. "Feiora can open you a Gate," he said.

"How are you still alive?" she asked, almost involuntarily.

He turned his back to her, holding his blade out toward Alin. He wore a plate of translucent green light, like part of a suit of armor that only existed in her imagination. "I like to come prepared," he said. As she watched, the spectral plate on his back flickered and went out.

Valinhall, she thought. *Why am I ever surprised when they have a new weapon? I should get him to make me a list.*

Feiora put a hand on her arm. Behind her, a two-foot-tall bearded man in a tall red hat burst through one of the blue windows, brandishing a pickaxe and screaming. Eugan shrieked at the gnome, flapping his wings to hover over the red creature's hat.

The Elysian choked and fell over, apparently victim to one of Avernus' psychic attacks.

The Overlord drew Leah back to the other end of the room, never checking to see if Eugan was safe. "It will take me a second to open an Avernus Gate. Stay here."

"Not yet," Leah said.

Feiora looked at her as though considering whether to knock her out and drag her into a Territory on general principle.

Leah flipped her left hand at an encroaching gold-armored dog, which had bounded through another broken window. A spike of crystal shot out from the tiles beneath it, enveloping the dog and sealing it in midair.

"You need me here," Leah said.

After a second, Feiora nodded, and then she turned back to the fight. She had gotten a spear from somewhere, although Leah would have sworn that she didn't have one before the fight began, and she began using it to poke a slithering, boneless blue cat away from Indirial, who had managed to swat a ball of gold light out of the air with the flat of his blade.

Just then, Leah realized what was missing.

"Where's Ilana?" she shouted.

No one answered.

Alin's head wouldn't stop screaming.

Leah's Ragnarus spear had blasted straight through an entire wall of Green Light, and he had barely been able to throw up a second shield in time, before the weapon destroyed his head as easily as it cracked the Green. The feedback from a broken Green shield was one of the few things that still pained him; Rhalia had once explained that the wall was constantly linked to him, which was why it felt like someone flogging his skull with burning whips every time a shield broke.

Currently, he was hurling blasts of Gold Light blindly at the Naraka waystation, trying to buy time until the burning in his head died down.

The noble citizens of Elysia were doing a wonderful job of earning time for him. Three of the Blue District jellies had been destroyed, and a handful of the gnomes were disabled, though their brothers kept fighting. Gold soldiers marched in formation against the side of the waystation, trying to knock their way into the walls, even as Violet and Silver creatures hopped or flew into the broken windows.

The Rose Light filled with compassion and horror at the number of living beings who were losing their lives crawling into that waystation, but Alin drowned out that voice with Gold. This was a battle, and he intended to win.

The Elysians swarmed the building, tearing chunks of stone out of the pillars to carve new entrances, slithering through cracks, hopping over shattered glass and into the windows. In fact, the most difficult point of entry might have been the gaping open hole where the doors used to be.

A Valinhall Traveler stood there, in the empty doorway, deflecting everything that Alin could throw at him and *still* managing to kill any summoned beings that got too close. At first, Alin had thought it was Simon, but when his vision cleared a little bit he realized that was ridiculous. This man, Alin had met only once: he'd pulled Alin away from Leah, just as Alin's rage had gotten the better of him.

This Traveler was older and taller than Simon, with lines of gray at the edges of his hair. He had the dark complexion of a villager, and he wore his shirtsleeves pushed up—even in this cold—to expose the black chains that wrapped up his forearms. He wore his cloak with the hood up, and when he moved, Alin could only see him for an instant. All he could see clearly was the flashing sword in his hands, which looked as though it had been notched and cracked by years of abuse.

The man grinned, bright and cheery, as he slapped away a bolt of Gold Light and sliced an approaching slitherback—one of the blue-skinned lizard-cats—into three equal chunks. Blue blood oozed down the stairs, mixing with red, purple, and yellow in a macabre rainbow.

Your people are dying, the Rose Light cried.

Put an end to this, the Gold advised. *The quicker the battle ends, the fewer lives lost on both sides.*

That sounded like good sense to Alin, so he summoned his golden blade.

It formed in his hand, an artifact created of Gold Light. Its blade was straight, its crossguard wide enough to protect him, its hilt long enough to hold in both hands if necessary. It wouldn't get rid of his reach disadvantage against a Valinhall blade, but Alin had other powers for that.

Red Light coiled around his legs, and he launched himself into the fight.

The raven's scream crashed into his mind, telling him to give up, to run away, to find a place to hide, and a thousand other conflicting instructions meant to distract him. He ignored that one; his bond with the Silver Light protected him. Somewhere, he could hear the Silver laughing at the pathetic attack.

A sheet of Violet Light fell like a luminescent blanket over the enemy Valinhall Traveler, covering him and hopefully providing an instant's distraction while Alin landed. It worked; the enemy dodged out from under the Violet with blinding speed, allowing Alin to end his jump by slamming into the stairs, legs braced and slightly bent under him. The lines of Red Light in his lower body absorbed most of the impact, flaring briefly brighter.

Then Alin realized a problem. He couldn't see the Valinhall Traveler. Where was he? Alin must be looking straight at him, given the direction he'd dodged, but there was nothing there. Nothing but a blurry shadow that Alin was, for some reason, having trouble looking at...

A burning line scratched his left side as the Traveler's curved Valinhall blade slashed straight through Alin's armor and scored a hit on his side.

Alin was calling Rose Light at the first hint of pain, and his wound flared pink as it healed. He swung his golden sword from left to right, hoping to take the other Traveler's head off.

The ball of smoke and shadow rolled to the right—he knew it must be the Traveler, but he still couldn't bring himself to focus directly on it, as though it slid away from his eyes. Silver flashed, and the sword was coming up from the ground, angled at Alin's neck. He put a single six-sided plate of Green Light in the way, and the tip of the blade slid off the shield like fingernails off a glass window. Alin retaliated by calling Blue Light out of the ground. It sprouted in tendrils, grasping for the Traveler.

But Alin had misjudged the other man's position badly, and he felt a stabbing pain in his back as once again the Valinhall Traveler practically ignored his armor. *Why* couldn't he look directly at the other man? What was he doing that would prevent Alin from so much as *looking* at him?

Alin knew he should have been beyond such emotions, but fury and frustration raged in him.

Stop holding yourself back, the Gold Light advised. *You're not a Traveler anymore. Don't fight like one.*

The Violet, Silver, and Red Lights agreed, so Alin gave himself over to the Incarnation of Elysia. He was thinking like a human, because that was all he had ever known.

But he was capable of so much more than that now.

Alin let his blade dissipate into motes of yellow, and threw his gold-armored hands out to either side.

Then he *really* called Blue Light.

The staircase of the Naraka waystation, the tiled floor inside, even the cobblestones behind him began to glow with a soft azure light. All of the Elysian creatures except those from the Blue District scrambled away: gnomes scampered over debris, Gold soldiers backed away from the way-station in proper military order, Silver constructs flitted out the windows.

They knew what was coming.

The Valinhall Traveler scored another hit on Alin's back, through the previous hole in his armor, but he had Rose Light ready. The wound closed almost instantly.

And the Blue Light rose to his call.

Tendrils and tentacles of luminous blue, each as thick around as a tree trunk, erupted from the ground. Many of them rose eight or ten feet in the air, and they glowed so brightly that everything was tinged in sapphire.

There was no need for Alin to see the Valinhall Traveler, so long as he didn't give the man anywhere to run.

He heard a few shouts from inside the building, and a muffled thud from what might have been a body collapsing. That would be better for them, in the long run. The Blue Light wouldn't kill them—he would extinguish it before it went that far—but it would keep them unconscious. After they woke up, he would be in control of Enosh again, and then he could teach them the truth.

The shadow of the Valinhall Traveler dodged in the forest of blue, landing two or three more cuts on Alin's arm, his neck, even alarmingly close to his eye.

Alin didn't bother dodging, or putting up a shield of Green. He kept pouring all of his will into Blue.

When the Valinhall Traveler fell to his knees, whatever power had kept him hidden fell away, revealing a cloaked man with a cracked sword in one hand. No longer smiling, he looked up at Alin, showing exhaustion in his eyes. He lunged weakly, and Alin let the sword land.

The tip of the Valinhall blade scratched Alin's armor. The strike had no strength behind it, but it used the last of the Traveler's vigor. He pitched over, sprawling halfway down the stairs with his chin resting on the street.

We should let him live, the Blue Light said. Alin was so deep in the Blue that the thought was a matter of course; any other alternative was unthinkable. Why would he *not* let the man live? Mercy was the hallmark of true strength, and only with mercy would Alin be able to show this man the error of his ways.

He's not the only enemy, though, the Gold Light pointed out.

It would be better if you could get Simon and Leah on your side, the Orange said.

Speaking of Simon, said the Silver, *aren't you forgetting something?*

Alin had actually taken another step inside before it occurred to him what the Silver Light had already started to realize. He whirled around, staring into the sky. The tendrils of Blue Light all bent over him, protecting him from the threat.

Then he saw Simon falling from the sky like a silver-and-black lightning bolt, heading straight for Alin.

We should catch him, the Orange Light suggested. *He might die, from that height.*

The Silver Light laughed, and Alin was inclined to agree. He filled his palms with Gold.

Protect yourself, the Green Light suggested. *Just in case.*

Alin spread a shield of Green over his head.

The Violet Light, always honest, started to panic. *Are you sure that will be enough?*

Reaching into the Green, Alin put another shield over that layer. And then another, to be safe.

Behind three shields of Green Light, his palms filled with destructive Gold, and surrounded by a forest of power-draining Blue tentacles, Alin felt as prepared as he ever could be to receive an attack.

You can handle this, the Gold said.

Then Simon struck.

He slammed into the first shield sword-first, with the impact of a falling catapult stone. The wall completely failed to hold, shattering like glass. It didn't even seem to slow him down; he was crashing through the second layer almost as soon as Alin registered the sight of him.

The pain of two Green shields breaking at the same time was enough to make Alin wonder if he would burn up from the inside out, but he channeled Red determination and put all his strength into the third layer. He could stop Simon here, bind him with Blue, and blast his defenses away with Gold...

Before he completely slammed into the third shield of Green Light, Simon slashed his blade across the emerald plates. How was it possible to move so fast?

The third shield of Green Light shattered, and Simon was *still* falling right on top of Alin. His view was filled by that horrible mask, silver and black and utterly without pity. Simon's blade flashed again.

Alin screamed in the pain of his broken shields, releasing the Gold Light in his hands.

It splattered inches from Simon's eyes, stopped by a spectral green helmet. The impact illuminated a full suit of ghostly armor. Had he been wearing that the entire time, invisible?

The Silver Light reminded him that he had seen such things before: when he fought the white-haired Valinhall Traveler back in Bel Calem. That armor could shrug off practically anything that Alin could call.

Well, good-bye, the Violet Light said. *We asked for a fair fight, and we got one.*

Simon's blade hit Alin at the collar, and it sliced its way down.

The blazing pain in Alin's body hardly compared to the burning in his mind from the shattered Green, but the fact that he felt it at all meant that he must be in real trouble. Too fast for Alin to see, Simon's blade passed through his upper-right breastplate, across his stomach, and cut across his left thigh. It sliced through his armor like it wasn't even there, spraying blood across the steps.

His blood shone.

It was still red, but it glowed with its own inner light, so that it looked like luminous crimson paint splattered on the stone in front of the way-station.

That's not right, he thought, absently. *Blood isn't supposed to be like that.*

You're not the same as you were anymore, the Silver reminded him.

Alin fell over on his back, staring up at the sky. The Blue Light started to dissolve, its essence returning to Elysia.

It's over, then, he thought. As last thoughts went, it wasn't much. He had always imagined himself dying with words of wisdom on his lips, or his true love's face in his mind's eye. But when he thought about dying now, he felt…nothing much at all.

The Gold Light sent him a feeling that didn't quite translate into words. It felt like a bleak secret, a dark joke, a grim smile.

Well, the Gold said, *I wouldn't exactly say 'over.'*

CHAPTER 13

INVASION

Lycus Agnos could tell: his sister wasn't paying attention.

Oh, she went through all the right motions. When he slashed at her legs, she hopped back and countered with a thrust to his neck. As he knocked her blade aside, she stepped in close, popping him in the nose with a quick punch.

Andra acted like she always did, but he knew her well enough to look beneath the surface. They had spent almost all their time together in the months since they had moved to Valinhall, as they had no one else to talk to. He knew her better than he ever had. Better than he wanted to, to tell the truth.

The biggest change had come when she got those chains on her arms.

As she punched him in the nose, he got a close-up look at the mark on the back of her hand. It looked like a black oval with squared-off corners, but he recognized it for what it was: the first link of a chain. All of the Valinhall Travelers had these chain-shaped marks, which began on their hands and wrapped up their arms like snakes twisting up a tree branch.

That knowledge hurt even more than the punch, since Andra's chain was only one link. That meant she wasn't drawing any strength from the House, and yet she was *still* beating him with less than half her attention.

Lycus' head snapped back and pain flashed through his skull, but he kept his sword up. He tried to focus through watery eyes, to see where her next attack would come from.

Andra wasn't attacking. She stood with her sword to one side, looking at him in concern.

"Are you alright?"

"I'm fine," Lycus tried to say, but it came out as though he were speaking through a heavy cold. He sniffed and wiped at his eyes, hoping that she wouldn't think he was crying. His eyes were watering because he'd been hit in the nose, that's all.

Andra glanced around the garden, tapping the tip of her sword against her boot. "If your nose is broken, you can go dip in the bath. I'll wait."

Lycus shook his head furiously, keeping his sword up to show her he could still fight. "It's not." He had broken his nose five times since coming to live in Valinhall, so he knew what it felt like. "Let's go."

Without another word, Andra brought her blade up and bent her knees, balancing on the balls of her feet, waiting for him to attack. The waiting was another sign that she wasn't taking him seriously. Andra always attacked, never started on the defensive, and she liked to make jokes while she fought. She made jokes most of the time, actually. If she was quiet, waiting for him to make the first move, that meant she was thinking about something else.

Lycus stepped forward and poked at her defense with a weak thrust, trying to prod her into attacking.

She parried gently, stepping to the left to force him to move, matching her.

At least they were fighting now, but it burned in him that he couldn't make her focus. No one took him seriously, that was the problem. He was the youngest around here, and by far the weakest. Even the Nye treated Andra like an adult, coming at her from the shadows, attacking her in pairs, dragging her out of her bedcovers with an iron chain around her neck.

When they attacked Lycus, they barely tried to kill him at all! Once, a Nye had even shaken him awake and allowed him to climb out of bed before whipping him with a chain. Lycus' mother believed that the Nye were an important and natural part of the House, testing its inhabitants to make sure that they were always alert, always ready for Valinhall's harsher tests.

If so, why didn't they test *him?* He was ready! If he couldn't conquer the rooms deeper in the House, how was he ever going to defeat Simon?

Lycus stepped once more to the side, but Andra didn't circle him. She stared at something over his shoulder, letting her sword fall again.

"What is *that?*" she asked, in a tone normally reserved for cockroaches and squirming reptiles.

They normally fought in the garden, but today Chaka had told them that their 'clashing and clanging' was getting on his nerves, and that they should take their 'limp-wristed flailing' somewhere else, before he taught them a lesson. So they had walked back through the House's main hallway and began sparring in the entry hall.

If Andra had seen something in this room, that could only mean that someone was opening a Gate. Valinhall Gates could be opened from anywhere outside, but they always led here, to the House's entry hall.

It was technically possible that Andra was baiting him, luring him into turning around so that she could attack him from behind. Lycus would actually have been relieved if that were the case, since it meant that she thought him dangerous enough to be worth tricking.

He turned around, hoping his sister would stab him in the back.

A Gate was indeed opening in the entry hall, but it didn't look...healthy. Normally, when a Valinhall Traveler opened a Gate, they sliced it from top to bottom, as though a curtain was being drawn back, revealing a different world on the other side. When they finished, the Gate would stabilize into a white-edged swirling doorway.

This time, the Gate was beginning in the middle, roughly chest-high on Lycus, not head-high on an adult. The edges weren't white, but red and angry. And while the blade that poked through the air had an edge of freshly polished steel, it certainly was not one of the gently curving Dragon's Fang swords that Valinhall Travelers used.

So if it wasn't one of the Dragon Army opening a Valinhall Gate, who was it?

Lycus took a step back from the Gate, glancing over at his sister. As much as he hated to admit it, she was supposed to be a fully-fledged Valinhall Traveler now. Maybe she knew something he didn't.

She glared at the hole in the world, fingers clenched around her Dragon's Fang. She looked dangerous now, in a way that she hadn't when she was fighting him. "Lycus, go warn someone. Something's trying to come through."

"Warn who?" Lycus asked. Simon wasn't in the House at the moment, he was outside doing whatever he did. Probably killing more people. Lycus had trouble thinking of Simon now without picturing him bathed in the blood of Damascan soldiers, men who had been supposed to protect Lycus and take his family to safety. True, Simon had sent the Agnos family to Valinhall, but it was to save them from a mess that he had created.

Besides Simon and Andra, Lycus only knew of three other Valinhall Travelers. Overlord Indirial only showed up when he was on business for his realm or for Queen Leah, and he never stayed long. Besides, he was an *Overlord*. Lycus wouldn't have called to an Overlord for help if he were drowning; he would have been afraid of distracting them from something more important.

Lycus didn't know Denner, who entered the House every once in a while, stayed for a day or two, and left without warning. He seemed the most normal of the Travelers, and he even told Lycus stories during his stays in the House. But Lycus had no idea where to find him now.

The other Traveler, Kai, was...odd. Lycus' mother had warned him never to talk to Master Kai without another adult present. He spent all his time talking to those little dolls, and Lycus got the impression that he would happily murder anyone who so much as mussed a single hair on a doll's head. Lycus was too scared to look in Kai's general direction most of the time. He had heard that Kai was staying deep in the House, deeper than Lycus had ever seen, but he didn't know why.

So all the Travelers were out. He supposed he could warn Chaka, but Chaka was stuck in the garden. What could he do about a threat in the entry hall?

"What about Erastes?" Andra suggested, keeping her gaze stuck on the growing red Gate. The blade slashed up, tearing a chunk out of the air, revealing a black-and-white tiled floor on the other side. And what looked like the body of an impossibly huge man in shining silver armor.

The sword worked slowly but steadily, as though sawing through the world was a demanding physical chore.

"Where is he?" Lycus asked.

The torn Gate was growing at an alarming rate. Soon the armored giant would be able to step through.

"Find him!" Andra snapped.

Lycus stayed where he was.

"Go!" His sister yelled. The Gate grew another two inches.

"I need to help you!" He couldn't leave his sister here, alone, to fight whatever was about to come through this Gate. What kind of brother would he be if he did that?

She gave him the look, the lopsided half-smile with a twinkle in her eye that she always used when she saw a joke that nobody else realized was funny. "You're a hero, Lycus, you really are. But what are you gonna do that I can't?"

A second dark link slid into being on her wrist, and a third was beginning to materialize. The chains of Valinhall were growing on Andra's arms, which meant she had called steel.

Lycus wondered what they would do if Overlord Indirial stepped through and demanded to know why they were pointing swords at him. They would get in a lot of trouble. The Overlord might even arrest them; he'd heard that some Overlords did that to people who got in their way.

That's probably all it is, he reasoned. *Overlord Indirial's going to come through that door, and he's going to yell at us for pointing swords at him.* He had never actually heard Indirial shout at anyone, but he could imagine it easily enough.

Then, with a screech like tearing metal, the Gate finished. It was two feet taller than a normal Gate, stretching from the entry hall's wooden ceiling all the way to its carpeted floor.

The armored giant stepped through, and Lycus saw that it wasn't a man at all. It looked like a man—two arms, two legs, a torso, a sword in its right hand—and it was covered in intricate gleaming steel armor, but it had no face. Its helmet was open, revealing thousands and thousands of metal gears inside where a human would have eyes, a nose, a mouth. It was like looking inside a man-sized clock. As it stepped through the Gate, it whirred and clicked and clanked. There was no flesh inside that armor.

Lycus felt like an idiot. Chaka reminded them every day of the first rule of Valinhall: it's *always* a threat.

He swore he would never forget that again.

"Stop where you are!" Andra called, and she sounded like she had the authority to make that demand. "Who are you?"

The helmeted head creaked as it swiveled on an armored neck. Twisting bronze gears surveyed Andra instead of eyes.

The metal giant spoke with a voice that sounded like grinding rocks. "I am Tartarus. I will not be stopped."

It marched forward, sounding with each step like a cupboard full of pots and pans crashing to the ground. The sword in its right fist had a blade as long as Lycus was tall, but it wasn't made of the same shining silver metal as its armor or Andra's Dragon's fang. The sword was solid, shining red, with twisting black lettering crawling up its flat surface. In the few moments of silence between the giant's footsteps, Lycus thought he heard the sword screaming.

Andra must have heard the same thing, because she gave the sword a wary glance. "Lycus, run. You need to find Simon."

With a shout, she jumped forward and thrust the point of her lightly curved blade up and into the shoulder, between the breastplate and the upper arm.

Sparks flew, and Andra stumbled back. Tartarus didn't slow down, walking implacably forward toward the hallway. Toward Lycus.

He stood frozen for perhaps a second, stunned. The Dragon's Fangs could cut through anything. He had seen those Valinhall-forged swords slice through trees, cut chains, and stab through stone walls. What was this giant's armor made of?

Then he realized that, if he didn't move from where he was, he was going to get an up-close look at the bottom of Tartarus' steel boot.

Hating himself, Lycus turned and took off running down the hallway. He would warn Chaka, and hopefully find Erastes. They could help Andra, even if he couldn't.

And maybe they would know where to find Simon.

Simon slammed into the street on his hands and knees, Azura skittering away. His skeleton rang like a bell, his knees and wrists felt like they had exploded, and his vision had whited out from pain.

But he clutched a single thought: he wasn't dead.

Rebekkah was laughing harder than he had ever heard her, or any of his dolls for that matter. She practically sobbed with laughter, and he was sure that if he could pull her out of his cloak, she would have a huge grin on her painted face.

That was, by far, the greatest thing I have ever seen anyone do, she managed. *Caela is going to be* so *mad she didn't get to see it.*

Simon crawled a few feet away, nudging his aching body across the rough cobblestones. His stone and steel had held out—in fact, thanks to the mask, they were still going strong—but he couldn't help but wonder what kind of damage he'd taken on the inside.

You know you wouldn't have made it without those shields slowing you down, Rebekkah sent. She had the tone of someone telling a joke. *I think he might have saved your life!*

I should thank him, he sent. Then he remembered that he'd landed a blow in the last instant before he hit the street. Alin was an Incarnation, true, but he'd seen Incarnations die from lesser wounds.

If his eyes would hurry up and clear, instead of showing him a blurry world full of phantom doubles, he could check for himself.

Hey Simon, Rebekkah said, still in her cheery tone. *Put your hand out to the right.*

Simon didn't question it; he reached blindly out and felt around on the street until something met his hands. It was a rough, round ball, about the same size as a coin, and it felt warm and slightly sticky.

His hand jerked back. Was she trying to get him to put his hand on a bloody piece of someone's body? What kind of gory prank was that?

Don't be a child. Pick it up.

Reluctantly, Simon did as she asked. As his vision cleared, he saw that he was holding something like a dried fig, only dark red. It didn't *look* sticky, or blood-covered, or anything else to account for the sensation, but it felt like it was trying to cling to his hands. It was too warm, and it seemed to almost pulse, as if it contained an impossibly small heart.

What is it?

Rebekkah gave the mental equivalent of a shrug. *How would I know? But it feels important. I bet you two hours that it's an artifact from another Territory. Probably Elysia. The Eldest will love that.*

Simon slipped the red fig into his pocket before he realized what she'd said. *Wait. Hours? You bet hours?*

Yeah, she said casually. *Hours out of the House. The only reason I came with you today is because I bet Otoku twelve hours that you'd earn the ghost armor. She thought you wouldn't be able to do it for* at least *another two weeks.*

But...you don't choose which doll I take, Simon sent. *I do.*

Rebekkah's mental voice took on a pitying tone. *Awwww, that's cute. You can believe that, if it makes you feel better.*

That idea became more disturbing the more he thought about it, so he put it out of his mind.

Speaking of time, you're almost out of it.

Almost, he sent. *Not quite.* He could feel the chains wrapping around him; they twisted down his legs and under his feet, until he felt like he was bruising his heels on steel links with every step. They bound his ribs and snuck up his shoulders, and he could feel them sliding up his neck. Once they wrapped around his neck, like a Nye's noose, he would be fully bound to Valinhall.

Here, now, that almost certainly meant Incarnation.

But it looked like he wouldn't have to risk it.

Alin lay less than five paces away, face-up in a pool of strangely glowing blood. His gold armor was split down the middle by a blow Simon didn't remember delivering, and pieces of metal had flown all the way to Simon's feet. Alin's eyes were still rainbows, but they were frozen; they didn't shift and change in the disturbing way they had when he was alive. His pale hair was matted and still, and he wore an almost comic look of surprise.

Simon's eyes burned, and he tried to wipe moisture away before realizing that he still had the mask on. Why should he care if Alin died? Simon had never liked him.

But he shouldn't have had to die. Alin had turned to Incarnation for no reason other than to save his sisters. He had taken over Enosh, and planned to take over Damasca, to prevent tragedies like it from happening again.

And he was from Myria. He wasn't the kindest, or the easiest to talk to, but Simon had grown up with him. He remembered Alin getting caught stealing at eight years old, and talking his way out of it.

Simon shouldn't have been the one to kill him. If the world was right, Alin shouldn't have to die at all.

In your fantasy world, sure, Rebekkah said. *In that magical Territory where nothing bad happens to anyone who doesn't deserve it. That's not reality, though, so take off your mask before you make this situation worse.*

Simon looked up at the waystation. None of the Elysian creatures had returned after Alin's death; in fact, they seemed to be backing up farther. Indirial was still sprawled on the steps, twitching and shifting underneath his cloak. Overlord Feiora marched out the doors, an armed bird-man in front of her holding a pair of swords, and a raven circling her head. Finally, Leah stepped out, the Lightning Spear in one hand.

"Did you get him?" she called.

Simon winced. "I got him," he yelled back. It sounded callous; they should have been mourning the death of a man they knew, not celebrating it.

Despite the steel, essence, and stone running through him, begging to be used, he forced himself to sit down. When he took off the mask, he'd collapse, so it would be much better if he didn't have quite so far to fall.

When he was seated on the street, he reached up to peel off the mask. Eugan the raven let out a single, shrieking caw.

Behind you! Rebekkah shouted. *Get him!*

Simon jumped up, banishing and re-summoning Azura into his hand with a simple effort of will.

Alin's body rose like a puppet pulled up by invisible strings. The wound across his chest sealed itself with a shimmering pink light, but his body still hung as stiff as a slab of meat on a hook. His arms dangled at his sides, his knees on the point of collapsing. He still stared as blankly as before, his rainbow eyes frozen mid-swirl.

Kill him now! Rebekkah sent.

Simon stood frozen. His every instinct in Valinhall was screaming at him to either finish Alin off or run, not to stand there like an idiot, but he had lost himself in regret for Alin's death. Now, he wasn't sure what to do.

He hesitated too long. Alin's eyes snapped to one color: blazing gold. His head jerked forward as though someone else was moving his body like a doll, his hand rising up, filled with gold light.

Simon may have hesitated, but Leah didn't.

The Lightning Spear flashed toward Alin so fast that Simon almost didn't catch it, even through the Nye essence. Alin should never have been able to react in time, but he managed to get one palm between his side and the spearpoint.

A gold flash, bright enough to all but blind Simon through the mask, met the Spear and blasted it aside. It flipped through the air toward the waystation, but Simon didn't stand watching it. He moved at last, drawing on essence and steel as deeply as he could. The world slowed, and he dashed toward Alin.

You have half a minute, at best, until the chains reach all the way around, Rebekkah warned him. *So finish him quick.*

Simon held Azura low in both hands, running for Alin. His golden armor wouldn't stop a Dragon's Fang, and he didn't have the reaction time to combat Simon with the Nye essence; this should be easy.

Alin's head snapped to the side, his eyes blazing gold, and he filled the street with a river of white-hot light.

Simon called ghost armor. It should have taken longer to regenerate, but under the effects of the mask he could call on his powers almost with impunity.

The destructive light filled his vision, blinding him, and crashed into the transparent green plates of the ghost armor. He braced himself against the onslaught, holding one arm in front of his face in an instinctive attempt to ward off the heat and pressure directed at his eyes. It still felt like getting pounded by a tide of molten steel, but he held on.

The ghost armor lasted long enough before it died like a spent candle, finally vanishing as the stream of Alin's gold light dried up. Simon survived, but he found himself fifty paces farther down the street, surrounded by cracked stones, glowing bits of metal, and rising wisps of smoke. The fronts of many of the houses were missing completely, and the entire street was covered in drifting ash.

Are you okay? he asked Rebekkah.

You don't have time for this! she snapped. *Run after him!*

Simon shot back down the street, only to see Alin throwing a bright lasso around something inside. He had seen Alin summon something like that before: he had used it to decapitate the serpent that had killed Simon's mother. This time, he was wrapping it around Indirial, who had woken up despite a bleeding head wound.

The Overlord stood on shaky legs outside the waystation steps, calling a distantly flickering version of ghost armor to keep the lasso from splitting him in half. It was obvious that the armor wouldn't last long, but Simon didn't need much time. In the waystation doorway, Leah had hefted the Lightning Spear and readied it to throw, her off hand braced against the door as if expecting an impact. Behind her, Overlord Feiora fiddled with what looked like a little leather bag.

While Alin had his attention entirely focused on the waystation, Simon drove Azura at his side with all the force of a fifty-pace charge.

The lasso didn't disappear, as Simon had half-expected. The red light coiled around Alin's feet flared, but Alin didn't even stagger backwards. The Dragon's Fang split his armor, penetrated the Incarnation's rib cage, and stabbed out the breastplate on the other side.

Blood leaking from a corner of his mouth, Alin turned his head to look at Simon. Slowly, he gave a bloody smile.

Despite himself, Simon jerked back. He had to fight the urge to pull his blade back out and run away, as fast as he could.

The Incarnation's eyes shone bright, but Alin wasn't behind them.

A hammer of gold light fell on Simon from feet above, and he yanked Azura out of Alin's flesh and held it up as though it could shield him from the attack. It did nothing, and Simon was blasted down into the stones of the street.

His vision was consumed in white.

He came to himself a short time later, realizing that he was sprawled in a tangle of aching limbs, Azura just out of his reach. His cheek was pressed in a pile of ash, and the smell of burning coals filled his nose. Dust choked his throat, and he coughed roughly until he felt like he could breathe again. He tried to stand, and his left leg sent a spear of pain through him. He stood anyway.

Then he became aware of Rebekkah shouting his name. *...don't have much time left, Simon! Wake up!*

I'm up, he sent. Even his thoughts sounded groggy.

You've got seconds left, Simon. Seconds. Get moving!

Simon forced his head up. Through the mask, he saw Alin calmly, methodically, blasting the corners of the Naraka waystation to rubble. The roof had already begun to sag, and Alin conjured another fist-sized ball of gold light, tossed it into the air like a juggler's ball, caught it, and threw it underhand into the corner of the building.

A sound like a falling boulder, and cracks spread out through the front of the waystation.

Anger surged through Simon, and a renewed resolve.

This wasn't Alin.

With all the steel, stone, and essence he could call through the mask, ignoring the pain in his leg, he jumped forward, summing Azura into his grip as he began a downward slash.

Alin caught the attack on a sword of golden light, but Simon was through pulling punches. He pushed with all of Benson's steel, cutting with the impossible quality of a Dragon's Fang, with the full intention of slicing *through* Alin's blade and down into his neck.

Loops of red light flashed on Alin's arms, then down his torso and into his legs, bracing him against the blow. He managed to turn Azura to one side, but his blade showed glowing yellow fractures.

Faster than the Incarnation could follow, Simon stabbed Azura through Alin's chest. He didn't wait to see a reaction, but kicked Alin off the end of his blade. Through the Nye essence, it looked as though the Incarnation was drifting inches off the street, even though Alin was already looking around, trying to find him through the concealing shadows of the Nye cloak, raising a hand that steadily filled with a whirlpool of golden power.

Simon leaped forward, bringing Azura down once more on Alin's chest. The Incarnation brought up the blast of gold he had conjured, knocking the sword away in time, but Simon still scored bloody hits across Alin's chest and the palm of his hand, shattering another plate of the armor and sending shimmering blood scattering over the street.

The force of the golden blast knocked Azura back, and Simon braced against it, skidding to a stop against the street. Alin had finally landed on his own feet, and was drawing both hands together, filling them with a ball of gold.

He was aiming it at Simon, but in the course of the fight, Simon had come to stand in front of the waystation. Alin was planning on blowing Simon and everyone in the waystation away together.

In his mind, Rebekkah cackled like a mad witch. *Duck, Simon!*

With the grace and speed of the Nye, Simon threw himself to the ground. Something loud and almost impossibly fast rushed by overhead in a blur of red, gold, and black.

The Lightning Spear caught Alin full in the chest, snatching him backwards and into a stone wall across the street.

I see what Caela said about that Leah, Rebekkah said. *She'd do well in Valinhall. Time's up, though.*

Simon didn't look to see if Alin had survived. His exhaustion and pain were piling up on top of one another until it felt like he wouldn't be able to swing Azura even if Alin rose up out of the ground. Folding his legs up under him, he sat down and peeled off the mask.

Then he fell over.

CHAPTER 14

BATTLE IN THE
HOUSE OF BLADES

The building was crumbling around Leah, she couldn't figure out what Feiora was doing, and Indirial was surely all but dead.

To top it off, her body was shaking with unspeakable pain after so many uses of the Lightning Spear. She was going to have to ask Indirial about that healing pool in Valinhall; she didn't think she would survive the day if she didn't get some kind of medical help.

But at least she had finally scored a clean hit.

"I'm going to start cutting a Gate," Indirial announced, his voice weak. He could barely hold his blade up with both hands, a sure sign that he had run out of whatever strength had kept him going this long. It took him three tries to get the point of his sword to stop shaking so that he could start slicing open the portal.

Leah nodded at him, too tired to say anything else, and mentally ordered the Lightning Spear to return. If she had it in hand, she would at least feel safe enough to try retrieving Simon from the middle of the street. As it was, she knew she was all but defenseless against the Incarnation of Elysia.

It took a second for her to recognize that the Lightning Spear still had not come. She called it again.

When it didn't show up the second time, she knew something was wrong.

"Indirial, work faster!" she called. "Feiora, do something!"

A scrape and a flash came from Feiora's corner of the waystation, along with the acrid smell of smoke, as though she had just set something on fire. "Sorry, Your Highness! I took the time to do my hair. Doesn't it look nice?"

Leah's gaze was stuck on the shadows of the other collapsing building across the street, where Alin's body had vanished along with her Ragnarus spear. On some level, she was convinced that if she turned around to look at Feiora, that would be the exact instant that Alin appeared and skewered her through the neck.

So she didn't turn around, but she did shout again. "What are you *do-*

ing, Overlord?"

Feiora muttered something, Eugan squawked, and the Traveler sighed. "There's an emergency measure that most Avernus Travelers have. We can Travel straight to our tribe's lands instead of to the point that *actually* corresponds to where we are. In this case, we can't cross over to Avernus, because the guards from Elysia would kill us and toss our bones into a fire. But I've almost figured out where this will take us, it'll just—"

Her voice cut off as a shining gold light appeared in the shadow of the broken building on the other side of the street. It began weak and steadily grew, like a rising sun.

"Seven stones," Leah breathed. She had seen four Incarnations in battle over the past six months, and she had started to think of herself as an expert. But none of them had taken this much damage and walked back out.

Alin's armor was crumbling around him, pieces of metal falling off and plinking to the ground. In his right hand, which glowed red, he held the Lightning Spear. The weapon shook and struggled, trying to respond to Leah's call, but helpless in the fist of an Incarnation.

In his left hand, he held a bolt of golden light.

To Leah's confusion, he didn't raise the light toward the waystation. Instead, he only lifted the hand a little.

He pointed at Simon's unconscious body.

There was one power that Leah hadn't used throughout the entire fight. She considered it a last resort, because its cost was too inconvenient to pay otherwise. Her father had taught her to always save it for a true emergency. She felt this qualified.

The ruby in Leah's Ragnarus crown blazed like a dying star, filling the street with crimson light.

Stepping forward, the Queen of Damasca announced her will to the enemy Incarnation. "Alin, son of Torin!" she shouted. *"Give up and die!"*

The order blasted out from her crown on a tide of red. Chains of scarlet light burst out of the Crimson Vault, binding the Incarnation's arms and legs, drawing him down onto his knees.

And one chain, the one that only she could see, crept up inside Alin's body, passing like a ghost through skin and flesh and bone. It sought out Alin's heart, and it began to squeeze.

When the Queen ordered you to die, she meant you to hurry up about it.

The Incarnation struggled against the Ragnarus binding, trying to fight his way up to his feet, lurching forward toward Simon—or maybe toward her—in a last-minute attempt to kill someone.

Then he relaxed. His eyes closed. He made a choking noise, probably in reaction to what her binding was doing to his insides, but otherwise remained silent.

When he opened his eyes again, they were no longer gold. They shone luminescent violet.

Strips of purple light, like unraveled bandages, whipped out from his hands and severed the chains of Ragnarus. In a violet flash, his body was cleansed of anything her power could do to him.

Then he casually rose to his feet, twirling a strip of violet light like a flail. He had released the Lightning Spear, though, so she called that back into her hand. It flew obediently, straight into her hand, and she snatched it from the air. She felt as though taking another shot with the weapon might kill her, but what choice did she have?

She raised the Spear, but then a hand grabbed her roughly by the shoulder and pulled her back, yanking her off-balance.

Leah got a good look at Overlord Feiora's grim expression before she was shoved through a white-edged Gate and into a forest. The scent of pine and fresh air overwhelmed her, after a battlefield choked in smoke and ash, and the calls of a thousand birds were almost deafening.

Feiora raised one leg to step into the Gate, but a whip of violet light wrapped around her arm. Her eyes widened in surprise and alarm before she was jerked backwards, off her feet. She slid across the debris-strewn floor, fighting the power of the Incarnation that was dragging her toward him.

Leah tried to shout, but her voice was silenced. Part of the crown's price. She lifted her spear for another throw, but then there was a violet flash and the Gate vanished.

Nothing but forest.

Avernus. She was in Avernus, a Territory hardly ever used for Traveling, and as such a Territory she was largely unfamiliar with. There was every likelihood that, while she was gone, Alin would kill Indirial, Simon, and Feiora all three.

What have I done? she thought. It was an old pattern, drilled into her by both her father and mother: the first thing to do, after a defeat, was to figure out what you had done wrong. Then you should never make that mistake again.

She had underestimated Alin. Even though she knew he was the Incarnation of Elysia, she had never taken him seriously. He hadn't even caused a massacre, like so many of the other Incarnations.

She had overestimated herself. She had been so sure that, whatever happened, she could handle it.

She should never have taken Grandmaster Naraka anywhere into enemy Territory. The Grandmaster would try to betray them, given half an opportunity, and Leah had *known* that. She and Indirial had discussed it specifically, and they had finally decided that she didn't pose much of a risk. Even if she did manage to close the Naraka Gate, they had said, that would hardly affect the success of their mission. They had, between them, four other Territories to choose from. If the Grandmaster closed off Naraka, they could escape in some other way.

Besides, her guards would have her under control in an instant if she tried anything. They most likely had her under control right now: even a Grandmaster couldn't escape a pair of fellow Naraka Travelers *and* a team from Tartarus. They had probably subdued her in seconds, then bound her hand if not cut it off.

But something had stopped them from re-opening the Gate. What?

It was a futile question to be asking now. The point remained: she had considered the benefits of taking Grandmaster Naraka along to outweigh the risks.

She had been an idiot.

And now Simon and Indirial were paying the price.

Oh, Maker, she thought. *Keep them alive.* Praying to the Maker wasn't a very Damascan thing to do; her grandfather, Zakareth the Fifth, had specifically banned the practice during his reign. But after two years with her aunt Nurita, she had picked up some villager habits.

Tightening her grip on the Lightning Spear, Leah amended her prayer. *At least keep them alive until I can get there.*

A panicked *caw* sounded from directly overhead, and her head jerked up, the Spear at the ready.

It was Feiora's raven, Eugan. She hadn't realized that the bird had followed her through the Gate.

It let out another squawk and flew through the empty space where the Gate had been. Flapping its wings frantically, it banked for another pass and flew through the space again.

Trying to get back to Feiora.

The sight tore at her heart, but she didn't let herself react. The only way she could get back and help Simon, Indirial—and even Feiora, if necessary—was to get out of Avernus.

And she was no Avernus Traveler, so she needed a guide.

Lycus was out of breath and holding back tears by the time he found Erastes, fighting against Benson in the skeleton's basement. Torches blazed blue on the walls, all dim enough to allow an ocean of shadows, and twenty-four hulking forms rested on pedestals all down the room. They were suits of armor, Lycus knew, and they could come to life to fight challengers.

The huge block of stone at the far end of the room was a rough-hewn throne, and Benson usually lounged on it, one steel leg hanging over the armrest, foot idly kicking. Now, the steel skeleton was swinging an axe at Erastes' head.

His news was urgent, but Lycus knew he couldn't interrupt a fight like this. If he shouted something and distracted Erastes at the wrong time, the man could die. Lycus took his responsibilities very seriously; he kept his mouth shut and made not a sound, even though his message squirmed inside him, trying to get out.

The old soldier ducked, moving like a man half his age, and brought a gleaming infantry sword up into the skeleton's chin. Benson leaned back, holding his wide-brimmed hat on his head with one hand.

Erastes pressed his advantage, stepping forward and bringing his sword down on his opponent's steel rib cage. The two metals clashed, sending up sparks, but he didn't let up. Lycus had always thought that Erastes was the perfect image of a Damascan soldier: his hair was iron-gray and cut short, his face weathered, his eyes cold. He looked like a man from the stories, like someone who would stare death in the eyes without ever blinking.

Benson, on the other hand, looked like Death himself. He was a skeleton made entirely of some shining silvery metal, his bones glittering in the blue light of the basement. The same light as the torches blazed in his eye sockets, and he wore an old, tattered, wide-brimmed hat on his exposed skull. The axe he wielded should have been too big to lift—it looked like it was made for two-handed use by giants, which may have actually been the case—but Benson spun the weapon over his head like a staff, bringing the double-headed battle-axe's blade crashing down on Erastes' head.

The soldier raised his short sword and caught the blow. His blade shone mirror-bright, like one of the Dragon's Fangs, though he had owned this sword as long as Lycus could remember.

Erastes strained under the blow, pushing up with both arms. One of his sleeves slid down, and Lycus saw the black chains printed on his arm.

With a final heave, Erastes pushed the blade away.

Benson chuckled, reversing the axe and grinding its head against the basement floor. "You're a quick one, aren't ya? Not a month with the steel in you, and you're already giving me a close run."

The soldier smiled, just a little, but Lycus saw his chance.

"We're under attack!" he yelled.

Erastes turned, his blade in one hand, his shirt soaked in sweat. "Where?" he asked. That was what Lycus liked most about Erastes; he took everyone seriously, even children. So many people thought of Lycus too lightly, but not him.

"Entry hall," Lycus said, and the soldier ran up the steps, taking them two at a time.

Benson managed to raise an eyebrow, even though his face was nothing more than a skull. "It's been a long time since we've been under attack in the House, kid," he said. He didn't go any further, but Lycus could hear the skepticism in his voice.

"Well, we are," Lycus said firmly. He hesitated, then added, "It would help if I had the steel, too. You know, so I could fight."

The skeleton grinned even more broadly than usual, tilting his hat down to cover one eye. "More than happy to. Come and challenge me whenever you're ready."

Lycus ground his teeth in frustration and ran after Erastes. He had challenged the basement practically every day for weeks, but he lost every time. Once, he had been hurt so badly that he had lain bleeding on the basement floor for four hours, until Simon noticed he was missing and carried him up to the pool. Since then, he hadn't been back.

His own weakness grated on him, even though the adults all insisted that he would grow out of it. He didn't want to grow. He wanted to help *now*.

But as it stood, the only thing he could do was run for help.

A crash like a whole cart being smashed to splinters echoed through the upstairs room as he was halfway up the staircase, interrupting his thoughts. He froze for a moment, trying to figure out where the noise came from, until he heard Erastes and his sister shouting over one another, followed by the sounds of steel on steel.

Lycus leaped up the last few steps, his own small sword clutched tightly in his fist.

The Tartarus Incarnation stood with its armored back to Lycus, the red-and-black Ragnarus blade in its right hand. It stood over the broken remains of the door to the forge, which it had apparently knocked off its hinges. The steel giant strained forward, pressing against the combined might of three Nye.

Each of the Nye had a long black chain wrapped around some part of the Incarnation's body. One of them had a chain around each of the giant's arms, and the third had its black steel wrapping its thick neck. They pulled against their chains, trying to keep it from entering the forge, stopping it from moving forward, as Erastes and Andra did their best to kill it.

Andra poked the Incarnation's armor joints with her Dragon's Fang, its blade spattered with black spots like ink. Every time she stabbed it, her strikes were deflected, as if she had been attacking the strongest parts of the armor rather than the weakest.

On the other side, Erastes whirled and thrust his blade two-handed into the monster's open faceplate. Erastes heard a sound like the grinding of gears, though the Incarnation said nothing, and then the sword popped out like a spring, launching into the forge and spinning across the floor.

Without missing a beat, Erastes lifted a chair and slammed it against the giant's face. One leg snapped off, but nothing else happened that Lycus could see. He smashed it into the intruder, again and again, until the chair was little more than splinters.

Then he tossed the last bit of wood aside, disgusted. For all their effort, the Incarnation strained against the chains no less than before.

And he was starting to gain ground.

The Nye slid across the polished wooden floor, trying to set their stance, but they might as well have been standing on ice. Slow, unstoppable, the Incarnation of Tartarus took one step forward. And then another.

Lycus had never been more aware of his complete lack of Valinhall powers. His sword hung heavy in his hand, and Erastes and Andra both were hitting the Incarnation harder than he could possibly manage. His arms were short enough that he'd have to practically leap on the giant's back before he could do anything, and even a Dragon's Fang couldn't pierce the Incarnation's armor at its weakest point.

Simon would do something, he thought. And if Simon could do it, Lycus had to prove that he was strong enough to do it too.

He ran toward the giant, not because he felt an outpouring of bravery, but because he was afraid that he needed his own momentum to keep going. If he hesitated, he might stop.

When he reached the Incarnation's metal legs, still braced against the House's polished wooden floor, he didn't hesitate.

He jumped.

Lycus didn't have Benson's steel running through his veins, so he didn't leap high enough to land on the giant's shoulders, as he had halfway intended. He managed to cling to the Incarnation's waist, which clicked and whirred beneath him as though he had grabbed on to a huge, living clock.

He scrambled up, finding more handholds than he expected, ignoring the horrified cries from his sister.

"Get down!" she yelled. "We can take care of this!"

Erastes ran into the forge to retrieve his sword. He didn't say a word, which encouraged Lycus enough that he found the strength to climb even higher. He didn't drop his sword, for which he felt a surge of pride.

The Incarnation's chest rumbled like an earthquake beneath Lycus' arms, and it twisted around, spinning at the hips until its upper body was facing backwards, and the gears it wore instead of a face stared at Lycus from inches away from his nose. The black chains of the Nye spun with the Giant as it turned, and out of the corner of his eye, Lycus spotted the three robed shadows gaining better footing on the wood, bracing themselves for a stronger pull.

They would be too late for him, though. The Incarnation seized him around the middle and lifted him up, inspecting him through the clicking clockwork inside its faceplate. Lycus tried to stab it, but the point of his sword scraped the side of the giant's steel helmet, doing nothing.

The giant didn't crush him, as he'd feared. It simply hefted him in one hand and threw him across the room.

Kai leaned against the edge of Valinhall's healing pool, his elbows up against the surface, relaxing. Only the waters of this bath dulled the pain in his back, like a tent peg being hammered into his kidneys every second. The second he left the bath, the wound would start getting worse, steadily burning more and more until the pain became unbearable, but for now it subsided into a dull bruise.

Beneath the suds on the water's surface, Kai felt something move. It was only the briefest of brushes, a soft current against his leg, but he had lived in this House for a long time. He lashed out with one foot, cupping the imp's skull under his toes, and then pressed it down against the bottom of the pool.

The water-imp's skin felt like rough, leathery bark, and its metallic nails scratched against his foot. He kept up the pressure on its head. Nothing it could do to him would hurt half as badly as the never-healing wound in his back, and the slices disappeared almost instantly inside the pool's water.

After a few seconds of being pressed against the stone at the bottom of the tub, its skull at the edge of breaking, the imp stopped fighting and started struggling to get away.

Over the years, Kai had learned that it was best to set them free at this point. If you kept an imp unto the point of death, others would come to defend it, and then you ended up having to kill a dozen of them. Which would then wake their mother, and he wanted to avoid that. Kai lifted his foot and let it swim away.

He had never opened his eyes.

When he was as clean as he was going to get, and his stab wound didn't hurt quite as badly as before, he climbed the stairs out of the bath.

As he did, his foot brushed Mithra's hilt.

To his surprise, the blade's emotions flowed into him. She felt determined, frustrated, and the sort of anticipation that prefaced a battle. So... she had been screaming to try and get his attention for minutes now, but he hadn't noticed. Now that she finally had him listening, she wanted him to go into battle *right this instant.*

Kai stepped away from the hilt, and the emotions stopped. Like Azura, Mithra rarely let him know what she was thinking. Unlike Azura, though, she was so insistent. Not nearly as polite, or graceful, or passionate as Azura.

He slipped into his clothes quickly, but not so fast as to make the sword think he was rushing because *she* wanted him to. When he finally picked Mithra off the ground, she smoldered with frustration.

He smiled. He never could stand passive ladies; he preferred his blades with a bit of a temper.

It only took him a second in the hallway before he realized what Mithra had been trying to tell him: a giant covered in Tartarus steel was marching in from the entry hall, an angry red Gate behind him. He had clearly torn his way into the House with a gatecrawler, and now he was locked in combat with the young girl Traveler, Andra. She was oblivious to his presence, her back to him as she swung Seijan in a futile effort to pierce the invader's armor. Her brother was nowhere to be found, which surprised him; he had thought those two were practically joined at the hip.

Far be it from me to disturb her, Kai thought, and he stopped at the seventh bedroom. Mithra practically shrieked in frustration.

He tried the doorknob, but it was locked. Only Azura's bearer, or those he specifically permitted, could enter the seventh bedroom easily. Despair rose in Kai's chest as he remembered how this used to be *his* room, but he put that aside. He had long thought about what he would do in this situation, when the desire to see his dear little ones became too much.

Calling steel, he pulled his foot back and stomped the door in.

The wood around the doorframe shattered, and the door swung open. The Nye would *not* be happy with him, but he was too happy to care.

His beautiful dear ones were talking.

I had a dream this would happen, Lilia said sleepily, her purple eyes content. *Or was it a nightmare?*

Delaine sighed. *I should have known it would be you.*

You should be helping, you know, Caela said, scowling from beneath her blue bonnet.

She's absolutely right, Angeline agreed.

Kai forced reluctance into his voice. "I would love to help, if only I had an advisor. It would be foolish to head into battle as I am now..."

The statement was met with sighs, jeers, and mocking laughter from the dolls. Kai was sure that Simon must have taken Rebekkah, or else he would have heard 'punch you in the face' included somewhere in the verbal abuse.

Otoku had her arms folded, though Kai hadn't seen her move. *Oh, and you don't think your advisor will show up soon? He's the* last *person to ignore a direct threat to the House.*

"Be that as it may, he's not here now. I'm afraid that I can't risk heading into battle without an advisor, it simply wouldn't be wise."

She grumbled a bit more, and her sisters joined in, telling him what a horrible person he was. His smile broadened; he *had* missed them.

Simon's not here, Otoku said at last. *So fine, I will allow you to borrow me. Only for today. And no baths!* She held her arms out for him to pick her up.

Tears burned at the corner of Kai's eyes. She had actually *moved*. For him! He picked her up as delicately as a sculpture of spun glass.

I hope you appreciate the sacrifice she's making, Caela sent. *Make sure you get rid of the Incarnation.*

He's absolutely wrecking *the House!* Gloria added.

The invader had given him a chance to use his beloved dolls in combat again. Far from killing him, Kai wanted nothing more than to shake the creature's hand and thank it, from the bottom of his heart.

But the little ones wanted him to take care of this threat, and that was what they would get.

He pulled open the door to the bedroom, and Otoku sighed. *Place me and Mithra on the ground.*

He couldn't conceal his surprise; she normally hated being set on the floor. It could smudge her dress. *Are you sure?*

No, I've given up my magical powers of prediction and now I'm wildly guessing. Hurry up.

Smiling to himself, Kai placed Mithra and Otoku on the ground. Then, to his surprise, he saw a body flying toward him.

For a second, as Lycus flew through the air less than a foot from the room's ceiling, Lycus marveled that he didn't feel any pain. Surely the Incarnation should have killed him, and he would die in horrific agony... compared to that, this seemed almost pleasant.

He had realized what would happen to him at the end of his fall, and the seeds of panic started to bloom, when his trip came to an abrupt halt. This, too, didn't hurt as much as he'd imagined. In fact, it almost felt like someone had caught him.

He looked up to see Kai's smile. His eyes were hidden behind clumps of his shaggy white hair, and he was smiling down at Lycus as though he held his own precious infant.

Lycus leaped out of the swordsman's arms as fast as possible.

Kai didn't seem to mind. He reached down and picked up one of his dolls from the floor: this one wore a long red dress with flowers on it, and her black hair hung loose down her back. He scooped her up, brushed off her dress, and placed her gently on his left hand.

With his right, he reached down and picked up a Dragon's Fang. It was easily as long as Simon's, covering more than half the room, and it had a smooth vein of gold running down the flat of the blade.

He must have placed the sword and the doll there before he caught Lycus. How had he known to do that? How had he found the time?

Kai looked at the Incarnation and cocked his head to one side. "So noisy, my dear, so noisy. You know I need my rest. Shall we stop the noise, so silence reigns supreme once more?"

The steel giant heaved its right arm, pulling one of the Nye off its feet, and then smashed a fist into the black robes. The Nye deflated as though it had been filled with nothing more substantial than air, flowing off like a snake made of black cloth and squirming blue-white light.

Erastes dodged one blow, and Andra hurled a decorative urn, which smashed against the Incarnation's armor. The other two Nye strained even harder, but the giant seemed to ignore them now. It ducked beneath the door to the forge, walking inside without looking back, then seized the handle to the workshop in one armored fist.

Lycus looked up to beg Kai to help, but the man was gone.

In his place hung a cloud of black smoke.

Smoke whirled through the room, flowing into the forge, re-forming into Kai, standing beside the Incarnation. He brought Mithra's silver-and-gold blade down on the giant's exposed neck.

The room rang with the sound of a bell cracking, and Incarnation of Tartarus almost dropped to one knee. That was more than Erastes and Andra had managed, and for the first time, Lycus thought they might actually be able to beat this thing. Kai was a full member of the old Dragon Army, not a new Valinhall Traveler like Andra or Erastes, and he could do things with his powers that Lycus couldn't imagine. If anyone could beat this creature, he could.

The Incarnation righted itself and slammed a skull-sized fist into the metal of the workshop door. At the first hit, the door dented. At the second, it caved in. At the third, it was knocked off its hinges and went flying into the room, crashing into a table and sending tools spilling all over the floor.

The Incarnation headed inside, and Lycus gasped as he heard his father, Caius, scream for help.

Lycus felt as though his heart would stop. His father almost lived in the workshop, some days, and the room wasn't that big. It would take the Incarnation significantly less effort to crush Caius than it had to crush the workshop door.

Erastes, Andra, and Lycus all ran forward, trying to help, even though the Nye had lost their grip on their chains. The two black chains now dangled from the Incarnation's shoulders and arm, flying behind him like streamers as he marched through the workshop.

The two Nye looked at each other, black hood meeting black hood, and then they backed into the shadows and disappeared.

"Hey, get back here!" Andra shouted, but they were gone.

Why did they leave? Lycus thought, astonished. Had they realized they couldn't beat an Incarnation, and therefore abandoned the rest of them to their fate? Were they trying to test the humans, to see if they were 'worthy' of defeating this invader? Or maybe they were trying to do something useful, and they had gone for help.

Now that he thought of it, Kai was standing there too. He stood with his head cocked, looking at the Incarnation's back, Mithra held in one hand and the black-haired doll in the other.

Lycus rushed past him, hoping desperately that the Traveler would decide to help. Kai was always strange, even frightening, but he was still an ally. Even a friend. He lived in Valinhall, too, which made Lycus think of him as on their side. The idea that he might stand aside and let the rest of them die...it hurt in ways that Lycus didn't even like to think about.

As terrible as Simon had been, that day when he killed the soldiers under Erastes' command, at least he hadn't abandoned his friends.

The Incarnation kicked and smashed at the tables in the workshop, destroying almost as an afterthought, as though it had been ordered to crush every piece of furniture it could lay its hands on.

Lycus' father, Caius, held a smith's hammer in both hands. He looked determined, but he had backed himself into a corner. He held the hammer out, as though it had the magical power to ward off Incarnations, and it looked like he was prepared to die fighting.

The Incarnation's helmet swiveled to look at Caius, and Lycus lunged forward, driving his sword into the base of the giant's breastplate, around the hip. That looked like a weak point, and there was *no way* he was letting this thing kill his father if he had a say in the matter.

The giant surveyed Caius for a second, then turned his gaze to a wooden table set with bags of precious stones. It swept the jewels off the table, then smashed its fist down into the wood, blasting the table to splinters.

Then it looked around, as though seeking something else to dismantle.

Meanwhile, Erastes plucked the hammer from Caius' grip. Holding the weapon one-handed, he jumped high enough to reach the Incarnation's head, driving the hammer down on its helmet.

Andra hacked furiously at the back of the giant's armored legs, trying to cut its feet out from under it, but as far as Lycus could tell, she was only scratching the metal.

Kai...still stood outside, in the forge, looking thoughtful.

Finally, the Incarnation caught sight of the blank patch of stone that held the hidden door to the gallery. Ignoring the futile attacks of the Travelers, it walked up to the wall and rubbed a palm over the wall, almost tenderly.

Lycus thought that it would hammer the wall into pieces, just as it had done the doors to the forge and workshop, but instead it reached out a finger and delicately flipped the disguised switch that opened the door.

The stretch of stone wall swung open to the tune of grinding machinery, and the Incarnation hummed in pleasure. "Efficiency," it said, in its rumbling voice. "Excellent."

Then it ducked, moving carefully to avoid wrecking the hidden door, and slid sideways into the gallery.

Lycus stared after it, wondering. Now that it was in the gallery, surrounded on two sides by stools and polished wooden bars, it appeared to be glancing around instead of attacking. It almost seemed like an interested foreigner, taking in the local sights. Like it was only *pretending* to be a monstrous destroyer.

Now that he thought about it, what was the Incarnation here for? It hadn't attacked the humans directly, instead moving deeper into the House. It hadn't tried to take anything, nor had it fought them seriously. It did nothing but move from room to room, breaking furniture almost absently, as if it couldn't be bothered to ruin a room completely before walking farther.

It didn't come to kill us, Lycus realized. *So why is it here?*

He couldn't figure out the answer, but the question bothered him. He didn't follow the giant into the gallery, though Andra and Erastes did.

Well, they tried to.

Kai stepped forward, though Lycus hadn't seen him move out of the forge. He placed a hand on Erastes' shoulder, lifting his gold-and-silver blade to bar Andra's way.

Both of them stopped, looking at him.

"Please," he said, bowing slightly. "Allow me."

He swung his Dragon's Fang around to point it inside the door, so it didn't get caught on the doorframe, and then he followed his blade inside. He moved with smooth grace, as though he was only one step away from starting a dance.

Honestly, it wouldn't have surprised Lycus if Kai *did* start to dance. He was the strangest adult Lycus had ever met.

Kai stopped and glanced back into the gallery, where Lycus noticed that the black-haired doll was sitting on one of the few workbenches to survive the Incarnation's rampage.

"Otoku, if you please?" Kai said sweetly.

Lycus thought he heard a distant, windy voice let out a sigh.

Then Kai popped into a cloud of smoke, which rushed behind and above the Incarnation, re-forming into an image of Kai standing atop the giant's steel shoulders. Kai drove his blade down, into the top of the shoulder joint, where the armor should have been weakest.

Nothing. His blow did even less than Andra's had. The Incarnation didn't even seem to notice, except that he absently swung his Ragnarus sword above his head, swatting at Kai like a horse's tail sweeping away flies.

Kai leaped back, his head skirting the tall ceiling, and landed lightly on the bar. He began to chant, or possibly to sing, a little above a whisper. "Hush, little one, there's naught to fear. It's just the wind, that's what you hear."

The Incarnation drove a steel fist at Kai so fast that Lycus couldn't see it, but the Valinhall Traveler ducked out of the way as though he'd known the hit was coming.

"Hush, little one, it's not the end. Just put your trust in steel...and wind."

Not for the first time, Lycus wondered if Kai was quoting something. Half of his little rhymes seemed made up on the spot.

Then again, there did seem to be something happening to his blade. It was almost invisible, like a heat haze in the desert, but the air warped around the Dragon's Fang. It twisted in transparent rivers around the sword's edge, and Lycus thought he could hear the rush of a breeze through the trees.

What power of Valinhall was *that?*

Kai jumped back up, onto the giant's shoulders. This time, the Incarnation seemed to be expecting it: the giant lifted its blade to drive into the Traveler's side.

Raising his own sword, Kai drove it down into the armor's shoulder joint.

At first, Lycus wondered why Kai had done it. The Tartarus armor had repelled his attack only seconds ago, surely nothing was different now.

Then he noticed that the Dragon's Fang was inches deeper than it should have been. It had driven through one of the weakest joins in the Incarnation's armor, the wound red-hot at the edges and dribbling molten steel.

Kai hopped back down to the floor, his blade still swirling with almost-visible wind. He ducked one of the Incarnation's slashes, then returned with an overhand cut of his own, landing on the wound he'd made in the giant's right shoulder.

He slashed through the metal, leaving glowing, heated links of steel chain in his wake. The Incarnation shouted, perhaps in surprise or pain, as its armored right arm slid off the shoulder, dangling only by a few bits of mail. The bronze, steel, and iron clockworks inside its arm clicked away, exposed to the air.

Humming to himself, Kai dodged a second punch from the creature's left hand. Then he took his blade in both hands, swinging with his whole body at the Incarnation's breastplate. He didn't bother aiming for a weak point, this time; he hit the giant square in the chest with the edge of his Dragon's Fang.

The Incarnation staggered back a step, grabbing a bar in its left hand for support. Kai kept pushing, long past the point where he should have realized that this wasn't going to work.

Then, to Lycus' shock, the edge of the Dragon's Fang actually pushed *through* the giant's polished armor. Kai's gold-and-silver blade tore through the breastplate and into the clockwork beneath, the edge of the wound dribbling melted steel.

Groaning, the Incarnation dropped to one knee. "You..." it groaned out. "Why...how..."

In one final motion, Kai sliced his blade all the way through the creature's chest. The sword emerged trailing drops of molten steel, and the Incarnation crashed to the ground in two pieces.

"Welcome to Valinhall," Kai said lightly. Then he flicked his blade as if to clear it of blood, and placed the Dragon's Fang on the bar.

Lycus passionately wished that he could be *half* that strong when he grew up.

The swordsman's head cocked again, but he didn't turn back to look at Lycus. "You were kept by urgent business, I trust?" he said.

In a rustle of cloth, the Eldest Nye drifted past Lycus. His robes were stormcloud gray, where most of the Nye wore black, and his sleeves drooped down almost the length of Lycus' legs. Andra and Erastes seemed as surprised to see him as Lycus was; Erastes took one careful step back, and Andra hurriedly lowered her sword so that the Nye could glide into the gallery.

He spoke to Kai, in his rasping voice. "You were here, as was the other one. I have more than a single matter to occupy my time."

"You're dealing with something more interesting than the invasion of Valinhall?" Kai asked. His voice sounded humorous, as though he found the whole situation funny, but Lycus wondered if he might actually be furious.

The Eldest chuckled unpleasantly. "This? I would hardly call this an invasion." His hood turned to the shadows at the corners of the room, and instantly a pair of Nye materialized, seemingly out of nowhere. Lycus had nothing to prove this, but he was sure they were the same two who had used their chains to try and slow the Incarnation down.

No one gave any orders, but the Nye bowed to the Eldest, then swept over to the Incarnation's body. It was still, though some of the gears still clicked and whirred. They began pulling plates off, removing gears, carrying them away.

"That will be valuable for study, I think," the Eldest said. "Someone has given us a present. I can only wonder why."

Kai nodded to the red-and-black blade that Lycus was sure came from Ragnarus. "What about that?" he asked.

The Eldest held one sleeve over the sword, just as Lycus might have held his hands up to a fire to keep himself warm. "Did he use its powers?"

With a shrug, Kai said, "He almost poked me with it once or twice."

The Nye's head swept from side to side. "We can be certain that was not its only purpose. Why, then, is it here?"

Kai walked away, leaving his sword sitting on the bar. As he passed, he glanced up at the four masks, hanging on the wall by their racks. "There is only one thing I can think of that has changed in this House," Kai said. "And the Incarnation headed straight for it."

"I did not ask you for speculation," the Eldest replied. "We will study the creature's body, and I will tell you what we find. In the meantime, be on your guard."

Scooping up his doll with one hand, Kai laughed. "On guard? What *would* I do without your sage advice?"

He walked away without a word for any of the other humans, whispering under his breath to his doll. Caius was holding on to a table with both hands, trying to catch his breath.

Erastes and Andra looked at one another.

"I'm going to go challenge another room," Andra said at last. "I've got a long way to go."

The soldier nodded, and almost smiled. Andra hurried out of the room, clearly upset with herself. Lycus knew his sister well enough to leave her alone for the moment, until she stopped blaming herself for not being able to help.

And what about me? Lycus thought. *I added nothing.*

The thought made him ache even more for the powers and privileges of Valinhall, but he couldn't shake something else.

Why did it come here?

He couldn't think of an answer.

CHAPTER 15

PRICES PAID

Zakareth faced the gates of Cana with the Incarnations of Helgard and Lirial behind him. His ancestors had constructed this wall, including the massive metal doors set into the stone. He couldn't begin to guess how many thousands of wagons and hundreds of thousands of people had passed through those doors over the generations.

He had always been proud of his family for bringing something like this into being, but since his...change...he had gained a new appreciation for these projects.

How much time had Queen Cynara the Second spent raising the walls of this city? How many workers? How many of them had died building defenses for their city, watering the stones with their blood? How many homes had gone untended, how many fields untilled, while these gates were formed and assembled?

It was all part of the price. If you wanted strong walls, you had to pay for them: in money, in time, in sacrificed opportunities. That was the way of the world.

Ragnarus simply made matters more...direct.

"Can you see them?" Zakareth asked.

"Of course I can," Lirial chimed, amused. "I can see everything." Her milky eyes stared through the walls of Cana, watching a battle in a Territory far away. "The time inconsistencies distort things, you realize, but Tartarus has been defeated. They are dragging his pieces away."

Lirial's crystal body shone a reflected red in the setting sun, the silver wire wrapping around her body burning with fiery sunlight. Helgard stood beside her, running a hand over the curling horns behind her ears. She stood in a small snow flurry that extended only a pace away from her; frost melted and ran in tiny rivulets at her feet. Zakareth wondered if she even noticed.

"And Elysia?" the King asked.

The melodic voice of the Lirial Incarnation grew distant. "It is remarkable. He has none of the control of his predecessors, but all of their power.

He keeps banishing my probes. By accident, I'm sure, but it's irritating nonetheless. And yet…the battle seems to have drawn to a standstill. Your Valinhall Overlord is badly injured, but still alive."

"The time has come, then," he said. With a thought, he summoned his crown onto his head. His shadow gained three tall spikes.

Lirial stepped into a sunbeam, her body becoming the crystal key to her Territory. In front of her, a Gate opened, swirling gray and silver at the edges.

"My constructions will guide you," she murmured. "Travel quickly, before the moons shift."

Zakareth stepped into the Crystal Fields without another word. He could tear his way free of any Territory, now, and the Lirial Incarnation would not be able to resist him once he escaped her Territory. She was afraid, and therefore she could be trusted. She would not lead him astray.

Helgard stood at his side, idly stroking the head of a furry, white, three-headed dog that hadn't been there a moment ago. "So this is Lirial… it's a bleak place, isn't it? I wonder where the Daniri kept their tombs."

She couldn't hide the greed in her eyes, and she didn't bother. It was in her nature, and they both knew it.

"This way," Zakareth said, tracing the lines of power in Lirial to a tiny, floating crystal. It bobbed in their presence and sped off, not waiting for them to follow.

One step in Lirial took them beyond Cana's walls, and a hundred paces closer to Leah's camp outside.

In the ancient days, before the Territories had come fully under humanity's control, walls had been an effective defense. High walls on a city meant that traditional attack was all but impossible, and only the best Travelers could bypass your protection to attack you directly. That age was long past.

In the end, his ancestors had paid their price for nothing.

The whole world had been washed in shades of purple and violet. He could dimly remember a moment before, when his surroundings had been made of gold, but the violet was so much more pleasant. His thoughts were clear now, even straightforward. Honest, that was the word.

Alin pulled the Avernus Traveler toward him, his Violet Light wrapped around her ankle like a lasso. As he dragged her across the stones, she scrabbled for purchase on the stone, her fingernails scraping against the stairs.

He didn't know this woman. She wore an armored black outfit, and her expression stayed rigid even as she struggled to escape.

I don't care about her, he thought. *I should kill her. That will keep her out of my way while I rescue Ilana, and take care of Simon and Leah.*

That brought another issue to his attention: did he have to kill Simon and Leah? Before, he had resolved not to hurt them any more than necessary, but he seemed to recall doing his best to destroy them both.

No, I don't need to kill them. Not unless it's too much hassle to keep them alive. I want them to live so that they can see how great I am.

Alin would never have admitted that before, even to himself; he marveled at the simplicity and freedom that honesty brought.

A sharp cry, like that of a hunting hawk, shattered Alin's ear. To his right, a blur of brown-and-white rushed toward him, feathers ruffled, beak sharp. One of this Traveler's Avernus bird-men, no doubt.

He didn't have to do anything. Fuzzy violet creatures—the Thrulls of the Violet District—leaped out of cover and landed on the bird-man. The bird should have been larger than all the Thrulls combined, but when their thin feet met the Avernus creature, the bird-man popped in an explosion of purple light and vanished.

The Thrulls raised their thin arms and grinned. "We don't like doing this, but we're obligated to serve you!" one of them cried.

Alin raised a fist in salute. "I shouldn't need to thank you! You have done nothing more than your jobs!"

The fuzzy, purple Thrulls bowed at the waist, and then scurried away.

He felt a strange lack of resistance on the end of his Violet binding, and looked over. The Avernus woman had escaped, somehow, and started limping her way back up the steps toward a black shape in the waystation.

No, wait, that's the Valinhall Traveler. The shadows that had concealed him before seemed weaker now. They flickered fitfully, like a guttering fire, and Alin wondered if the Traveler had run out of whatever power kept him hidden.

Idly, Alin twirled a strip of Violet Light around his finger as he walked up to the Naraka waystation. Simon lay in a heap behind him on the street. He was taken care of; Alin would have a long talk with him whenever Simon managed to wake up.

He didn't see Leah or Ilana, though. That was interesting. Perhaps these two had agreed to buy time for them until they got away. He should use Silver Light to search the city, he knew that, but somehow the Silver had never felt so distant.

I've given myself entirely over to Violet, he thought. *It was likely a defensive reaction to keep me from dying.*

That made sense, but he couldn't help feeling a little irritated that he couldn't call on his other powers. Not to mention the fact that he never should have been pushed that far to the brink to begin with.

The Avernus Traveler had made it behind the man from Valinhall. She rummaged through her pockets, pulling out an empty leather bag and what looked like a handful of herbs and feathers.

Alin didn't care. He was in no hurry. Red gnomes circled the crumbling building, and the roof was covered by blue floating jellies. Come to think of it, he never had learned what those jellies were called. He should find out.

With trembling hands, the Avernus Traveler poured the handful of herbs into the bag. She started to say something, but Alin didn't wait to see what it was. He flicked his long, violet bandage like a whip, cracking it into her hand.

The bag and its contents vanished. Finally, the Avernus started to show fear. Her skin paled, and she swallowed visibly, but she ground her jaw and forced herself to meet his eyes.

In front of her, the Valinhall Traveler had finally lost his concealment. He stood, looking years older than he had earlier, the black chain-marks peeking through the top of his shirt as they showed on his collar. He swayed as he stood, and he held his cracked sword in both hands as though he didn't have the strength to hold it one-handed any longer.

Somehow, the man smiled reassuringly, despite his obvious fatigue. "This is unnecessary. Nobody has to die today."

Alin heard the words, he weighed them, and he found them less than honest. "You've killed many of the citizens of Elysia." He gestured to the steps and to the street, where corpses of all colors bled a rainbow of blood. "A dozen dead, maybe two, I'll need to get someone in here to check. Do they not matter to you?" He was honestly curious. "Is it because they're not human?"

"I'm sorry about that," the Traveler said easily. "Nobody *else* has to die today."

Unlike his previous statement, *that* one was true. "You're right," Alin said. "Surrender yourselves, and I'll take you alive."

Alin waited.

The Traveler waited.

His eyes flicked toward Simon's body, and his shoulders seemed to slump. "I'm sorry, I can't do that. It's gone too far."

The man's shoulders firmed. His bright smile grew steadier. The point of his sword stopped wavering in midair, and stayed pointed at Alin's chest.

The woman behind him let out a bleak laugh. "You always have to be the hero, don't you?" Her eyes drifted to Alin. "I'm not going to surrender either, but I won't be so dramatic about it."

Alin wanted to answer. He tried to make his voice work, but something had stuck in his chest, as though he had swallowed a bone.

You always have to be the hero, don't you?

Through the ruthless honesty of the Violet Light, he took a look at himself. And he finally saw.

He was the powerful, all-but-immortal Incarnation standing tall after a harsh battle. He was the menace, looming over a weary swordsman who kept his blade raised in futile defiance. He was the uncaring master, carelessly discarding minions by the score, their bodies strewn all over the street. He was the traitor who had beaten Simon bloody for trying to protect Alin's own sister.

At last, the Violet Light showed him his own appearance in a cruel, unrelenting mirror.

He looked like a villain.

Alin drifted back, away from the Travelers, until he felt a wall where he could brace himself. He leaned with one arm against the cracked wall, the Violet Light fading from his body.

When the Violet faded, the other voices returned.

The enemies are still there! the Gold Light raged. *Go get them, you coward!*

This is wrong, said the Green.

Sadness radiated from the Silver. *There were so many other ways you could have handled this.*

Spare them, the Blue begged. *Please. For your own sake.*

They were your friends, the Orange said.

The Rose Light whispered, *What have you done?*

And then a smaller, more distant voice, one he almost didn't recognize. *Who am I?*

Overlord Feiora Torannus watched the Incarnation of Elysia limp away to lean against the building on the opposite side of the street. For her life, she couldn't figure out what they had done to drive him away.

But she intended to take advantage of it.

"Indirial, make a Gate," she ordered.

The other Overlord looked as stunned as she felt, and even more bruised and battered. "Why did he leave?" Indirial asked.

Feiora clapped her hands loudly. "Indirial! Gate!" She pointed to the blue jellies floating over the roof, their giant tentacles dangling down.

Indirial shook himself, gave her a sheepish smile, and started cutting one of his Valinhall Gates. She could have opened a Gate to Avernus, but her scouts had told her about the guardians on the other side of this place, and she had no wish to run into them. The only token she'd brought that would send her directly into safe lands had gone with Leah, who had probably followed Eugan straight to a comfortable Corvinus tribe lodge.

The thought of her raven was too painful to focus on, so she hurried as best she could over to Simon, keeping one wary eye on the Incarnation, in case he changed his mind and returned to sanity.

Her shins would be nothing more than a set of massive bruises tomorrow morning, her fingernails were scraped bloody, and she was sure she'd twisted her left ankle. But somehow, she managed to lower herself and scoop Simon into her arms, cloak and all.

She almost fell, and her knees sent bolts of pain shooting all the way up into her spine. He looked small, but this kid was *heavy*. He had put on more muscle than it looked, apparently.

Feiora staggered over to Indirial, leaving Simon's sword lying in the street. If she had learned anything about Valinhall from watching them today, it was that they could banish and summon their swords as they liked. Even if it wasn't as easy as she imagined, she simply couldn't carry the sword and him both. So that was that.

The Elysian creatures had started growing restless, shouting and growling and shrieking around them, but they still didn't charge. They seemed as confused by the Incarnation's change of heart as Feiora herself.

When she reached Indirial, his slice in midair had snapped into a proper white-edged Gate. An old-fashioned, well-appointed sitting room rested on the other side.

Indirial wasn't looking through the portal, though; his gaze remained locked on the Elysian Incarnation.

"What happened?" he wondered aloud.

Feiora shoved Simon through the Gate, onto the carpeted floor beyond. She couldn't carry him any farther, and if she tried, they were both going to pitch over. "I don't know," she said. "And I don't care. Let's get out while we still can."

Indirial shook his head, took one last look at the Incarnation in his shredded remnants of gold armor, and then walked into Valinhall.

The Gate zipped shut behind them.

Something grabbed Ilana, and she struggled, but she wasn't strong enough. They grabbed her, a whole crowd of creatures and two-foot-tall men in hats, dragging her out the broken window of the waystation. She screamed, but it was swallowed up in an explosion from outside, where Simon and her brother fought in a battle she would never have believed a few weeks ago.

She lashed out with a foot and kicked one of the gnomes in the chin.

He didn't seem to mind. In fact, he took the kick on his bearded chin and nodded approvingly. What kind of weird, twisted people were these?

Ilana didn't stop fighting. She punched, kicked, screamed, clawed, and bit until she was exhausted.

When her strength ran out, she realized she was lying on a bed of soft grass, looking up at a golden sky. She glanced around, seeing nothing but a grassy horizon occasionally broken up by flowers. Surely this plain of waving grass didn't go on forever. It had to stop at some point, right?

When she turned back the other direction, she was met with bright blue eyes and a fuzzy white snout.

She yelped and scrambled backwards on all fours. The dog—which, she now noticed, was wearing plate armor of bright gold—bounded after her. It let out one bark, which rang in the emptiness like a bell echoing in a castle.

Ilana was no Traveler, but she knew a Territory when she fell headfirst into one. And this dog was wearing armor, so that was another clue that she wasn't in her world. Dog-armor. There was only one reason for that: someone expected this dog to fight in a battle. This was obviously a vicious warrior-dog, protecting the Territory from intruders. Intruders like her.

She got to her feet and backed slowly away—somewhere she had heard that if you moved slowly, dogs wouldn't chase you.

The dog sat on its hind legs, puzzled. It scratched at the armor around its neck and whined.

She glanced over her shoulder to make sure that she wasn't about to step into a pit full of armored snakes, or whatever other horrors this Territory had in store for her, but when she turned back to the dog, there was a face three inches from hers. Golden eyes stared straight at her.

Ilana screamed, the face screamed back, and the dog barked happily and started running around in circles. That was when Ilana realized that the face was upside-down. Long, gold-blond hair dangled from the top of this upside-down girl's head, almost reaching to the tops of the grass. She wore a white one-piece dress, belted in the middle by a gold sash.

Strangely, Ilana found herself wondering how the woman's skirt stayed up, when by all logic it should have flipped down and covered her completely, but Ilana's instincts ran away without her.

On pure panicked reaction, she punched the woman in the nose.

Her fist slammed into a surface that felt like metal, but *looked* like a six-sided plate of green glass that floated in front of the other woman and definitely hadn't been there a second before.

Pain shot up Ilana's fist and into her arm, and she backed away from the floating woman, cradling her hand. It wasn't the first time she had punched someone, but it was the first time she had tried to punch somebody who could conjure armor out of nowhere. This woman was obviously a Traveler, and that meant that Ilana's chances of getting out of here alive had shrunk to almost nothing.

"Oh, I'm so sorry!" the other woman said, drifting around so that she looked Ilana in the eye again. She was still upside-down. "Here, let me help you with that."

Ilana wasn't fooled; she kept her distance from the weird floating Traveler. "What are you, a Traveler? A ghost?"

The other woman shrugged, which looked particularly disturbing when she was hanging upside-down. "A little of both, actually," she responded. Then she gave a bright smile and flipped right-side-up. "My name is Rhalia, and you must be Alin's sister!"

She stuck a hand out for Ilana to clasp.

Ilana bolted.

Whatever reason this Traveler had for dragging her here and persistently trying to touch her hand, it couldn't be good. Maybe they could kill with a touch, she didn't know. Half the things Simon and Alin were doing before she left, she would have sworn were impossible.

She managed to run for perhaps ten paces—the armored dog easily keeping pace with her the whole time, like he thought it was a game—before she slowed to a halt. She couldn't help it.

A wall of white stone, gold edges, and silver plating rose in front of her, seemingly a hundred paces in the air. It was definitely miles long, as it stretched around a city bigger than anything Ilana had ever seen or imagined. Tower-tops rose over the wall in every color she could think of, silver and gold and ruby and white and green...

Now that she thought of it, even the walls were worked with a variety of colors. Emeralds spiraled in complex patterns over a seemingly insignificant stretch of wall, next to a mural of a rising sun made out of precious stones.

She stood, stunned by her own wonder, as a column of light like solid lightning rose from somewhere in the city and blasted into the clouds.

At least I know what Territory this is, she thought.

Rhalia drifted up beside her, smiling like a proud mother. "Isn't it wonderful? You should have seen it when Travelers lived here to hold Gates open, and people came and went..." She sighed. "Sadly, they're all gone. For now."

"What about my brother?" Ilana asked. "You mentioned him. This is his Territory, isn't it?"

"It's his Territory, yes, but I wouldn't call him a Traveler any longer."

Elysia was plenty warm, but Ilana shivered. "Why did he bring me here, then?"

Rhalia's eyes widened. "Oh, no, he didn't bring you here. I did!"

"Why?"

The other woman floated behind her, pushing gently to guide her toward the city gates. "There's someone I'd like you to meet," Rhalia said.

Chapter 16

THE FOUNDER'S HEIR

When Simon woke up, he couldn't move.

He lay on his back, staring up at the plaster ceiling of his bedroom back in Valinhall. As far as he could see from craning his eyes, he was still fully clothed and wearing his Nye cloak. The bed was soft beneath him, but he wasn't wrapped in a sheet. Someone must have taken him here and dumped him on his bed. Bits of his clothes were still damp, and the rest was stiff, as if recently dried—someone had taken him on a trip to the healing pool.

He was grateful. If they had dumped him here without healing him, he would have felt burning agony instead of paralyzing numbness.

I guess we won, then, Simon sent.

A few of the dolls tittered, some scoffed, and a few groaned. The total effect was like one long, exasperated sigh.

No one died, if that's what you're asking, Caela told him.

Not as far as we know... Lilia added.

Not even Alin! Rebekkah said, irritated. *You waste way too much time standing around when you're wearing that mask. Leah almost got him, but he ended up going crazy and letting everyone get away. You should have punched him harder.*

How did I get back here?

Ask him, Angeline sent.

Before Simon could ask who she meant, a dark hood leaned over his bed, giving him an eyeful of the void the Eldest Nye wore for a face.

His whole body twitched, and his heart hammered against his ribs. Everything he'd learned in Valinhall was screaming at him to jump up and stab the Eldest through the chest, before the Nye could draw a chain around his neck and choke the life out of him...

"Be still, son of Kalman. I have not come to kill you while you sleep away the effects of your mask." He leaned closer. "Though my mind could always change."

"What...you want?" Simon grunted. It was the best he could manage through his all-but-paralyzed throat.

The Eldest held up a shriveled fig the color of blood, pinching it through his sleeve. "Why did you bring this here? It's not a weapon, it cannot be attuned to us. If it were planted here, it could be the end!"

What is it? Simon tried to ask. It came out sounding more like "Whatsit?"

In a flicker of one black sleeve, the Eldest made the object vanish. "It is a seed of the Crimson Vault's domination. It is *vile*. It is *disgusting*. And it is not something the Founder's heir should ever touch!"

He seemed genuinely angry rather than simply menacing or threatening, and maybe that had led the Eldest to speak carelessly, but Simon felt sure he had let something important slip.

With a monumental effort, Simon craned his head forward and spoke clearly. "Founder's heir?" he asked.

The dolls went totally quiet.

The Eldest hesitated. "The point remains that you were careless, bringing this here. This seed is not something we can make our own! I am afraid even to destroy it here, in case we awaken it through careless action. You have put us all in danger!"

Simon refused to be distracted. "Tell me."

The Nye's hood twitched from side to side, as though trying to think of a way out. At last he began to speak, forcing the words out as though they pained him. "This Territory...it began as dozens of empty shards, splinters of a world that came before. Perhaps all Territories begin this way. In our case, Valin was the man who bound our splinters together into one new Territory. He was, and is, our Founder."

He drifted out of Simon's sight, but from the rustle of shuffling robes, Simon got the impression that he was pacing. "When he was taken from us...we discovered that Valinhall needs a Founder. It is a relationship of equal exchange that we have with our Travelers, you see, and without a Founder, the two sides do not balance. Our Travelers take more from us than they give. We needed our master back, but we could not have him. So she selected a replacement."

"Who?" Simon grunted.

Mithra, Angeline sent. The other dolls remained silent.

The Eldest's hood flicked over to the dolls' shelf, but he addressed Simon again. "Mithra was always Valin's blade. Whoever inherits her, inherits the responsibilities of Valinhall's Founder."

"Kai," Simon said.

A laugh scraped its way out of the Eldest's robes. "Kai? He shirked his duties even *before* he was crippled by Ragnarus. Now, if someone does not make up for his lack, our world will fade away, another dead splinter adrift on an endless void. Just like before."

Simon tried to ask another question, but his throat wouldn't cooperate. *What responsibilities?* he asked the dolls.

Angeline dutifully repeated his question to the Nye.

"I have said too much, daughters of wind," the Eldest replied. "He will learn fast enough by doing as he is instructed." The Nye flowed over to the door, out of Simon's field of vision. His voice floated back to the bed. "I am taking this demonic seed with me. Perhaps I can find a way to dispose of it."

He made no other sound.

Is he gone? Simon finally asked.

No, he's behind you! Otoku called.

He's gone, said Angeline.

You're no fun.

Simon found himself mentally rehearsing the Eldest's speech, and it didn't comfort him much. *What does he want Kai to do? You know, don't you? Does he expect that of me?*

Gloria sighed. *Oh, honey, I don't think it would be wise to talk if the Eldest doesn't want us to.*

It sounds smart to me, Otoku said. *What can he possibly do to us? Oh, I'm sorry, I meant what* can't *he do. That list is much shorter.*

I'll tell him, Rebekkah said casually. *He needs to know.*

It was a good life while it lasted, Lilia sighed.

The Eldest told us not to! Angeline put in.

A few of the others started to argue, until it sounded like a whispered twelve-sided debate in the middle of a windstorm.

Finally, Caela's voice cut through the rest. *Actually, I believe I've thought of a solution,* she sent, her mental voice pleased.

The others stopped for a second, and in the moment of quiet they all seemed to come to some sort of agreement.

Oh! That's a good point.

If anyone would know, he would.

I'm sure he's not afraid of the Eldest.

What would he have to be afraid of?

Finally, Simon cut in. *What are you talking about?*

There was a brief silence, which Simon felt certain was filled with condescending pity.

Think about it, Simon, Caela said. *Who knows everything there is to know about Valinhall? Who would gladly tell you anything the Eldest won't?*

Then Rebekkah jumped in, as subtle as ever: *Who is currently stuck in the graveyard with nothing to do but answer your questions?*

Simon felt like an idiot. *I should have asked Valin these questions a long time ago, right?*

You're learning, Otoku said.

I'm surprised it only took him this long, another doll sent.

He may be slow, but at least he's... Lilia's voice trailed off.

Thanks, everybody. Thank you. Simon leaned back against his pillow and sighed. *Now if only I could move.*

It had only taken Simon about six hours to climb to his feet, according to the clock beside his bed. Someone had pounded on the door a few hours before, but since Simon was physically incapable of shouting or rising to answer it, the mysterious person was on their own. It was probably Andra anyway.

The dolls had taken turns entertaining Simon with their favorite stories during his paralysis, some of which had involved Kai. Many of them were embarrassing incidents featuring him. For some of those, he hadn't even had a doll with him.

He almost called steel so that he would turn into an Incarnation and be done with it. By the time he was strong enough to limp to the hallway, he almost wept with relief.

You're welcome! Otoku called, cheerily, as Simon left.

He breathed a sigh of relief as he reached the hall, though it took all his concentration and both hands against the wall for him to stay upright, much less walk.

To his surprise, Overlord Feiora was waiting for him. She wore solid black, though her armor from the day before was missing, and her blunt face hardened on seeing him. "Good, you're awake. You need to take me back."

"Sorry," Simon said, pushing himself a few feet down the hall. "I can't help you right now."

"You can and you will," she said. "I have business that can't wait."

"Same here." Maker, how long would it take him to get down this hallway? It had never seemed so long before.

Feiora stared at him as though she couldn't figure out what he was talking about, and was stuck deciding whether or not to break his legs. "It's an order from an Overlord, Traveler."

"Not from Damasca," he said. "Sorry." Later, he would probably regret talking to her like this, but he had spent hours being bullied by the Eldest and embarrassed by his own advisors. He wasn't exactly in the right mood.

"You're from the village of Myria," she said. "I'm an Avernus, and I like to know who I'm working with. Myria is as much a part of the kingdom as Bel Calem."

"Who says?"

"Centuries of tradition! Thousands of maps!"

"Get new maps."

That didn't even slow her down. She started talking about how the kingdom could be falling apart, and he was stopping her from saving lives, and he couldn't imagine what was at stake, and a few other things that he didn't much pay attention to.

He'd known that he shouldn't have tried being clever with her. It never worked. So he resorted to his old habit: saying nothing. Simon pulled himself along the wall, through the House, and into the garden.

Overlord Feiora didn't stop until he shut the door to the rain garden almost on top of her. She couldn't open it, but she did pound on the stone for a while, shouting something muffled that sounded like curses.

Simon was already relaxing in the beautiful sounds of the steady rain and the wind through the nearby plants—and the glorious lack of anyone speaking to him—when he realized that, since the graveyard had moved, the courtyard wasn't directly accessible through the rain garden anymore. He had gone the old way. If he wanted to do this without doubling back, he was going to have to cross through *six* rooms, and in at least three of them he'd have to fight his way through.

At the thought, he almost cried.

Two hours later, panting and covered in shallow slashes, Simon arrived at the graveyard.

Valin wasn't there.

The sheets of emerald lightning rolled overhead, lending the usual green cast to the headstones and ivy-shrouded pillars. Simon usually saw Valin sitting on one of the tombstones, or else locked in combat with Kai.

Today, he saw no one.

Simon walked forward on shaky legs, concentrating on not falling over. Valin wasn't behind the first stone column, as he had half-suspected, nor was he behind the second. He glanced over behind the first row of graves...

And there he saw Valin, crumpled in a pile of tangled limbs. He couldn't have been sleeping; no one could sleep with their legs twisted at different angles. Besides, one hand was outstretched toward the hilt of a sword that rested a foot away on the grass. Either he had been crawling toward it, or he'd dropped it when he fell.

Simon collapsed to his knees by the Wanderer's body, feeling the man's neck for a pulse. Nothing. His skin was waxy and cold, and his gray eyes stared blankly into the dirt.

So he's dead, Simon thought. *Again. I wonder if it will stick this time?*

The strangest thing, to him, was that he couldn't see any obvious wounds. He would have thought that, if a room guardian were killed, it had to be the result of someone challenging the room. But if Kai had killed his former master at last, there should be some evidence of it. Blood, sword wounds, something.

Maybe the Eldest Nye's resurrection technique had been temporary, and Valin had simply returned to his natural state. That would make sense, but if that were the case, why had the Eldest given him a position as a room guardian? He should have known that Valin could pitch over dead at any time.

Then Valin heaved a great breath and bolted upright, his eyes widening.

Simon almost fell backwards, startled but not surprised. He hadn't really expected the Wanderer to stay dead.

Valin squeezed his eyes shut, at the same time pulling a dagger away from Simon's throat.

That, on the other hand, surprised him quite a bit. He hadn't even noticed that Valin had a knife.

"How long has it been?" Valin rasped, his throat sounding caked with dirt.

"I saw you yesterday," Simon responded. "Or…maybe the day before, I'm not sure."

Valin blinked his eyes open and gave Simon an easy smile. "At least it wasn't twenty-five years, this time. Are you here for training?"

Simon eased himself onto a gravestone, trying not to fall off. "I met the Eldest today."

"Oh, I get it." Valin pulled one arm over his head, stretching sore muscles, then he cracked his neck with a sharp sound that made Simon wince. "You've got questions."

"Yeah. My first one: does this happen to you every time? The dead thing, I mean."

Valin rolled his chain-wrapped shoulders, working them loose. "I'm only around when the room needs me," he said. "Usually, that's when a Traveler's here. When nobody's around, I get weaker and weaker until, eventually, I keel over and die." He paused for a moment, then added, "It got worse after what I did for you the other day, calling on my old power for a few minutes. Turns out that wasn't such a good idea. Who knew?"

"So you're not…" Simon stopped. He wasn't even sure what question he wanted to ask, much less how he was supposed to say it.

The older man flexed his fingers, opening and closing his fists. "I don't understand how the Eldest brought me here. I wonder, sometimes: was I actually dead? I feel like myself, and yet…thin, somehow. Sort of hazy, like a ghost." The Wanderer looked off into the distance, far past Simon. "I don't know how he did it, but I wish he hadn't."

Simon waited, wary of saying something to set him off.

"But I'm here now," the man continued, brushing dirt from his pants. "And I don't think you have to worry about ending up like me, so you can relax. I'm Valinhall's Founder; it's as much a part of me as I am of it. Not to mention that I was an Incarnation at the time, so..."

He shrugged. "Was that it? Were you worrying about having to share a room with me? I have it on good authority that I don't snore while I'm dead."

"Not quite," Simon said. The thought of ending up like Valin had never occurred to him, but it didn't sound so bad. No matter what the Wanderer said, working as a room guardian in Valinhall still had to be better than dying. "The Eldest mentioned that you were the Founder, and I'd never heard that before today. What does that mean, exactly?"

Valin glanced in his direction, and then away. He stepped forward, putting his short sword through a casual three-part combination that de-limbed and decapitated an invisible opponent. While he moved, he spoke. "He's setting you up as the Founder's heir, is he?"

"Uh, yes. Yes, he is. I was hoping you could tell me what that means."

At the end of a thrust that skewered another non-existent man through the heart, Valin shrugged. "I'm not too surprised it's you. From what I hear, Kai hasn't done much in the past two and a half decades, and there had to be *some* reason why the Eldest gave the Nye essence to a new kid. Why do you think he picked you? Instead of, say, Denner or Indirial."

Valin was picking up speed, slashing imaginary opponents behind him, to either side, and even above. Simon took one prudent step back; the Wanderer seemed to think that friendly, good-natured violence was all in good fun, and he was more than capable of attacking without warning. As he had proven often enough in the past.

"The Eldest said everyone else had turned him down," Simon responded.

"That ought to tell you something, don't you think? If the Nye passed up two—well, Kathrin's still alive, so three—highly trained and experienced Travelers, and he's trying to put you in charge...I can only think of one reason." Valin spun, his sword blurring to a halt in front of Simon's nose. Simon didn't flinch; for Valinhall, this wasn't worth noticing.

"He wants a Founder who will do what he says. Seven stones, *I* never listened to him, and it seems like Kai isn't listening to anybody. Kathrin would do what she wanted even if the Eldest had his chain around her throat, Denner takes every chance he can get to leave the House, and Indirial would probably bring everything to his *Queen* first." Valin spat to one side. "That leaves someone new, preferably someone young and ignorant enough that he'll do whatever the Eldest tells him."

Simon bristled at the comment about his ignorance, but he cast his mind back over his early conversations with the Eldest. It seemed to fit. He had always known that the Eldest was trying to scam him into a bad deal, but his real question remained: how bad of a deal *was* it, really?

"He hasn't asked me to do anything terrible, so far," Simon said. "Nothing I might not have done on my own."

Valin propped one leg up on a headstone and leaned down on it, stretching out the muscle. "I know how he works. You've done exactly what he wants, but somehow you always end up deeper in his debt than before. Am I right? You brought him some new artifact or something, and then he acted like he was doing *you* a favor by letting you use it."

Simon thought back to the mask. "Yes, actually."

The Wanderer laughed, shaking his head. "When you get to be a few centuries old, I guess you never change. Listen. All the Eldest wants is the expansion of Valinhall at all costs, because the healthier and stronger this Territory is, the more power he's got. He'll want you to raid other Territories for weapons and creatures, find enough bearers for all thirteen Dragon's Fangs, anchor the deep rooms so that they're passable again, and ideally bring a population of human servants here to work under the Nye. It's a lifetime of work, and he'll never be satisfied."

"He *did* ask me to find the lost Dragon's Fangs," Simon said. "That was one of the first things he asked me to do."

Valin whirled on Simon, sword clenched in one fist. "Lost *Fangs?* Plural? They're not here, in the House?"

Simon shook his head.

The bald man plopped down on a gravestone, driving his sword into the ground with more force than necessary. "How many do we have left?"

"Six, I think," Simon said. "Indirial, Denner, Andra, Kai, and I all have one. Plus Kathrin is supposed to have one, but I've never met her."

"They lost *half* my swords!" Valin exclaimed. "More than half! I don't—all right, kid, look. The Eldest is right about some things, and he's wrong about others. He may be old and mysterious and creepy as a Strugle—"

A what? Simon wondered.

"—but he can be wrong, like everybody else. He's right that, if things keep going as they are, Valinhall's going to drift apart. It'll end up like I found it, and that's..." He shuddered. "Believe me, nobody wants that. And if he thinks we need a Founder to prevent that, he's probably right. But listen to me, and listen *close.*"

Valin leaned forward, and Simon found himself unable to look away. The Wanderer's gray eyes shone with a hint of metallic silver, as though the Incarnation of Valinhall spoke through him. "If we need a leader, we need one who knows what he's getting into, and who *chose to do it.* This Territory was left in the hands of four people who didn't want to take responsibility for it, and it's falling apart. Using lies and traps to snare a Founder won't work. We need someone to step up, do you understand?"

He did, and the words sounded great in theory, but he was worried about something a little more practical. "How am I supposed to say that to the Eldest? Right to his face...er, his hood."

Valin grinned and leaned back. "The Eldest forgets that, if he puts you in charge, then you get to be in charge. Ultimately, that means you do what *you* want. Not what he wants. Sometimes, you have to remind him of that."

Simon sat in place for a moment, mulling it over. He didn't want to lead Valinhall. Ideally, Kai or Indirial would do it. But the *Eldest* wanted him to lead, and that meant that, for once, he had some leverage.

He stood and, after a moment's hesitation, bowed to Valin like one of the Nye. "Thank you," he said simply.

Valin waved away the thanks. "Don't forget to come by and resurrect me every once in a while, okay? I don't want to wake up and find out I've missed a quarter of a century. Again."

Simon left the room, heading for the Nye's lair. The Eldest had taken something from him, and if he wanted to start acting like he was in charge, he needed to take it back.

As soon as the kid was gone, Valin rose back to his feet and called out, "So what did you think?"

A patch of shadow slid out from behind a column, resolving in to the figure of the Eldest Nye. "You told him far too much," the Eldest rasped. "And you are turning him against me."

Valin gave him an insolent grin, purely out of spite. The Eldest hated being mocked. "I thought you'd like that." With one hand, he tossed his sword high into the air, almost high enough to hit the lightning that danced on the ceiling. "I'm right, and you know it. He can't be what we need if he only does what you tell him."

"If he does not do what I tell him, he will not survive," the Eldest snapped. "I will move him like a *puppet* if I must, but I will not go back to what I was. Little more than a shadow."

"He seems like he's coming along," Valin said, catching his sword by the hilt as it came down. "Correct me if I'm mistaken, but it seems like he doesn't have much of a life outside Valinhall. Right?"

The Eldest said nothing, which Valin took as agreement.

"Well, then. That's the game half-won. He has nothing to lose by doing what you want. Maybe he won't do it the *way* you want, or *when* you want, but he'll be working with you instead of against you."

Slowly, the Eldest shook his hood. "You do not know him as well as you think. At times, the son of Kalman is a boulder rolling downhill. He decides that he must do something, and he lets nothing stop him. Even when it would be wiser to stop. But that is only sometimes. The rest of the time, he is a leaf in a breeze. He does not know what he wants, so he does what others tell him. It is an irritating combination."

Valin stared up at the lightning crackling on the ceiling. The Eldest had argued against the construction of this very room, but it had always been one of Valin's proudest achievements. "There's your mistake, Ka'nie'ka. You're trying to keep him from deciding, so that you can steer the leaf wherever you like. I don't want a leaf. I want a boulder. We don't want to stop him from making up his mind, we want him to make up his mind *in a way that helps us.*"

He looked back down to see the Eldest looking thoughtful. He decided to press his advantage. "You're well on your way. In a year or two, perhaps as many as five, he'll be ready. You've got to win him over, instead of tricking him into serving you."

"Kai stands in the way," the Eldest rasped, but he sounded contemplative rather than angry.

"You're worried about Kai? The Kai I remember might have been a problem, but *that* Kai would have made an excellent Founder. This one…"

Even more than seeing the state of his Territory, even more than realizing his students had betrayed him, even more than remembering how he betrayed his students, Kai had been the greatest disappointment to Valin. He remembered an eccentric genius who practically radiated potential, not this…broken wreck who wanted nothing more than to play with his dolls.

But then, it was Valin who'd broken him.

"Kai would trade Mithra for Azura if Simon so much as suggested it," Valin said at last. "He's practically begging for the chance. He won't be a problem, as long as we can get Azura to agree."

The Eldest put his sleeves together and bowed, unintentionally mimicking Simon's gesture from moments earlier. Or maybe it was intentional; Valin had never been able to understand any of the Nye, much less this one.

"I will consider your words, Master," the Eldest said at last. "Now, I must go. I suspect the son of Kalman is searching for me."

"What does he want?"

The Eldest shivered, his many layers of cloth and shadow rustling. "A seed of that which imprisoned you."

Valin felt like he'd been dunked in a bath full of ice water. "Burn it. Cast it out. Get Kai to open the Nexus, and hurl it as far away from us as you can."

"I'm not so certain that would be a…permanent solution," the Eldest said. "Besides, I believe it was you who advised me to let the boy make up his own mind."

Valin wrestled for a moment with his own rage, with the Incarnation of a warrior Territory rising up in his mind, before he could make himself relax. The Eldest was right. Simon had the right to decide, and it seemed that he was even friends with that Ragnarus girl. Maybe he could persuade *her* to destroy it.

"You're right," he said at last. He forgot, sometimes, that this wasn't his Territory any longer. He was nothing more than a passenger.

The Eldest glided toward the door, and then paused. "I respect your motivations today," the Nye said. "But do not oppose me too often. I can just as easily return you to the state in which I found you."

Valin grinned and raised his sword in a salute to his old friend. "I might say the same to you."

After the Nye vanished, Valin put himself through a few more sword forms. He wanted to fit in as much exercise as he could before he died again.

His steps felt lighter, and he found his smile lingering. He had a new student to train, a Territory to rebuild, and an old friend to outwit in a lethal contest.

Life didn't get much better than that.

Chapter 17

CAPTURE

In the House's entry hall, Indirial placed his sword onto its rack. Vasha's cracked blade gleamed in the lamplight, reflecting Feiora's irritated expression.

"What are we still doing here, Indirial?" she demanded. "You said he would show up."

"Relax. I know where he is. There are a few ways in and out, so I don't know exactly where he'll pop out, but this is a pretty safe bet."

She paced restlessly up and down the room. "They've been alone for too long now. I didn't fully complete the transfer process, so they could have ended up practically anywhere! We need to *do* something."

Just to show her that he was capable of relaxing, Indirial walked over to a plush sofa, sat down, and propped his feet up on a table. "It hasn't been as long as it feels. You know how this works. I'm sure Eugan is fine, and I *know* Leah is." That was one of the major purposes of the Damascan royal family's trial: every Heir and Heiress was sent off to live essentially on their own, teaching them self-reliance and practical survival skills. Leah would be well-prepared for surviving in Avernus, especially with Eugan as a guide.

Not to mention the fact that, in direct combat, a Ragnarus Traveler could eat any number of Avernus tribesmen alive. As long as she was willing to pay the price.

"What if she's not?" Feiora demanded. "Are we supposed to bring the crown to Adessa, hm? Or how about her older sister?"

"Feiora," Indirial said, "I'm as eager to act as you are. You have to understand that there is nothing we can do! A couple of hours ago, Simon was too weak to lift a fork, let alone a Dragon's Fang. And with the way his chains had grown, I wouldn't be surprised if he'd Incarnated the second he tried to open a Gate."

"I still don't see why—" she began, but Indirial gently spoke over her.

"I can only take you two places. The Latari Forest, or straight back to Enosh. That was the last place I opened my Gate. Simon, on the other

---

217

---

hand, opened *his* Gate exactly where we want to go. Even if I *did* take you to the forest and you Traveled from there, it would take you, what, a whole day to get where you're going? And that's if they're there. It makes far more sense to wait."

Indirial had made the argument before, but he didn't blame her for her agitation. Avernus Travelers shared a bond with their birds that he didn't fully understand, but they became almost dangerously overprotective when their advisors were in danger.

Besides, he knew how he would feel if his family had been trapped in another Territory. He had almost dissolved in panic when he found out how Cana had been sealed, thinking his wife and daughter were inside, until he remembered that they'd left the city before Enosh attacked. They waited for him even then, safe in Leah's camp. Well, as safe as anyone was, with the Incarnations loose.

"How long *has* it been for them, in Avernus?" Indirial asked, mostly to make conversation.

"It's hard to say, exactly," she said. "Avernus is like Helgard, in that the flow of time fluctuates in patterns. Unlike Helgard, though, Avernus is notoriously hard to predict."

Indirial nodded along. He had learned this years ago, but for her sake he tried to look studious and alert. The longer he could keep her talking, the more patiently she'd wait for Simon.

"If it's been one night outside, in Avernus it could be...half that. A quarter. Less. Or perhaps as much as seven-eighths, I can't say for certain."

Indirial smiled as though that solved the matter. "See? For them, it's barely been any time at all."

"Far too much time," Feiora began, but she stopped when a rug lifted in the center of the room. It bulged evenly in the middle, as though a door had been opened beneath it. Which was, of course, exactly what had happened.

"Hey," Simon called out. "Is there somebody out there? I don't want to call steel right now."

Indirial leaned down and tossed the rug out of the way, then gave Simon a hand up. He had climbed up a ladder that stretched all the way down into the bowels of the Territory, well out of the reach of the light.

"Thanks," Simon said, then he looked suspiciously from one Overlord to the other. "What are you doing here?"

"Waiting for you," Indirial responded. Then he saw Simon slip something in his pocket. Something that had been hidden in his hand. "What have you got there?" he asked, but Feiora shouldered him aside.

"I already told you what we want!" she said. "Open a Gate to Cana!"

Simon looked at Indirial. "Oh, that's right. You opened the Gate from Enosh, didn't you?"

Indirial turned and lifted Azura's gleaming blade from its rack. Since he hadn't called steel, it took him both hands. "If you would, sir."

He hesitated to take his sword. "I don't want to call steel right now." He pulled the collar of his cloak aside, revealing black chains that were starting to retreat down his back. "Is there any other way..."

"No, there isn't," Indirial said, as gently as he could. "We do need you to do this." His own chains wrapped around his midsection, and he was reluctant to call any more power. Simon's were in even worse shape, but there was no other choice. He hadn't heard from Denner in weeks, not that being unable to contact Denner was in any way unusual, and Kai had retreated back to the deep rooms, where Indirial was reluctant to follow.

More importantly, he had no idea where Kai's Gate would come out. That left Simon.

To his credit, Simon didn't hesitate any further. He seized the blade with one hand, and the chains on his back began to creep upward as he called steel.

Simon had gotten faster at opening Gates; it only took him half a minute to slice open a portal leading straight into the inside of a tent that Indirial recognized from the camp outside Cana.

Feiora stepped through without a word, and Indirial followed. "Thanks, Simon. Report back here after another night, and we'll see what we can do about finding these Incarnations."

The boy had already placed Azura back on its rack and released his steel; he sagged in place, just strong enough to remain standing. He nodded to Indirial before the Gate vanished altogether.

Feiora was already gone, no doubt to open a Gate of her own to Avernus. Indirial couldn't blame her.

But he had his own work to do.

The first thing he did was inform all his officers and high-ranking

Travelers that he had returned, which was a visible relief to them. It wasn't often that two Overlords and the Queen vanished for almost a full day after heading out on what was supposed to be a short-term scouting mission.

Next, he asked about the team of Travelers who had been assigned to guard Grandmaster Naraka during his disastrous mission to Enosh. To his shock, they were all unharmed, and the Grandmaster was back in custody. She had escaped long enough to close the Gate and then seal the waypoint somehow, which even the two Naraka Travelers working together couldn't undo.

The three Tartarus guards, meanwhile, had clubbed the Grandmaster over the head and bound her with chains "so tight she couldn't sneeze without picking three padlocks." They had remained in Naraka until the seal on the waystation dissipated, at which point they'd glanced through the Gate and seen the building in rubble. At that point, wisely, they had trekked back to the camp and informed their superior Travelers.

They all five seemed anxious that Indirial would blame them for what happened; on the contrary, he complimented their quick thinking and devotion to their duty. It was *his* fault that he had allowed the Grandmaster as much freedom as he had, not theirs. He thought of himself as somewhat of an expert at fighting Naraka Travelers, and he'd never seen one seal a waystation completely. He hadn't considered it possible.

After that, he indulged himself by spending half an hour describing to Grandmaster Naraka, in detail, the punishments she had earned by endangering the Queen. Justice would catch up to her at last, and there was something poetic about that.

He spent the next two hours poring over reports. Nothing of significance had happened while he was gone, but everyone under his command had to tell him that, in triplicate and signed if possible. With that taken care of, mostly, his next priority was to help find the Queen. He and Feiora had agreed that she would take care of that, and since Leah was in Avernus, Indirial should technically have deferred to the other Overlord. But the situation was volatile enough with all the Incarnations missing; they couldn't afford a missing monarch as well.

However, he could allow himself a short stop on the way. The sun had just set, so Nerissa and Elaina would be sitting down to eat. Perhaps he could grab a bite or two.

He ducked into his family's tent, already grinning. "Here I am, back from the dead!" he called. "It took two Incarnations and a..."

The gold medallion he wore grew cold against his chest. *Danger...* Korr whispered.

Korr, his advisor, rested inside the black gem at the heart of his medallion. Korr wasn't the most talkative advisor of the thirteen, and he only gave advice when he thought it would be needed.

A violet flame, visible only to Indirial's eyes, burned inside his tent. He turned, and for a moment he couldn't accept what he was seeing.

It wasn't the inside of his tent. It was a swirling window onto another world, its red edges wide enough to scrape the edge of the tent.

Indirial looked onto a cavern lit by rough scarlet torches. A pair of silver doors, each carved with half of the face of a one-eyed king, had been flung open, giving him a look inside the Crimson Vault.

Without hesitation, he backed out of the tent. Leah had not opened this Gate, and that meant that someone else had. He would bet everything he owned that it wasn't one of the remaining Heiresses—one of them still exiled to Lirial, the last he'd checked, and the other gibbering and weeping in an Asphodel asylum—and that left only one possibility: the Ragnarus Incarnation.

The camp was under attack, and his family had been the first victims.

His heart burned to go inside, to kill whoever he needed to kill to get his wife and daughter back. No Territory was as good for fighting Travelers as Valinhall, not even the Crimson Vault.

But the fact that this Gate had been left open inside his tent meant that this attack, or at least its initial stages, had been aimed at him personally. He wasn't enough of a fool to give the enemy what he wanted.

"We're under attack!" he bellowed, as loudly as he could, as he emerged from his tent. "Incarnation in the camp! Raise the—"

A violet flame burned to life in the corner of his vision: Korr's warning. Something white and gleaming streaked toward his stomach, so fast that the human eye could barely track it.

So it was a good thing he'd called Nye essence the instant he recognized a Ragnarus Gate.

Summoning Benson's steel, he slapped the projectile out of the air with the flat of his hand. It looked and felt like an oblong ball of ice, and it still tore through the tent next to his after he knocked it aside.

"Fascinating," the Helgard Incarnation said. She stood outside his tent, curly white hair flowing behind her spiral horns. The emerging starlight shone on her blue skin, and her glacial eyes were curious. "Is that reaction time something that you learn in your Territory, or a power you are granted? Does it work if you are caught completely off-guard?"

Vasha shimmered like an illusion and appeared in his hand, phantom chains crawling across his flesh. "Return your captives," said the Overlord of Cana.

Helgard ran a hand down the white fur that covered her like a dress. "Don't worry, they're completely—"

Indirial lunged. He didn't have to move far, considering Vasha's length, and then he brought his blade down diagonally across the Incarnation's body. A bar of black ice spun into being, meeting the Dragon's Fang with a nearly unbreakable surface.

He had expected that. He bore down with all the power he could draw from Valinhall, every drop of liquid steel he could summon from Benson's blue-lit basement. His strike didn't cleave the dark ice in half, but the force of his blow drove the ice downward. Vasha, with a bar of dark Helgard ice on the end, slammed into the Incarnation's left shoulder like a hammer.

Bone crunched, and she tumbled down and away, coming to a halt five paces away. Her white fur was speckled with dark blue blood.

"That wasn't a yes," Indirial called. She wouldn't have died from a hit like that, so she got the message. He raised his voice once more, blue-white mist puffing out of his mouth as his Nye essence drained. "Incarnation in the camp! Travelers, to me! Incarnation in the camp!"

Soldiers boiled out of the nearby tents, but most of them had the good sense to keep their distance. Distantly, he heard a horn as his warning was picked up and spread throughout the camp. Then another horn, and another.

Soon, he would be surrounded by allied Travelers. He only had to stall until they got here.

He could do it. He had fought this Incarnation before, and even though he didn't think he could kill her, he could certainly stall until backup arrived. At which point they would capture this Incarnation and find out where she was keeping his family.

Assuming nothing else went wrong.

Danger! Korr hissed.

He turned to see a slight flash out of the corner of his eye, little brighter than a reflection of moonlight off a spearhead. He spun, swinging the flat of Vasha's blade toward the light.

It was like a star the size of his fist, speeding at him out of the darkness. The light exploded when it hit his sword, instantly searing his hand and sending him stumbling backwards, almost knocking the Dragon's Fang from his hand with the force.

A second Incarnation strode out of the darkness. It was another woman, this time made entirely out of smooth crystal that flowed as she walked. Loops of silver wire wrapped her limbs and neck loosely, then tightened around her torso in a solid sheet of armored metal. Her body was almost completely transparent, but her eyes were the more typical milky-white crystal that Indirial associated with her Territory. She wore a slight smirk, and three more of those stars orbited her head in a pale halo.

"Lirial, I presume," Indirial said, calling ice. His body flooded with cold even deeper than the steel and Nye essence could account for, numbing all his injuries at once. Even the tearing burn in his right hand subsided to a dull throb, so he didn't drop his blade.

"Valinhall, is it?" she said. "In my day, we didn't—"

Indirial jumped backwards, propelled by all the steel he could draw. He felt a little ridiculous doing it—Valin had always warned them against unnecessary acrobatics—but when he reached the height of his jump, he flipped in the air.

He landed on top of the Helgard Incarnation, driving Vasha down into her chest. If he had one chance of surviving this fight and going on to find his wife and daughter, he had to eliminate one of the Incarnations early. He stood practically no chance against two of them, but one-on-one he could at least draw out the battle until reinforcements arrived.

The point of his Dragon's Fang met a shield of black ice.

Helgard's glacial blue eyes snapped open, her wounds already beginning to freeze over. To his eyes, slowed by the Nye essence, she seemed to drift to her feet, stretching slowly with a series of disgusting cracking sounds, as if her bones were snapping back into place.

He flipped up the hood of his cloak and swung Vasha overhand at her neck, taking advantage of the fact that she wouldn't quite be able to see him.

Two of Lirial's white stars blasted into the ground on either side of him, and the third crashed into his back. She had cast all three at him in the hopes of hitting him, since she couldn't pinpoint him exactly.

It had worked, but fortunately he'd anticipated her.

Instead of slamming into his unprotected back and pushing him forward into the Helgard Incarnation, the third star crashed into a plate of ghost armor and dispersed.

He turned and ran at Lirial. His initial strategy had been to overwhelm Helgard while she was injured, but since that obviously wasn't working, he would take out the weakest link in the chain first. Lirial was like Avernus: no matter how powerful the Traveler, they wouldn't be as useful in battle as most of the other Territories. He should be able to at least drive her off, keep her separated from her ally.

Down the row of tents, a few red-robed Naraka Travelers ran with leather-wrapped Endross Travelers, lightning already playing around their hands. Some of them carried storms the size of their two hands together, and they were headed toward him.

Good. He wouldn't have to hold out long, and then they could begin the *real* search: finding his family.

He stepped forward and drove Vasha into the Incarnation's crystal chest. Well, he tried to.

When he tried to maneuver his sword for a stab, both of his hands moved, jerking him off-balance. Both his hands had been cuffed together in solid crystal.

He didn't even let that slow him down. Without a moment's hesitation, he jumped forward, intending to slam his stone-encased hands onto the Lirial Incarnation's head.

In midair, he slammed into dark ice. Before he had a chance to react, the bar seemed to reach all the way around him, freezing into a wide circle of ice around his middle. The ice slowly levitated back down to the ground, locking him into an awkward position: twisted at the hips as if to stab, both hands clutching an immobile sword in front of him. The skin around his stomach was already starting to burn from the cold.

"I've been trying to do that since the fight began," Lirial confided, running a hand over her crystal head. "Do you know—"

Indirial's legs were still free. He jumped up and slammed both his feet into the Incarnation's diamond chest.

With a satisfying crunch, she flipped over backwards, spinning a full revolution in the air before she crashed into the ground.

A second later, he fell into the bar of ice on his back, slamming into his ribs, and only the Valinhall ice he had called into himself prevented him from screaming out in pain.

But seeing the Lirial Incarnation's face right before his boots slammed into it had been worth every second of agony.

Helgard peeked over at him as the shouts from the allied Travelers grew louder. A bright orange fireball shrieked into existence over him, but it snuffed out in a flurry of wind and snow almost before it finished forming.

"You're unspeakably interesting, did you know that?" Helgard said. "What keeps you going?"

He struggled, trying to stretch Vasha's point closer to the Incarnation. With her bar of ice around him, surely she would be less protected now.

"I keep waiting for one of you to open your mouth," Indrial replied. "Then I attack. You'd be amazed how many people choose to talk instead of fighting."

A pale bolt of lightning crashed into a nearby tent, setting it ablaze. "I see," the Helgard Incarnation said, even as Lirial pulled herself up and brushed dirt from her jeweled skin.

"It was my own mistake," Lirial allowed. "I should never allow myself to be anything less than perfectly attentive."

Helgard flicked a blue hand in her direction, and a screaming orange wasp the size of a small dog froze solid and dropped before it reached Lirial. "Hmph. Of course it was."

"Shall we go?"

"The Gate is still open."

Indirial screamed and yelled, but the Incarnations met any attack from the crowd of Travelers without seeming to pay attention. The band of ice around his ribs dragged him into the air, pulling him behind them.

And into the Crimson Vault.

As soon as he vanished into the tent, his Travelers tore the fabric apart, blasting it into shreds and ash inside a second, trying to catch sight of him again. Indirial caught a glimpse of a few desperate, friendly faces before the red Gate sealed shut.

Leaving him at the entrance of Ragnarus with two Incarnations. Or...possibly three.

The sounds he typically expected from a trip to the Crimson Vault were all missing: he didn't hear the growls of a distant beast, or the rushing of a river that didn't exist, or the clatter of a dozen legs on the stone beyond this cavern. He heard only what might be a faint breeze blowing through a crack in the rocks, and nothing else.

But there was another detail that had changed from most of his visits: the silver doors, instead of staying closed, had been thrown wide open.

And through them, deep in the Vault, he could see a woman with red skin lounging on a dark chair. He thought she was looking at him, but it was hard to make out detail when staring into the depths of Ragnarus.

It wasn't any of the living Heiresses, he was sure of that, so it had to be the Ragnarus Incarnation. Had someone else in Cana trapped the Incarnation while the city was sealed? Had the Incarnation done it to herself?

Something inside him relaxed. He had been afraid, all this time, that when the barrier of Cana fell, they would find that Zakareth had Incarnated and had been soaking the city in blood. He knew that there had been a Ragnarus Incarnation sealed under the capital for hundreds of years, but somehow he'd always worried about seeing Zakareth with bright red skin or burning scarlet eyes.

At least his friend and king was truly dead, fallen in battle. In that, at least, he could relax.

Lirial and Helgard chatted with one another about the weapons here, and the history of the place, and who the Founder must be, and whether the weapons were added regularly or if there were an unlimited number.

At first, he listened attentively, trying to sift through the banter for a clue to his release. But then two things happened at once: first, he realized that they were passing time waiting for something, and second, his ice ran out. Suddenly, the actual, physical ice wrapped around him seemed to burn, and his crystal-encased right hand flared as if he had dipped it in molten steel.

He almost screamed, but bit his lip. In front of some Incarnations, he'd be better off tossing bloody meat to a pack of wild dogs than releasing a scream. He didn't think Lirial or Helgard would be that vicious, but he couldn't take any chances.

Lirial was examining a levitating javelin, silver-white crystals whirling around every inch of the weapon, when another Gate opened.

The Ragnarus Incarnation must have opened it for them, because it was an ordinary red-bordered Gate to Ragnarus, leading out into the royal palace. The Blue Room had been decimated, its shattered blue tiles held together by twisting red wood and stone evidently summoned by the Ragnarus Incarnation, but he still recognized the remnants of the rooms.

Helgard and Lirial left, Helgard walking out of the shadows with a dissatisfied look, and Lirial giving one last, longing gaze to the vault full of weapons.

Helpless, Indirial drifted behind them, suspended in a prison of black ice.

He had spent most of the last twenty-five years in the royal palace, so it only took him a few minutes to map the passages in his head and realize where they were going: the throne room.

A sick feeling grew in his stomach, and he struggled against his bonds even as the last of his steel ran out and the pain threatened to overwhelm him.

Much of his job as King Zakareth's bodyguard had taken place in the throne room. When they reached the great double-doors, etched with a nine-pointed star and a bright red eye, Lirial flicked a single wrist toward the hall. Two crystals flew out, pushing the doors open.

The room had greatly changed since his last visit. He remembered it as a high, wide room with the royal throne at the end, and a row of tall windows on the east side. Banners had hung from the ceiling, and tables for documents and chairs for petitioners were often laid out on the wooden floors.

Practically the only thing that remained was the throne. The windows were gone, replaced by black stone that glowed with veins of sullen red, providing bloody light to the room. The banners were gone, replaced by spiked iron cages dangling from the rafters. Most of them were empty, and a few held corpses, but on first inspection he didn't see any living prisoners.

The throne remained intact and unchanged from when he'd last seen it: a solid block of ruby hewn into the shape of a wide chair, and ornamented in lines of gold. A man filled the throne, one elbow propped up on the left armrest, his chin held in one hand. He wore a tall, spiked crown, and in his right hand he gripped a tall ruby-headed staff. From the bulk of his silhouette, he seemed to be wearing plate armor, and his left eye burned with a bright red light all its own.

Indirial almost screamed, trying to call more steel, trying to shatter his frozen bonds. But his steel had run out, and nothing he could do would call more.

"Welcome home, Indirial," King Zakareth said. He leaned forward, and Indirial got a better look at his face.

Patterns of red and gold swirled up over his skin, as though he had been painted with whorls of metallic paint. The mesh seemed to glow softly, but not enough to overshadow the light from his left eye, which gaped empty. Instead of the stone, which Zakareth had given to Indirial personally, his left eye was composed entirely of swirling crimson flames. His right eye, which still looked more human, had turned red instead of its usual icy blue. Even his hair hadn't escaped unaltered: most of it was still iron-grey, but it showed odd threads of bright gold or ruby red.

Indirial's greatest fears had come true. He had been afraid of any Ragnarus Incarnation, but in the same distant, vague way he would fear any Incarnation: not someone he would choose to fight if he got the chance, but not anything that would cause him to lose sleep at night, either. He was a Valinhall Traveler, after all. He feared very little that other Travelers could do to him.

But Zakareth...Zakareth *knew* him.

And that meant he could hurt Indirial very badly indeed.

"You know why I brought you here," the King said, and his voice was so much the same that it filled Indirial with a mixture of revulsion, relief, and anger. Even his way of cutting straight to the topic at hand, without any sugar-coating or dancing around, proved that this was the real Zakareth.

"You want something from Valinhall," Indirial said. "You're holding my family hostage until I give it to..."

He trailed off. That couldn't be right. Zakareth knew Indirial, better than almost anyone else. Surely, the King would know that Indirial wouldn't betray his Territory to save his family. He would do everything he could to save his wife and daughter, and if that failed, he would do everything in his power to end those responsible.

He wouldn't give in, and Valinhall could strengthen his body and fortify him against pain. So what did Zakareth want that taking Indirial's family would get him?

Cold washed through Indirial like a breath of Nye essence. "You want me," he said.

Zakareth nodded.

"Why take Nerissa and Elaina, then? Zakareth, you can let them go. They're unnecessary."

Pleading with King Zakareth the Sixth's pity was an exercise in futility, but appealing to his sense of efficiency could often work.

Then again, he realized, the King had never needed to take Indirial's family to get him here. The two Incarnations could have made sure of that on their own. And that meant...

He still needed them for something.

"I do need you, Indirial," King Zakareth said, his voice as blank and expressionless as ever. "It would have worked with any Valinhall Traveler, but when the fates were unkind to me, I decided to exercise my will more directly. And that meant I got to pick the Traveler I wanted."

"All you had to do was tell me you were alive," Indirial said. Maybe if he kept the King talking, he would reveal something about Nerissa or Elaina.

The King drummed his fingernails on the arm of his throne, and they clicked like stone-on-stone. "You would never have obeyed me as I am now. It is not within you. Not as you are."

"Of course I would have!" Indirial lied. "I would always serve you."

"On that, we agree." Without any visible signal from Zakareth, two of the cages above began to lower, their chains rattling. Indirial wasn't sure whether the King was doing it himself or whether he was getting Lirial or Helgard to do it for him, but that thought soon left his mind.

Nerissa, his wife, huddled in one cage, her back pressed against the bars, her knees drawn up to her chest. His daughter Elaina slammed her fist against the bars of the other, shouting his name, telling him to run.

He had expected it, but the sight of his family still acted on him like a spark on tinder. He wrenched the last drop of liquid steel from Valinhall, surging to his feet and stumbling three feet toward the throne before tipping over forward, almost impaling himself on his own crystal-frozen blade.

"I will hold them here," Zakareth said. "I am in no rush. I require only one thing of you: survive, Indirial. If you don't, neither will they."

The crystal holding his hands together vanished, and with a crack like a calving glacier, the ice around his middle dispersed into dark snowflakes. He shivered uncontrollably and pitched over, Vasha falling from numb hands.

His steel and Nye essence were completely out, and would take minutes to regenerate. He had other powers he could call, but none of them were likely to help him here. Worse, his chains wrapped almost all the way around his shoulders. He had to wait until his steel was back, but even then, would he be able to fight his family free before he transformed into another Incarnation to threaten them?

A bare foot, hard as stone, met him under the ribs and kicked him up. He landed on his knees, a flower of pain blooming in his chest, his breath leaving his lungs. The Lirial Incarnation stood over him, dispassionate, glancing into a crystal lens she held in her left hand as though she were more interested in what was happening far away than in his torture.

King Zakareth leaned back, resting against the throne. "We have time, Indirial. We don't eat. We don't drink. We don't sleep. And while you're here, neither will you. How long will you last, I wonder?"

Indirial couldn't help it: he called stone. The next kick hardly hurt, but when he tried to grapple with the Incarnation's crystal leg, he didn't have the strength to knock her on her back, as he intended.

The King wanted him to Incarnate. If he wanted to win, he would have to remain himself at all costs. But that meant not calling upon Valinhall, which would surely result in his death, not to mention the deaths of his only remaining family.

He would simply have to draw it out as long as possible. He'd endure as long as he could without Valinhall powers, and—once he called them—hold onto them as long as he could.

If he could only survive long enough, then at some point, he'd think of a plan. He always did.

Korr whispered into his mind, more worried than Indirial had ever heard him. *So much danger...*

CHAPTER 18
A CONVERSATION IN AVERNUS

359ᵀᴴ YEAR OF THE DAMASCAN CALENDAR
1ˢᵀ YEAR IN THE REIGN OF QUEEN LEAH I
3 DAYS SINCE SPRING'S BIRTH

Leah marched through the undergrowth, her whole body burning from the aftermath of the fight in Enosh. She hardly knew how long it had been since she'd found herself in Avernus, but she and the raven, Eugan, had spent one night huddled under a wide-leafed bush, sheltered from the rain. She seemed to remember that time in Avernus moved more slowly than in the outside world, which meant two whole days may have passed in Damasca. Perhaps as many as four in Valinhall.

Leah tried to stop herself from wondering why no one had found her yet. She was capable of speech again, finally, but the other part of her crown's cost had yet to wear off.

She still couldn't summon Ragnarus. Even the Lightning Spear was nothing more than an ordinary weapon to her now—she had tried to throw it at a bird that startled her the night before, and the Spear practically flopped into a bush.

Leah didn't expect to be able to open a Gate to the Crimson Vault. That never worked in a Territory. But she could usually call on her Ragnarus weapons no matter where she was; it was the crown's price that prevented her from speaking and from using any other weapons from the Vault. After she used the circlet to issue one absolute command, it took time to release her from the price, usually in proportion to the strength of the order. She had put everything she had into binding Alin, but it rarely took longer than twenty-four hours for the curse to wear off. If that remained true this time, she should be getting her Ragnarus powers back any time now.

Worse was her physical condition. She had suffered only minor wounds in the fight against Alin, but she was still painfully bruised in her left leg, her right hip, both her elbows, and her neck. She was covered in more scrapes and cuts than she liked to think about, and hiking through the Avernus wilderness wasn't helping that. More than that, throwing the Lightning Spear the way she had took its toll on her body. The pain that tortured her with every throw was more than in her mind, and her limbs still shook with echoes of that agony.

"How much farther?" she asked Eugan.

He screeched, and Leah may not have been an Avernus Traveler, but she got the message: 'Don't ask stupid questions.'

Then she pressed through the next clump of underbrush and found that she was standing on the top of a hill, overlooking a wide camp of wooden outbuildings and crude tents.

She looked over at Eugan, who had perched on a branch beside her head. "You could have told me," she said.

The raven opened his beak and let out a raucous laugh.

Leah's whole body ached with pain, and she hadn't slept last night, crouched as she was beneath a leaf and soaked with freezing rain while birds screamed practically in her ear. So, all things considered, her brain wasn't moving at its customary speed.

But she was still embarrassed when she realized she had stood there, staring at the Corvinus tribe Avernus outpost, for five minutes without making a move. She'd been wearily trying to construct a stealthy plan of approach that would allow her to survey the area and find a loyal Damascan Traveler who could open a Gate for her, but that was an idiotic plan. For one thing, she was a Lirial Traveler. She wouldn't need to go down there herself; she could summon a couple of scout crystals, send them down there, locate an appropriate Traveler, and then send Eugan to guide them back to her.

More importantly, everyone down in the camp had a mind-reading raven. They'd known she was coming long before she had.

Abandoning any attempt at stealth, Leah slipped and slid down the front of the muddy hill. She briefly considered concealing her identity: in Avernus, the Travelers tended to live based on tribal affiliations rather than national allegiance. There could be as many Enosh Travelers down there as Damascans, and even a substantial group who owed nothing to either side.

It wouldn't do her any good, though. The Avernus Travelers couldn't pull any specific thoughts from her through her crown—it was one of the crown's many protective functions, and she'd been thankful for it often—but they could still sense her presence, and likely that of Ragnarus as well. If a young woman came into their outpost whose mind they couldn't examine, carrying artifacts of the Crimson Vault...well, it wouldn't take a genius to draw the right conclusion.

So she entered with her head held high, as though she expected nothing more than generous treatment. She didn't pretend that she wasn't tired, because that would have been transparently ridiculous. She was wearing villager clothes that looked like they had been through a mudslide and a fire, not necessarily in that order. But she'd been taught that half the journey toward getting people to obey you was expecting people to obey.

Therefore, she walked into the Corvinus tribe as though she owned the whole outpost, nodding to everyone she met. Most of the people she passed wore feathers and soft leather, even children that were clearly too young to be Travelers. Small groups huddled in the doors of their cabins, whispering to each other as she passed.

Seven stones, how long is it going to take to get someone's attention?

Ravens flew everywhere, and for the first time since entering the Feathered Plains, she saw and heard nothing of any other type of bird. Only the black-feathered hunters like Eugan, perched on rooftops or fenceposts, occasionally fluttering out of doorways to get a look.

All of them staring at her with dark eyes. And all of them could surely sense her thoughts, if not read them in detail. So why wasn't someone here to help her?

At *last*, after she had walked half the length of the outpost, an Avernus Traveler walked up and bowed to her. She wore the same calf-length soft leather dress as most of the others, with black feathers arranged around her collar and in her sandy hair. A bronze-and-pearl badge at her chest, in the shape of a fan of brown-and-white feathers, marked her as a Traveler of Damasca rather than just someone living in the village.

"Your Highness," she said. "Traveler Galene, at your service. If you would follow me, please, I can take you to the one who will serve you."

Leah glanced up at Eugan. He had stuck with her all of last night, so he was the closest thing to a native guide and a friend that she had in this place.

The raven cawed and landed on her shoulder, which she took to mean that she was doing the right thing. She nodded at Traveler Galene, who bowed again and walked off, clearly expecting her to follow. Leah did so, ignoring the whispers that drifted along behind her.

She ground the butt of the Lightning Spear into the mud, using it more and more as a walking stick. Her strength was starting to leave her, which put her on her guard. She needed to find a safe place where she could rest soon, or else a Gate out.

Galene finally stopped at a broad tent, much larger than the others, almost a campaign tent. It was propped up on smooth wooden poles at the corner and at the center, and the flap was secured by a complex knot in a white rope. It took Traveler Galene a moment to undo the knot, and when she drew the tent flap aside, Leah couldn't see anyone inside. Only a few candles burning, even though it was midday outside and the light filtering through the canvas should have been enough to see.

She thought she caught a glimpse of a spread wing and a few loose, drifting feathers, but that shouldn't have been a surprise—this was Avernus, home to ten thousand species of bird.

"After you," Leah said. She wasn't about to trust the word of a Traveler she'd never met about the safety of a mysterious tent in a foreign Territory.

Traveler Galene shook her head, shooting a fearful glance into the tent. "I'm sorry, Highness. I'm not allowed."

Who was in the tent? It wasn't Overlord Feiora, or the woman would have marched out and demanded to know why Leah looked like such a wreck. It can't have been Overlord Lysander, because—unless some other Lirial Travelers had been hard at work without her permission—he was still sealed in a crystal coffin on a hillside outside a random country village.

Which left the regional commander of this outpost, whoever it was. How could he or she inspire this much fear in their Travelers? Unless...

Goosebumps prickled along her arms, and she took a healthy step back. Then she twisted her left arm so that the crystal she wore there, suspended on a fine silver chain, caught a ray of sunlight.

It took her a long moment, and far more concentration than usual, all the while Traveler Galene insisted on interrupting her with questions that she, in turn, ignored. Finally, her call to Lirial was answered.

After another few seconds, her viewing lens fell into her hands. It was roughly the size of a dinner plate and made of smooth, translucent crystal.

With a slight mental effort, she focused on the person she wanted to see: the only Incarnation that she and Simon had managed to actually seal back into its Territory, these past six months. The only Incarnation they hadn't either watched escape or been forced to kill.

The Incarnation of Avernus.

Sure enough, the image resolved in her lens almost instantly: a face almost like a human woman, with eyes of a bird of prey and soft brown feathers instead of hair. Two pairs of wings rose in layers from her back, each wing a different color: one the deep black of a raven, one the gentle white of a seagull, one gray, and one a startling jade-green.

"Come on in, Leah," the Incarnation's voice said from within the tent and inside the crystal at once. "I'm much more myself this time, compared to when we last met."

When they'd last met, the Incarnation of Avernus had been a screeching madwoman who'd controlled the minds of the Damascan citizens around her, directing them like puppets.

"Just a moment," Leah said. Then she turned to leave.

Eugan hopped up from her shoulder and flew into the tent. After he flew out of her view, he let out a sharp caw. She was sure that meant he wanted her to follow, but that made her walk faster. Of course he thought she should enter the tent; he was part of Avernus. He would likely laugh as his Incarnation stripped the flesh from Leah's bones.

Leah almost ran straight into a man's chest before she realized that the inhabitants of the outpost were all standing in her way. Hundreds of ravens covered every nearby surface, staring at her, and the humans stood in front of them, silently barring her way.

Traveler Galene stepped up, blushing. "This...isn't what it looks like, Your Highness. She doesn't want to hurt you. She only wants to talk."

Leah couldn't imagine a worse time to be without her Ragnarus powers. If she had been at full strength, she would feel much more confident about facing an Incarnation of Avernus. Even though Avernus had accounted for hundreds of lives during her rampage, before Leah had managed to put a stop to it, she still wasn't much use in combat against another Traveler. With Ragnarus, Leah might have been willing to climb into the tent.

Without it, Leah was little more than a Lirial Traveler. And if there was any Territory that was just as unsuited for battle as Avernus, it was Lirial.

A voice sounded in Leah's mind, like one of Simon's dolls. *I have news about your father.*

Well, that was hardly fair.

I swear that I will not attempt to harm you, the Incarnation went on. *You are free to come and go as you wish. I foretold that you would be abandoned in Avernus, which is why I asked Eugan several days ago to bring you here. I think Overlord Feiora told you, didn't she?*

Come to think of it, the Overlord had said something about Leah going to Avernus. And the Incarnation certainly wasn't acting like any other hostile Incarnation she'd ever met—which meant, essentially, that she hadn't tried to blast Leah to pieces or capture her for study.

And she'd promised news about Leah's father. It could have been a simple lie, but she would never forgive herself if she didn't at least find out for herself. Like any good Lirial Traveler would do.

A voice of caution sounded in her mind, a voice that sounded a lot like Indirial. It begged her not to take this risk.

But she went inside anyway. Sometimes, if she wanted to make the right decision, she would have to risk herself. She kept her connection to Lirial open anyway, tapping into her Source in case she needed to encase anyone in crystal.

She may have been taking an intentional risk, but she didn't have to be stupid about it.

Leah walked into the tent calmly, as though she were the one who had arranged this meeting. The interior was plainly furnished: a cot, a desk, a small chest, a pile of what might be mouse carcasses. Only the bare necessities for this Incarnation. She didn't let herself look shaken, adopting a careful mask of polite neutrality. The Incarnation couldn't read Leah's mind, so if she kept her expression blank, she ought to have an advantage. If her mind was blocked from influence, she had nothing to fear from this particular Territory.

Then she realized that the Incarnation had somehow managed to speak with her, in her mind, through the protection of her crown. At least she managed to keep from bolting out of the tent.

Avernus herself sat on a stool to the right of the entrance, her four strikingly different wings folded up behind her. The bronze feathers that served her instead of hair had been tied back into a single tail, which ran between her wings, and she was wearing the same softened leather outfit as everyone else in the outpost.

"Feel free to have a seat," the Avernus Incarnation said smoothly. She picked up a teacup that Leah hadn't noticed before, lifting it to her lips. "I'm sorry I only have the one cup. Just because I see pieces of the future doesn't mean I don't forget things. Would you like me to have another cup brought?"

"No, thank you," Leah said. She didn't think anyone in Avernus would need to poison her—they would likely try and invade her mind directly, rather than through more subtle means—but she didn't know much about the plants of this Territory.

Besides, a quick nap on the bare cot in the corner looked more inviting than an entire pot of hot tea.

"I wanted to speak with you while you were here, because I didn't think I'd get another chance. As one of the last active Ragnarus Travelers, perhaps the last, you should know the truth behind what your family has been doing for three and a half centuries." She spoke carefully and precisely, with no accent, as though she sculpted each word before it left her mouth.

"I appreciate your candor," Leah said, though her tone remained a bit too dry.

The Avernus Incarnation chuckled and took another sip of tea. "But you have no reason to trust the truth from one of the mad Incarnations. Tell me, do I seem insane to you?"

Leah had to admit that she didn't, but crazy didn't necessarily mean foolish. An Incarnation as in control of herself as Avernus might be able to pretend sanity long enough that she could fool all but the most careful watchers.

"Incarnations become much less, after some time in their home. When a few months have passed, they will be Incarnations no longer."

That made sense to Leah. "That's why we get a reprieve after sealing the Incarnations into their Territories. For a few months, at least, they still exist as Incarnations, before they...fade away."

"This is knowledge that has been lost throughout the years," the Incarnation said wistfully. "I remember when that was not the case. I remember when the information was lost. I remember when the second Queen Cynara sealed me. I remember the rage..."

Her voice trailed off, and for a moment her raptor's eyes began to glow slightly, as if she had started to become once more the force of nature that she remembered. But then her eyes dimmed, and Leah relaxed.

"What has been lost?" Leah finally asked. "The knowledge that you're not insane?"

Avernus chuckled over her teacup. "Hardly. The knowledge that an Incarnation, in her own Territory, becomes nothing more than another native. We can't call on our full powers, we can't summon or banish, and we can't appear in the Unnamed World unless we are summoned by a Traveler."

The Unnamed World. It was the oldest title of the outside world, what some called the 'real world': the place outside the Territories. The ancient scholars had feared that to name their world, as they had the Territories, would somehow reduce it, and that by giving it a name they would be contributing to a potential apocalypse.

Leah's tutors had been of the opinion that these original scholars had simply been afraid to name their world, because that would make it seem more like a Territory. The idea that they were all living in the largest Territory instead of a whole, unique world was simply too terrifying for them to consider.

Either way, very few used the term 'Unnamed World' anymore, and it drove something home to Leah: this Incarnation was from a different age, when legends walked the earth and the Territories were still wild and free, rather than tools of war, trade, and commerce.

She would have to screen the Incarnation's words appropriately.

"We have that knowledge today," Leah said. "That's why we sealed you here. If you seal an Incarnation back into its Territory, they fade away, and we earn a period of time during which no other Travelers can take its place."

The Incarnation of Avernus held out both hands, palms-up, and moved them up and down as though imitating weights on a scale. She had talons instead of fingernails.

"Hmmm..." she said. "True, but incomplete. An Incarnation *is* part of its Territory, no matter where she is. That's why, when she walks around outside, the world around her shapes itself to resemble her Territory. The

Unnamed World seeks to correct a mistake."

"What mistake?"

"The Incarnations are not meant to exist in the Unnamed World," Avernus said firmly. "They never were. Incarnation only happens to Travelers who upset the balance, and only because they draw too much of their Territory's power into themselves. Through Incarnation, they become part of their Territory, which means they are supposed to stay *inside* that Territory. Do you understand?"

Leah thought she did: Travelers in the outside world should rarely be able to Incarnate, except under certain specific conditions. However, she saw at least one flaw in the argument. "If that's true, then why are there so many Incarnations running around in the Unnamed World?"

The Incarnation shook her head. "I wondered that for years. What do you know about the history of the Incarnations that Queen Cynara sealed?"

"Led by the Elysian Incarnation, they attacked the young nation of Damasca," Leah said. "They were encouraged to gather as much support from their Territories as they could, so that the Damascan Travelers wouldn't be able to oppose them..."

Leah trailed off as if she had finished, but in reality she had been struck by a sudden thought. She'd always imagined the ancient Incarnations as monsters from long ago, like mythological monsters that mothers used to frighten their children into behaving. Even after she found out what the sacrifice was for, and that the Incarnations were in fact sealed beneath most Damascan cities, she'd still thought of them as impossibly distant.

Now, it was striking her for the first time that she was sitting directly across from an ancient Incarnation. This woman had actually served under the first Incarnation of Elysia, marching against Queen Cynara the First and, later, was personally sealed by Cynara the Second.

Avernus smiled a little, as though she knew what Leah was thinking. Maybe she did. "I was a young Strigaia, a simple fortune-teller. A group of people approached me, saying they worked for the Elysians. They claimed they could teach me a way to see farther, to sense more, to grow closer to Avernus than I'd ever dreamed. I didn't trust them at first, but they seemed respected by the older Travelers, and some of my teachers even encouraged me to study with them. So I did."

She took a sip of tea, and then sighed regretfully. "It took me only a few months to Incarnate. When it first happens, you're almost over-whelmed by your new instincts. I lashed out mentally, and I'm afraid I crushed the minds of quite a few bystanders whose only crime was to be standing near me. But, above all, I struggled to get back to my Territory. Those teachers, the supposed Elysians, stopped me. They held me back.

"When my mind was my own again, they explained to me that, if I returned to my Territory, I would be trapped. I didn't want to go after hearing that, so they found it easy to persuade me to join with Elysia. I want what Avernus wants: true community, on an honest and open level, nothing hidden. Complete loyalty and dedication...They said I could achieve that among all the Avernus Travelers, and even including some Travelers of other Territories. We would be one, and I would get a chance to understand people I had never met."

The Incarnation's face crumpled up, either in disgust or in suppressed tears, Leah wasn't sure. She tilted her head back and drained her teacup in one shot.

Silently, Leah pulled apart the Incarnation's story. It fit the facts, but it would be easy for her to craft a lie that Leah couldn't possibly see through. With events that happened so long ago, what objections could she have?

Above anything else, she was sure that the Avernus Incarnation wasn't giving her this information out of the goodness of her avian heart. She was building up to something, and Leah had to find out what it was.

"I suspect the other eight had similar stories," Avernus continued. "Well, perhaps not Elysia, but certainly the other seven. What about the modern Incarnations? Valinhall, Ragnarus, that second Endross Traveler?"

"Ragnarus is an ancient Incarnation," Leah said, confused. "It was sealed before you were. Isn't that right?"

Avernus rubbed her forehead with a taloned hand. "I get ahead of my-self, I'm sorry. Valinhall and the second Endross, then."

"No. No, we're not going to switch topics because you think the timing isn't appropriate. Tell me what you were going to say about the Ragnarus Incarnation. Is it my brother? My father?"

Leah held her breath, fearing and hoping. If it was her father, that meant he was alive—in a manner of speaking—and that she could deal with him. If Talos had somehow survived and Incarnated...well, at least killing him would be easier than dealing with King Zakareth the Sixth.

The Avernus Incarnation sighed. "Your father."

She nodded, too sick to say anything. It was one thing to suspect, but quite another to have her fears confirmed at once.

"I'm sorry, Leah. I truly am. But please, concentrate on the questions I asked you. Why did the Valinhall Incarnation and the second Endross give in? What happened to them?"

Leah answered automatically, her mind still focused on her father as an Incarnation. "Valinhall was the one who created the Territory. His name was Valin. If I recall correctly, he Incarnated because he had some sort of personal vendetta against my grandfather. Or perhaps because he opposed the system of sealing the Incarnations under the Hanging Trees, I'm not completely sure."

Avernus was chewing on her bottom lip, a surprisingly human gesture from a woman with two sets of wings. "The Founder of Valinhall became an Incarnation? I thought the two were mutually exclusive...would it make him more powerful, I wonder, or simply unique?" Abruptly she shook herself, and all the feathers on her body ruffled at once, then flattened. "I apologize. But notice that, either way, he was driven to Incarnation in order to oppose the reigning trend of keeping us sealed. Indirectly, he Incarnated because we did. And the other Endross?"

"He was a follower of the ancient Endross Incarnation. When we killed the first one, he saw his chance to become, as his own followers believed, a demigod. There were almost a dozen of them trying anything they could to transform, and he was the first to succeed."

The Incarnation pointed at Leah with a taloned finger. "That's it. You see? He intentionally chose to do it in order to imitate an Incarnation he'd already seen. There is a pattern at work here, not simply unfortunate chance."

Step by step, Leah worked it through in her mind. If the Avernus Incarnation was telling the truth—and for the sake of argument, she had to assume that was the case—then at least eight of the original nine Incarnations had been *lured* to transform outside of a Territory.

The Avernus Incarnation leaned in, her hawk's eyes sharp on Leah. Her wings had stretched out now, so that the white and the emerald feathers were actually pressing against the canvas of the tent. "You see it," she stated, with absolute certainty. She folded her wings back in and crossed her legs, wearing a smug smile. Idly, Leah noted that her feet were complete bird talons.

"Why would anyone do this?" Leah asked. "Who benefits from creating wild, murderous Incarnations instead of allowing them to serve their Territory?"

Avernus raised her teacup to her lips, realized that it was empty, and tossed it behind her. It landed on the ground with a tinkle of broken porcelain. "No one, as far as I know. But that's not what happened, is it?"

Behind her, a pair of hands reached in underneath the canvas. They scooped the shattered teacup into a dustpan and then quickly retreated.

Leah spoke her thoughts aloud. "The Incarnations were born here, instead of in their Territories. There was a war, and they were sealed."

"So for three hundred years…"

"…we haven't had to deal with any Incarnations," Leah finished. The implications were unsettling.

"When the Incarnations exist in our own Territories, we advance our own goals, even at the expense of foreign Travelers," Avernus said. "Many Incarnations would destroy outposts, waylay or deceive merchant caravans, or seduce Travelers into their service. So who benefits from nine Territories free of any Incarnations?"

Leah thought of the single, dominating factor that had allowed Damasca to prosper and flourish under her family for the last three-and-a-half centuries. They didn't need an intricate system of roads or communication, because messages and goods passed through Territories. They never had to fear drought or plague, because they could always get their crops from Avernus or Asphodel. Their borders were secure from all but Enosh, because the ways in and out of each Territory were secured by semi-permanent outposts. Until recently, the Overlords had been kept in line because only the royal family could deal with the Hanging Trees…and the creatures sealed beneath their roots.

If anyone turned a profit from Territories that were easier to control, it was Damasca.

At last, Leah answered the question.

"I do," she said.

Chapter 19
CREATING INCARNATIONS

Indirial hadn't eaten in two days. He hadn't slept. Neither he, nor his wife, nor his daughter had been given a drop of water. None of his bones had been broken, and he wasn't bleeding badly enough to endanger his life. The Incarnations were very careful to preserve him as they kicked him, taunted him, sent phantom noises into his mind, lured his eyes with illusions, tore his skin and bruised his flesh…

And through it all, King Zakareth sat on his throne and watched. Indirial didn't think the man had moved in forty-eight hours. He sat on the ruby throne of Damasca, leaning on his elbow. Watching.

"Don't be a coward, Indirial," the King said. "Face the challenge and overcome it. Fight for freedom. Earn it."

Every few hours he would make similar announcements, appealing to the Valinhall philosophy of fighting for what you wanted.

He didn't realize that Indirial was already fighting. Not for his own desires, but to keep his enemy's plan from succeeding. He was fighting not to call on his powers.

He'd been forced to draw on Valinhall to stay conscious, to see through illusions, to burn poison from his veins, to deflect a spear launched at his daughter. Now, as the Ornheim Incarnation lifted him in one rocky fist, preparing to drop him one more time to the floor below, he could only feel one thing: the black chains wrapping around his throat.

They were too close. His time was almost up. It was a miracle that he'd lasted this long without going over the edge.

Ornheim dropped him, and he fell.

When he hit the tiles, he heard the damage to his body more than he felt it. It sounded like a solid, meaty *crunch*. Maybe he had finally reached the point where he was too numb to feel anything else. If so, he thanked the Maker for it. That meant death was close; he could die with a clean conscience.

His neck was twisted around against the tiles. Not enough to snap his spine, no matter how much he wished that were the case, but enough to force him to stare at Nerissa and Elaina in their cages. Nerissa had stopped whispering words of encouragement yesterday, when she had apparently lost her voice. She sat huddled in her cage now, her ice-white eyes strangely blank and locked on him. Even Elaina had stopped fighting, though both her fists were scraped and raw from where she'd hammered on the bars of her dangling cage. Her eyes were closed, but she jerked and whimpered at every sound.

They wouldn't survive him long. That was what the King had promised, and Indirial didn't doubt that he meant it. Once Indirial was dead, Zakareth had no reason to keep Nerissa and Elaina alive or around. He would either execute them and toss their bodies out as refuse, or leave them here until they died. Indirial prayed for the former.

King Zakareth held up one hand, and the Ornheim Incarnation froze. It looked like one of the Territory's golems, but intricately carved with the detailed features of a tough older man, his skin lined with years. The Incarnation was made out of a fine white stone, with lines of every color running through him. In other circumstances, Indirial would have called this creature beautiful.

"Get back to work," Zakareth ordered. The Incarnation rumbled deep inside its stone chest, glaring at the King with what Indirial recognized as restrained hatred. Its marble fists slowly closed, with a sound like grinding gravel.

He almost expected Ornheim's eyes to be gemstones—that was the tradition in Ornheim golems. Instead, they were far more bizarre for looking disturbingly human, as though someone had imprisoned a man's eyes in a statue. The effect was doubly disconcerting when they shone with hot rage.

But the King rapped his staff down on the floor, and Ornheim simply bowed at the waist and walked out, its footsteps crashing on the tiles.

Indirial let himself relax against the floor. Maybe he would be able to snatch a few minutes of sleep, or at least fade into unconsciousness to forget the damage to his body. If he was lucky, the King would lose his patience and execute him while he slept.

Zakareth gestured again, and a stream of silver mist flowed in the doors.

Indirial struggled weakly, thrashing and trying to persuade his body to move. He almost pushed himself up, but his arms were too weak.

Is it worth calling steel?

He considered for a moment, sorely tempted. He would have plenty of strength to get up and fight this new Incarnation, at least as long as his steel lasted. But the price was too great.

No, that's what he wants.

Indirial fell back down, his elbows collapsing under his own weight, chin smacking against the floor.

The boots of the Asphodel Incarnation clicked against the floor as he walked past Indirial without a word. The Overlord couldn't see anything of his enemy above the knees, but the boots seemed to be made of gracefully flowing wood and decorated with vines that sprouted tiny, brightly colored flowers. A wave of Mist flowed behind Asphodel like a cape.

King Zakareth liked to move the Incarnations around in rotation, using their unique abilities to torment Indirial in new and unexpected ways. Over the past two days, he'd seen six of the nine Territories: Avernus, Naraka and Tartarus had yet to make an appearance, but he'd personally witnessed that Avernus had been sealed back into her Territory. That left Naraka and Tartarus. Maybe Zakareth hadn't been able to recruit either of them, or maybe he was saving them for some hideous torture later.

But of everyone he'd seen so far, the Asphodel Incarnation was by far the worst.

Asphodel swept a bow, his mist-cape billowing behind him. "Zakareth, allow me to compliment you on your excellent health and keen sense of color coordination." A smile shone through his words, though Indirial couldn't see his face. "How may I serve the throne today?"

Each of the Incarnations had reacted differently, confronted with the man who had effectively imprisoned them for three hundred years. Indirial kept track of these reactions in the hope that, against all odds, he would be able to use the information against his enemies someday.

Lirial and Helgard seemed to let their curiosity overwhelm their resentment, but every once in a while their anger would burn through. Ornheim had stated his objections clearly, and Endross had openly tried to kill Zakareth every time he was summoned, but Zakareth forced them both into line with his Rod of Harmony. Asphodel was the only one who seemed genuinely not to care about his three centuries of inactivity and torment.

It was entirely in character for him. Asphodel Travelers, as a rule, didn't allow themselves to experience much emotion. The Incarnation wouldn't have feelings, he'd simply feed on the feelings of others.

"Educate the prisoner," King Zakareth ordered, his burning crimson gaze returning to Indirial.

Asphodel bowed once more. "Yes, Majesty. And I must remark once more on how intimidating you look. Sitting there in your bright red throne, left eye glowing, cages dangling overhead...not to mention the implicit threat of the Rod in your right hand, and the whole armor-and-spiky-crown image. Your enemies must positively *quake* with fear."

The whole speech was delivered in the same smooth, content, slightly disinterested voice, as though he were complimenting a poorly paid gardener.

"I have many uses for your time," King Zakareth said, not shifting position in the slightest. The ruby on top of the Rod of Harmony flared. "Stop wasting it."

The Asphodel Incarnation waved away the threat, turning to walk away from Indirial. The floor tiles cracked as a vine as thick as an oak tree curled up from the soil beneath, blooming into a flower big enough to swallow a man whole. Asphodel settled back into the soft yellow petals, which contoured around his form to make a seat.

"Ah, Ragnarus," the Incarnation said with a sigh. "Territory of overt violence and instant gratification. Mine is the art and science of subtlety. The *audience* should be quiet and watch."

King Zakareth's face hardened even further at that, and Indirial dared to hope that he would take the time to teach Asphodel a lesson. The King had never learned how to take orders, and Indirial couldn't believe that Incarnation had changed that about him.

But the Incarnation of Asphodel didn't seem to care *what* Zakareth did. He lounged in his flower, plucking petals from his hair.

This Incarnation was somehow both more and less human than many of the others Indirial had seen. He didn't look like a monster, which already put him above Endross and Ornheim, but he was covered in clothes made of living roots and blooming flowers. His skin was pale, but it was the white of a lily, not of healthy living flesh. His hair flowed down to his shoulders in locks of silver, ornamented with a circlet of yellow, red, and blue flowers. His eyes were soft lavender, and he wore an amused expression as he stared down his nose.

Straight at Indirial.

Asphodel's head snapped up in alarm. So did the King's.

"Go find—" Zakareth began, but then a door-sized section of the stone wall blasted inward, scattering the throne room with rubble.

Simon shot in through the hole in the wall, nothing more than a blur of black-and-silver to Indirial's exhausted eyes. The boy dropped his huge Tartarus steel hammer to the floor, pulling Azura out of midair as he ran.

Still moving, he swung the Dragon's Fang in a gleaming arc through Asphodel's neck. The Incarnation had raised one hand as if to stop him, but it did no good. When Asphodel's head rolled across the tiles, it still wore a look of mild surprise.

Simon brought Azura down with both hands onto the King, who managed to block with his staff. The Rod of Harmony wasn't made for melee combat, though, and Simon's Tartarus steel blade sent a chip of gold spinning off into the distance.

Red light leaked from the Ragnarus weapon, and even Zakareth's eyes widened in alarm.

Simon threw himself backwards as the Rod exploded, sending shards rocketing everywhere in the hall. In their hanging cages, Nerissa and Elaina cowered, protected from the debris by the bottoms of their steel prisons. Indirial himself tried to keep his eyes open despite the almost overwhelming desire to squeeze them shut: he had to *see* Simon strike the final blow, had to know that his torment was finally over.

The throne had been broken into pieces by the explosion, lying in boulder-sized chunks of ruby. Of King Zakareth there was no sign, but a larger pile of rubble in the back corner of the room shifted.

Then Simon was there, helping Indirial to his feet. The pain that shot through him felt like being hit by an Endross lightning bolt combined with having Benson beating him into the pavement, but he didn't complain.

"Did you..." his voice gave out, so he tried again. "Did you get him?"

Simon was wearing that mask of his, half his face silver and the other half black, so Indirial couldn't see his expression. His voice echoed hollow. "No, I just stunned him. We have to hurry; can you make a Gate, if I hold him off?"

Indirial considered for an instant. He'd have to call steel to keep himself on his feet, and then summon Vasha and cut the Gate. Considering how much space his chains had left…

"Barely," he said. "You'll have to save my family."

Simon nodded, and King Zakareth rose from the pile of rubble, his burning eye almost a blood-red bonfire. He pointed the Rod of Harmony in Simon's direction, though Indirial wasn't exactly sure what it would do when used against Simon in the mask. The Rod was meant to turn a Traveler's own powers against him, but since Valinhall's powers were internal, would it even work? The mask had originally been an artifact of Ragnarus; would that change anything?

Is this real? he wondered. It certainly *seemed* real, and he didn't doubt that Simon would have headed off to Cana as soon as he learned that Indirial had been captured.

But he had to know for sure.

Valinhall offered a host of powers to deal with physical threats: he could make his bones and muscles stronger, armor his skin, burn away poison, increase his body's ability to heal, numb pain, block direct attacks…practically any threat he might face in battle could be blocked or reversed by the forces he could summon from the House of Blades. But against mental attack, they only had one real defense.

Until this point, Indirial had avoided using it. He had even survived Asphodel's last visit without it, by reminding himself over and over that the images he saw of his family being tortured to death were within his own mind. But this…this didn't seem like the kind of thing the Asphodel Incarnation could make up. How would he even know who Simon was?

Just in case, Indirial called diamond.

All at once, the world clarified. It didn't slow, as when he called the essence of the Nye, nor did his senses heighten. Everything simply…made more sense, as if the weight on his thoughts had finally lifted.

Indirial glanced at Simon, who was pulling his hand away from Indirial's shoulders, preparing to charge Zakareth.

How did he find out I was missing? Only the Damascan camp knew, and none of them could have gone to the House. Besides, Simon's still recovering from the last time he used the mask. If he wore it again, he would become the Valinhall Incarnation before I got a chance.

"This is a pathetic attempt, Asphodel," Indirial called. "I hope you didn't expect me to believe this."

The scene wavered and blew away like smoke in the wind, the masked Simon vanishing to nothing. The Asphodel Incarnation sat, unharmed, in his blossoming chair, idly chatting with Zakareth. "...the information comes from within them, you see," Asphodel was saying. "All I have to do is nudge it, give it form."

King Zakareth hadn't twitched. He still leaned with his elbow against the arm of his throne, Rod of Harmony on the other hand, looking at Indirial.

Indirial was actually standing, which was remarkable. He had thought everything about the scene must have been an illusion, but evidently the Incarnation had coaxed him to his feet even through his body's pain. Remarkable.

He felt that same agony now, but he set it out of his mind. It was only pain.

"It seems you are to be congratulated, Asphodel," King Zakareth said. There was no triumph in his voice, only utter confidence.

The Asphodel Incarnation buffed his fingernails on the edge of his flower-petal shirt. "Well, I hate to brag, but I *am* the best."

"Congratulations," Indirial said, "I've called on Valinhall." He knew with perfect clarity that, a moment ago, he would have released the diamond immediately, fearing to push himself past his limit. If his debt to Valinhall grew too great, he would Incarnate.

But so what?

Zakareth wanted him to become an Incarnation because the King was certain he could control Indirial with the Rod. But, as Indirial had wondered earlier, he wasn't even certain the Rod of Harmony would work on a Valinhall Traveler, who kept all his powers within himself. Beyond that, King Zakareth had obviously been unable to control Valin to any degree, or the original Valinhall Incarnation would still be living under Damascan control.

So the situation became utterly clear.

Situation: the enemy is holding two priority targets hostage. He has left me the freedom to call on my Territory because his objective is to get me to do so.

Primary Objective: free the hostages, take them to Valinhall.

Secondary Objective: total destruction of all enemy forces.

Question: do I allow him to accomplish his objective in order to accomplish mine?

Nerissa was pressed against the edge of her cage now, calling something, but Indirial didn't listen. It wouldn't be combat-relevant information, so he didn't waste his attention.

Indirial glanced between the Incarnations of Asphodel and Ragnarus. Could he take them both? Asphodel was hardly a threat; with the diamond protecting his thoughts, he could destroy that Incarnation in short order. So would he be able to kill an impossibly powerful Ragnarus Traveler in one-on-one combat?

I can't be sure, he concluded. *There's too much in the Crimson Vault that I'm not aware of. As far as I know, he has some weapon that controls Incarnations without any possibility of resistance, and the cost was simply too expensive for him to pay while he was a human. I should release the…*

Something in his thoughts clicked together as the last link of chain formed around his throat.

…what was I thinking? Of course I can win an open battle.

I am Valinhall.

The Avernus Incarnation settled back on her wings, holding a newly delivered tea-tray in her hands. This one held a pot and two cups, in case Leah might change her mind.

This time, she accepted. There had been water out in the wilderness, but she was still thirsty. Besides, whether Avernus was lying or not, Leah thought the threat of being poisoned had passed. And she wanted something to do while they talked.

Leah took a sip of her own tea, and found it a balanced blend of savory sweetness. She supposed she shouldn't be surprised; much of Damasca's tea was imported from the Feathered Plains. The Asphodel blends were better, but most people didn't trust tea leaves harvested from a Territory known for poison and mental deception.

"Who would try to control the Incarnations like that?" Leah asked, trying to steer their conversation back on track.

Avernus ruffled her feathers in what looked like her equivalent of a shrug. "Other than your ancestors, I have no idea, though I had some passing familiarity with Queen Cynara the First. She seemed genuinely enraged at the Elysian Incarnation's manipulation of us, calling us abominations and all that. Perhaps she was simply an excellent actress, I don't know. And as for the one who first led us, the Incarnation of Elysia herself..." Avernus shook her feathered head. "She was honest to a fault, which I suppose came from her Territory. She never told a lie or ordered another to do so, even when it would have been tactically sound. And I never sensed any deception or ambition in her, just a warped desire to guide us to a better future."

At last, they were beginning to get to the portion of the conversation where the Avernus Incarnation started to conceal how much she knew. Leah had wondered when they'd get to this part. "As I understand it, you Incarnated during a war between Ragnarus and Elysia. If, as you say, someone manipulated you into it, then how can you possibly believe it wasn't someone representing one side or the other?"

Avernus looked down into her cup, swirling one talon idly on the surface of the tea. "It is more accurate to say our Incarnation ignited the war, rather than occurred as a byproduct. As for who placed the pieces on that particular board...I must admit that I don't know."

Very carefully, she set her teacup aside and leaned in toward Leah, her raptor eyes gleaming in the candlelight. "However, I've told you all this for a single purpose: to illustrate to you that this current system is *unnatural*. It was engineered! This whole, messy business with all nine—or eleven, I suppose—Incarnations running around, it would never occur in nature. You simply have to find a way to restore the original balance."

As reluctant as Leah was to accept the advice of an Incarnation regarding the current policy toward her kind, she would be foolish to turn down any source of information about old Damasca. No matter how biased the source. "What would a balanced world look like, then?" she asked. "As you helped me realize, I would ruin myself if I allowed the Territory outposts to be destroyed."

Avernus smiled. "That's the beauty of it! You don't have to give up the outposts. Simply run them according to the Incarnation's laws, not yours. The Territories have a symbiotic relationship with their Travelers, and most Incarnations know it. So, for instance, if the Naraka outpost were subject to its own justice system outside of Damascan law, the Naraka Incarnation should be perfectly satisfied. The Asphodel Incarnation...well, I have practically no idea what the current Asphodel Incarnation wants, but in general those outposts should remain untouched as long as everyone knows to steer clear of the Mist."

"And what about Avernus?" Leah asked pointedly.

"Arrange the outposts according to tribe rather than according to national allegiance," the Incarnation said.

Leah thought of the outpost in which she sat: Damascan and Enosh Travelers lived together with their families, and she had seen no birds but ravens. "That seems to be the trend already," she said dryly.

"Then you truly have nothing to lose."

If the whole situation was as simple as the Avernus Incarnation seemed to think, then Leah would give up her crown to her insane sister Cynara and go off and live as a hermit in the most desolate part of Lirial. For one thing, she couldn't see the Endross Incarnation standing for an outpost under any circumstances. Even if he agreed to it initially, there was nothing to stop him from blowing it to splinters when a violent mood took him.

There were other holes in the plan as well. "Am I to believe that, if we sorted out all the current Incarnations into their original Territories, that all my problems would be solved?"

"No, of course not," Avernus said, picking up the corpse of a dead rat and casually biting off its head.

Leah was rather proud of herself for keeping her composure at that moment. She even managed to take a casual sip of her tea.

"There's no stopping human nature," the Incarnation said, munching on the rat's bones. A bit of blood dribbled down her chin, and Leah took a quick gulp of scalding tea to keep herself from becoming sick. "Travelers would still Incarnate here and there, but this whole mess with nine people Incarnating at the same time would never happen again without direct intervention. All you would have to do is deal with the Incarnations as they pop up, which should be relatively simple."

Simple? Would it be simple when a Naraka Incarnation emerged in the center of Bel Calem, burning an entire city block to the ground before her Travelers could get there and seal him? Leah couldn't believe that Avernus didn't see these problems—maybe she was reducing the problem for the sake of rhetorical argument, but Leah still thought she was painting over some fairly serious objections.

Even more than that, what motivation did she have to listen?

"The Hanging Trees have worked for my ancestors for generations," Leah said, watching the Incarnation for a reaction. "Why should I value your solution over theirs?"

Very carefully, Avernus set the decapitated rat down on the tea tray. "The time beneath the Tree was...unpleasant. It was like a restless sleep, plagued with nightmares, in which I could *almost* wake up, but never quite enough. During those times when I slept the lightest, I could feel the Tree feeding on me, draining my power away one sip at a time. It was like having leeches all over my body, taking away my blood drop by drop. For three hundred years. Time still moved for me, there under the ground, even if I slept through most of it. Instead of three centuries, it felt like... let's say, one. Would you like to be trapped under the ground for a hundred years?"

To keep her reaction blank, Leah took a sip of tea.

"Birds are meant to fly free, with the entire sky behind them," Avernus went on. "Being locked in the earth for so long...I can't describe it to you. It's the reason why I insisted on a tent this big—" she waved around her, indicating the high ceiling—"but also why I demanded a tent at all. If I didn't keep myself inside, I'm afraid I would start flying and never stop..."

Her voice trailed off, and in spite of her determination not to let an Incarnation's words sway her, Leah couldn't help but ache for her. She had never thought of it quite like that before: unable to move, buried alive for generations, fed upon by a vampiric tree from another Territory. Death would be a welcome relief.

"Thank you for your perspective," Leah said, and stood. If Avernus was lying, then Leah had done nothing more than waste a few minutes in exchange for a quick trip back to the outside world. If she was telling the truth, then Leah had gained valuable information. Either way, it was time to leave. "Please have one of your Travelers send me back to my camp outside of Cana. If I wish to consult with you further, will I still find you here?"

The Avernus Incarnation didn't stand, but she did stretch out both pairs of mismatched wings, reaching from one wall of the tent to the other. "The next time you set foot in Avernus, wherever you enter, you don't need to worry about finding me. I'll find you."

She opened her mouth and made a sound like a raven's caw, and two ravens fluttered in. One of them, Leah somehow recognized as Eugan— she couldn't remember him flying out, but he must have left the tent at some point. They fluttered over to Leah, landing one on each of her shoulders.

"Take Eugan back to his Overlord, if you would," the Incarnation said. "She's looking in entirely the wrong part of this Territory, and I can see that you will encounter her before I will. Murin, on your left shoulder, is my gift to you. She does not belong to you, but I have no doubt that you will find a use for a mind-reading raven in the Damascan court. She will serve you for as long as you wish, and help advise you on the matter of the Incarnations."

Murin made a sound in Leah's ear that sounded like a gurgling purr. She couldn't think of a way to get rid of the raven short of killing her and enraging the Incarnation, so it looked like Avernus had managed to literally perch a spy on Leah's shoulder. Even if everything else the Incarnation had said was completely accurate, this alone would have reminded Leah never to trust anyone who tried to ambush her for a meeting.

She hoped the raven would at least learn to speak a language she could understand. If she had to interpret a code of squawks directly into her ear, she would go deaf before she even got a chance to do whatever the raven wanted.

"I'm overwhelmed by your generosity," Leah said, smiling warmly to cover up the irony in her voice.

"Galene will take you home," the Incarnation said, but then she hesitated. "However you choose to deal with the Incarnations, I hope you remember this one thing. We are not pure evil, no matter what you think, nor pure forces for destruction. We are, as our name suggest, simply incarnations of our Territories."

"I've tried to believe that," Leah said honestly. "But it's hard to do, when we can lay such a toll in death at your feet."

Avernus sighed. "An Incarnation in the Unnamed World is like a hawk pushed into a river. At first they panic. The instant an Incarnation is created, the very first moment when they begin the transformation, that's when they're the most dangerous. The compulsion to act according to their Territory is overwhelming, and it's not until later that their own will comes back into play. For hours, even days...well, I'm afraid at that stage there's no appealing to reason. You just have to try and survive."

Chapter 20
Old Friends and
New Enemies

There was a straight sword in his left hand and a Dragon's Fang in his right, and Indirial was in the air, falling toward King Zakareth. He didn't know how it had happened. He didn't remember jumping or summoning either sword, but now he hung in the air, ready to draw blood.

He hadn't called Nye essence, nor did Benson's cold steel flow through his veins. And yet, somehow, the world slid slowly by. He felt enough power in his hands to rend steel.

He didn't need to hold the diamond anymore—the power was part of him now. His every thought was precise, filtered to absolute clarity by the focus of the Valinhall diamond. In that clear, cold light, his future became simple.

He was going to kill Zakareth. Then he would kill Asphodel. After that, he would begin the selection process: there were too many Travelers, too many people, who weren't strong enough to hold their own in combat. He would be doing them a disservice if he didn't attack. They would learn or they would die, and if they failed, he would be sparing them a worse death in the future.

It was so simple, he couldn't believe that he hadn't seen it before.

Vasha struck first, because of her length, but King Zakareth brought up a black-and-gold shield directly from his Territory. The tip of the Dragon's Fang skittered to one side, repelled by something more than simple metal.

Indirial reversed the infantry sword in his left hand, driving it down like a dagger toward the Damascan King's crown.

Zakareth's expression didn't falter, though the red light of the room glittered in the odd ruby and gold swirls on his skin. He met the second blow with the shaft of Rod of Harmony. The Ragnarus artifact didn't shatter, as it had done in Indirial's vision, so the King managed to knock both of Indirial's strikes aside.

He remained motionless, focused, determined. Indirial knew him well enough to guess his thoughts: the King truly believed that the future held nothing but victory, so not a single wrinkle of worry marred his expression. He was that confident.

Indirial landed with both feet on the stone, but he drew one leg up and kicked Zakareth in the chest.

Red bolts of lightning, like tiny flickering worms, crawled all over the King's black armor. The ruby at the center flared, but some power of the Crimson Vault had scattered the strength of Indirial's kick.

It hadn't worked, and Zakareth was bringing his Rod of Harmony forward, so Indirial dropped his swords and fought bare-handed. He slapped the Rod aside with the back of his left hand, bringing the right up to wrap around the King's throat.

King Zakareth's command flared with the light of the Crimson Vault, sending another flash of light rolling through the hall. He spoke only one word: "Surrender."

Indirial's hand unclenched without his will, as though a muscle spasm had seized his fist and forced it to open. His knees buckled, and he flopped to the ground at the King's feet.

Without a look of triumph or celebration, the Ragnarus Incarnation raised the Rod of Harmony. He didn't look like someone who had defeated a worthy foe. To him, the outcome of this fight had never been in doubt.

Indirial, on the other hand, felt *fantastic*.

This is what I was missing, he thought. He had never realized how long he'd lived without a real opponent. Sure, he had Travelers to kill every once in a while, and some of them even posed something of a challenge. Other times, an enemy would catch him off-guard, and he would suffer a severe injury.

That danger had given him an illusion of satisfaction, but now the veil had been ripped from his eyes. He wasn't satisfied. He had never been satisfied! Valinhall wasn't meant for crushing the weak, it was meant to challenge those with even *more* power.

So as the King activated the Rod of Harmony, a single spark of light igniting in the tip of the ruby, he must have seen something in Indirial's grin. He hesitated.

Indirial felt it when the chains on his skin turned to steel.

The marks of Valinhall had never grown up to his scalp or down over his face, as they had with Valin. They began at his wrists, wrapped around his midsection and down to his feet, but they ended in a collar around his neck. And all of a sudden, they flashed from black to shining steel.

Doors opened in Indirial's mind as though he walked through the House of Blades, throwing open each new room and devouring the power within. He called no specific power, but the ruby light binding him was a simple thing to throw off, if he had a moment of spare concentration. And the King had hesitated.

Indirial bent all his focus to the commands of the Ragnarus crown, and he sliced through that power like a Dragon's Fang through a length of twine. Still wearing his grin, he strode toward King Zakareth.

For a fraction of a second noticeable only because of the half-frozen world around him, the Incarnation of Valinhall stared into the eyes of Ragnarus.

Zakareth's eyes widened—the first time his expression had changed since the fight began—and the jewel at the top of the Rod of Harmony flashed.

The red light crashed around Indirial like a warm wave, but he'd called no external powers from the House. The Rod found no purchase, nothing to turn against him, and he exulted in the freedom.

That was one gamble won...but it wasn't even much of a gamble, was it? Of course he'd won. He was unstoppable.

Indirial summoned Vasha, and he could fully sense her personality for the first time. Every other time he'd held the blade, he could only feel Vasha as a distant mind. At times, he'd wondered if she was even real.

Now, her cold hunger for battle flowed through him, matching his own. But there were other things that didn't feel quite right, so he stood in place, trying to figure out what was wrong.

Ah, that's right. The King had banished his medallion, Korr, almost as soon as Indirial had been captured. Incarnation of Valinhall or not, he wanted his advisor.

Ordinarily, he couldn't summon his advisor directly from the House, but it seemed so straightforward now. He simply willed it to happen, and Korr vanished from Valinhall and appeared, hanging on a gold chain around his neck.

I'm sorry, Indirial, Korr whispered. That almost threw him off. Korr never apologized, and he couldn't remember the last time the medallion had actually used his name.

But, well, at least Korr was here now. He didn't feel comfortable fighting a battle without him. Speaking of which...

He was already reaching out to summon the Nye cloak from Valinhall when he stopped. He didn't need the cloak anymore, and who knew how it would react to his new eyes? He needed something better. Something more.

Shadows crawled from the House, folding into a hood that crept over his forehead. The shadows flowed down behind him, spreading into a cloak that fell almost to his feet. After a quick mental adjustment, the fabric retreated to leave his arms bare.

Vasha, Korr, his cloak...perfect. Now he was prepared for a *real* fight.

The Ragnarus Incarnation surprised him, leaping over his own throne in a jump that might have been fueled by Valinhall's steel. King Zakareth wasn't showing his age, but then again, Indirial wasn't sure such mundane concerns even applied to Incarnations. He had the Lightning Spear in both hands, and for a second Indirial was surprised; hadn't Leah held that spear? But then the steel spearhead was driven toward his chest, and he had to slap it aside with one hand, driving Vasha toward Zakareth's throat as he did.

The length of their weapons was almost exactly equal: the Lightning Spear drew a slice across the inside of Indirial's arm as Vasha cut a piece off of King Zakareth's cheek.

The King's wound healed in a sizzle of scarlet sparks, and Indirial's flesh knit together with a spray of green and gold.

So neither of them could be permanently injured. "This should be interesting," Indirial said happily. He couldn't imagine a better fate than two immortals, locked in combat. The only problem was going to be finding a challenge to top this one, after the King was taken care of.

"Asphodel!" King Zakareth called, turning another strike from Vasha with the end of his spear.

Maker, that's right! Indirial thought. He'd almost forgotten about the other Incarnation, focused as he was on Ragnarus.

He knocked the Lightning Spear aside and jumped backwards, though he hated to do it. More distance favored the man who held the devastating ranged weapon, but he had to get some space to see what Asphodel was up to.

The Asphodel Incarnation was…still lounging on his chair of petals.

He noticed Indirial looking at him, and a broad smile split his pale face. "Oh, excuse me, gentlemen. I'm afraid I'm entirely outclassed."

A blue-edged Asphodel Gate spun open beside him, and he casually strolled inside. "Oh horrors, it seems that he's caught me. No, help, I'm bound in my Territory. Ah, cruel fate."

He turned toward King Zakareth and waved good-bye as his Gate shrank behind him. "If you need me, Your Majesty, you know where to find me."

The Asphodel Gate winked shut.

What was wrong with him? He had decided to seal himself permanently into his own Territory instead of seeking out a perfectly good fight?

King Zakareth shook his head. "I never have understood Asphodel."

"Me neither," Indirial said. Then he leaped straight up.

Sure enough, the Lightning Spear blasted into the tiles at his feet, driving a hole straight through and into the ground beneath. A rough-edged crater of rubble and dust now dominated the center of Zakareth's throne room, and through the cloud of dust, the Spear flew back to its owner.

Indirial whipped Vasha to one side, then the other. She bit through the ordinary steel, slicing through the chains above his wife and daughter's cages. The prisons fell alongside Indirial and he threw Vasha to the ground in order to free up both his hands.

Then, reaching to either side, he caught each cage by the bars.

When his feet hit the ground, he had to hold the cages up to the sides to prevent them from slamming to the ground and injuring his family. The bars warped and bent under his grip, the bolts at either end of the cage popping out, but his strength seemed limitless. He hardly felt the strain.

Delicately, he placed the cages down, hardly noticing the tears that wove their way down his wife's face, or his daughter's look of unrestrained horror.

He summoned Vasha back to his hand and slashed her down from head-height all the way down to the floor. Earlier, all his Gates would have been the same size, and it would have taken him the better part of a minute to open one.

Now, the Valinhall Gate opened easily.

His family screamed questions at him, but he didn't bother to answer, tossing the cages through the portal. He willed it shut in time, as the Lightning Spear blasted toward him from the cloud of dust.

Danger, Korr said, and the violet flame burned on the end of Zakareth's spear.

Indirial had never felt anything so intoxicating. He could die here, right now, and if he did, then he would go to his grave at the hands of a powerful enemy.

On an instinct, he dropped Vasha again.

If this didn't work, the Spear would blast him to pieces, and he would see what the immortality of the Incarnations was worth.

But he couldn't resist the chance to try.

He clapped both hands together on the head of the Spear, catching it between his palms.

The sheer force of the blow knocked him ten paces backwards, the bottom of his boots skidding along the shattered tiles. He ground to a halt at the end of the throne room, the Lightning Spear quivering in his hands.

But he'd *caught* it.

He grabbed the weapon around the shaft as it tried to jerk out of his grip, attempting to fly back to its master. It struggled, but he wouldn't release it.

The Ragnarus Incarnation had lost, but by the Maker, he'd put up a good fight. He was worthy. Indirial would let him live; in the coming world, he would need warriors like Zakareth.

He started to say so, but then the column of dust and smoke cleared.

King Zakareth stood next to a huge Ragnarus Gate. Another woman, red-skinned and clothed in scarlet light, sat inside the Territory, perched on something that looked like an impossibly massive barrel tipped onto its side so that Indirial was looking down its deep, dark mouth. If the woman on the top of the barrel was any indication of scale, it looked like it could swallow a wagon and a team of horses.

Indirial didn't know what was supposed to come out of that barrel, but he liked the look of it. Maybe this would be a true test. He dropped the Spear and summoned Vasha, holding her in both hands.

We're both dead, Korr whispered.

"There's no one else like you, Indirial," King Zakareth called. "But I can always build another palace."

Red light swelled deep within the barrel.

Indirial called ghost armor.

The room vanished in a tide of red light.

Leah, stepping out of the Avernus Gate with a raven on either shoulder, was swarmed by officers, clerks, and concerned well-wishers.

"Thank the Maker!" one woman said. "You were gone, Overlord Feiora was gone, Overlord Indirial was gone...we were afraid you were all dead."

Cold fear settled into the pit of Leah's stomach. "Slow down a moment," Leah said. "Indirial's gone? Where did he go?"

Then the Lightning Spear vanished from her grip, and she was afraid she knew.

When Indirial regained consciousness, his entire world was dark. Practically every part of his body felt torn and broken, but in a distant way, as if he had simply heard of someone else being tortured. He tried to reach up and feel his way forward, but his arm wouldn't respond.

Then it began to heal, and in the gold-and-green sparks he was able to see a bit of his prison. The arm itself was twisted around like a wrung-out towel, bone and blood and muscle showing through the torn skin, but Indirial was sure that his powers would sort that out in a moment. More importantly, a slab of rough stone the size of a palace ceiling hung only inches away.

For a second, he wondered if he had been sealed underneath a Hanging Tree. Panic seized him: would he be down here for decades or centuries with no weapons? No one to fight? He would rather die.

Then the stone above him scraped and moved, and he realized that there were no roots twisting around his flesh, hungering for his blood.

He relaxed and waited to see who would pull him free. Whoever it was must have been strong enough to move a whole wall's worth of stone, which meant that they were worthy. Anyone that powerful had earned their place in Valinhall.

Finally, the stone slid to one side, and the sun shone down in Indirial's eyes. Once, it would have been blinding. Now, he didn't even blink.

King Zakareth stood over him, his armor flaring with red light as it provided him the strength to push tons of rock out of the way like he was sliding the lid off a coffin.

He raised the Lightning Spear in one hand.

"I have paid the price for you again and again, Indirial," he said, his voice once again certain and commanding. "Will you obey me at last?"

Indirial couldn't help himself: he began to laugh. "With persistence like that, you would have done well in Valinhall. Not to mention your weapons."

He reached out a hand to the Ragnarus Incarnation. Not that he needed the help up; it was symbolic, and Indirial remembered that such things were important.

"I'm with you," he said. "You've earned it."

The King's eyes flared with something like satisfaction, and he hauled the Incarnation of Valinhall to his feet.

The Eldest stood before two caged human females, studying them both. The older one had explained the situation, asking him politely who he was, begging him to let them out. Everything he would have expected from a human captive. The younger one had alternated between threats and stubborn silence.

That one might have a future here.

They both insisted on using Indirial's name as much as possible, as though he couldn't see Indirial's presence hanging over them like a banner.

"I will free you," he said at last. The older woman's eyes filled with hope, but the younger's narrowed in suspicion. Yes, she would have a future here. He would make sure of it. "Before I do, I have a few conditions of my own."

If their story was to be believed, Indirial had succumbed to his chains at last. The Eldest wondered if that should be counted as a loss or a gain. On one side of the scale, Incarnations were notoriously lacking in self-control. Getting him to do anything productive would be like getting a newborn Nye to walk in the light. On the other side, the Eldest now had a powerful avatar of the House wandering around in the outside world. Surely, there must be some way to turn that to his advantage.

"You will spend some time as my guests," the Eldest said at last. "I must decide what is to be done about Indirial."

A pair of valuable pieces had fallen into the Eldest's grasp, and it was finally his turn. If he played this right, he might be able to walk away with a new Founder after all.

One way or another.

CHAPTER 21

DAUGHTER OF WIND

359ᵀᴴ YEAR OF THE DAMASCAN CALENDAR
1ˢᵀ YEAR IN THE REIGN OF QUEEN LEAH I
6 DAYS SINCE SPRING'S BIRTH

"No one's heard from Indirial?" Simon said.

"...and tell them they can decrease the guards on the Avernus side," Leah murmured to a servant in a messenger's uniform. "I don't think we'll have any trouble from them anytime soon."

The messenger bowed and departed, and Leah turned back to Simon. "Indirial was last seen in the camp five days ago, screaming about an Incarnation in the camp. Some soldiers witnessed him fighting what may or may not have been an Incarnation before he vanished. Into a Gate, some say." Her lips tightened. "Into a red Gate."

Simon paced restlessly, trying to work off the feeling of doom that had been hanging over him ever since his fight with Alin. Now that Indirial was gone...well, Indirial could handle most anything, but they had perhaps eight Incarnations unaccounted for. Images flashed through his head: a man, charred and burned on the ground. A shriveled woman, held in the fangs of a giant snake.

He hadn't been able to do anything to help his parents, but Indirial had saved him. He burned for the chance to return the favor.

But he couldn't do anything if he wasn't there.

"Let's say it was a Ragnarus Gate," Simon said, pausing his pacing to stop directly in front of Leah. "Where would it come out?"

Leah shook her head wearily. "He could be anywhere by now, Simon. And without Indirial, it's even more important that you stay here."

"I came after *you.*" Simon hoped that would make enough of an impact to end the argument, but Leah's mouth quirked up into a one-sided smile.

"Yes, and look how necessary that turned out to be. We're not even sure it *was* a Ragnarus Gate. If it was red, it could as easily have been a Gate into Naraka, or even parts of Ornheim. It could have been an Elysian

Gate, for all we know."

Simon turned that over in his mind. It still irked him, a little, that Alin was still alive and free. Not that he wanted Alin dead, exactly, but it almost insulted his pride that an Incarnation had fought him one-on-one and escaped virtually unharmed.

Would Alin have kidnapped Indirial? Simon still wasn't sure what the Elysian Incarnation might be capable of, but Alin himself wouldn't have targeted the Overlord of Cana. It might not have even occurred to him to do so. If he came after anyone, it would be Simon or Leah. Or perhaps Grandmaster Naraka, who was still bound, gagged, and guarded somewhere in the camp.

He couldn't believe that Alin would plan and execute a trap to capture Indirial, but it seemed that *someone* had. And even though Vasha was missing from the entry hall, Indirial hadn't entered the House in over a week, as Valinhall reckoned time.

Simon had recovered enough from the mask that Valin and the dolls had pronounced him fit for duty. The chains hovered around his shoulder blades, but he could feel their cold links crawling back down even as he met with Leah.

"I don't think it's Alin," he said. "You have to say, it makes more sense if it's Ragnarus."

Leah sighed and nodded. "It does. That's why I have the camp on alert. We've been avoiding Cana ever since the barrier went down, waiting for someone to contact us, but so far no one has. The people are getting restless; most of them have family in the city. We're going to send a few parties of Travelers in later."

"When do they leave?" Simon asked.

"I would rather you stay here," she said. "An Incarnation, possibly two, infiltrated the camp only a few days ago, and we haven't heard from our most powerful combat Traveler since. We need you in case of an attack."

It made sense, but Simon didn't have time to explain the powers of Valinhall to Leah. As long as he had a mask and Indirial didn't, Simon had a better chance of pulling him out of Cana. In his mind, he had a responsibility to try.

"If they were going to follow up with an attack, they would have already done it," he said reasonably. He was interrupted by the raven on

Leah's shoulder.

He'd tried to ignore the bird throughout their conversation, which was what Leah had advised him to do, but it was getting harder. The bird stared at him, stared *through* him, in a way that made him nervous. He couldn't help feeling that the raven knew his thoughts and didn't approve.

Besides, it was shouting in Leah's ear, which made it hard to ignore.

Leah didn't seem as irritated as he would have expected, given that a bird was shrieking at her. Instead, she reached out and pulled the Lightning Spear from out of nowhere, her eyes searching the sky. He didn't know what she was looking for, but she obviously knew something he didn't. He called steel.

A screech, as though from a hunting bat the size of a horse, echoed through the camp. The noise of the people dulled to a muted roar as many froze, waiting to see whatever had made that sound.

They didn't have to wait long.

A man, blazing with blue-white lightning, rocketed through the sky. His eyes shone like a pair of thunderbolts, and even his hands and feet were shrouded in bright, flickering light. A set of wings streamed from his back, seemingly made from smoke...no, from stormclouds. They, too, flashed with light from deep within.

The Endross Incarnation screamed again, and this time it sounded like laughter.

A dozen bolts of white, unnaturally straight lightning hammered down from a clear sky, all over the camp.

Leah and Simon stood on a hill rising above most of the tents, so Leah would have a better view of the camp's overall layout. Where the lightning bolts struck, fires burned, and smoke began to rise. Meanwhile, rolling thunderstorms the size of donkey carts flowed through the rows between tents, spitting out hissing snakes, giant lizards, and creeping vines that shot sparks.

Simon summoned Azura, looking up to judge the distance between himself and the Endross Incarnation.

Leah was faster.

The Lightning Spear shot forward like a streak of dark lightning itself, headed directly for the Incarnation. She staggered as if in pain, clutching Simon's shoulder for support.

The Spear tore through Endross's side, sending him shrieking and plummeting into the ground.

With his free hand, Simon had already grabbed Leah, pulling her into a nearby tent. "Keep down," he said. "This attack will be aimed at you."

Her eyes were determined even as she staggered after him, leaning on his arm for support. "I can take him out of the air more easily than you can."

"I'm going to lead him away from you," Simon said, overriding her objections as he pushed her through the tent-flap. "You can throw the Spear if he gets too close—"

"*Caw!*" yelled her raven.

The Lightning Spear tore through the side of the tent and smacked into her hand, then she leaned out of the flap and threw it again.

The Endross Incarnation rose from the camp in a fury, trailing smoke and ashes behind him. He shouted at them, his voice choked and barely understandable, his eyes locked on Leah: "I HAVE THE—"

The Lightning Spear crashed into the top of his skull, sending him flipping over backwards in midair. His head was a ruined, bleeding mess that resembled nothing so much as a smashed melon, but it began to rebuild itself even before he fell beneath the line of tents.

"Your turn," Leah said, panting. She leaned back into the tent, and Simon stepped away. Immediately, he flipped up the hood of his cloak. When the Endross Incarnation burst out of the row of nearby tents, roaring, Simon called the essence of the Nye.

Leah was in the tent, out of the Endross Incarnation's view. And if this Endross was anything like his predecessor, he would aim straight for whatever target he could see first.

Then again, none of that would matter if Simon hit the Incarnation before it had a chance to strike.

Endross had no more than an instant to look confused before Azura hit him in the neck.

At least, it should have. The blade actually paused an inch or two from the Incarnation's skin, held at bay by a shield of dense air.

Simon jumped back as the Endross Incarnation gestured, and a thunderstorm Gate opened where Simon had been standing. A reptilian head reached out of the Gate, snapping hungrily on empty air, sparks flying from between its teeth.

It occurred to him that finding himself so close to death would have been a traumatic, horrifying experience for him before his time in Valinhall. Now, narrowly escaping death didn't warrant his attention. He stepped away from the gnashing Endross creature and thrust Azura at the Incarnation.

…who suddenly wasn't there, having taken wing and flown off, tossing lightning bolts across the camp.

Simon started to run off, but Leah jumped out of the tent and seized his arm.

He almost pulled her off her feet before he realized that he was supposed to stop and wait for whatever she had to say.

"There's something wrong here," Leah said, after she had regained her balance.

Simon looked down the hill, across the camp. Columns of smoke rose from tents and patches of grass where the Incarnation's lightning had struck, and Endross creatures snapped at the heels of practically everyone he could see.

"Yeah," he said. "We're under attack."

She stepped closer, and the raven on her shoulder let out a soft sort of mewling sound. "Then where are the bodies?"

Simon stopped and looked closer, wishing he'd brought a doll. Down there, one royal soldier pulled another from a burning tent as an Endross crocodile looked on…and did nothing more threatening than snarl and blast lightning into the sky. A giant snake slithered through a crowd of washerwomen, snarling at each but not biting anyone. The Endross Incarnation himself swooped down on crowds, making a startling show of lights and sounds, but now that he thought about it, Simon couldn't remember seeing him kill anyone.

"What does this mean?" he asked.

Leah shook her head. "I don't know," she said. "But something else is coming, and we need to be ready."

Simon grabbed her by the shoulders and steered her back toward the tent. "Then let's start by getting you inside."

King Zakareth stood on the walls of Cana, watching the destruction in his daughter's camp through a spyglass. Ragnarus had many tools, but all of them had some application as weapons; the Vault held nothing to let him see supernaturally far. Perhaps he could rectify that himself, once he'd pulled Elysia down and looted its treasures for his own.

Indirial stood next to him, the chains on his arms turned to steel, a cloak of shadows flowing from the top of his head all the way down to the stone behind him. His eyes were seas of black, on which floated circles of burning violet.

That surprised the King, deep in a part of him that was still capable of experiencing surprise. He had thought the only colors of Valinhall were black and silver, and he wondered if irises of violet flame were Indirial's choice, somehow.

That was an idle thought, and had to give way before more practical concerns. Indirial's new appearance was more intimidating, which meant more effective.

Indirial smiled like a proud father. "Leah almost brought down Endross on her own. I think if she'd been forced into a full-on fight, she might have won."

"The weapons of Ragnarus have great power," King Zakareth said, wishing he'd seen the fight in more detail. Why could Valinhall have a power to increase eyesight, but the Vault didn't?

That was an irrelevant thought, and he couldn't afford distractions. He had to stay focused.

Indirial squinted. "Is that...Simon down there?"

"Where?" Zakareth asked. Through his lens, he had seen Leah as a crimson dot, and the hill she stood on an island in a sea of burning tents. She was missing now, but he had trouble making out details at this distance. Even the Endross Incarnation was little more than a bright spot among the veil of smoke.

"There was someone in black with her before," Indirial said. "But now I see no one. It's enough to make me wonder if we waited too long."

"Do you think he's recovered from the mask by now?" Zakareth asked, keeping his spyglass trained on the hill. Indeed, there did seem to be a patch of shadow atop the hill that gleamed strangely, as though the darkness concealed a length of polished steel.

But then, it could easily be a trick of the light.

Indirial leaned forward to rest his elbows on the edge of the wall. "I'm not sure," he said. "I never was familiar with the mask, and it wouldn't do me any good now. All it does is allow them to draw on Valinhall more deeply, just as I do."

When the mask had been a part of his Vault, it had been intended to strengthen other Travelers, to increase the reach and depth of their powers. In its original state, it had a series of safety measures built in to keep Travelers from delving too deeply and burning their life away. Then, in a battle long ago, it had been shattered.

Malachi had used it for years in its broken state: all of the power, none of the restraint. Zakareth could hardly imagine what this mask—built from the remnants of the old one and attuned to a new Territory—was capable of. But if the Valinhall Incarnation didn't know either, then that could be cause for concern.

"If Simon is down there," King Zakareth said, "his blade will be as well. Do we dare continue?"

Indirial chuckled, pulling his cracked and pitted sword from midair. "If it's Simon alone, we can take Azura from him at any time. Besides, I'm glad he's not in the House. I don't want to fight him in a *group*, or as part of an *ambush*." He spat out the word 'ambush' as though it burned his tongue, grimacing in distaste. "I want to fight him man-to-man, when he's at his best. He's the only one to win a fight against the last Valinhall Incarnation."

His burning violet eyes grew distant, staring off at Leah's hill. "In fact, why not now? Why don't I do that first? If he is down there...but if he's not, I might be able to find Leah. She might be something of a challenge..."

Zakareth laid a gauntleted hand on Indirial's shoulder. "We have a job to do," he said.

Indirial shook himself and nodded, walking over to a relatively clear stretch of wall. He didn't seem to notice how the stones smoothed and cut themselves into tiles as he passed.

Out of idle curiosity, King Zakareth glanced down at his own feet. The stone of the wall was turning red in a steadily expanding pool, as though blood spilled from his feet in a constant wave.

That was appropriate enough.

"This would be easier if we had Asphodel along," Indirial commented, raising his Dragon's Fang.

"We do not," Zakareth said.

"Or even Avernus."

"You know exactly what happened to Avernus."

Indirial sighed. "But does it have to be Ornheim?"

The Ornheim Incarnation shuddered to life from where he had been crouched against the side of the wall. The stone had actually started to grow around him, forming a little cave complete with tiny stalactites.

He grumbled, loud and low in his throat, his pale stone skin shivering. He was shot through with jagged lines, like marble, but these veins came in every color. He looked like a statue designed for decoration, not war.

And his all-too-human eyes were locked on Zakareth in an expression of pure hatred.

The King couldn't even remember a time in his life when that might have bothered him.

"Ornheim is what you have been given," King Zakareth said, in tones of command. "If you can take their swords, he will be enough. If not, I have kept Helgard with me, and I can send her in reserve. Lirial goes ahead to prepare the way."

Indirial sighed and sliced open a Valinhall Gate. "Well, since I can't go myself, I guess two Incarnations are all right. If they can get the job done."

Ornheim tried to shoulder Indirial aside with a stone arm as he walked into the Gate, but the Valinhall Incarnation didn't budge.

From inside the Gate, Zakareth could sense two expressions of Ragnarus. The first was shaped like a sword, and was one of the Vault's various gatecrawlers. With an effort of will, he banished the device at a distance. He didn't want to leave it there long enough for the Valinhall creatures to attune it to their Territory.

The second throbbed and pulsed in time with the beat of Zakareth's own chest. The Heart of Rebirth wasn't a pleasant artifact, and it had taken several citizens of Cana to pay enough of its cost to make it functional.

But now the price would justify itself. He clapped once, sending out his will in an invisible wave.

Deep within the House of Blades, the Incarnation of Tartarus began pulling himself together.

For an instant, Zakareth felt another expression of Ragnarus power, pulsing to a different beat. It was more distant, and in another direction... it seemed to be coming from the hill on which Leah stood.

That made sense. Leah was the only active Ragnarus Traveler left. She had almost unrestricted access to the Vault, so it was no surprise that she would have something of his. He recognized the Lightning Spear she held, though. This was something else, something he almost remembered...

But once again, he put aside irrelevant thoughts to focus on the mission at hand.

"Do what you must," King Zakareth said. "It's time for me to slip the muzzle back over my hound." Then he stepped out over Cana's wall.

His foot came down on a tower of packed snow that hadn't been there before. Helgard waited at the foot of the wall, holding a book in front of her frozen eyes. Zakareth walked forward, each step landing on a slightly lower tower of snow, as though he walked down a staircase that existed only because he needed it.

Behind him, the Incarnation of Valinhall was giving orders. The King allowed himself to feel a small spark of satisfaction. For once, he had paid for a weapon and received even more than he was expecting.

Indirial was far more than a weapon, like the other Incarnations. He was a warrior, and a trusted servant.

He would get the job done.

Indirial watched the Ornheim Traveler take the first few steps into the entry hall and look around for threats. This was one reason he hated working with Ornheim: he would measure twice before cutting once, and all Indirial needed this time was a sharp cut.

"The swords," he commanded. "Get the swords."

Ornheim didn't stop looking around. He even lifted up a sofa as though to see if there was something dangerous underneath. *Maker, what could possibly be threatening about a sofa?*

Finally, the Incarnation seemed satisfied, turning his head to the sword-racks. He reached out for Seijan, its blade short and speckled with ink.

A black chain looped around his wrist, pulling him short.

"Don't worry, it's just a Nye," Indirial said.

Ornheim slammed his free fist down on the Nye's shadowy form...but before the blow could land, that hand was bound by a different chain.

Then the Nye were everywhere. They filled the room like a hill full of ants swarming a carcass, and Ornheim was covered by so many black chains that Indirial could barely see the stone beneath.

The see of black parted, and a hunched figure in dark gray slid past, gliding up to the Gate. "We have so few of the Fangs left," the Eldest hissed. "You would steal them? Even you?"

Indirial met the Eldest Nye's empty hood without looking away. In his current state, he could sense each of the Nye, like knowing his shadow trailed behind him without having to look. They were more than expressions of his power; they were at the heart of whatever made Valinhall the way it was. He had never fully appreciated that before.

But that didn't mean he had to do what they told him.

"The Dragon's Fangs will be returned, along with all that we're missing. The King has ordered me to collect them, for now, so that the other Travelers of Valinhall cannot interfere with our mission." It had been his idea to disarm the Dragon Army, actually, not Zakareth's, but the orders to do so *had* come from the King. "They will be re-distributed to the worthy."

The Eldest's own chain, rough and heavy even compared to those of the other Nye, ran between his sleeves in a hissing, clinking river. "Not only have you lost control, you have sold your home to the King of the Vault. My master would rip your throat out with his teeth."

"Your master is imprisoned in a graveyard, where he belongs," Indirial said. Behind the Eldest, the sea of black chains bulged and pressed upwards as the mountainous strength of the Ornheim Incarnation strained against the combined might of the Nye.

The Eldest didn't look behind him, but he did consider for a moment. "I have your wife and child with me. I can make sure that they take months to die."

Indirial shrugged. He would prefer his family to live, but if they did not...well, that meant that they couldn't handle the trials of life. "If they're worth saving, they'll save themselves."

"You speak like the true Incarnation of Valinhall," the Eldest whispered. "But still you plot to give your own power to Ragnarus."

That wasn't exactly true, but nothing Indirial could say would sway the Nye's belief, so he let the Eldest think what he wanted.

In the background, the Ornheim Incarnation had risen fully to his feet, and was tossing Nye away from him like a child splashing in the waves.

The Eldest ran his chain through his sleeves again. "I cleaned this room only yesterday. But it seems I must have missed a pebble or two."

He practically vanished, even from Indirial's vision, and when he reappeared he was standing behind Ornheim. His thick chain was wrapped around the Incarnation's neck, and the Eldest heaved, pulling Ornheim over onto his back.

The Ornheim Incarnation struck the floor of the House with a booming crack so loud that Indirial wondered if the others could hear it even in Valinhall's depths.

Rocky white fists flailed at the Eldest, but he dodged each strike without even seeming to pay attention.

The Nye had swarmed again, rushing at Ornheim's prone form and lashing him with the ends of their chains. Indirial couldn't help it; he was a little impressed. They were managing to take chips of stone from the Incarnation's solid skin with each strike.

So it was a good thing he had a backup plan.

It started with a rhythmic pounding, as though someone in the distance had decided to strike up a beat on a vast drum. When the sound rose to drown out even the Nye's treatment of Ornheim, the beat vanished.

The Eldest raised one sleeve as though he were about to issue an order, and then the floor of the entry hall exploded.

Tartarus, the gleaming ten-foot giant in the mirrored steel armor, landed on the edge of what had once been the trapdoor down to the Nye's basement. Evidently they had kept his pieces down there, never realizing that he could be pulled back together at King Zakareth's will.

Blades flashed into the Tartarus Incarnation's grip, and he impaled Nye after Nye with seemingly unlimited shards of metal. Wherever his clockwork gaze fell, another cloaked shadow was pinned to the wall.

After only a moment, the Ornheim Incarnation unfolded and stood next to Tartarus, equal in height and strength. Spinning rocks appeared out of nowhere, lashing forward like shooting stars and tearing through black robes.

"I know what I'm doing, Eldest!" Indirial called. "I came prepared."

The Eldest appeared completely focused on Indirial, though he dodged spikes and flying rocks almost as an afterthought.

"Did you?" he rasped, and somehow the sound cut through even the din of battle.

Then the Eldest raised his sleeve again.

And, all over the entry hall, the *furniture* joined the battle.

The sofa curled up its legs, leaping onto Ornheim's arm, its scarlet cushions working like a great mouth. It growled and snarled like a pack of wolves, sending handfuls of gravel up into the air.

One of the tables reared like an angry horse and kicked Tartarus hard enough in the chest that he staggered backwards. A rug lifted off the floor and seized a nearby chair with one tassel, slamming it against the back of the Tartarus Incarnation's helmet. Somehow the chair didn't break, and the rug knocked the Incarnation again and again.

The room was a flurry of flying stone, metal, cloth, and wooden splinters as the two Incarnations smashed furniture and the furniture smashed back.

He'd had no idea they could do that.

Now that he looked with the eyes of the Valinhall Incarnation, it seemed obvious. The tables and chairs of the entry hall remained hidden and innocent unless called upon, like a sleeping guardian. But now, through his violet eyes, he could see the dormant potential lying within each plank of wood.

Against all reason, he felt a surge of pride in his Territory. How could anyone ever choose to Travel Naraka or Helgard when Valinhall was this magnificent? Even the furniture rose to defend it from outsiders!

Not that sofas and lamps had any chance of defeating two Incarnations, but they could be rebuilt, and the House would be stronger than ever for this battle. He would make sure of it.

In a matter of seconds, the room looked like it had been trampled by a herd of oxen. The walls bristled with spikes of mirrored steel, and fist-sized rocks were scattered across the ground. The air was filled with drifting bits of cushion stuffing, and the floor covered by splinters. One grandfather clock against the wall had been gutted, spilling gears and springs everywhere, and every mirror in the room was reduced to shards.

The sofa pulled itself across the floor on one leg, snarling weakly, before it finally collapsed, weak and inanimate once more.

There was no way someone in the House hadn't heard that commotion, and all the Nye were slithering away like snakes of shadow and light. It was only a matter of time before someone showed up, and he had to complete his mission before that happened.

"Back to work," Indirial said.

Seconds later, the two Incarnations tossed him three Dragon's Fangs. A Valinhall Traveler in the outside world could summon his blade from the House, but no Traveler in the House itself could summon their blade from outside. And once he got the Fangs into a different Territory—in this case, Ragnarus—they wouldn't be able to banish the blades back to Valinhall, either, unless they got close enough to touch the weapons directly.

Effectively, by keeping the Fangs sealed outside the House, he was disarming the other Travelers of Valinhall. Kathrin and Denner wouldn't be able to return and fight him, Andra would never get a chance to progress until he found her worthy, and Simon and Kai...they would have an opportunity to kill him in a duel, but only when he allowed it.

Indirial glanced at the pile of Tartarus steel waiting for him at his feet. Counting Vasha, that made four out of six. "We're missing two," he said.

Azura and Mithra were missing. Simon was probably down on the hill with Leah, so Indirial would be able to recover that one at his leisure, and Kai was undoubtedly challenging a room deeper in the House. That seemed to be everything to his life these days.

But those were the two most dangerous Travelers whose blades he didn't have, so he decided to be certain.

"Tartarus, go check the seventh bedroom," he said. "Down the hall on the left, marked with a large circle and two smaller circles."

The Incarnation's armor creaked as he stared at Indirial with blank clockwork eyes, as though trying to figure out who was giving him orders.

Indirial stared back, until finally Tartarus turned to march down the hallway.

If Azura was anywhere, it was probably with Simon, but the Fangs could sometimes be kept in the bedrooms instead of the entry hall. There was no telling where Kai or Mithra were; as far as Indirial knew, Kai had never used Valin's bedroom, even though Mithra would have granted him access. It wasn't worth chasing down all the possibilities looking for Kai, not when Kai was far more likely to lock himself in the House anyway. That was what he'd done for practically twenty-five years. If Azura was in the bedroom, then Simon was disarmed, and that was a bonus. If not, then Indirial got the chance to challenge the boy for his blade.

Either way, it was a win for him.

Then he noticed the Eldest was missing.

Kai stood on a circle of earth in a sea of darkness.

All around him, in every direction, was complete emptiness. He could still see, somehow, as though he and his little chunk of rock and dirt were outlined in dim light. Not that there was much to see, in this room.

Idly he wondered if the room had a name. Probably not; it served no function, and as far as he knew, granted no power. It did, however, have a guardian.

Standing on his circle of earth, knees bent, Mithra held before him in both hands, Kai waited.

As usual, he heard the guardian before he saw it: the ringing rattle of steel against steel, growing until it was louder than thunder, getting closer. He closed his eyes, focusing on the sound. For the tenth time that minute, he wished for his dolls.

Then he threw himself to the side as a chain the width of a house drove through empty space, missing him by a hair.

The chain seemed to scream like an enraged bull, its links whipping by one after the other, wider around than his body, faster than a speeding horse. He ran Mithra's edge along the chain, letting her blade throw up sparks against the chain's seemingly infinite steel.

It roared again. As the guardian chain stretched out, it seemed miles long against the darkness, its head looping up and around to come lung-ing back down toward Kai like a striking snake.

He leaped from his circle of earth, suspended over the void for one long second before he crashed back down onto a second floating island of soil and stone.

The chain's head slammed into the circle where he had first stood. It didn't blast straight through the earth, as he would have expected, but pushed it down instead like a hammer driving a nail.

Then the darkness seemed to peel away from itself, black becoming storm-gray, and the Eldest Nye stood beside him on his little island.

"Ah, and here you are, to spoil another wonderful day," Kai said.

For once, the Eldest wasn't in the mood to trade insults. "The House is under attack."

From the void, the head of the steel chain gleamed, rushing up at him like a blacksmith's hammer big enough to knock the tower off a castle. He was too far away from the next island to jump, even with Benson's steel run-ning through him, so he focused on his target destination and called smoke.

As usual, turning into smoke felt like having his body pulled apart. It was oddly painless, but he had the disturbing sense of falling, of drifting apart, of becoming nothing.

And then, in a black cloud, he puffed back into existence on the distant circle of earth. The giant chain circled the island he had left like a con-fused snake whose prey had disappeared.

He could see, now, why Valin had never liked to call smoke. He couldn't see or hear anything in transit, and there was no changing his route mid-way. Once he called smoke, he wouldn't reassemble until his pieces reached their destination. It was risky, and prone to manipulation by a clever opponent.

Besides, he felt like he was going to drift away and ceased to exist every time he used it. He wasn't sure he'd ever get used to that.

"You have inherited this responsibility," the Eldest hissed, right in his ear. "You must defend the House."

Kai almost groaned. He had dared to hope that the Eldest had been killed when the chain attacked the last island. The Nye could manipulate and communicate with the intelligent guardians, but some of the creatures this deep in the House had no minds to speak of. This chain was likely incapable of processing any thought other than 'destroy all intruders,' so the Eldest would not be able to exercise any authority over it.

That was a very comforting thought. If Kai weren't completely sure he would die the instant his steel ran out, he would live here permanently.

"Lead the way through the dark, O shifting shadow," Kai said, with a bow. Without another word, not even a taunt, the Eldest took off. He leaped from island to island, heading for the door floating in space.

Kai followed, his steel waning. He still had a few minutes left, enough to get him through the House, but he tried to keep his steel called as often as he could, now. The cool power rushing through his veins was the only thing that calmed the throbbing burn in his back. Perhaps it was time for another healing bath, to push back the fire behind his kidney.

After he dealt with whoever was attacking Valinhall.

When the Tartarus Incarnation reached the seventh bedroom, he reached two ginger fingers out and turned the doorknob. Nothing happened. Indirial had ordered him to avoid damage to the bedroom doors if possible, because he wanted to limit Valinhall's destruction as much as possible. He would need the Territory intact.

A face full of clockwork gears turned toward Indirial, awaiting new instructions.

The bedroom doors were a part of Indirial now; he could sense them in his mind, feel them refusing to give in to the strength of Tartarus. He twisted his thoughts, granting the Incarnation permission to enter the room.

Tartarus tried again, but nothing had changed.

Indirial crossed his arms, thinking. Maybe the bedrooms were bound to the Dragon's Fangs in a rule of Valinhall so deep that even he couldn't change it. Or maybe he could, if he was in the Territory itself, and not standing on the brink of a Gate. For a moment the temptation to enter the House was almost overwhelming; he belonged inside, it was a part of him, just as he was a part of it. He belonged in Valinhall like water belonged in the ocean, and he *knew* that if he stepped inside, everything would be all right…

He moved back a pace or two. As tempting as it would be to set foot in the House, the King had earned his loyalty. Who would he be if he denied proper rewards to the warriors that earned them?

Besides, there was one law respected in Valinhall above all others: force.

"Break it down," he ordered. The Tartarus Incarnation stared at him with eyes of blank metal gears—he didn't know Indirial, and clearly didn't fully understand why he had to follow the Valinhall Incarnation's orders. Indirial stared back, calm and unmoving. "I represent the Incarnation of Ragnarus in this matter," he said, in cold tones appropriate to the Overlord of Cana. "If you disobey me in this, you will answer to him. Now, when I command you to destroy, you *destroy.*"

The Incarnation snarled, a sound like a quick avalanche, but he drew back a fist to do as commanded. His blow shattered the door, and his shoulders broke the frame as he forced his way inside. From the cracks and bangs issuing from within the bedroom, Indirial assumed that Tartarus was stretching his command to destroy as far as it would go. It was the action of a petty child, breaking whatever he could reach, but anything in that room could be replaced.

Then Indirial heard the screams.

Kai flew through room after room, passing at last into the familiar parts of the House. "Where are the others, may I ask?"

"I locked the family in their gallery," the Eldest responded. He didn't seem to be moving any faster than a walk, but somehow he was matching Kai in speed. "Simon is away, and Denner has had his Dragon's Fang removed. I doubt he is aware, or he would have banished it and re-summoned it already. I fear that Ragnarus will soon prevent that course of action entirely."

"I'm surprised you spared the girl and the old man," Kai said idly, dodging around the yellow-lit columns of the courtyard.

"They face two Incarnations," the Eldest said. "That would not be a test, it would be murder. I am no murderer."

Kai chuckled at that as he leaped over the healing pool, landing on the rough stone of the other side without slowing. "Of course not," he said. "Just a killer."

"There is a difference."

The Eldest pulled open the bathroom door and Kai sped out, into the room beyond.

Then he stopped.

He could see the hallway from there, and the bedrooms on either side. One of the rooms was shattered, the door broken off its hinges. Distant, whispered screams, threats, and horrified gasps drifted from inside.

Kai didn't remember calling smoke, but the next he knew, he had re-formed inside the seventh bedroom.

The shelf holding his precious little ones, the shelf he had carved, polished, and installed himself, had been destroyed. His dolls were scattered all over the floor.

And they were hurting. He could feel their pain like it was his—no, this was worse because it *wasn't* his.

Rebekkah's left arm had been half torn off at the shoulder. She clutched it with her right, glaring murder at the Tartarus Incarnation and threatening death in her mind. Lilia crawled away from the metal giant's stomping boots, her white dress torn and both her feet crushed. Gloria wept into her hands, her hair and dress torn, her chest cracked. Still others had cracks, or fractures, or were simply frightened.

But Otoku lay on the floor under Tartarus' feet, motionless, staring up at the ceiling with one eye. The other side of her face had been crushed, torn away, ripped casually from her head.

Kai knelt beside her, ignoring the ten-foot metal giant standing behind him. He laid Mithra down on the ground, and gently took Otoku up in both hands. He smoothed her dress. He straightened her hair.

Well, she sent, her whispered voice weak. *At least I'll look good while I die.*

And so she did.

CHAPTER 22
GRIEF

The Endross Incarnation hovered over the Damascan camp on storm-cloud wings, occasionally throwing a bolt or a ball of lightning. He was making some speech about how the world would burn, all its citizens his fearful subjects, and Simon had finally stopped listening. It didn't make any sense.

He stood inside the same tent that sheltered Leah, peeking out the tent-flap to watch the Incarnation. He kept his hood up in case he was spotted, calling as little Nye essence as he could. At this rate, he should remain shrouded from the Incarnation's sight for…five, maybe ten more minutes.

Simon drove Azura into the ground at an angle, trying to figure out what Endross was up to. It looked like he was trying to avoid killing any-one, against all reason. Simon had fought the last Incarnation of Endross, and even been present when this Traveler had snapped and Incarnated. More than any other of their kind, the Endross Incarnations acted like natural disasters, tearing the land and the people around them apart.

The Endross Incarnation should be anything *but* restrained. So what was going on?

Leah had spun out three or four floating Lirial crystals, which zipped out of the tent to collect the reports of various Travelers around the camp. None of them had seen any actual casualties that could be directly at-tributed to the Incarnation. The Endross Travelers were baffled. Some of the monsters they saw running free were more than capable of tearing through crowds of soldiers like a fox through a henhouse. But they were acting like leashed hounds.

"Maybe he really is in control of himself," Leah suggested, after review-ing the latest report in one of her crystals.

Simon didn't say anything, but he couldn't believe it. In his experience, assuming that the enemy was *less* dangerous than he looked would lead straight to gruesome injury or horrible death.

"Surely it's possible," she said defensively, as though he'd spoken his doubts aloud. "The Helgard and Avernus Incarnations could carry on perfectly intelligible conversations. So could Alin, and so can this Endross, it seems. A measure of intelligence suggests some free will, don't you think?"

"I don't think they're stupid," he said. "Not most of them. And it's not like I think they're out of control. I think that whatever they're doing…it makes sense to them. It's the only logical thing for them to do."

Leah's blue eyes were distant, considering. Her raven let out a *caw* that seemed approving.

"It's like when I fought Valin," Simon went on. "He didn't think he was going crazy, killing everybody he ran into. He was attacking people to see if they were strong enough to handle it. He thought he was *helping* them."

"So what does this Endross think he's doing?" Leah asked. Simon had no response to that.

But something else had started to bother him.

A sense of dread had begun creeping over him, raising goosebumps, filling his heart with a feeling of sickening tragedy. It was the strangest thing: they didn't feel like *his* emotions, as though someone were pressing their feelings on him from the outside. He could think about it intellectually and realize that there was no reason to feel this way, but that didn't shake the nauseous dread.

"I think…I think something bad happened," he said. He knew it sounded stupid, and Leah raised one eyebrow at him, but he couldn't think of a better way to say it. Somehow, he knew something terrible had happened to someone. Or maybe…was about to happen.

Above the camp, behind the Endross Incarnation—who was still giving a speech that made him sound like a newly installed tyrant—a dark figure rose slowly into the air. It looked like a man in armor, wearing a helmet covered in dark spires and holding a staff. His armor was black, edged in gold, and set with rubies. Another ruby capped his staff, and nestled in his crown above his forehead.

His skin glistened in the sunlight, as though he wore whirling metallic tattoos of red and gold, and one of his eyes blazed red.

"Leah," Simon said, his voice dry. "You need to come see this."

She hurried over to the tent flap without a word, pushing him aside so she could see out. "Oh, no," Leah whispered. "Oh, Maker, please no."

She seemed to realize something, and she jerked her head around, searching for something along the ground in the tent. When she saw the Lightning Spear lying nearby, she snapped out a hand to summon it into her palm.

It vanished.

All the dolls were absolutely silent.

"Mithra," the Tartarus Incarnation rumbled. He bent at the waist to pick up the Wanderer's silver-and-gold sword.

Kai started to laugh.

It started in his chest, an involuntarily convulsion that shook him, tearing out of him until he couldn't help but cackle, chortle, positively *choke* in spasms of mirth. This was too much. He'd finally left them alone, tried to stay away like they wanted, respected Azura's choice. And this was what happened. *This was what happened.*

He laughed until tears streamed down his face as the Tartarus Incarnation scooped up the sword and started to walk away.

Abruptly quiet, Kai held out a hand to the crowd of dolls.

"Caela, if you would," he said smoothly. Caela rose to her feet and hopped up onto his arm without a word. Reaching up with her wooden hands, she tightened her bonnet.

Go, she said.

Kai exploded into action. His steel had been running out, but he did not accept that. As he'd done once before, he reached deeper into Benson's basement until the steel skeleton's burning blue eyes loomed in his mind.

Kai, my friend, Benson began, *you look—*

Kai *ripped* the power from him, and steel flowed through his muscles in a torrent. His leap took him over the Tartarus Incarnation's shoulder, until he almost hit the ceiling, but as he passed over the Incarnation, he seized its breastplate in both hands.

When he landed in the hallway, he pulled the Incarnation down with him.

The giant flopped over onto its stomach, blindly waving Mithra. The edge of the Dragon's Fang scraped at the walls and doorframes of the hallway, leaving shallow gouges. With its free hand, Tartarus pulled a steel spike out of midair and drove it at Kai's neck.

Behind, Caela snapped.

Kai leaned his head to the right, and the spike drove through empty air. He grabbed it with his own free hand, jerking the weapon out of the Incarnation's grip and tossing it to the ground.

He kept walking forward, dragging the ten-foot titan behind him like a struggling child.

He didn't walk back to the entry hall, though he was vaguely aware of a stone giant and a shadowy figure back there, as well as a swirling Gate. Now, he had a new plan. Someone had sent this Incarnation into his Territory, into his home, to kill his dolls.

Kai wasn't satisfied with breaking the enemy's weapon. He would break the enemy.

When he finally reached the door to the forge, Kai picked up the Tartarus Incarnation with both hands and used him as a hammer, slamming him once, twice, three times against the door until it broke inward.

This is the second time he's broken this door, Kai thought. *Naughty, naughty.*

Inside the next door, the Agnos family waited. They screamed and scattered as he walked in, dragging an Incarnation behind him. Andra and Erastes stood in front of the others, Erastes clutching a Tartarus steel infantry sword and Andra a smith's hammer.

Kai paid them no heed. When the Tartarus Incarnation reached out for a workbench to try and pull himself up, Kai broke the bench into splinters. When he tried to throw a blade at one of the bystanders, Caela warned him, and Kai stomped his hand until it crumpled.

When he finally reached the gallery, he heaved the Incarnation in the room ahead of him. Behind, the hidden door slid shut.

The Incarnation placed one metal hand on the counters to either side of him, pushing himself up. One of his gauntlets still gripped Mithra's hilt. Above, five complete masks—one more than last time—looked down on them.

"I am bound by honor to tell you that I was operating under restrictions the last we fought," the Tartarus Incarnation grated out.

Kai didn't care. He looked up at the masks on the wall. "You have no guard," he said. "No trial. No way to release your power." He pointed at the Incarnation, still looking up at the masks. "So with my own trial, I will prove my worth."

Tartarus struck at Kai with Mithra's blade, but Caela called out, and Kai ducked. He never glanced at his opponent.

"The enemy is strong," he continued. "The enemy is here. The enemy threatens us all. It's carrying Valin's own blade, and if that's not enough for you, then I don't know *what else you want!*" By the end he was screaming at the masks, at the room, at Valinhall itself.

The sword fell like an executioner's axe, and Kai stepped to one side. *If defeating the same Incarnation twice in one room doesn't count as earning a power, I don't know what does.*

Caela's mental voice was grim. *If it doesn't, then tear this House down and build it again,* she said. *Because I won't want to live here anymore.*

Tartarus swung the sword at Kai's neck, and Kai stepped forward, inside Mithra's reach, calling stone.

His skin hardened, and he struck upward, driving his fist at the Incarnations' descending wrist.

The metal arm collapsed in on itself with a deafening crunch, and steel fingers flew open. Blindly, Kai reached out and snatched Mithra's hilt with his left hand, the blade reversed.

Then he called wind, letting the power flow down into his sword, strengthening and sharpening.

Blades appeared in the Tartarus Incarnation's hands, but not fast enough.

Mithra passed through the Incarnation's neck, sending his head clattering to the floor in another spray of gears and molten metal. The body jerked and twisted, but it didn't attack anymore.

But Kai wasn't one to lose the same way twice.

He slashed through the Incarnation's breastplate with a wind-enhanced strike, tearing open the gears and springs inside, ripping the armor away plate by plate and severing each limb. When the Incarnation was little more than scrap metal, he reached in and pulled out something that looked like a red, pulsing, metal heart.

Ragnarus, he thought, and rage swelled within him. *I will tear apart the Crimson Vault with my bare hands.*

I...don't think it was Ragnarus, Caela said reluctantly. *I feel someone outside the Gate. A Valinhall Incarnation.*

Kai froze. Last time they had entered the House through a gatecrawler, so he had assumed...but the Gate was clean and white, not angry and red. He remembered the shadow he'd glimpsed outside, at the end of the hallway.

One of his own, betraying him, attacking him in the House.

Again.

Kai collected what he needed from the gallery, stalking out into the workshop. "Take the scrap metal to the furnace," he said, on his way out. No one said anything.

The Eldest was waiting for him in the forge, so he tossed the Ragnarus heart at the Nye. "Cast this into the void. Let it drift away from existence for all time."

He bowed, his sleeves folded together. "It shall be done."

The tip of Mithra's point winked under the Eldest Nye's hood, and Kai slowly moved the flat of the blade upward, lifting the Nye's head. "If I find that you have tried to bend it to your will, you will answer to me," Kai said softly. "Destroy it."

The Eldest bowed again, and Kai walked out of the hallway to the entry hall.

The Gate had vanished.

Indirial felt Kai's rage, felt one of the daughters of wind die, felt the destruction of Tartarus.

He couldn't help but wonder if he'd made a mistake.

When the Ornheim Incarnation left Valinhall, Indirial considered for a moment leaving the Gate open. Kai would certainly charge after him in a rage, and they would have their showdown. After all, Kai had beaten him once. Maybe he could do it again.

The thought was tempting, but the mission came first. And Kai wasn't much of a threat, not after twenty-five years of isolation and slow, creeping insanity. Indirial would be better off cherishing the memories of their first fight.

Ornheim gathered up the three Dragon's Fangs, and the two of them began walking along the wall, preparing to jump off. They needed to reach King Zakareth as soon as possible, so he could seal the Fangs in the Vault. There, they couldn't be banished, and the remaining Valinhall Travelers would be all but powerless...until they were tested and proven worthy.

One Incarnation for three Dragon's Fangs and, essentially, control over Valinhall. King Zakareth would probably consider that a good trade.

Ornheim stepped off the wall, landing in a crater far below, and set off at a jog toward Leah's camp. Indirial began to follow him when something burned at the back of his awareness, like a mole trying to burrow its way into the back of his skull. He turned and saw an angry red light where the Valinhall Gate had once hung.

Five spiked black fingers stuck out into midair, clawing the Gate back open.

The black gauntlet: Valinhall's gatecrawler.

The call of the frozen horn would seal even this Gate, and for a moment Indirial wondered if he ought to try. It would be a race to see whether the horn's powers ran out first or the gauntlet's, and it would eat up precious time.

Now, it seemed like he would get the fight he wanted.

With Vasha gleaming and ready at his side, Indirial grinned.

With the spiked fingertips of his black gauntlet, Kai gutted the world. He tore a gaping red hole where the Gate used to be, and stepped through it. Wind tore at his clothes, at the hair over his eyes, as he walked onto the mighty walls of Cana.

The stones of the fortifications had been marked by the presence of Incarnations. One stretch of rock was dyed red as though it had been soaked in blood. The Crimson Vault. A few paces away, the wall's bricks had melted and flowed into a small cave set with sparkling crystals. The Maelstrom of Stone. Outside the walls, pillars of snow and ice lowered in a makeshift staircase heading toward a distant camp. The Tower of Winter.

And a few paces away, the stone formed neat squares of smoothly polished tile. The House of Blades.

And on those tiles, the Valinhall Incarnation stood ready for battle.

His boots were dark and practical, his pants black, his shirt crisp white and missing the sleeves. The chains that spiraled up his tanned arms glistened in the sun, reflecting light like a steel mirror. An otherworldly cloak, woven from what looked like solid shadows, rose from the ground behind him. It flowed like a cape, untouched by the breeze, and rose in a cowl over his head.

Two things shone from inside the darkness of that hood: the twin violet circles of his eyes, and his bright smile.

Of course it was Indirial.

It had to be Indirial, because Kai had once let him live. This was all Kai's fault. If he had killed Indirial a quarter of a century ago, then he wouldn't have to worry about this. Or if he had let Indirial kill him. If he hadn't taken in Simon, then Azura would never have abandoned him, and he could have protected Otoku as she deserved.

But then, if he had killed Indirial, then Indirial would never have saved the child Simon's life. And then Azura would never have had the chance to choose another.

No matter how he twisted it, everything came down to Kai's poor decisions.

Indirial leaned forward, Vasha in one hand, Korr dangling from his neck. "Challenge me, Traveler," he said. "Come on!"

The wound in Kai's back burned, but now he didn't care about the pain. It felt like a fire at his back, driving him forward. His minutes were numbered, now that he'd left the protection of the House and the poison of Ragnarus could work at its full capacity. Besides, no matter how much power he'd taken from Benson, it would wear out eventually. And his chains had already reached past his shoulders, from his work in the deep rooms and his fight against Tartarus.

Indirial could move faster than Kai, could hit harder, could last longer. But Kai only had to last long enough to see him die.

The mask Kai pulled from his belt wasn't as deadly looking as Simon's. It was half white and half gray, with two rectangular slits for his eyes and no mouth. He slid the metal up, under his bangs.

If this doesn't work, I will tear Valinhall down to its foundations.

Oh, I wouldn't worry about that, Caela said.

When he moved his hand away, the mask stayed. Steel coursed through him in a rolling, icy storm. Chains crawled across his skin even faster, but what did he care? He could *fight*.

Indirial blurred toward him, powered by the Nye essence that Kai had never earned. If he were on his own, he would never have been able to react.

But he wasn't alone.

Left, Caela called. *Left, then right, then straight ahead.*

Kai stepped forward and swept Mithra up and to the left, knocking Vasha's cracked blade wide. Indirial came in with another strike to the left side, but it was a feint. He reversed the blow, his blade flowing from the right, but Kai turned it aside again. When Indirial brought Vasha down with both hands, Kai raised Mithra and caught the edge of his blade on his own.

The gold-and-silver Dragon's Fang of Valin, the Wanderer, met the cracked and pitted blade of his first student. For a moment they stayed evenly matched, quivering with tension, Kai's mask only a pace from Indirial's grin.

Then, in a puff of smoke, Kai vanished.

He'll expect you behind him, Caela sent, as he dispersed. He'd anticipated that.

Which was why he formed above Indirial, falling toward the Incarnation's head, his blade reversed so that he could drive his blade down and through Indirial, pinning him to the stone like an insect to a board.

That was the plan, anyway, but something made the Valinhall Incarnation look up, and he almost seemed to blur as he sidestepped, moving so fast that Kai couldn't see it. He called wind anyway, and when he landed, his sharpened Dragon's Fang drove into the stone wall of Cana as if into soft mud.

Vasha's blade flashed toward his throat, but he disappeared into another cloud of black smoke.

They continued that way, evenly matched, for a tight handful of seconds that stretched on like minutes. Indirial was too fast for Kai to land a clean hit, but between Caela and the smoke, Kai could avoid any hit the

Incarnation delivered.

Thanks to the mask, they were evenly matched in strength. But with every second, his wound tightened and burned worse, until even his fury couldn't ignore it. And the ends of his chain-marks had started creeping up to his neck.

I won't be able to finish this before the chains reach their end, will I?

Not unless he throws himself off the wall, Caela said. *Probably not even then.*

Indirial ripped a chunk of stone out of the wall with one hand and hurled it at Kai. Mithra sliced it in half, the two pieces flying off to either side, but it was a distraction: Indirial flew straight toward him, violet eyes glowing, Vasha pointed straight at Kai's chest.

He swung his blade with both hands, Mithra meeting Vasha strength-for-strength. The force almost knocked Kai off his feet, and he stumbled several paces backwards, almost knocking himself over onto his back.

His time was running out. At this rate, he'd never be able to avenge Otoku.

I need a new plan, he thought.

Simon watched as King Zakareth the Sixth, Incarnation of Ragnarus, defeated the Endross Incarnation in an entirely staged contest.

He and Leah stood with their cheeks pressed almost together, trying to see out the tent-flap without opening it. He felt a little ridiculous, like a child trying to spy on an adult's conversation, but two facts remained: they had to know what Zakareth was saying, and they couldn't risk being spotted. That meant peeking out of a tent like an eight-year-old.

Zakareth rose in the sky on a glowing platform—glowing red, of course—and stood there, with a staff in his right hand and the Lightning Spear in his left. If he'd been serious about attacking Endross, he would have thrown the Spear from the ground, not levitated up to fight him one-on-one.

The Endross Incarnation growled and spun when he realized Zakareth was there, throwing out both hands and blasting a double-fistful of lightning at the Ragnarus Incarnation.

The ruby on the top of the King's staff flashed, and there was a blinding explosion.

When Simon could see again, the Endross Incarnation was plummeting to the ground, trailing smoke. The King raised his staff again, and all the Endross Gates around the camp were swallowed by red light. Even the summoned creatures vanished.

"How did he do that?" Simon asked.

"I couldn't tell you," Leah said, in a flat voice. She seemed to be handling news of her father's survival and Incarnation better than Simon had thought she would.

King Zakareth raised his staff again, and the Endross Incarnation was hauled back up into the air by his throat. A glowing red collar wrapped around his neck.

"There's no Ragnarus weapon that does that many different things," Leah said. "He's cheating somehow."

Simon suspected that Incarnations were allowed to 'cheat' when it came to their own Territories, but he said nothing. Zakareth was already faking the fight; why not fake the extent of his own powers?

"I am the King of Damasca," the Incarnation announced, his voice carrying easily through the whole camp. "I have come to protect my people."

A few isolated cheers went up from around the camp, but even most of the soldiers in the royal army seemed too stunned by the turn of events to react.

"If you yield to my rule and guidance, Incarnation of Endross, you shall keep your life...though not your freedom. Do you submit?"

Simon couldn't imagine anyone believing a scene like that, even from a King. It sounded like Zakareth was reading off a page, like Alin reciting an old, memorized story around a bonfire.

"I humbly submit myself to you," the Endross Incarnation said, thus cementing his place in Damascan history as the worst actor of all time.

"Then kneel," the King said. Endross went to one knee in midair, effortlessly hovering.

If this wasn't practiced, how did he know that the Endross Incarnation could kneel in open air? Simon wondered. *I wouldn't have expected that.*

Not for the first time, he wished he'd brought a doll. The inside of his head seemed a lonely place without one of them around.

"Kneeling on air," Leah muttered. "That's a neat trick."

"Exactly!" Simon said. "Thank you. That's what my dolls would have said."

Out of the corner of her eye, she gave him a strange look.

In the sky, King Zakareth raised his staff and spear above his head. "People of Damasca! I have returned to you."

This time, there was a definite cheer from the camp below.

"I have been away for some time, securing the city of Cana. At this time, the city is open to you. You may now return to your homes."

The cheering grew louder, accompanied by a series of quiet murmurs.

"I regret to inform you that some of your friends and family, husbands and sons, wives and daughters, did not survive the war in Cana these past six months." His voice hardened. "For make no mistake, there was a war. But I—and the loyal citizens of Damasca still in the city—have emerged victorious."

"A war against who?" Simon asked, but Leah's tan skin was growing a shade paler with every word her father spoke.

"The Incarnations now bend knee to me and me alone," the King continued. "As should you. As will Enosh, very soon."

There was no cheering at this, but the confused murmurs intensified.

"You all have followed my daughter for half a year, and for this I commend you. She is my Successor, and a worthy Traveler of Ragnarus. But now I have returned, and I have no need of Heirs or Successors. With the full power of the nine Territories, I will lead you against Enosh. I will never leave you, I will never fail you, and I will crush them at last."

As he spoke each word, the ruby glow grew brighter and brighter around him, until at last he was surrounded by a scarlet aura like the one that had sheltered Cana for months.

The roar from the camp was almost deafening.

Simon didn't know what to make of half that speech, but the part about not needing any Heirs or Successors was fairly clear. "That's it," he said, reaching for Azura's hilt. "We need to get you out of here."

Leah laid a hand on his arm, stopping him. Her eyes shone with anger.

"He can follow me into the House," she said. "Especially if he was the one who took Indirial." Simon flinched at the idea that the Ragnarus Incarnation might have the Overlord of Cana under his control, but he had to admit that it seemed likely. "I need to Travel through the one place where he can't follow me. Or won't, at least."

She placed her palm flat against the empty air, and space bloomed into a swirling red Gate, opening onto a pair of silver double doors.

Leah and her raven stepped into Ragnarus.

"Find out what happened to Indirial," Leah ordered, as she walked through the Crimson Vault. Her red dress blended in perfectly with the light. "See if you can get the Valinhall Travelers all together; we might need them. And find out what my father wants. It sounds like he intends to attack Enosh, and if that's true..." She took a deep breath. "We might need to work with Alin."

Simon flinched at the thought, but he swept a bow anyway. He'd been working on that, and this time he thought he'd done a pretty good job.

She turned slightly and smiled at him. "Not bad, Simon."

He straightened. "When I've done all that, how will I find you?"

She shook her head, returning her attention to the silver doors. "When I've done what I need to, I will find you."

The Ragnarus Gate shrank, and Simon looked back out of the tent to find the King's blazing red eye locked on him. He reached for Azura.

Whatever she says, I think everything would be a whole lot simpler if I killed him right here, he thought. But Zakareth didn't attack.

And when Simon's grip closed around his Dragon's Fang, he realized whose fear and pain and panic he'd been sensing for the past few minutes. Azura's.

Her dread and grief crashed into him, and the pain hit him like the death of his mother all over again. A tear crawled down his cheek, and he didn't even know why.

What's going on? he asked, trying to send his thoughts to her the way he would with a doll.

She didn't say anything he could understand, but he felt another surge of grief, and a single image:

Otoku, half her face torn away, staring at the ceiling of the seventh bedroom, nothing more than lifeless wood.

Steel flooded him, and he raised his blade to begin cutting a Valinhall Gate right there in the tent. Someone had attacked his Territory, and if he had anything to say about it, they would never get a chance to escape.

No, wait…

He dropped the Gate. That wasn't the right place to go, and he knew it. No…Azura knew it. The enemy wasn't in the House. *So then, where?*

Behind him. He pushed out of the tent and saw, miles distant, the stone walls of Cana.

The enemy was there, sure as he knew his own name. But even with steel and essence in him, it would take minutes for him to cover that distance.

Simon didn't have minutes. Otoku's killer might be escaping even now. He pulled out the mask.

CHAPTER 23

A PAIR OF MASKS

The first time Indirial had fought with Kai, he hadn't expected much. Kai had been shorter, weaker, and slower…but somehow it hadn't mattered. With the help of those dolls of his, and some scary ability of Kai himself, the kid had been able to *predict* everything Indirial did. It didn't matter that Indirial was faster and stronger, with better reach. Kai anticipated every move Indirial made and positioned himself to meet it.

Before, that had driven Indirial half-crazy. He'd been fighting Kai to save Kai's life, in part. He'd seen through Valin's insanity, though Kai hadn't. He still wondered, sometimes, how they would have changed—how the world would have changed—if Kai had lost that day.

For one thing, there would have been no Travelers from Enosh on a rainy day nine years ago, looking for Valin's Hanging Tree. Simon's parents wouldn't have died, and he likely would have never become a Valinhall Traveler.

At the time, Indirial had known he was right, and Kai's resistance had filled him with frustrated anger.

Now, on the walls of Cana, he feinted at Kai's left side, changed direction to sweep at his throat and force him to back off, and then summoned a spear from the Valinhall armory to thrust at his chest. Kai didn't even blink at the feint, leaned back far enough to let Vasha's point scrape the chin of his white-and-gray mask, and then grabbed the spear below the head and pulled it, jerking Indirial off-balance. In one smooth motion, he pulled Indirial toward him and drove Mithra through his stomach.

Far from frustrated, Indirial didn't think he'd ever had a better time.

Valin had always spoken of the joy of battle, how there was no game greater than wagering your life in a contest of strength and skill between two evenly matched opponents, but Indirial had only ever caught glimpses of that in himself. He enjoyed using his Valinhall powers; how could he not? He could leap to the top of a tall building and look out over Cana, enjoying a view that only the Avernus fliers got to see. Unlike them, he didn't even have to worry about falling. Travelers held very little fear for him, because he knew that in a straightforward combat scenario, he would always hold the edge.

But he'd rarely felt the sheer thrill, the enjoyment of battle for its own sake. Not until now.

So he let Mithra slide in through his stomach, relished the distant pain of his mortal body. Kai had *earned* that. It was a beautiful move, and had Indirial been only human, that would have been enough to outplay him. Taking this hit was something like applause from an appreciative audience.

"Well done!" Indirial said, through a genuine grin. "I mean, wow, I've never seen anything like it."

While Indirial was talking, Kai released Mithra's hilt, pulled a two-headed battle-axe from the armory, and swung it at Indirial's neck. Indirial ducked under it—which felt a little more awkward than usual, considering the six feet of steel sticking through him.

He coughed up a little blood, idly wiping it away, and then pulled Mithra out of his stomach inch by inch. He tossed it underhand, back to Kai.

In a spray of green and gold sparks, his stomach knit itself back together.

Kai stepped forward with Mithra in both hands, working the forms as beautifully as if he were practicing in front of a mirror. He swept the blade diagonally up, then across, driving Indirial back. At some point, Indirial knew, his back would hit a wall. Kai was backing him into a corner. It was such a classic move that Indirial almost wanted to let him land it, but that would remove the spirit of the game, so right when he sensed he was about to be backed into a wall, he jumped. His strength as an Incarnation let him soar over Kai easily, even considering his reach with Mithra.

Kai had been waiting for him.

He hadn't banished the battle-axe after all. He had only dropped it. Indirial had stopped paying attention to the weapon after it left Kai's hand, but that was a mistake.

Kai scooped up the axe, big enough to bisect an ox, and hurled it one-handed. It spun over and over on its way to meet Indirial in the air.

He got Vasha up in time to deflect the axe-blade, but he didn't expect Kai to be right behind it, leaping after the weapon to clash with Indirial in midair. Indirial managed to twist out of the way, avoiding a Dragon's Fang through the chin by mere inches.

Indirial had tried that move earlier with a simple chunk of stone he'd torn off the wall, and now Kai copied him with a *battle-axe?*

He was falling down to the wall, but he already had his feet under him, and with the Nye essence it felt like a casual glide. "Is it the scroll?" Indirial called up. "Is that how you're doing this?" Kai had always claimed he had a power called the 'iron scroll,' or the 'black scroll' or some such thing, and that allowed him to understand the flow of combat better than anyone else. Indirial had never found such a power, but Kai definitely had some edge.

Indirial landed lightly, and Kai hurled a spear after him. He deflected it with the flat of his blade, watching Kai hit the wall in a crouch, Dragon's Fang held out to the side. Under his shaggy white hair, the white-and-gray mask was featureless. Pitiless. Cold.

It hadn't been long since Indirial had hated the masks, hated the very idea of them. Calling more power at the expense of increasing your debt to Valinhall seemed like the exact trap that had ensnared Valin. The same trap that had ensnared him, if he was honest.

But now? He liked the look of the masks. They would be the faceless executioners of Valinhall, and the last sight the unjust or unworthy would take to their graves would be a blank plate of gleaming metal.

Come to think of it, Indirial thought, *what about that debt?*

He glanced up at Kai's neck.

The black chains were only one link from completion.

All his life, Indirial had heard horror stories about what happened when two Incarnations existed at the same time. Most of them, it seemed, simply died. Others lost all their powers and went insane, or one lost their powers and the *other* their sanity. Valin always said that he'd personally witnessed a double Avernus Incarnation, where each Incarnation had *physically fused* with the other, creating a horrifying monstrosity with extra parts, both bird and human, constantly tugging between two wills.

Indirial wasn't quite sure how that would be possible, since all of Valin's life had passed while the Incarnations were sealed beneath the Hanging Trees. But he'd taken the stories to heart.

He let Vasha vanish and raised his empty hands.

"We should do this again, Kai," he said. "If I was…like I was before, you'd have killed me right now. But I'm not, and you can't. Now take off the mask."

Kai had paced back and forth on the wall while he was talking. He seemed to be limping, favoring his left leg. But when Indirial stopped, Kai puffed into smoke and swirled in Indirial's direction.

Look out, Korr warned. The violet flame burned at the heart of the smoke, flying along with the black stream, and came to rest in front of him.

So Kai was going for a frontal assault, then? Fine.

The white-haired Traveler manifested in front of Indirial with the point of his sword an inch from Indirial's heart. He pushed it up, skewering straight through the heart like a knife through an apple.

Blood welled up and flowed through Indirial's lips, filling his mouth with the taste of copper, but he finally had the chance he'd been looking for: he grabbed Kai's shoulder with one hand and his mask at the other, prying with all his strength and the full will of his Territory, trying to peel the mask off his old friend.

Kai jerked back, tearing the mask from Indirial's fingers. It was still stuck, so the Incarnation tried another tactic.

When Kai tried to pull Mithra out of Indirial's chest, Indirial held onto the blade and stepped forward.

Then he kicked Kai in the ribs.

Kai brought the Dragon's Fang with him, pulling it out of Indirial with a sucking noise. He flew through the air, blood trailing from his blade, and landed hard on his back at the foot of the still-open Valinhall Gate.

He writhed on the ground, in even more pain than the fall could account for. *That's right; he must have fallen on his wound.* So much the better for Indirial's purposes.

This time, when Indirial reached down to peel the mask away, Kai didn't resist.

The last link around his throat was half-formed, but if Simon's experience with the original mask was any indication, Kai wouldn't be able to call any powers from Valinhall for hours, if not days.

"You should have...left her alone," Kai said, choking up. "She didn't... deserve that."

Indirial let his joy fade a little; it wouldn't be appropriate to keep grinning in the face of Kai's obvious grief. "I didn't want any of them to die," the Incarnation said. "They're part of me, now. As are you."

He reached down and grabbed Mithra, summoning Vasha again so that he held a Dragon's Fang in each hand. All of the Wanderer's remaining swords were now in his possession, except for Simon's Azura. "Can you make it through the Gate, Kai?"

Laughter burbled up in Kai's throat, sounding like he had a throat full of blood.

Indirial sighed. "Kai, I can't believe how often we seem to have this conversation. Get back through the Gate, or you're going to die. The fight's over. I won."

"Hmmmm?" Kai said, his voice smooth. "Did you?"

He reached out, and the air shimmered as he summoned something from the Valinhall armory: a giant hammer, mirror-bright Tartarus steel from head to hilt.

With an audible click, the black chains around his throat snapped together.

Indirial's mind shattered, re-formed, shattered again. He was vaguely aware of falling to his knees, but he also felt the cold stone against his back, the burning Ragnarus sword wound in his back, and an overwhelming grief for a broken doll in a red dress. Steel shifted and pushed like needles beneath his skin, as patches of his flesh painfully hardened.

He was looking up into his own eyes, which burned with violet flame like a warning from Korr.

No, wait…that *was* a warning from Korr.

Danger! His advisor shouted.

With the last of his strength, Kai tossed the Tartarus steel hammer over the wall.

And Simon rose up from the walls of Cana, masked in mirrored steel and dark iron. His cloak trailed black behind him, the hood raised. In his right hand he held Azura, long and gleaming silver, and with his left hand he plucked the falling hammer from midair.

He seemed to hover for an instant, a specter of shadow and bright steel like an Arbiter of Naraka come to deliver judgment.

Indirial had one moment to think, *That is exactly how a Traveler of Valinhall should look.*

Then Simon struck.

That glimpse of Simon was the one clear look that Indirial got. As soon as the boy started moving with his hood up, the essence of the Nye flowing through him, Indirial had a hard time looking at him straight on. He wondered briefly if certain Incarnations had an easier time looking through the Nye cloak than others, but then Simon was on him.

His first strike was a slash with Azura, which Indirial had to nudge with the Dragon's Fang in his left hand. Simon followed up with a one-handed swing of the hammer, aimed at Indirial's head.

Ordinarily, he would have dodged, continuing his attack from a lower angle. Perhaps ducked under the hammer and driven his sword up into Simon's stomach. But he had a good sense of Kai's strength when he was wearing the mask, and he didn't *really* want to kill Simon. The boy wouldn't give him the same fight as Kai, but maybe in twenty or thirty years he'd turn into something truly spectacular. Indirial the Overlord, Indirial, son of Aleias, and the Valinhall Incarnation were all in agreement: they wanted to see Simon reach his potential.

So he caught the blow one-handed with Vasha. Assuming that Simon in his mask was just as strong as Kai had been, Indirial wouldn't need to meet the attack with his full strength.

Indirial had already begun planning his next strike—stepping forward and hitting Simon in the head with the flat of Mithra's blade, hopefully tripping him up and letting Indirial subdue him unharmed—when he realized that the hammer was *still coming.*

Under the Nye essence, the instant had felt much longer, but the Tartarus steel head of Simon's hammer met Vasha and didn't even slow down. It was headed straight for Indirial's temple.

In a split second, he redirected all his strength as the Valinhall Incarnation into supporting his one-handed defense, pushing against the hammer with everything he had.

Superhuman strength or not, there was only so much he could do against momentum with poor footing and no leverage.

The hammer, along with the back of his own blade, smacked Indirial in the face.

Even as an Incarnation, he felt that pain. The hammer smashed the side of his head, whiting out his world and sending him flying into a stone wall. He hit hard enough to crack the bricks, along with most of his bones, before flopping down to the ground. Which, he couldn't help but notice, was also solid stone.

As his body knit itself together in a blinding display of gold and green, he came to a realization: *That mask is stronger than the other one.*

Oh. So that's how Valin lost.

Still, Simon didn't have the Ragnarus blade that had crippled Kai and killed Valin—however impermanent *that* had turned out to be. No matter how strong the boy was, he didn't have a way to kill Indirial. And he was still shackled by Valinhall's chains, so he was working under a time limit. The only thing Indirial had to do was stall—

His world shook again. He was staring up at the blue sky, his white hair falling into his eyes, then he was on his hands and knees, staring at the stone, then he was Kai again, whose skin was slowly turning to steel…

Kai was transforming. He had already half-changed into an Incarnation, and if he kept going, either he or Indirial would die.

Indirial's hand grew numb and began to shake. He tried to make a fist, but he couldn't control his body. Indirial and Kai both shook at the same time, and Kai and Indirial felt both sensations together.

With a supreme effort of will, Indirial wrenched his consciousness back into the right body. He forced himself up.

Black-cloaked Simon, with his cold metal expression, was swinging the hammer in both hands. It came straight for Indirial, and he was having trouble remembering why that was supposed to be a bad thing…

The hammer hit him like a falling star, and for a while he knew nothing.

When he came to, he was lying on the floor of the hallway in the House of Blades. He glanced to his left. Yes, there was the bedroom where he'd spent most of his life. Where was Valin? *The graveyard,* part of him murmured. Where were the others? *The graveyard.*

Gold and green sparks flickered in front of his eyes—or possibly *in* his eyes—and he leaped to his feet.

The Gate! He had to reach the Gate.

He was there almost as soon as he'd thought of it, his body reacting with superhuman speed. He pressed through the Gate, and it was like walking into an invisible screen door. He could almost walk through, but the air itself pressed against him, holding him back in a solid barrier, as though the world itself wanted him on this side. He strained and pushed with all his will as the Incarnation of Valinhall, but the screen never tore.

He reached out for Vasha, and realized that she wasn't at his side.

Where was she? Not on the rack, all the racks were empty. He tried to summon her, but she didn't come. Where...

He looked out through the Gate. There, on the walls of Cana, where he'd tossed every other Dragon's Fang he could find, Vasha lay. Unreachable.

Outside the Gate, Simon peeled the mask away and collapsed. Inside the Territory, Indirial pulled up a padded chair and sat in it backwards, straddling the back.

He'd thought he would have felt bitter at being so thoroughly defeated, but he felt more pride than anything else. Simon and Kai had both surpassed his expectations, and both of them for the second time.

Maybe he should learn to stop underestimating them.

"Well played," he said.

CHAPTER 24
THE END OF A TRAVELER

Simon commanded his body to move, to do anything other than sit slumped against the edge of the wall, but he could barely raise one trembling hand. At least he hadn't lost consciousness this time; he hadn't worn the mask to its absolute limit, so he could stay seated, and could even move his limbs an inch or two at a time. That was about as far as his body would take him.

But he needed to do more than sit here. He needed to help Kai.

Kai lay on the stones less than a pace away, covered in blood and steel. It looked like the Incarnation had begun with his hand and then gone terribly wrong: one hand was encased by a mirror-bright gauntlet of metal that ended at the wrist, but the rest of his body was practically torn apart. A metal spike had burst from his elbow, beneath the skin, trickling blood onto the ground. Two blades pushed out from his shoulders, also dripping blood.

Patches of mirrored steel had replaced his skin seemingly at random, and clumps of his hair had started to transform as well. Most of the hair hung naturally: shaggy, grimy white, smudged by dirt and blood. The transformed patches didn't look like real human hair. It was bright white, strangely stiff-looking, and blood seemed to flow through it without leaving any spots behind.

The whole of Kai made him look like a hideous abomination, like a man and an artificial creature from deep in a Territory had been blended randomly together.

That's almost exactly what happened, Caela sent. *Oh, Kai.*

Kai's body shook again, with another spasm, and a dagger-blade pushed itself up from inside his rib cage. His white-gray mask clattered to the ground, the force that held it onto Kai's head vanishing. Simon forced himself to look away.

Call Andra or Erastes, Simon ordered her. *We have to get him into the pool.*

Caela lay by Kai's body, staring up at the sky from under her blue bonnet. Simon wasn't sure if it was coincidence or not, but one of her wooden hands lay on Kai's arm.

Not the pool, she said. *We need to get him into the bedroom.*

How will that help?

That's where he wants to die.

Simon refused to accept that. Kai's chest still rose and fell with each breath, and his head moved from side to side. If he could still communicate with Caela, he could still be saved.

He looked over at the shadow-cloaked Incarnation sitting in the entry hall. "Indirial, can you move him?"

Indirial waved at the Gate. "You saw what happened when I tried to leave. Besides, the pool won't save him."

"If you can't help, then get someone who can."

"No one can."

"Then get the Eldest!" Simon shouted. "Go find him, and promise him whatever he wants to get him here *now.*"

Finally, Simon managed to push himself up to his feet. He swayed and almost fell when a wave of dizziness caught him, but he caught himself with one hand on the edge of the wall. Good. He was recovering much faster than before. His chains were still reaching up to his neck, so that could be a problem, but he surely had enough time left to drag Kai through the House.

Where's Andra? Simon asked Caela.

On her way, the doll responded. *She and Erastes will take him.*

By the time Andra hurried into the entry hall, carrying an ordinary sword and looking ready for a fight, Simon had managed to stand on his own. He stood, wavering, just outside the Gate, trying to muster up the strength to drag Kai on his own.

Andra stopped at the edge of the hallway, staring at Indirial's shadowed form. Warily, she raised her blade. Erastes hurried in behind her, chain mail jangling, and his Tartarus steel sword was out of its sheath and pointed at Indirial before he even made it into the entry hall.

"Leave them alone, Indirial," Simon said, trying to inject some authority into his voice. He was worried that he only sounded tired. "Don't hurt them."

Indirial's eyebrows lifted. "You defeated me in combat. I won't stand in your way." His violet eyes turned to Kai. "I won't help you, either, but I won't get in your way."

Another spike pushed out of Kai's skin, and he groaned weakly.

"Help him!" Simon demanded. Andra and Erastes glanced at each other, and then they were out of the Gate, bending down to grab Kai under the shoulders.

"What happened to Seijan?" Andra asked, as she pulled Kai into Valinhall, moving carefully to avoid cutting herself on his spikes.

Her Dragon's Fang, Caela reminded him.

"Oh, right. It...I mean, he...she?" Now that he knew the Dragon's Fangs could think for themselves, at least a little, what was he supposed to call them? "You should probably banish it and re-summon it," he said at last.

Indirial smiled a little over the back of his chair. "You should hurry up about it. The King can seal them in the Vault, and then you'll never get them back without his permission."

Andra stuck one arm out, past the Gate, and in the entry hall Seijan appeared. It was half the size of Azura but roughly the same shape, with its shorter blade speckled with spots of what looked like ink. Andra glanced behind her and sighed with relief, then turned back to Kai.

"Take him straight to the pool," Simon said.

Erastes nodded and started pulling Kai toward the hallway, but Andra hesitated. "Your doll said..."

"I don't *care* what she said," Simon snapped. "Take him to the pool." Was he the only one who hadn't given up yet?

Andra and Erastes pulled Kai into the hallway, and Simon glanced behind him. The top of Cana's wall was little more than a ruin. Not only had chunks been broken, crushed, or sliced out of the stone, the evidence of the Incarnations' presence remained: pools where the bricks had turned red, a cave where the rock had flowed into something resembling a natural formation, a stretch of tile shaped by Valinhall that had been shattered by Valinhall's powers.

On that ruin lay three Dragon's Fangs.

He'd dropped Azura when he needed to use the hammer, and there she sat, shining in the sun and almost seven feet long. A few paces away, Vasha—bigger and thicker, riddled with cracks—sat where it had flown from Indirial's hand. At the foot of the Gate, in a pool of Kai's blood, lay Mithra.

The Wanderer's sword looked much like Azura except for the line of gold running up the blade from hilt to point. The three blades sat there, visible from the Territory, and Simon knew he'd need to pick them up. They were too valuable to leave sitting out in the open, but how was he supposed to carry them? He could banish Azura, but he wouldn't be able to lift the others without calling steel. He wasn't sure he could call on Valinhall at all so soon after using the mask, but even if he could, it might do to him what it had done to Kai.

He pictured spikes stabbing out of his skin from the inside, and shuddered. *I don't want to die like that,* he thought, but then he stopped himself. *No. Kai's not dead yet.*

With a thought he banished Azura, and she appeared on the rack across from the Gate. He managed to bend over without falling, scooping up Caela and tucking her into his cloak. Then he looked for Indirial, to see if he could help.

His chair was empty.

He left minutes ago, Simon, Caela said softly. *Did you not notice?*

That was stupid. He was letting himself slip because he was exhausted, and all but powerless, and maybe about to pass out. So what? He wasn't wounded. Kai had taken far more damage today than he had.

Caela shifted inside his cloak pocket. *It's not just today. It's all piling up on you, Simon. You need to stop pushing yourself.*

The dolls were always trying to stop him from using the mask. He couldn't fight an Incarnation without it on, certainly not the Valinhall Incarnation, so he would have to live with the risk until the danger was past.

He was trying to figure out another way to get the swords when the Eldest appeared in a flutter of black robes. "I hear you have lost another two of the swords," he hissed. "Every time I think you have stepped forward, you show me that you have actually taken a step back."

Simon met the Nye's empty gaze, trying to project an image of confidence and strength. If he wanted the Eldest to take him seriously, he had to act like he was in charge. "I will get them back. I will get them all back. But you need to hold up your end of the bargain and save Kai."

The Eldest paused for a moment, and then he began to chuckle. "You get one miracle out of me, and you begin to expect them on command. I am loath to disappoint you, O exalted heir, but Valin was an exception in more ways than one. It was no great thing to bring him back. I am more impressed that he managed to die at all."

You know he's right, Simon, Caela said, but Simon didn't let that sway him. The Eldest might sound convincing, but that didn't mean he was telling the truth.

"You've bargained with me before," Simon said. "Why not now? Do you want Kai to die that badly?"

"I don't care how long he lives before he dies, but he was transformed halfway into an Incarnation. That is a death sentence. The merciful thing would be to put a chain around his neck right now."

Simon forced himself to march forward and grab a double handful of the Eldest's robes. He'd never tried to fight the Eldest directly, but he'd do what he had to for Kai.

"Save him!" Simon commanded.

"I cannot."

Simon's hands were shaking on the Nye's robes, and he forced them to unclench. "I'd better…" he began, but he wasn't sure how to finish.

What was he supposed to do?

Let's go see him, Caela urged.

Step by step, Simon marched down the hall, toward the bathroom. He felt like he was marching toward his own funeral, and his mind kept racing toward a way out. The Eldest had said Kai's transformation into an Incarnation had been interrupted.

Because of Indirial, Simon realized. There could be only one Incarnation at a time. Just because Indirial had been sealed into the Territory, he hadn't lost all his powers yet. So what if Simon killed Indirial? Would that help Kai?

Simon shook his head, forcing his thoughts back in line. That wouldn't help Kai, it would only put Simon in the same situation. He didn't want Indirial to die either. *None* of them should have to die; this whole situation was ridiculous! He wasn't even sure why they'd been fighting in the first place.

It all came back to Valin's question: *What do you want?*

Why was he fighting? What was he willing to fight for?

To keep Kai alive, he resolved. *That's a good enough reason for anyone.*

We're here, Caela announced.

No, we're not. We're still in the hallway. The bath is still…

Then Simon realized that the seventh bedroom, his bedroom, had been torn open. Andra and Erastes stood within, and they'd been joined by Caius, Lycus, and Olissa. The five of them stood in a half-circle around Kai's bleeding, transformed body.

But that wasn't what held Simon's attention. The floor was scattered with walking dolls. Walking, moving, *broken* dolls.

Rebekkah's arm was bound in a sling that it looked like she had tied herself. As he watched, she tossed her red braid back over her shoulder and tightened the sling with her teeth. He hadn't known that she could move her jaw.

And there, Angeline was carrying Lilia on her back. Both of Lilia's feet had been crushed, and the hem of her flowing, white dress torn away. Gloria sat nearby, her hair and dress ruined, sniffling and wiping at her eyes as though to brush away real tears.

All of the dolls moved around on the floor; for the first time since Simon had seen the room, their shelves were completely bare. Even the dolls he hardly ever spoke with—Delia, Reka, Sara, the twins—they all moved and helped the injured.

Then he saw Otoku.

Kai clutched her to his chest, stroking what remained of her long, black hair. Half of her face had been shattered, as if with a hammer, and the remaining half stared up at the ceiling with an expression of mild surprise.

It finally hit Simon that he'd lost someone. Again.

Ever since he'd gotten his powers from Valinhall, he'd managed to save everyone who needed it. Now Otoku, who should have been safe, was gone. And Kai...

One by one, the dolls walked up to Kai. Some of the injured and broken had to help each other, but they each stopped and lay a hand on Kai's forehead. Serious Angeline bent over to plant a wooden kiss in his hair, and the twins actually threw all four of their arms around him for a hug.

No one said anything.

When all the dolls had finished, they stood around Kai's body in a complete circle, facing inward. Simon's mind was still racing: *Were they doing something? Maybe they could save him.* He'd never understood the powers of the dolls—maybe *they* could bring Kai back.

He was surprised to realize that Caela had crawled up out of his cloak and was sitting on his left shoulder; he hadn't felt her at all. And she never moved so much.

Good-bye, she said, softly. Several of her sisters echoed her. Kai smiled, and he let out one last, contented sigh. "My little ones..." he said.

Then his hand, still brushing Otoku's hair, stopped moving.

That was it. Simon had waited long enough. He called steel and stepped forward, brushing aside the nearest few dolls, reaching for Kai. He would pick the man up and drag him to the pool, no matter what he wanted, and if that didn't work he'd take Kai to see Valin...

Somebody stood in his way, and Simon tried to push past, but he couldn't. They were holding his shoulders, and they were just as strong as he was.

Erastes, he realized. Simon didn't hesitate; he drove his fist into the old man's gut.

Filled with steel, the soldier didn't make a sound. He stepped in front of Kai, blocking Simon's vision. "He's dead, son," Erastes said, his words characteristically hard.

Simon knocked his hands away and tried to push past, but Andra was holding his left side, and Erastes his right. He struggled against them for a moment before he realized it was useless.

You can't do anything now, Caela said.

No, he couldn't.

And he cried for that as much as anything.

Leah walked into the middle of the Crimson Vault, standing between the rows of weapons on their marble shelves, with their delicately carved labels. She stopped in what she guessed was the center of the long gallery, and turned to the raven on her shoulder.

Murin purred, or the raven equivalent. It sounded like she was gargling birdsong, but Leah got the impression that the raven did sense another mind. Another sound, almost a soft bark, and Leah understood that this person was quite close.

It could be convenient, having a raven that could sense, read, and possibly manipulate thoughts. But Leah hoped that one day the bird would learn to communicate more clearly. Having to interpret each little sound, even with Murin's mental assistance, was becoming a noticeable inconvenience. Still, at least she was getting better at it.

Leah looked around at Ragnarus, at the glittering weapons that surrounded her, and she raised her voice. "I've come to talk with you," she said.

For a few seconds, only silence answered. Then a woman stepped into Leah's view. She walked as if she had exited a door, but Leah could clearly see a straight hallway in either direction. There was no way for this woman to have hidden anywhere.

Even if she *would* blend in.

Her dress was scarlet light folded into waves of solid fabric, and her skin a dusky red that looked painted on. Her eyes were shaped like those of an ordinary human, which Leah hadn't expected, but their irises were clearly red.

The former Ragnarus Incarnation put a hand on her hip and smiled with one side of her mouth. "I suppose you're the daughter."

"Queen Leah the First. And which of my ancestors are you?"

The red woman's smile widened. "Queen Cynara, also the First of that name. A pleasure to meet you, Highness." She bent her knees in an ironic curtsy.

Leah had been somewhat prepared for this. She'd already thought through all the possibilities of exactly *who* could be sealed beneath Cana's Hanging Tree. It couldn't be Queen Cynara the Second, since that Queen of Damasca had remained alive to seal the other eight Incarnations. That left either her mother, Cynara the First, or one of the Ragnarus Travelers of old, before the Vault was sealed by the Elysians and re-opened.

She had considered this possibility, but her expectations paled before the reality. She was standing before the first Queen of Damasca, the woman who had torn away the seal on Ragnarus, bound the Territory to her bloodline, defeated the last Elysian Incarnation in single combat, and formed Damasca into a unified nation almost singlehandedly. Leah had grown up hearing legends of this woman's adventures, both historical and mythical.

So she was proud that her voice didn't waver as she said, "The pleasure is mine."

Cynara nodded, accepting the compliment. "You approached me. You wish to bargain?"

"I wish to stop my father."

Leah's hand brushed the ring-box in her pocket. Even a former Incarnation of Ragnarus would surely ask for payment, so hopefully a lost artifact of the Crimson Vault would do the job.

Queen Cynara paced slowly across the Vault's broad floor, seemingly lost in thought. "There is the matter of payment...but we will get to that. How do you know you want to stop your father? Do you even know what he wants?"

"If he's the Incarnation of Ragnarus, then he wants power," Leah said. "He doesn't care how or where he gets it, so long as someone pays a price." Murin fluttered her wings and squawked, agreeing.

Cynara nodded, once. "True and wisely spoken. Still, why stop him? He would make a better ruler than some."

Because he's an insane, murderous Incarnation, Leah thought. "Because I don't trust his judgment," she said.

"Ah." Queen Cynara pondered for a moment, tapping a finger against her lower lip. "Take it from me, his judgment is certainly questionable. As was mine, until...recently. But you want more than to stop your father. Be specific."

If that's the way she wants it, Leah thought. "I need the answers to three questions. What is my father planning? How do I stop him, and the other Incarnations? And how do I deal with the Incarnations as a whole?"

She wasn't sure Queen Cynara would have an answer to the last question, given that she had apparently failed to control the Incarnations the first time around, but it would be worth comparing what she said to the Avernus Incarnation's advice and then comparing notes.

"The last one is easy," Queen Cynara said, shrugging one red shoulder. "Simply return each Incarnation to its home Territory. The longer I spent in the Unnamed World, the more my thoughts began to bend to my new nature. And now, the longer I spend in my Territory, the more I remember who I used to be." Her eyes grew distant. "I wish I'd known that before I saved your father from the brink of death."

Leah, too, wished that she had simply let Zakareth die on the Vault floor. "So, if I return the Incarnations, everything works out?"

Cynara waved a hand. "Of course not. Nothing ever 'works out' simply or easily. You'll have to create a team of Travelers dedicated to finding and stopping Incarnations. That's what the Elysians did, in my time, but now I'd recommend that Valinhall of yours. Or at least I *would* have, except that Zakareth attacked them. I don't know how it ended up, but we do have two of their *excellent* swords here in the Vault."

Leah's first thought was to run and go tell Simon, but if the attack was over, then he surely already knew. And she had better things to do than to worry about a bunch of Valinhall Travelers in a fight.

She decided to ask the ancient queen the same question she'd asked Avernus. "The Territories would become more difficult to colonize and control if I left the Incarnations loose," she said. "Why don't I use the Hanging Trees again?"

Cynara stiffened visibly at the mention of the trees, and she began rubbing her left wrist. "Even if you were willing to bear the moral burden of the yearly sacrifices, which I suspect you are not, the situation is much worse for the Ragnarus Incarnation. The Trees were never meant to work on our kind." Cynara's eyes blazed, and her voice shook with remembered pain and grief. "I never fully lost consciousness as the Tree fed upon me, do you understand? Not for one moment. I was even aware of the outside world, able to sense events to a certain degree. I cannot imagine a more complete state of agony."

Leah managed to repress a shudder. She would subject the Incarnations to that if she had to, to preserve the security of the realm, but she would certainly prefer another way. A way that Avernus and Cynara seemed to be offering.

"Well, then, on to my other questions. What is my father planning, and how do I stop him?"

Queen Cynara released her own wrist and composed herself, brushing off her scarlet dress. Her smile returned, and this time it had an edge. "In this, help and payment are one and the same. Here is my price: I will give you the information you seek, and in exchange, you will embrace the power that you now hold."

"I will not become an Incarnation," Leah said at once. She had decided on that before coming here. The last thing they needed was *another* Incarnation taking her father's place.

"Not that," Cynara said irritably. "Why does everyone assume I speak in riddles? The power you now *hold*. In your hand."

Leah's hand clenched on the ring-box, and she drew it out of her pocket. "This?"

"The Eye of Ages," Queen Cynara said, her smile broadening. "I'll help you replace your eye, and tell you your father's plans...not that he's been keeping them secret. All you have to do is accept."

Leah rattled the ring-box in front of her. "What do you gain from this?"

Queen Cynara rested her chin in her hand as though thinking. "That wasn't one of the questions I agreed to answer, was it? No, it was not. Let us say that our interests coincide, for a time."

I can't see a trap, Leah thought. *Which means there must be one somewhere. What angle is she playing? What am I missing?*

The problem was, she didn't know enough. She knew practically nothing about the Eye of Ages, or about Queen Cynara. What could possibly motivate the woman?

"What do you think?" Leah muttered to Murin. She hadn't quite decided whether to trust the bird—she *had* come from another Incarnation—but it seemed that Leah's interests and the interests of the Avernus Incarnation should align on this issue.

Murin ruffled her feathers in what looked like a shrug. From everything the bird could tell, Queen Cynara had no secret agenda.

Which meant that her move was *so* subtle that even a mind-reading raven couldn't ferret out its meaning. That made Leah even more nervous.

Cynara hadn't stopped pacing. Or smiling. "One eye in exchange for wisdom. There are worse bargains."

Leah's father had a saying about bargains. *It takes two people to make a deal: a desperate man and a winner.*

So far in her life, Leah had always tried to be on the winning side. In this bargain, she was afraid she knew where she fell.

But she *was* desperate.

"I have some conditions," she began, but Queen Cynara spoke over her.

"No, you don't!" she said sweetly. "You're quibbling to make it look like you haven't given ground. Come now, I'm a weapons dealer, not a merchant. Let's get started, shall we?"

Cynara clapped her hands, and a chair slammed into the backs of

Leah's knees. She collapsed backwards, sinking in the soft, padded fabric. Murin took off from her shoulder in a flurry of black wings.

Her parting *caw* had a distinct flavor of *You'll get no help from me.*

Queen Cynara leaned over the chair, with her red eyes and ruby smile. "Just relax and let me take care of everything. It'll all be over soon."

Then she reached for Leah's eye.

NEWFOUND POWERS

359ᵀᴴ Year of the Damascan Calendar
1ˢᵀ Year in the Reign of Queen Leah I
7 Days Since Spring's Birth

Simon sat on the grass of the graveyard, looking at the newest headstone.

He realized that he'd never even known Kai's full name. What was his father's name? Or his family's, if he was Damascan? Simon didn't know. He knew so little about the man who'd given him a new life.

And now he may never know. The tombstone read, simply:

KAI AND OTOKU

That was it. No birth date, no cause of death, no prayer to the Maker or mention of family. Valin had added Otoku's name without Simon having to ask for it, for which Simon was grateful, but he still felt like it wasn't enough.

Valin stepped up beside him. "Nine graves, huh. Better than I'd expected. I'd have thought there would be thirteen, by now. Then again, I also thought we'd have overthrown the Damascan throne, so what do I know about making realistic predictions?"

Simon said nothing. He didn't have anything to say.

The Wanderer sighed and ran a hand over his bare, chain-marked scalp. "Sulking, huh? Seven stones, I was good at sulking when I was your age. I'd had a lot of practice, you see."

He thought *grieving* would have been a better word than sulking, but Valin wouldn't appreciate the difference. This was the man who had founded Valinhall—he wasn't likely to overflow with compassion and pity.

A shadow stepped up to Simon's other side. *Speaking of pitiless...*

"He's still dead," the Eldest Nye said. "As I said he would be. Watching the rock will not bring him back."

"Not that it would change much if he did come back," Valin remarked idly, scratching the back of his neck with a dagger. "He didn't do much but lounge around the House all day. He'll probably be happier dead, all things considered."

Simon looked up at him, feeling surprisingly…blank. This was an obvious attempt to provoke him, for some reason. The Eldest and Valin were trying to get a reaction out of him.

So be it. If they kept it up, he'd kill them both, and then they would stop. Was that what they wanted?

The Eldest folded his sleeves. "He had such promise as a child. To think he never accomplished anything of worth. It's an unforgiveable waste."

Simon hadn't brought Azura with him, and he couldn't summon or banish anything within the House. It seemed Kai had known how to do so, but that secret, too, had died with him.

But Simon never went anywhere in Valinhall unarmed.

He didn't attack the Eldest first. Since the Nye had been last to speak, he would be prepared for an attack. Instead, Simon pulled the dagger from his belt and struck at Valin, slashing at the man's legs.

Valin stepped back, but Simon pressed the advantage, pushing the knife toward the Wanderer's bare middle. The older man caught his wrist in a grip that didn't budge under Simon's steel-enhanced strength.

He had expected as much from Valin, but this gave him the opportunity to try a move that Kai had demonstrated but never properly taught him. He dropped the dagger and grabbed on to Valin's wrist with his newly empty hand, pulling himself up and off his feet. Then he drove a knee into the Wanderer's face.

Valin's nose crunched, spraying blood down his chin, and he staggered back. Without a pause, Simon turned and drove a fist at the Eldest.

His knuckles slammed into the Eldest's upraised arm, which felt like punching a steel bar wrapped in yards of thick cloth. The Nye started to speak, but Simon kicked his dropped dagger up, snagging it out of the air with his left hand and driving the blade into the Eldest's hood.

The Nye swayed backwards, bending almost entirely in half. Simon kicked at his waist, forcing him to take a step back, and then turned the dagger back to Valin.

He scored a long hit across the Wanderer's chain-marked chest, but Valin didn't seem to notice. He stood smiling, his nose and his chest both bleeding freely.

"I guess you can fight like the Valinhall heir should," Valin said.

The Eldest flowed around to stand side-by-side with his former master. "If Kai had brought us the Founder's heir, then perhaps his life was not such a waste after all. If, instead, he only brought us a single worthless recluse to replace him...I would be very disappointed."

The Eldest Nye took one step to the side, and beside him, driven at an angle into the earth of the graveyard, was a slightly curving sword almost as long as Azura. A single line of gold ran from the hilt to the tip of the blade.

"You defeated me when I held Mithra," Valin noted, ticking the point off on one finger. He held up a second finger. "You were Kai's choice as his apprentice." Third finger. "And technically you defeated a *second* Valinhall Incarnation." Valin spread his hands. "Mithra wouldn't abandon her previous bearer, but now Kai is dead. You're the obvious choice."

Simon had spotted the setup between King Zakareth and the Endross Incarnation earlier, and he wasn't about to miss this one. He looked to the Eldest Nye. "This is what you want from me. This is where you've been steering me since the first day. And...is this why you brought him back?" He nodded to Valin.

Pressing the ends of his two sleeves together, the Eldest bowed slightly. "I brought him back for many reasons, some of which you could not comprehend. This was but one of them. As for you, I did not 'steer' you anywhere. I had to practically choke you with this."

Valin wiped blood away from his chest with one hand—his wound had already closed on its own. "I'd hoped to have this conversation with you in five years, when you'd...filled out a bit. But time moves on and nothing stops it, not even a Territory like this one."

On the surface, it seemed that they were offering to put him in charge. But that wasn't quite right, was it? They didn't want to give him more authority; they wanted somebody to take responsibility.

A few quick objections flicked through his mind—*I'm too young, I'm not ready, there are better choices*—but he set them all aside. There were two questions that needed answered.

First, did this need to be done?

And second: was he willing to do it?

The Wanderer's earlier question, separate from but related to the first two, passed briefly through his thoughts: *What do you want, Simon?*

Valin spoke up again, wiping blood away from his mouth. "Kai died in a fight with another Valinhall Traveler, and I hear Indirial became an Incarnation. Those things should *never happen*. It's a mess around here, and we need a Founder to take charge, to make everyone march in the same direction. Essentially, to keep everyone alive."

So it did need to be done, then.

If you boiled it down, this was the same problem that had gotten him to leave Myria in the first place. People needed help, and no one else was going to help them.

What do I want to do?

When he put it like that, there was no choice at all. He'd made his decision the minute he walked away from his village.

He stepped over to Mithra and put his hand on her hilt. Then he hesitated. "Wait. What about the dolls? They're bound to Azura, aren't they?"

"You will take a new advisor," the Eldest said, in his raspy voice. "He will guide you forward not in battle, but in the order and governance of Valinhall as a whole."

Guilt pecked at his insides like a sparrow plucking seeds from dry ground. He couldn't abandon the dolls, not now. Not when they were broken, and scattered. Kai would never forgive him.

"Azura doesn't have a new bearer yet," Valin pointed out. "Until she does, you'll still be able to come and go in the seventh bedroom. And the dolls can always talk to you, if they wish, though I understand it's harder for them to communicate with the bearer of a different Fang."

At least he wouldn't have to abandon them immediately. Not until Azura chose a new Traveler.

Valin leaned close. "So, Simon. Did Kai waste his life, or not?"

Simon wrapped his hand around Mithra's hilt, and he felt a surge of satisfaction that he didn't think came from him. He still held steel—though he was starting to worry about his chains—and he pulled her from the soil, adjusting to the balance. She felt much the same as Azura, but was shaped slightly differently, and perhaps a few inches shorter. He would have to practice even harder now.

It took him a moment to notice that something had changed.

The grass, which usually rippled in a gentle breeze, had stilled. Even the crawling nest of emerald lightning overhead was completely frozen.

Simon stood in a lake of absolute quiet and stillness; for a moment he thought he'd called as much Nye essence as he could hold, but he felt no ice in his lungs.

The Wanderer had his eyes shut, and the Eldest drew a deep, rattling breath through his hood, as though savoring a new scent.

"It has been too long since we were complete," said the Nye.

"I can already sense the difference," Valin responded. "The scales are swinging, I'm sure you know that."

"But this time, they will settle on balance." The Eldest took one more breath, and then the world snapped back into motion.

Simon stood holding Mithra in one hand, feeling like he'd missed most of what had passed between the other two. "What now?"

The Eldest turned to him. "Now? Someone created and controlled an Incarnation of Valinhall, sending him to lead an attack against us and steal our weapons."

"And I think we all know who," Valin said, his voice hot with anger.

"The Ragnarus King has delivered us one insult too many," the Eldest continued. "I have spoken with Indirial, and I can be sure that the blame for this latest injustice lies at the feet of Zakareth the Sixth. He has, in effect, murdered Kai, corrupted Indirial, and declared war on the House itself. You tell me, Founder's heir, what should be done about a man like that?"

Anger grew in Simon even as his fist tightened on Mithra's hilt. Zakareth and his family had sacrificed thousands of lives over the years to protect the people from Incarnations, and now he was killing people as an Incarnation himself.

More to the point, for Simon, King Zakareth was the man responsible for Otoku and Kai's death, as well as Indirial's Incarnation. He had set himself up to oppose Leah, and if you looked at it from a certain perspective, set into motion the events that led to the death of Simon's mother.

And now he was a reckless, deadly Incarnation, who was rallying the other Incarnations under his immortal rule.

No matter how Simon looked at it, the man needed to die.

"I'm going to find him," Simon said. "I'm going to take our swords back, and in the end I'm going to chop his head off."

Valin jabbed a finger at him. "With that attitude, you'll do well around here."

Simon started walking to the graveyard door. He wasn't exactly sure how much time had passed in the outside world since Kai's death, but he knew that he needed to meet up with Leah. It might already be too late for the defense of Enosh, but in case it wasn't, he'd need to contact Alin. And for the fight itself, he'd have to mobilize everyone who could possibly carry a Dragon's Fang. They'd need the two lost Fangs back, and maybe he could persuade Benson to lend Lycus some steel...

He was lost in thought when he realized that he'd forgotten one very important question.

"I almost forgot to ask," he said, turning back to the other two. "Who's my new advisor?"

Valin looked at him. The Eldest looked at him. Then the Nye pressed his sleeves together and gave him a little bow.

The Wanderer started laughing.

"No," Simon said in horror. "Please, Maker, no."

The Eldest bowed deeper. "I am pleased for this opportunity, son of Kalman. We shall be working together much more closely in the future."

When Leah left the Crimson Vault, her world had changed.

Everything seemed flatter, for one thing. As she picked her way over the rubble of the royal palace—Ragnarus Gates only had one exit—she stumbled and fell no less than six times. Her hands were scraped raw from catching herself on rough stone, but she couldn't seem to judge distances properly with one eye. Her father had apparently adjusted, so she would have to as well.

Besides, the other advantages more than made up for the drawbacks.

The place on the ground floor where the Hanging Tree had once stood, she still saw as the ghost of a crimson door, towering over the ruins of the palace. That, she was sure, marked the exit of a Ragnarus Gate. Other ghosts hung in the air: sparkling white stars that bobbed down the street, drifting fireballs with screaming faces, miniature towers sculpted from ice. Remnants of Travelers' powers.

When she glanced at Murin, the raven swirled with feathers of white and bronze. The bird was bound to Avernus, which was obvious even without her crimson eye. But she found it most interesting that the bird apparently was bound to the Territory and Leah in equal measure: a thin red line connected the bird's leg to Leah's shoulder.

So the raven was connected to Leah, not the Incarnation. That was cause for relief and suspicion at the same time. On the one hand, she was glad not to be carrying a spy around on her shoulder. On the other, the Avernus Incarnation's motives were unclear. How did she benefit from the Queen of Damasca carrying around a loyal advisor? Did she want Leah to think better of Avernus?

As Leah snuck up to the walls of Cana, she had more disturbing things to occupy her mind than the possible plans of the Avernus Incarnation.

For one thing, the top of the wall was crowded with transparent specters. Golems of ghostly light patrolled along the wall, under a steady snowfall and a rain of blood. Ornheim, Helgard, and…Ragnarus, she thought. She was certain her father could have figured out exactly what each of the different Incarnations were doing here, but she still wasn't used to the Eye. She would have to learn its powers one by one.

Black chains, seemingly made of shadow, crawled over everything. If the chains had any connection to the marks on Simon's arms, then this meant someone had called on Valinhall in great measure. Perhaps even a Valinhall Incarnation.

Fear gripped her chest, but she forced it away, walking among the chains. Even if there was still a Valinhall Incarnation around, worrying about it wouldn't do any good. It could kill her the same whether she was prepared or not.

Murin gave a soft caw and flew in a broad circle around her head, sending a flood of reassurance through their mental bond. The raven didn't sense another mind nearby, which did help Leah to relax.

Only a moment later, she reached her destination: at the center of the web of chains, there stood the ghost of a door. It was made of wood, and carved with the emblem of a sword—long and slightly curved, like Simon's—but bound in chains.

She had no doubt that this was the door to Valinhall. Someone had opened a Gate here, and not long ago.

Reaching deep into Ragnarus, she withdrew what she needed. A straight sword, its blade twisting with black and red in a vaguely shifting, nauseating pattern, appeared in her hand in a flash of red light. This was one of the Vault's several gatecrawlers, though she couldn't recall its name at the moment.

She had promised Simon that she would contact him when she needed him. Well, she needed to talk to him now, and she wasn't sure how to send him a message without tearing open his Territory. Hopefully he'd see the need.

Holding the sword in both hands, Leah jammed it into the translucent door. The steel edge of the blade glowed red, and the red-and-black lines twisted and danced. Leah sawed back and forth, tearing open the Gate one inch at a time.

Now that she thought of it, she'd never operated a gatecrawler personally before. She'd never had to; there was always another capable Traveler around to do it for her. Somehow, she had never quite realized that they were so much *work*. It was like chopping down a thick tree with a dull spade. She was sweating before she got the Gate halfway finished, and her arms ached and burned by the time she finished, and the Valinhall Gate snapped open.

She found herself staring down seven feet of a silver-and-gold blade, looking into Simon's hooded face. An old soldier at Simon's side held a Tartarus steel infantry sword—she thought his name was Erastes, from the last time she had entered the House. Beside him, Andra Agnos had her long blond hair bound up in a tail, and chains were crawling up her forearms. She held her short, black-spotted blade in both hands.

So they had reacted to a gatecrawler as if to an attack. That was…not unexpected. In Valinhall, even the most innocent actions could conceal an attack, and tearing open a foreign Territory wasn't usually the action of a friend.

If it was just Simon, she might have apologized. But Erastes and Andra were there as well, and they were proper Damascan citizens. They needed to see their Queen composed.

Leah pushed aside Simon's blade and stepped into Valinhall, letting the gatecrawler vanish back into the Vault. "I need to speak with you, Simon. I've gained some information regarding the enemy's next move."

Behind her, the Gate slid slowly shut.

That reminded her.

"Ah, before I forget..." She stepped to the edge of the Gate and reached both hands into the air of the outside world. Then she summoned two more swords from the Crimson Vault.

These swords were reasonably sized, compared to a few of the other Valinhall blades, but she still felt every ounce of their weight when she held one in each hand. She turned without showing the effort.

"I believe these belong to you," she said.

Simon's eyes widened, and he tossed his own gold-streaked blade onto a nearby sofa, freeing his hands to pick up the new blades.

"Diava," he said, hefting the short-handled, red-wrapped sword in his right hand. This blade had a more pronounced curve than his own. "And..." He glanced at the second blade, which had a strangely long handle to pair with its short blade. "I don't know the name of this Fang, but I've seen it here. I guess it's Kathrin's."

He looked at Andra, who shrugged and placed her sword on one of the wooden racks.

Erastes was still on his knees; Leah hadn't even noticed him kneeling. "You may stand," she said absently. She really needed to change that tradition.

Simon placed the blades on a couple of nearby racks, a few spaces away from Andra's. "Where did you find these?"

Leah arched an eyebrow at him. "It seems they were sealed inside the Crimson Vault. I removed them during my visit there."

Simon stared at her left eye. "Oh. Yeah. How...is it? The eye?"

Queen Cynara had managed to transplant the Eye of Ages in a quick procedure that involved no blood or unpleasant tools, and had only taken a handful of seconds. By contrast, it had taken Leah six hours to get over the pain. Her eye still throbbed, and she was constantly fighting the urge to scratch the socket.

Not that Simon needed to know any of that.

"I can see farther than I ever have before," she said, which was a mysterious enough answer to suit even her father. It was true, though. The chains on Simon's arms didn't stop at his skin. She could now see them twisting off into the distance like black ribbons, disappearing into the air of the Territory.

As he used his powers, he was binding himself to Valinhall in some way. Hopefully he knew already, but just in case, she would have to tell him about it later.

"More importantly, I need to speak with Indirial," Leah said. "Have you found him?"

Some emotion twisted Simon's expression for an instant, but he smoothed it again. "He attacked us. We had to seal him here."

It took a few seconds for the full impact of the words to sink in.

If Indirial had attacked the House of Blades, that meant he had been working for Zakareth. Cynara had explained that his first step would be to destroy or recruit the Valinhall Travelers, as they would be the most capable of defeating him *or* the one remaining Elysian.

And if he had been sealed in the House…

"I see," Leah said, fighting the sick feeling in the pit of her stomach. "He will be missed." She hadn't spent much time with the Overlord of Cana the past few years, that was true, but he had once been more of a father to her than King Zakareth had ever been. Now…he might be lucid, but there was no telling how much of *him* would be left. Some Incarnations were little better than monsters.

Leah took a deep breath, steadied herself, and walked over to the tallest table in the room. It was different than she remembered: slightly smaller, and carved in a different pattern. Freshly carved, if she wasn't mistaken. She spread out the map that always covered the table and nodded to Simon. "I need you to call the other Valinhall Travelers. We're going back to Enosh."

Simon, Erastes, and Andra walked up to the table, and Simon met her gaze. His eyes were even darker than usual.

"I can't call anyone else," he said. "This is it. Now, what's the plan?"

It had been a few days since Simon had visited the camp outside of Cana, but tonight it looked almost completely deserted. Trash, discarded weapons, wagon ruts, and torn-up grass were all that remained of the army of refugees who had followed Leah for six months, aside from a couple of patrols and a few isolated tents.

With Andra and Erastes trailing her, Leah made her way through the dark to one of the remaining tents. Every once in a while, her bird gave a peaceful-sounding gurgle, which she seemed to interpret as helpful advice.

"We can get to Enosh through any number of Territories," Simon muttered. He kept his voice low; they weren't sneaking, exactly, but she had said to avoid attracting attention as much as possible. "If we can send Alin a message, he might even be able to send us some bears. There are other ways."

Leah turned to him, one eye blue and the other glowing red. She smiled. "Trust me," she said.

Simon wasn't sure he'd ever get used to the Ragnarus eye. It reminded him uncomfortably of her father, though at least she'd managed to avoid the scar running across his eye socket.

Although, now that he thought of it, Leah might look good with a scar. Everyone could use a few scars; Maker knew he had his share.

I can't believe I have to tell you this, Caela sent, *but keep your mind on the mission.*

We're not in Enosh yet. I can't defend the place until we get there.

Certainly not, she said reasonably. *Hey, Queen Leah: you should get into more knife-fights. Simon would like you better with a few prominent facial scars.*

Simon stumbled and caught himself, face flaming. Andra, Erastes, and Leah had all turned to stare at him before he realized that Caela hadn't *actually* cast that thought in Leah's direction.

Judging from her peals of laughter, though, she did find his reaction hilarious.

His cheeks burning, Simon shook his head. "Dolls," he said.

Without a word, Leah beckoned the guards at the front of the tent. They opened their mouths when they recognized her, but she put a finger to her lips and then waved them closer.

"I hereby order the prisoner punished," she said, after a brief, whispered consultation with her raven. "Beat her, but don't inhibit her permanently. While you're doing that, accidentally loosen the restraints on her hands."

One of the guards, a Naraka Traveler, cleared his throat. "I'm not...certain that's wise, Your Highness."

Leah feigned a look of surprise. "Oh? Are you unable to have an accident on command, Traveler?"

The guard sighed. "No, Highness. But she could very easily kill us all."

"She won't," Leah said confidently, and the raven croaked alongside her. "She'll be looking for a different opportunity."

The two guards saluted at the same time, and then headed into the tent. Within seconds, the thud of fists on flesh floated out, along with their grunts of effort.

Grandmaster Naraka made not a sound in protest.

"She'll head in a line straight for Alin," Leah said, her eyes flicking over the tent. "And...I see her deep in the fires of Naraka. She craves justice for the other Grandmasters."

"There are other ways," Simon said again. "Just have one of those other Naraka Travelers take us."

Leah didn't respond. She stared at the tent, her mind obviously elsewhere. "Simon, how many Incarnations can you handle, if you had to?"

The question caught him off-guard, though he understood why she was asking. According to her mysterious information, King Zakareth was preparing to attack Enosh with everything he had, hoping to destroy Alin and Elysia. With Valinhall and Elysia gone, he would have all of the Territories under his control.

That meant he would be attacking Enosh with all the Incarnations he could command. Counting himself, he had at least five Incarnations, perhaps as many as seven.

Far more than Simon could handle on his own.

He pulled down the collar of his cloak, revealing the chains stretching up to his neck. "I've been using the mask too much, lately. I've only got a few minutes of power left. With that...one, maybe two, if they don't work together. Andra and Erastes, perhaps one more. And let's say that Alin can get one."

"That's as optimistic as we can be," Leah murmured. "Minimum, that still only takes care of the Incarnations under the King's command. Not King Zakareth himself."

Another slap of flesh-on-flesh echoed from the tent, as the Grandmaster endured her beating. She still made not a sound.

"Which means that we have no choice but to fight in Elysia," Simon said. He'd tried making this argument before, but Leah hadn't been much interested in taking advice. "I can still draw on my power in another Territory, but most of the enemy Incarnations won't be able to use their full strength. If Alin can call up the City's whole army, we might have a chance."

Leah shook her head. "We need the City as a fallback position," she said. "If we leave Alin exposed outside, he'll be overwhelmed and eliminated in seconds. He can't enter the Territory or he'll be trapped, and that means he probably won't let any of his citizens enter either. We'll form lines outside of a Gate and fight a retreat into Elysia, as planned."

Simon didn't see why they had to fight for the city of Enosh at all. As far as he was concerned, the city was lost. All they could do was stop the Incarnations after they weakened themselves to assault the City of Light.

"And you're sure you can't contact the other two Valinhall Travelers?" Leah asked, for at least the third time.

"You're the Lirial Traveler," Simon said. "You find them."

Kathrin's advisor is capable of long-distance communication, Caela noted. *It's too bad Kathrin's not here to contact...Kathrin.*

Leah was thinking again—he knew that look. It was like she was absorbed deep in some book, and she would come back to reality in a few seconds with a random question.

"Do you have that mask here?" Leah asked, finally.

Unfortunately, Caela sent.

Simon dug around in his pockets for the mask, and his hand encountered something round, warm, and slightly tacky. He pulled it out for a better look.

Oh, that's right. He'd almost forgotten the red stone that the Eldest had tried to take from him. He'd mentioned something about the Crimson Vault in connection to the stone, and Simon had intended to tell Leah, but somehow he had forgotten.

"Do you know what this is?" Simon asked, holding it up to the starlight.

Leah hissed, her eyes widening. She snatched it out of his hand, dropped it immediately, and then almost fell to her knees scrambling to catch it before it hit the ground. When she managed to snatch it out of the air before it hit dirt, she heaved a sigh of great relief.

Simon could only stare. He didn't think he'd ever seen her so startled.

Andra and Erastes moved closer, readying their swords as if to defend her from some threat, but Simon waved them away.

Leah rose to her feet, brushing herself off with her left hand and holding the stone up in her right. "I don't believe it," she breathed. "Why didn't you tell me you had this?"

"I didn't know what it was. I still don't," he added, hoping she would take the hint.

She shook her head wonderingly. "I can see now. No wonder…"

Simon had to restrain his impatience, but he refused to ask the question again.

"It's a Seed of the Hanging Tree," she said at last. "Maybe the last one, as far as I know."

He took a step back from it, wary. He didn't know what a Hanging Tree would do to an ordinary Traveler, but he knew what it did to Incarnations, and he had no wish to spend three hundred years as living compost. He pointed to the Seed. "Can we use it?"

"I think…yes, I think we can. Simon, I can't believe you had this. This might mean the difference between living and dying." She gave him the most genuine smile he'd seen out of her in years, and her red eye did nothing to ruin the effect. "This could be exactly what we need."

He cleared his throat. "Then, uh, I'm glad I found it." *Completely by chance,* he added in his head.

You should always take credit for your own good luck, Caela said. *After all, who else will?*

"You realize what this means," Leah added. "The Seed can't be planted in a Territory. It seems we'll have to fight in Enosh after all."

I don't know why I'm surprised, Simon thought. *We suddenly find something that could turn the fight around, and it supports Leah's battle plan over mine. Naturally.*

Maybe she *should inherit Valinhall,* Caela said thoughtfully. *What do you think, Mithra?*

The sword, thankfully, remained quiet.

The sounds from within the tent had stopped, and the two Naraka guards emerged. One of them was nursing a split knuckle. They bowed to Leah and took up their posts outside the tent.

The raven purred in the back of its throat.

"Not long now," Leah whispered.

After a few more minutes of silence, during which Andra lay back on the grass and began snoring softly, a flash of orange light brightened the tent.

Andra snapped awake, waving her Dragon's Fang wildly.

"Open a Gate!" Leah ordered the Naraka Travelers, marching forward with Simon and the other two on her heels. This was one part of the plan that she hadn't explained to Simon.

"There will be traps," one of the guards said, but he continued waving his hand in preparation to open a Gate.

"Your turn," Leah said, and Simon stepped forward.

Sure enough, as soon as the Naraka Gate opened, a screaming orange fireball hurled itself from the Territory's depths.

Simon called ghost armor, throwing up his arm between the Gate and the Traveler. The fireball shattered inches from his forearm, broken by a plate of spectral green armor.

A disgusting smoke-and-sulfur smell wafted from the Territory. "Do we *have* to go through Naraka again?" Simon asked.

Leah shot him a look. "It's that or fly."

Simon was prepared to try flying.

Erastes stepped up, preparing to enter the Gate. "Should we follow her, Your Highness?"

Leah pushed past him and stepped into Naraka first. "I can track her," she said. "And we know where she's going."

"I don't see how having her along will help us," Simon remarked. "It practically killed us last time." Maybe if Leah gave up this idea, they could Travel through another Territory. *Any* other Territory.

"Trust me," Leah said again. She was leaning on his trust fairly hard, tonight. "We'll have a hard enough time winning Alin over. That's why this time, we're bringing a present."

CHAPTER 26
STRATEGIC PLANNING

359TH YEAR OF THE DAMASCAN CALENDAR
1ST YEAR IN THE REIGN OF QUEEN LEAH I
8 DAYS SINCE SPRING'S BIRTH

Alin didn't sleep anymore, so he spent a lot of time thinking. All night, he'd been meditating on the same topic that had haunted him for the past week: his own failure.

You proved yourself an enemy to those who should be your friends, the Orange Light said.

You let them get away! said the Gold.

The Violet Light had a different opinion. *You lost control,* it told him.

He was inclined to agree.

Alin knew he was an Incarnation, and for the most part that fact didn't bother him. His Incarnation allowed him to think more clearly, to bond fully with the essence of his Territory. What harm could there be in the manifestation of Elysian virtues? He was honest and compassionate, wise and patient, valiant and loyal, merciful and diligent.

So how had he allowed himself to be taken over? When he'd let the Gold Light control his body, he hadn't been patient, or loyal, or merciful. The Light had consumed him in valor, so much that he needed to *prove* his bravery through victory.

But today, after a week of meditation and productive work, he was finally under control. He wouldn't be making the same mistakes again.

In the Gate next to him, Rhalia drifted over the grass of Elysia, her golden hair shining in the sunrise. "How are you feeling today?" she asked.

"In control."

Rhalia smiled, watching the sun peek over the city walls. "Ah, so then you've learned nothing. That's what I suspected, but it's good to have confirmation."

Irritation shot through him before the patience of the Green Light ground it down. "I am complete, Rhalia. In balance."

"Not without the White, you're not," she added cheerfully, juggling a few balls of Gold Light. She'd been in a better mood ever since the fight in Enosh, in direct contrast to his own feelings. He wondered what had happened.

He elected to overlook her comments about the White Light, which were becoming more frequent these days. "I will not let one battle throw off my balance this time. I will remain composed."

Rhalia frowned out the Gate, letting her golden lights vanish. "That's good to hear, because I think you're going to get a chance to prove it."

Silver constructs approached from practically every direction, radiating something like panic. A winged silver eye flew up to him and began delivering its report, though he could feel the urgency flowing from it in waves.

"Cordon in Helgard is breached—"

Another Silver construct, like a spider of polished steel, clattered up on the cobblestones and spoke over the first messenger. "Our outlook in Endross was destroyed—"

A golden hummingbird came up from behind him, delivering its message in a disturbingly deep voice. "Over the city walls, Eliadel. You should come and see."

He leaped toward the walls with Red Light flowing through his limbs, lift provided by a cushion of orange. He was practically flying as he soared over the city, landing with a crunch on roof tiles or cobblestones and pushing off again. The specifics of the various messages were different, but the core intent was clear: he was under attack.

Alin's heart tore in a dozen different directions.

His Rose-colored compassionate side broke at the thought that the citizens under his protection might be in danger. His Blue mercy urged him to surrender, his Orange loyalty to protect those beneath him at any cost.

But today, he felt more in line with the Gold Light.

At last, he thought, with a sigh of great relief. *An enemy.*

When he landed on the golden walls of Enosh, he realized how right he was.

The army wasn't as large as he'd expected. Only a few thousand soldiers, mostly Travelers, had lined up in the wasteland between Myria and Enosh. More important by far were the five figures standing at the front, surrounded by a host of vicious creatures.

Helgard, a horned woman with blue skin and white fur, stood stroking the head of a giant blue cat. It was practically a desert out there, but she moved in her own private snow-flurry, a trail of melted snowflakes following her wherever she walked.

Lirial stood next to her, a woman of white crystal and silver wire. She gleamed like a star in the sunrise, and Alin was only sure of her identity because of the open Lirial Gate next to her. She sent flashing crystal probes in and out, apparently communicating with someone.

Ornheim was next, a giant of white stone standing nine or ten feet tall. He crouched in the sand, absolutely still as stalagmites rose from the ground around him. One of them broke off, the rock forming into a three-foot-tall man-shaped golem. It staggered drunkenly around before dissolving into gravel. The Ornheim Incarnation didn't react. Veins of every color ran through him, so that he seemed designed for decoration rather than war.

Endross never stood still, pacing up and down the line of other Incarnations. His wings were formed of black stormclouds flashing with heat lightning, his eyes blazing like lightning bolts themselves. Even his hands and feet glowed with lightning, the rest of his body shrouded in what looked like snakeskin. Creatures of Endross burst into existence around him in a cloud of sparks, hissing and crawling through the sand, growling and spitting at the other Incarnations. No one seemed to care, least of all Endross himself, who stared without ceasing at the walls of Enosh.

Finally, King Zakareth the Sixth stood at the end of the line.

Alin recognized him, even at a distance, even with the significant physical changes that the King had undergone during Incarnation. Alin had been the one to kill the man, after all, though it looked like transformation had saved him. His skin swirled with designs of gold-and-ruby, his stone eye replaced by a rolling fireball of crimson. He wore the same black armor as last time, set with rubies and trimmed in gold, and even his gray hair was speckled with the occasional hair of red or gold. In his left hand he held a ruby-topped staff, and in his right a spear. The same spear that Alin had seen him use to fight off half a dozen Grandmasters and highly trained Enosh Travelers.

The King was speaking, giving orders to his fellow Incarnations, but his eyes were fixed on Alin.

You will likely die today, the Violet Light pointed out.

Alin considered that and found it true. The fact didn't bother him much.

Then I will die defending my city and my Territory, he thought. *At the very least, I will die a hero.*

The Gold Light approved.

Then an explosion from behind him caught his attention. He didn't stop and stare; he hurled a cloud of Silver Light behind him, sensing the location, and his body flared with Red and Orange Light as he hurled himself backwards off the wall. He was in the air and flying toward the source of the noise before the explosion even finished.

It was in the Blue District. The ruins of the Naraka waystation, naturally, because it seemed that he couldn't have a disturbance anywhere else in his city. He hadn't seen a Naraka Incarnation under Zakareth's control, but it had been long enough since Alin had destroyed the last one. It was certainly possible that King Zakareth could have kept Naraka in reserve, to send saboteurs through to weaken Alin's defenses.

A familiar presence glowed in his mind with Silver Light.

No... he thought. *No, I couldn't possibly be that lucky.*

Grandmaster Naraka stood outside the ruined Naraka waystation, her red spectacles turned up to watch him.

He landed in front of her, hands trembling, all the old emotions surfacing at once. *She* was the one who had destroyed his hometown. *She* was responsible for the deaths of two of his sisters, and the escape of the third. *She* was the one who had caused him to give up his humanity in the first place. She was even the one who had taught him to Travel.

No matter how he turned the situation over in his mind, she had brought him here.

His palms filled with Gold Light, almost on reflex, but he banished the force before it could fully form. He didn't need to blast her down in cold blood; he wanted to do this *right*.

Naraka's mouth twisted into a smile, and she spoke in her usual, creaking voice. "I come for justice, Eliadel."

"And justice you shall receive," he said. That was a line from a story, but whether she understood the reference or not, he didn't care.

She shook her head slowly. "It's difficult to become a Naraka Incarnation. Far more difficult than it is for Elysia, it seems. It's not only a matter of drawing too much power, you see. You have to flee justice, and yet hunger for it at the same time."

Grandmaster Naraka raised her right arm, which no longer ended in a smooth stump. Her right hand was a shriveled black claw, crawling with orange flame. "I escaped the Queen of Damasca and my well-earned punishment for betraying her. I come here, now, to a place where the law says I could be executed."

She smiled widely, and as Alin watched, her canines elongated into fangs. "I come because I have only one desire: to bring you to justice. You, who killed my fellow Grandmasters. Who ruined everything good in this city. You, Alin, deserve justice."

Her other hand burst into flames, and Grandmaster Naraka cackled loudly enough to shake the streets of Enosh. The Silver Light warned him that a handful of other people were scrambling out of the Naraka Gate behind her, but he didn't care that she'd brought backup. The Incarnation would be the real threat, and his eyes were stuck to her transformation.

The glasses slipped from her nose, red lenses shattering on the ground. Her pale white eyes turned orange, like live coals, her body twisting and stretching into a hunched, serpentine form. She spat out a tongue of flame.

Then Leah's voice echoed through the street, supernaturally loud. "We allowed her to come to you, Alin," she said. "A peace offering. Do with her what you will, and none of us will interfere."

For an instant, the hideously transformed Grandmaster Naraka looked as surprised as Alin felt. But then she turned back to him, unable to look away for very long. A red, pebbled tail shot out from under her robes, spikes on the end scratching the stones.

Fury pounded in his heart, the Gold Light crying out for victory.

But he had regained control of himself. Did he dare give in to his desire for vengeance now? What would that do to him?

Then again, there was an Incarnation here on his streets. Surely the *right* thing to do would be to destroy her before she ran rampant and killed his citizens. Yes, he was sure that in this, what was right and what he wanted were one and the same.

In her Gate beside him, Rhalia was whispering advice, but he didn't listen. He called Gold Light.

Then there was a streak of shadow and steel, and Simon slammed a giant hammer down on Grandmaster Naraka's head. She crumpled with a noisy crunch, though ash sprayed out instead of blood.

Simon looked up, meeting Alin's gaze. His hood was down, and his eyes were angry.

"I'm sorry about that," Simon said. "She didn't tell me what she was going to do."

Bones popped and slid as the Naraka Incarnation pulled herself together, flesh sliding back into one piece, her head rising out of the pile of her body. Fire gathered in one of her hands.

Then Simon slammed the hammer down again.

He ground the head of the weapon into her body, leaning casually on the handle. "We heard the King was going to attack you, and we wanted to come help. He already tried to destroy Valinhall, now he's moving against Elysia."

Elysia? The King was trying to destroy not just Enosh, but Elysia? Alin glanced over at Rhalia who was looking thoughtfully at Simon. "You know, I like his approach," she said. "It's efficient."

"Are they really going to attack the City?" Alin asked.

"I wouldn't be surprised," she said, her voice grim. "It's been tried before, and it was futile, but we had many Travelers then. Now, you can't even set foot in the Territory, and I can't leave unless I'm summoned...on our own, against six Incarnations—"

"Five," Simon interrupted, slamming his hammer down on Grandmaster Naraka again.

Rhalia laughed. "Five, right. Five Incarnations, on our own...they could do it. Bring down the walls of Elysia."

Simon had tossed his hammer aside, and had started driving a sword into the pile of flesh, bone, and ash that had once been Grandmaster Naraka. This was a different sword, Alin noticed: roughly the same length and shape, but with a line of gold running down the middle. The gold sang to him, shining brighter than the ordinary metal should have. It couldn't be from Elysia, could it?

"See?" Simon said. "You need our help. The enemy of your enemy is... us." He frowned down at his own cloak. "Stop laughing, he knows what I meant."

An old man in chain mail and a gray uniform had stepped up beside Simon, stabbing his infantry sword into Grandmaster Naraka. A blond girl of maybe thirteen or fourteen joined him, cutting off limbs and pieces of bone with her own short, slightly curving blade.

Everything was happening so fast, Alin couldn't get a grip on himself. But one thing was clear: he couldn't attack them, now that they'd named themselves his allies. None of the Elysian virtues would allow that, no matter how much the Gold Light grumbled that he needed to finish the fight.

There was one thing, though, that Alin himself wanted. He pointed to Naraka.

"Step away from her," he said. "She deserves justice."

None of the Valinhall Travelers listened. Simon looked up at him with evident surprise. "And you don't think she got it?"

When Alin didn't budge, Simon finally ordered the other two back. That was interesting: Alin would have expected the old man was in charge, but he and the girl both stepped back when Simon said so.

Grandmaster Naraka...didn't look like much anymore.

She was little more than a man-sized pile of ash, with bones and pebbly bits of lizard skin sticking up at odd angles. Without the shattered spectacles lying in front of her, Alin would have never known who these remnants had been.

His impotent fury rose up again. How *dare* they take her from him? He had spent six months searching for her, and now Simon killed her before he got a chance? Simon had circumvented justice! He deserved to be punished!

That's not justice, the Blue Light pointed out.

All you wanted was vengeance, the Silver Light said.

It was true, and the Violet Light confirmed it. What he *wanted* to do was challenge Simon to another fight out of sheer frustration, defeat him, and use that to proclaim his superiority. But the *right* thing to do was let it all go and accept the help.

He raised his voice to include Leah as well. "You are welcome here," he said. "We can always use more allies." Leah, he noticed, had replaced her left eye with a glowing red substitute. He wondered if that should bother him more, but his own eyes were anything but human.

With a deep breath, he drew on the Green Light and banished all thoughts of vengeance. They were beneath him, now.

"Maybe you can learn after all," Rhalia said thoughtfully.

"I don't know what he's waiting for," Leah said. "But we need to take advantage of this time and come up with a plan."

That's why Simon had suggested meeting in Valinhall: whatever time they had would be doubled, here.

Alin's eyes flashed silver. "He's bringing his forces through various Territories, so they won't all reach at the same time. He will be waiting until his side is in position, both in this world and in each Territory. We should have at least an hour."

That sounded reasonable. He spoke with such confidence that Simon had to believe him, even though for all Simon knew, Alin could have been making it all up.

For the first time since Myria, Simon stood in a room with Alin and Leah. They each stood around a table in the House of Blades: the only neutral location where they could be sure they wouldn't be observed.

In each of them, the changes couldn't have been more apparent.

Alin, of course, was no longer human. He was clad head-to-toe in gleaming golden armor, and his hair matched. His skin was a shade paler than it had ever been, and his eyes shimmered with slices of every color in the rainbow. More than that, he carried himself differently. His face was all but expressionless, and he had the tendency to stare at something for long minutes without blinking. He had always laughed and told stories for anyone who would listen, radiating warmth and confidence like a bonfire. Now the fire was cold and distant, like a star.

In some ways, the changes in Leah were more dramatic. She had taken command of any situation, even before Simon had known who she was, but now she wore a long, expensive dress of pure red, with a silver circlet on her head. The pale crystal on a chain around her wrist seemed like a lady's ornament, now, rather than simple jewelry worn by a villager. And she only had one blue eye left. Her red eye shone bright, seeming to stare right through him. The raven on her left shoulder let out a *caw*, and then began preening its wing. The whole of Leah, with the raven and the eye and the crown, left her looking like the powerful Queen out of some Territory, not the ordinary ruler of an earthly kingdom.

And then there was Simon.

The cloak makes you look like a bad actor in some cheap play, Caela commented. *You don't even have the sword right now, but if you did, it's way too long to take seriously. You look like a child playing with your father's weapon. The mask looks like it was hammered by an amateur with a pile of scrap metal, which is almost the truth, and—lest we forget—you're carrying around a doll.*

I always did feel ridiculous carrying you around, Simon admitted.

What? No, I make you look much better. 'I don't know who that idiot is, running around in that cloak like he thinks he's an assassin, but where did he get that beautifully crafted doll?' That's what people are going to say about you.

Simon considered and discarded half a dozen possible responses before realizing that, no matter what he said, Caela would win in the end. *I'm... sure you're right, Caela,* he sent at last. *That's exactly what they'll say.*

"We need to lure them over the wall," Alin was saying, when Simon turned his attention back to the discussion. "Fight them on our terms."

"*Can* we fight them, even on our terms?" Leah asked. "We only have, at most, three Valinhall Travelers."

Alin frowned. "Of course we can. I am Elysia, and I will destroy them all."

Leah raised one eyebrow. "Honestly, Alin?"

After a moment, Alin's irises flared violet. "Honestly, no. I can account for two Incarnations, as long as one of them isn't Ragnarus. The King is too dangerous on his own."

It was disturbing, listening to Alin change his mind so fast. It was almost like they were having a conversation with more than one person in the same body.

"Why didn't you bring more Travelers?" Alin continued. "You're the Queen, surely you could have ordered a few along with you."

Leah toyed with the bracelet on her left wrist. "I could have brought some, but there are many who would say I stopped being the Queen the moment my father revealed that he was alive. No matter what state he's in, he's still the King. Anyone I brought would be just as likely to switch sides at any moment. The real threats are the Incarnations anyway; once we destroy them, I can command the remaining Damascan Travelers to return home."

Simon studied the map on the table, which had been switched from a map of Damasca as a whole to one specifically showing the city of Enosh. The Nye knew what they needed, and prepared accordingly. Judging from the layout of the city, Simon realized that he knew precisely nothing about predicting a battle based on the layout of a city. He could have used Indirial's instruction, but the Incarnation had vanished somewhere in the House, and Simon wasn't sure he wanted to know where. If he chased blindly after Indirial, he might find the Overlord consumed by his Incarnation powers, trying to murder Simon in the hallway.

Then again, this was an emergency.

"Eldest," Simon said, and instantly the Nye in the dark gray cloak was standing by the table. Leah took a step back, and Alin's palm filled with gold light, but the Eldest bowed.

"Where's Indirial?" he asked.

"In his new room," the Eldest rasped out. "With his family."

Leah's eye flicked between Simon and the Nye. "Indirial's here? Bring him out. We need his advice."

The Nye shook his hood. "He is a room guardian, now. He cannot leave the gallery. And I do not think he would welcome visitors, at the moment, no matter who they are. He is…struggling with himself, you could say."

So they wouldn't get any help from Indirial. That was a disappointment that might well get them all killed—his experience was invaluable. With him on their side, he could almost believe that they would win. Without him…well, at least he could leave a Valinhall Gate open and retreat when things got too rough.

You wouldn't do that, Caela said confidently. *If you would, Mithra would have never chosen you. Neither would Azura, for that matter.*

No, he admitted. *But at least I'll be able to order Andra and Erastes back.*

A flash of light caught his eye, and he happened to glance up at the weapon racks on the wall.

The empty weapon racks.

Only two blades still rested on their racks: Azura, long and gleaming and silver, and Indirial's Vasha. The others were all empty.

A distant hope rose in Simon's chest. Maybe, just maybe, they'd have more backup than they expected.

But there was no need to count on theoretical support. He'd have to rely on what they had, and then hope for the best.

"Kai and Indirial were our two strongest fighters," Simon said. "Working together, Andra and Erastes and I can take care of two, maybe three Incarnations before we run out of power. That's if we can take them one at a time."

"Which are ideal conditions," Leah added. "That's not likely."

"Yeah. The problem is this." Simon pulled out the mask and placed it on the table. Leah gasped and her hand jerked forward as if she wanted to touch it, but didn't trust herself to do so.

"Simon, is that…was that…"

"It's the same mask I used to fight Alin the other day," Simon said. Alin's eyes had gone flat and gray at the sight of the mask. "It allows me to draw much more power from Valinhall, maybe as much as an Incarnation, but there are…drawbacks."

Leah's fingers drifted through the air above the mask, tracing something that Simon couldn't see. "It binds you to the House," she said. "I can see the chains. The House practically eats you alive when you put this on, doesn't it?"

Simon had never thought of it quite that way, but it sounded accurate. "That's the problem. If I put on this mask, I'll be a match for any of the other Incarnations. Even Ragnarus, I think. But I can only wear it for a couple of minutes, the way I am now, and then I'll run out of power completely. If I keep it on any longer than that…"

"Double Incarnation," Leah said, nodding.

Alin's eyes were back to rainbows again, though the violet slices were shining bright. "Which means you die. That's a pity. We could have used a Valinhall Incarnation on our side."

Simon couldn't keep the irony from his voice. "Yeah, that's tough for you." He tapped the mask with one finger. "This is the Valinhall weakness. We're almost unbeatable in battle, but only for a few minutes. If we don't win quickly, then Erastes, Andra, and I are going to end up either useless or dead."

The three of them stood around the table, looking at the map, lost in thought. Simon couldn't escape the vision of himself ending up like Kai:

metal spikes shredding his body from the inside out, dying slowly and painfully in a way that the pool couldn't heal. He wouldn't mind dying in battle, if he had to, but he had trouble imagining a worse death than Kai's.

"How many Travelers do you have, Alin?" Leah asked.

"Almost two hundred," he said, and Simon's hopes lifted again. Why were they even worried about a handful of Valinhall Travelers if they had *two hundred* other Travelers to call on?

Leah didn't seem as excited as he felt. She simply nodded, as though that was the answer she'd expected. "And how many more fighters from Elysia?"

"Perhaps five hundred." His eyes flashed silver, and he added, "Closer to six hundred, actually, and roughly a thousand ordinary soldiers equipped for battle. Enosh isn't large."

She sighed. "That's what I thought. We have enough to match the force outside, without the Incarnations."

That's why, Caela said. *If they have you to defeat the Incarnations, then they can focus on the ordinary battle. As it is, you have enough force to defend against the army or the five Incarnations, not both.*

Leah rolled the Seed of the Hanging Tree between her fingers. "And then we have this. I didn't want to use it, but we'll take whatever weapons we can get."

Alin's eyes flashed gold. "So you *did* steal that from me. I'll have it back, now."

Leah's mouth quirked up into a smile. "Hmmm…no, I don't think so."

They matched stares for a few moments, red eye meeting rainbow, until Simon finally cleared his throat to get their attention.

"It was hers to begin with," he pointed out. "Besides, aren't you both going to use it for the same reason? As long as she uses it to trap one of the Incarnations, who cares which of you plants it?"

They eyed each other for a few seconds before Alin finally nodded and turned his attention back to the city map.

I hate doing that, Simon thought.

Doing what? Caela sent. *Speaking common sense to two people who were bragging and posturing over something senseless?*

Keeping the peace, he responded.

Oh. Well, get over it.

Such sage advice he got from his dolls.

Over the next hour or two—as time passed in Valinhall—they came up with a plan. Leah expected Zakareth to lead with his Incarnations and follow up with the army, but whenever the Incarnations were committed, Leah would join Andra and Erastes in separating their five enemies from one another. Simon and Alin working together had the best chance of actually finishing off an Incarnation, so they would engage any Incarnation by itself, kill it as quickly as possible, and move on to the next one. Whichever of the five was left by itself at the end would earn the Hanging Tree.

The plan was clear, simple, and Simon hated it immediately.

For one thing, it relied on the fact that they knew practically nothing of King Zakareth's real plans. The Ragnarus Incarnation had shouted to practically the entire nation that he was going to attack Enosh, but he hadn't given any specifics. Leah wouldn't reveal how she had learned that the King was going to be here today, or that his real goal was Elysia, but she had claimed that her source was reliable. And she couldn't use Lirial to scout out the enemy for more specific intelligence, because they had a Lirial Incarnation on their side. None of her scout crystals would return, so she didn't bother sending them.

So that was one hole in their plan: they were relying on the assumption that King Zakareth would be attacking all at once, with overwhelming force. True, that was apparently his favorite strategy, but the King wasn't an idiot. If he had decided that one huge assault was the appropriate tactic, that meant that he thought it had the best chance of success.

"We're basically relying on him not knowing that we're here," Simon pointed out. "Does that seem stupid to anyone else?"

Alin and Leah didn't say anything, but they didn't seem to like having their intelligence insulted, even by implication. Simon forged on nonetheless. "They've got the Lirial Incarnation, so they probably have eyes everywhere. And he could probably sense you, Leah, as soon as you stepped into the city. Why wouldn't he expect us to be here? Where else would we be?"

"I would like to suggest something," the Eldest said, and Simon almost jumped. He had forgotten the Nye was in the room. "The King of Ragnarus forced Indirial to embrace Valinhall and become an Incarnation. It is safe to believe that he knows, by now, that the assault on this House has failed. If that is the case, then let us assume that he knows all. We have lost two of our strongest warriors, and the only full Traveler of Valinhall available to us is this boy. Imagine, for a moment, that he knows all this."

Simon pictured the situation from King Zakareth's side, and he had to admit, the situation looked pretty bright for them.

"If that is the case," the Eldest continued, "then what need has he to account for you in his plans? He may expect his daughter to resist him, and he has surely planned for the Incarnation of Elysia, but to him, Valinhall is broken. We have been disposed of. Even if we brought all our force to bear, in his eyes we are only one Traveler. A Traveler who cannot even become an Incarnation and thereby challenge him, because Indirial has yet to fully rejoin the House."

The Nye spread his black sleeves. "It seems to me that your greatest advantage lies in being underestimated."

Leah tapped her chin thoughtfully at the Eldest's words. "Even if what you're saying is true, he will surely have considered the possibility that there are other Valinhall Travelers left."

"Perhaps he has," the Eldest said. "However, you have forgotten the one great weakness of the Incarnations. They are slaves to their nature."

"Present company excluded," Alin said, in what was probably an attempt at a joke.

The Eldest Nye stared at the Elysian Incarnation for a moment before he continued. "Ragnarus, for all its strength, is very straightforward. He pays the cost, unleashes the weapon, and destroys his target. In his mind, the target called 'Valinhall' has been destroyed. It is in my mind that you may count on some surprise, at least from the House."

"That does help," Simon said. "A little. Thank you. It's not like we have much to surprise him with, though."

"You may be surprised yourself," the Eldest said, and Simon could practically *feel* a smile through the impenetrable darkness of the Nye's hood. "One week ago, I took the liberty of dispatching messengers to the ends of the realm. I did not expect the Dragon's Fangs to be taken hostage, but if I have timed this correctly—ah, see. No matter how old I get, I can still fit a trick or two in these sleeves."

A pair of Valinhall Gates were opening at almost the same time, cutting the entry hall with slashes of white light. Simon had never seen two

Gates open simultaneously before; instead of overlapping, they simply slid to the side where the edges of the Gates connected, pushing each other apart.

At practically the same time, the two final members of the Dragon Army stepped into Valinhall.

Denner wore, as usual, a brown dirt-stained traveling cloak. His clothes were rough and worn, and he wore three days' worth of stubble. He carried his Dragon's Fang in one hand, and under his other arm he had tucked a huge book bound in red-and-gold: his advisor, Hariman.

Simon recognized the other Traveler by reputation alone. Her solid gray hair was cut very short, close to the skull, so that she initially reminded Simon of Erastes. Her face bore the faint marks of a dozen small scars, as though she had taken many cuts to the cheeks while fencing. She wore armor that was both practical and simple, and she held her short-bladed Dragon's Fang in both hands. Her eyes were bright green, and they surveyed the entry hall with distaste.

The Eldest rasped out a chuckle. "As you will recall, son of Kalman, my only joy is that of a good entrance."

Simon felt his spirits lift. He had given up on contacting Denner and Kathrin weeks ago, because there was no way to find them, much less send them a message. But the Eldest had managed it. Adding two Travelers shouldn't have made much difference to their side's chances, but since they were from Valinhall…that might mean another dead Incarnation.

Kathrin glanced around the hall, expression flat and hard. "You redecorated," she said.

"The room was destroyed," Simon said. "Incarnations."

Denner sighed. "I'm sorry to hear that. And, uh, who are they?" He nodded to Alin and Leah.

"For that matter," Kathrin put in, "who are you? And why couldn't I summon my sword yesterday? I was almost killed by pirates. *Pirates,* you hear me? The beggars of the sea, and they nearly got me."

"He's Kai's apprentice," Denner said, before Simon could say anything. "But I was wondering about the Dragon's Fang myself. Before the Eldest's messenger found me, I thought Diava had stopped listening."

Kathrin marched over, threw herself on the sofa, and propped both feet up onto a nearby table. "Where *is* Kai? Hasn't killed himself yet, has he?"

Simon didn't know what his reaction looked like, but Denner took one look at him and sighed heavily.

"I'm sorry," he said. "You can tell us everything later, but for now: who are we fighting?"

CHAPTER 27

WAR IN THE CITY OF LIGHT

The battle began only an hour later.

Simon and the other four Valinhall Travelers waited in the Violet District of Enosh, crouched in a house that was painted a blinding purple. According to Alin, the house had elements that would hide them from opposing Lirial scouts, but the hiding and waiting portion of the battle was almost over.

He knew the fight had begun when the earth shook beneath them, setting the house rattling so that it felt like it would collapse at any second.

"Let's hope that was the King exploding," Andra muttered.

Kathrin held her Dragon's Fang to one side and threw the door open, glancing up and down the street in sheer defiance of her orders to keep hidden. "The first one to attack will be Endross," she said. "He'll head straight for the Elysian Incarnation, and you can believe that." She banished and summoned her Dragon's Fang, then did it again, in what seemed like a nervous tic. "Can't believe they attacked Valinhall...show them what it means to break into *my* House..." Her voice dissolved into angry mutters.

Denner sighed.

"I hope Endross does come alone," Simon said. "We can take him down together. But we need to wait for Leah's signal."

"The Queen," Erastes corrected. "Show her some respect."

Caela giggled. *Yeah, Simon. You should learn to speak respectfully, like me. I could have chosen Angeline,* Simon sent.

Chosen? We decided that I should go with you because I know you best, and I could help you work through Kai and Otoku's death. Even Angeline agreed.

Simon was about to respond, but a silver-white crystal spun into the room, flashing and screaming.

"THIS IS THE SIGNAL," the crystal yelled. "THIS IS THE SIGNAL. THIS IS THE SIGNAL."

All five Valinhall Travelers hurried out of the violet house, as much to escape the shouting crystal as anything. "Somebody shut that thing up,"

Kathrin said.

"Not me," Andra said. "I got the last one."

Jogging down the street, headed into a fight, was a different kind of anticipation than Simon had ever experienced. Sure, he'd run toward fights before, but he was usually forced into them by circumstances. When the options were fight or die, he had little trouble making up his mind. But this time, he was running into an open battle against a superior force, and anything that went wrong would—to one degree or another—be his responsibility.

It was similar to the normal thrill of fear he felt when headed into a fight, combined with the dread of speaking in front of the entire village. He couldn't decide if he liked the feeling or not.

He glanced up, where Alin hovered over the city, glowing with red and orange light, hurling balls of golden force at the walls. Or at the rubble that had once been a wall. That explained the earth-shattering explosion earlier: the opposing Incarnations must have knocked down the city's walls as their opening move.

Alin glowed like a sun, shouting battle cries with superhumanly strong lungs, and generally drawing all the enemy's attention toward himself. He waved a golden blade, his armor shining in the sunlight, occasionally throwing a blast of power at the assembled enemy. In short, he made an obvious target.

That was the heart of the plan, and it looked like he was holding up his end.

It was time for Simon to uphold his.

"Spread out underneath Alin," Simon said. "If any Incarnations show up, split them up, try to get them alone. I'm going up to support him."

"Why?" Kathrin asked. "We have a specialist right here."

Without slowing, she clapped Denner on the shoulder.

The Endross Incarnation, as expected, blasted straight toward Alin on wings of cloud and lightning. He laughed with a sound like thunder, hurling a bolt at Alin that shattered on a shield of green light.

Simon didn't have time to argue about this. "Denner, can you take down Endross?"

Denner looked up and sighed, but he nodded.

"Then you support Alin, and I'll stay below."

Without another word, Denner leaped on top of the nearest building, banishing his Dragon's Fang and summoning a spear from the armory.

As planned, the four remaining Valinhall Travelers took up positions beneath Alin, each standing at one corner of the block. Simon could see Andra on his right, and Kathrin around the corner to his left. This was the Red District, and everything seemed to be organized in perfect squares, which helped when he needed to keep an eye on two streets at once.

At first he was surprised that the streets had been so empty. They hadn't seen anyone or anything between the Violet District and the Red.

They're all fighting at the walls, Caela reminded him.

What's headed our way? Simon asked.

Surprisingly…not much, she sent.

He supposed he should be grateful. No one coming meant that he could go longer without calling on his Valinhall powers, and his chains would stay where they were. But he couldn't escape the thought that he was playing right into someone else's plans.

Correction: we've got a few pets on the way, Caela sent. *A pack of dogs from Naraka, headed straight for us. Kathrin should get them.*

"Kathrin, on your left!" Simon called. He couldn't be sure whether she heard him; she did wave in his direction, but she didn't turn her attention from the battle overhead. Simon didn't bother to look up, though the flashes of light and sudden sounds made it difficult. Between Denner and Alin, they should have no trouble with Endross.

Six ash-gray hounds with manes of smoldering flame burst around the corner, lunging at Kathrin.

She didn't take her eyes off the battle in the sky. With her short-bladed Dragon's Fang held in both hands, she jabbed one dog through the throat as it lunged, spun and gutted the second, shattered the third's spine with a reversed stroke, kicked the fourth through a nearby window, crushed the fifth hound's skull beneath her boot, and impaled the last one through the ribs.

Kathrin covered her mouth as she yawned, wiping her blade absently on a dog's gray coat. She still seemed more interested in Denner's fight than her own. "Don't tell me I got out of bed for this," she called over.

Simon didn't say a word.

Andra! Caela called, and Simon summoned Mithra. An Endross serpent appeared next to the blond girl in a flash of lightning, coiling up to strike. Andra didn't back down; she pulled her own Dragon's Fang back to cut the snake's head off.

A streak of white light flashed past Simon, singeing his arm. It blasted a smoking hole through the giant snake, sending the monster's body to the ground, where it twitched and sent off sparks.

Simon looked back to where the light had come from, only to see Kathrin standing six feet behind him, looking over his shoulder. She banished the same huge steel bow that Valin had used against him in the graveyard, already walking back to her corner. Her eyes were already on Denner and Alin. "That's seven for me," she yelled back to him. "You're going to make Mithra cry."

The Endross Incarnation's body hit the street next to Simon an instant before its head, which rolled almost to Simon's feet. Its eyes were nothing more than smoking sockets.

He looked up to see Alin and Denner. The Incarnation was still shouting battle cries and hurling bolts of gold, while Denner sat on the roof nearby, panting and emptying a waterskin over a burn on his right arm.

Nothing else happened.

Simon could hear the distant battle over by the walls, and Alin was obviously shooting at *something*, but where were the Incarnations? Their primary objective was to eliminate Alin and, if possible, Elysia. So why weren't they going for it? Was the trap that obvious, or had something gone wrong?

Leah still hadn't ordered him elsewhere, but Simon called steel and hopped up to a second-story window ledge, and from there to the top of a two-story house.

He couldn't see much of the battle: a group of soldiers, supported by red gnomes from Elysia, engaged a handful of Ornheim Travelers a few streets over. Other than that, mostly all he could see were wheeling birds, bolts of lightning, and flashes of colored light.

Caela, where are the Incarnations?

Don't rush me, she snapped. *There are a few thousand bodies down there, and it's not as easy as you think to tell them apart. Truly, only someone as skilled and talented as I would even bother to try...*

After a few more seconds, she gave him the mental equivalent of a frustrated sigh. *They're not there,* she said. *I'd bet a thousand hours on it. The only Incarnation on this battlefield was Endross.*

So the King *had* anticipated them and set them up. The thought almost made Simon feel more comfortable—he wasn't sure what he'd do if a plan went exactly as he expected it to. Die of shock, probably.

Simon shouted some quick orders to Andra and then hopped to a nearby rooftop. "Lead me to Leah," he said.

You're talking out loud again, Caela reminded him, but she still gave him directions.

Predictably, Leah was standing behind a wall of golems and Travelers, giving orders. The fact that these soldiers weren't Damascan probably hadn't occurred to her, and they seemed to salute and obey her quickly enough. Even the gold-armored, winged warriors of Elysia listened to her, running where she pointed.

Simon hopped down from the house and released his steel as soon as possible: the chains were creeping up onto his neck, and he needed to delay as much as he could.

"The Incarnations aren't here," he said.

With her red eye, Leah scanned the nearby battle: a bunch of bird-men engaged against a giant blue jellyfish floating in the sky. It was odd to think that he was on the side of the jellyfish.

"I know," she said. "We saw them before the battle, but they disappeared shortly before Endross attacked, presumably into a Territory. There's no telling where they'll come out."

"Oh." It was good to know that Leah was aware of the problem, but she didn't seem as upset as he had expected. "What are we going to do about it?"

"That's why I keep a bunch of Valinhall Travelers around," Leah said, tapping a nearby golem on the shoulder and pointing toward the bird-men. The creature of living rock hefted a stone axe and turned its emerald eyes to the battlefield, lumbering slowly down the street.

"We will engage the Incarnations when we see them," Simon said. "We'll try to slow them down until you can get there."

Leah nodded, her red-and-blue eyes still on Simon. "*Just* slow them," she said seriously. "Don't throw your life away for Alin's. I'd rather have you back alive than him."

Awww, how sweet, Caela sent.

"I'm not sure how I can protect him without risking my life," Simon said, but he owed her more than that. He met her eyes and gave a little smile. "Sorry. I'll do my best."

She returned the smile, and he left.

He was almost back to his corner of the fight, underneath Alin, when a swirling blue-edged Gate flashed into being right next to Kathrin.

Caela and Simon shouted a warning at the same time, but a torrent of force blasted out from the open Gate: lightning, stones, a spear, some sort of flashing crystals and jagged ice, and maybe a hundred other things bursting from the Territory with the force of a titan's hammer.

The wrath of the Incarnations met ghost armor, and Kathrin was launched backwards, down the street, her Dragon's Fang falling from her hand.

She's alive, Caela said hastily, *and she'll be coming back. But that surely broke her ghost armor, so she'll have to be careful.*

The four remaining Incarnations piled out of the Endross Gate, along with a single Endross Traveler in loose-fitting white clothes. Now that the Endross Incarnation was gone, the remaining Incarnations could all Travel through Endross as a unified group.

King Zakareth, the patterns on his skin shining red and gold in the sunlight, held out a hand. The Lightning Spear smacked into his palm, and he raised it to throw.

Andra ran from the other side of the building, rounding the corner to come face-to-face with four Incarnations.

Helgard waved a hand in her direction, and the black ice sharpened into a jagged icicle pointed straight at Andra.

Lirial raised both hands toward the far side of the building, where Simon knew Erastes waited. The old soldier only had the steel; he couldn't stop a bolt from an Incarnation.

Ornheim stepped forward, raising a red-and-black sword in both hands. Simon felt like he'd seen that sword before, somewhere, but he couldn't quite place it. The Incarnation thrust the blade into the air and began sawing slowly through the air.

A gatecrawler. While everyone else was distracted, the Incarnations had decided to cut their way into Elysia and bring down the City of Light behind Alin's back.

All of this flashed through Simon's mind in a single instant, but one thing rose above all the rest: Andra and Erastes were in danger. They were entirely outclassed…and for that matter, so was he.

He reached into his cloak pocket.

I have to, he sent.

I know, Caela said, sadly. *It's what Valin would have done.* Mithra felt somehow both resigned and eager.

Simon put on the mask.

Only a few minutes since Alin and the brown-cloaked Traveler finished off the Endross Incarnation, the Silver Light alerted him to something down below. It felt like a Gate opening, and four impossibly bright individuals walking out.

He flew over, prepared to unleash Gold Light on them, when someone stuck a burning, jagged blade into his mind.

Gatecrawler, the Silver Light whispered.

And then Leah's spear was blasting toward him. He summoned a shield of Green Light, as thick as he could, and the spear struck with only enough force to send a crack running through the plate and give him a splitting headache. He retaliated with a two-handed blast of Gold Light, but the King caught it on his shield.

"Duel me with honor, Elysia," King Zakareth called, in the dramatic voice of a trained orator. "Let us not settle for these—"

And then he was blasted off his feet when Simon slammed into him.

To Alin's vision, he was little more than a black-and-silver blur cloaked in shadows, but it couldn't be anyone else but Simon. He hit the Ragnarus Incarnation's shield with his shoulder, knocking the King off his feet and onto his back, but he didn't stop moving.

His blade passed through the Helgard Incarnation's wrist in a sheet of shining gold, so she dropped her spear of ice. Her expression was annoyed, rather than surprised or pained. Then, without seeming to move, Simon was ten feet away, standing in front of the Lirial Incarnation, deflecting her incandescent white bolts with his flashing blade.

The King regained his feet, but not before Simon kicked Lirial up, across the street, and onto a nearby roof.

We shouldn't waste that opportunity, the Gold Light pointed out, and Alin agreed. He called Gold from Elysia in a hammer that fell from the sky on top of Lirial, blasting her down through the roof and through two floors of the house.

Simon, meanwhile, had managed to go blade-to-blade with Ragnarus. The King held his spear in both hands, sweeping the butt of his weapon at Simon's feet and managing to get his spearhead between every one of Simon's strikes, in spite of the Valinhall Traveler's impossible speed. Alin couldn't see the details of the match, thanks to Simon's cloak of shadows, but Ragnarus was clearly on the back foot.

Helgard, meanwhile, was engaged in combat with the blond-haired Valinhall girl. Actually, the Incarnation didn't seem particularly engaged at all: she was focused on fitting her severed hand back onto her wrist, where it froze back on to her arm. Her ice was doing all her fighting on its own, spinning and parrying every one of the Valinhall girl's strikes.

Alin lowered himself to the ground.

They need you to even the odds, the Orange Light said, and he had to say: he was looking forward to it.

He summoned his sword of golden light and swung it at Helgard's back in a Red-enhanced fist.

A second length of black ice appeared out of nowhere, catching his strike. Helgard turned slowly to look at him, her eyes flashing with every color of winter.

"Alin, son of Torin," she said. "Elysia. I have always wanted to see the City of Light."

Then the whole street froze.

Snow simply *appeared,* perhaps summoned from Helgard, and every exposed surface was suddenly covered in a layer of frost. Even his armor crawled with white, growing like moss over the surface of his golden breastplate. Snowflakes whirled through the air in a white flurry.

Alin opened himself up to Violet, planning to banish every inch of this snow, but he hesitated. He couldn't dive in too deep to the Violet Light, or he would end up like he had the last time he'd fought Simon. He couldn't afford to lose control now.

And in that moment of indecision, a frozen hand formed out of the snow, grabbing him by the shoulders and pulling him to the ground. A layer of black icicles flashed up to meet him, stabbing through his armor and driving into his flesh. The cold was at least as shocking as the pain, which remained as distant as ever, but his Rose Light flared at every wound. The spears of ice drove into his flesh as quickly as he healed, tearing his wounds even deeper, pushing in agony so deep that it reached him even through his Incarnated body.

For the first time in six months, he screamed with actual pain.

His honest, wordless cry summoned Violet Light, which flailed blindly from his body in long, bandage-like strips. Scoops of snow vanished wherever the Violet struck, and it only took a second to clear out the icicles that were driving into his ribs. The Rose Light began repairs instantly.

But Helgard had been busy.

A blue-skinned hand big enough to juggle an ox wrapped around Alin's middle and tossed him into a building across the street.

Alin surrounded his body in a bubble of Green, filling himself with Red an instant before he hit. He crashed straight through the solid wall, tumbling and rolling to a stop on the second floor.

He caught a glimpse of a room filled with hand-carved wooden toys, perhaps a child's bedroom, before he was falling again.

The floor hadn't given way—there was *already* a hole in this floor, and he had simply rolled into it.

He caught himself with Orange Light before he hit the ground, the Rose still repairing the damage from Helgard's icicles. He let himself drift gently down to the floor.

When his eyes were blinded by a flash of light, he realized he wasn't alone.

His head blasted backwards as though he'd been hit with a hammer, and he heard a woman's mocking, crystalline laughter.

Ah, the Silver Light noted. *This is where Simon threw the Lirial Incarnation.*

You're blind, the Rose Light added. *Nothing we can do about it for a few seconds, at least.*

So Alin called Silver Light.

The world appeared before him, drawn in shades of white and shining gray. Inanimate objects—the walls, floor, the rubble around him—were somehow indistinct, as though he were looking at them from the bottom of a lake. But Lirial shone with perfect clarity, a trio of stars whirling around in a halo behind her head.

Another blast hammered into him, but this one he caught on a shield of Green Light. Then he reached out and grabbed Lirial's head in a hand filled with Red.

With Red Light coiling through his whole body, Alin hurled the crystal Incarnation through an undamaged section of wall.

That, it seemed, was too much for the building. With a slow roar, the house collapsed in on itself, sagging and sliding down to the snow in the street below. Tons of debris collapsed on Alin's head, but he covered himself with a shield of Green and Orange. The large chunks floated away from him, the smaller pattering against the six-sided plates of Green. He walked out unscathed.

The Rose Light had already completed its work on the rest of his body, and had started repairing his eyes. The world went from fuzzy outlines to clear, distinct colors as he exited the building, and he took a look around.

The Lirial Incarnation was nowhere to be seen, but Helgard's blue giant was rampaging down the street. It towered above all the buildings he could see, its entire face nothing but one huge eye. Its head turned, that eye swiveling to look at Alin.

There were beings he could summon from Elysia to match this titan, but they would all be needed to defend the City in case Enosh fell. No matter what this giant was capable of, he would be no match for the Incarnation of Elysia.

The one-eyed titan reached down and scooped up the Helgard Incarnation, lifting her to stand on its shoulder. Helgard raised her hands, and a blizzard howled down the street, covering everything else in a blanket of white.

Simon couldn't understand why the Ragnarus Incarnation wasn't dead.

He planted his foot in the old man's chest, kicking him with enough force to crack a stone pillar. The King flew up and back, flipping in midair and landing on his feet on top of a nearby building. Simon leaped after him, vaguely aware of a towering blue giant and a flowing cloud of snow rushing along beside him. Helgard was Alin's problem now, and Simon only had enough time to deal with one opponent at a time.

Deep in the Nye essence, Simon flashed toward King Zakareth, sweeping Mithra in wide arcs to back him up. Once the Incarnation had his back to the ledge, Simon could launch a real attack and finish him.

That was the plan, but the King was proving a match for him even with the Nye essence. The point of the Lightning Spear caught the flat of his blade and knocked it up, leaving a gap in his defenses that he had to step back to cover. From there, the Ragnarus Incarnation had the advantage, and his Spear seemed to be everywhere. It was all Simon could to do turn each blow with Mithra's edge, knocking the spear aside high, then low, then sidestepping as the Lightning Spear reached for his throat.

Panic gripped him by the gut. He wasn't worried about losing the fight, not with the mask, but he was running out of time. There were only half a dozen links left in his chain before it closed around his neck, and he died. Like Kai had.

You've driven him away, Caela said. *Leave him! There's nothing he can do on his own.*

The second I turn my back, he'll put the Lightning Spear through me, Simon said, slipping past a strike from the same spear. *I need...*

Help, Caela finished. *Fortunately, you've got some coming.*

Behind Zakareth, Erastes climbed up the side of the roof. The King would never be able to read Simon's eyes behind the mask, but he still tried not to look directly at the other Valinhall Traveler, for fear of drawing the Incarnation's attention.

It didn't matter. Zakareth cocked his head to one side, as though listening. His expression never changed as he pivoted smoothly, hurling the Lightning Spear straight at Erastes.

The soldier had no chance. He only had the steel, not the essence, and he would never be able to react in time. His eyes barely had time to widen before the Spear...

...shivered to a stop in mid-air, frozen and hovering.

To your right! Caela called, and Simon glanced over to see Leah standing on the next rooftop over, red eye blazing, with one hand outstretched toward the Spear. Her raven whirled overhead, screaming.

The Spear started to float toward Leah, but then Zakareth beckoned sharply, and it flipped back into his hand.

"Hello, father," Leah began, but Simon didn't have time to listen to a conversation. He threw himself back at the Ragnarus Incarnation, trying to push the old man around so that Erastes could have a shot at his back.

Unbelievably, Zakareth got even faster. He ducked a strike from Simon, spun around and tripped Erastes with the butt of his spear, then completed the turn and thrust the Lightning Spear at Simon's chest.

So that's what happens when you use Ragnarus enhancements on an Incarnation's immortal body, Caela said. *The Nye will be interested to know that.*

What can I do? Simon asked, the chains on his neck closing around him like the hands of a murderer. But when Lirial alighted on the building, firing a series of white bolts at Leah, he knew the answer.

Nothing.

Leah had come to fight directly, even though she knew she shouldn't have. Murin thought she was an idiot for doing so, and she couldn't help but agree with the bird. Direct combat wasn't her style; that was why she had Simon and Indirial.

Or...just Simon, now. She would have to get used to that.

She was preparing to call Lirial crystal and seal her father's feet, maybe at least trip him up a bit, when Lirial herself drifted to the rooftop, her dress of silver wire flashing in the sun. Lirial struck with her version of a star-net, blasting Leah with a mixture of crystals and bolts of solid white light.

She called crystal out of the roof, and a jagged spire of pale stone met the bolts, defending her for a moment. Only for a moment. If she could summon the Lightning Spear, she would be fine, but her father held that weapon in an iron grip.

She did have one card yet to play, though.

Kneeling behind her spire of crystal, Leah pressed both palms to the roof and stretched her will out to Ragnarus.

"Cynara the First, Queen of Damasca, your daughter calls upon you," she said. The Queen had insisted that her summons should be appropriately dramatic, or she wouldn't bother answering.

For a few seconds, the Lirial Incarnation continued chewing through Leah's crystal shield, and she started wondering if she should repeat the call again, though with some more flowery language.

Then there was a red flash, and Cynara stood over her.

Her dress of scarlet light flowed against the wind, crimson flesh standing out like a spot of blood against the white snow on the roof. Her eyes were locked on Lirial, and there was a small smile on her lips.

Leah didn't know what price Cynara had taken for her help, but whatever it was, it left her feeling like she was on the edge of passing out. "I'm glad...I met...with your approval," she managed to say.

Cynara waved a hand. "Good enough," she said. "Now, I don't have quite the power I once did, but since Zak isn't using it..."

Leah had a second to think, *Zak?*

Then Cynara pulled the Rod of Harmony from the Crimson Vault, and stepped in front of the Lirial Incarnation.

The bolt from the star-net crashed into a wave of red light from the ruby on top of the Rod. Lirial screamed, and then the bolt appeared an inch from her eye, slamming into her forehead and flipping her over backwards.

Queen Cynara was already on top of her, moving with a grace and athleticism that Leah would never have expected. The Rod was gone, and she was driving a heavy mace down on Lirial's crystal head.

There was a flash of white light, and Lirial was floating across the street. Cynara walked to the edge of the building, next to Leah, her stride casual. The mace was missing, and she held a gold-and-ruby dagger in each hand.

Cynara bent her scarlet legs as if to leap after Lirial, but she evidently thought better of it. The twin daggers went back into the Vault, and a wide, shallow bowl came out.

"Watch yourself," she called to Leah.

Leah wasn't sure what she was meant to look out for, but she backed up as far as she could. Simon was still locked in battle with King Zakareth, two or three roofs over, but the old soldier Erastes was gone. Dead?

Then Alin's gold-armored figure came hurtling out of the snow like a falling star. He flew straight toward the bowl that Cynara held, which she angled to catch him. In a flare of red light, Alin froze ten feet from the bowl, hovering in midair. When he stopped, a blast of wind shot out from him, as though the force of his flight had been dispersed into the air. Snow blasted away from him in a ring.

The snow that had started to melt on the roof, even what had half-melted to slush, froze solid. Leah started shivering again; the temperature seemed to drop into the depths of winter in the span of a few seconds.

"The Bowl drains heat," Cynara explained, levering the bowl to the side. Floating in the air, Alin moved along with the artifact, falling on to the ceiling when she dumped the bowl over. "That's the only price, though I'm not entirely sure why."

Alin rose to his feet, brushing snow from his shattered armor. "Thank you," he said, then he gave Cynara a closer look.

"You're the former Ragnarus Incarnation?" he asked.

Cynara smiled more broadly, then gave him a mocking curtsy.

Alin stood for a moment, thinking. After a few seconds, he held out one golden hand.

"Please, Rhalia," he said.

A woman popped out of the air in front of him. She wore a long white dress belted with a golden sash, and her blond hair almost reached down to her feet. She spun a loop in midair, her arms and smile wide. "You should have summoned me *ages* ago! It's a lot whiter than I...remembered..."

Her loop slowed to a crawl, and she drifted down to the roof, staring at Cynara. The two summoned women stared at one another with wide eyes. Even Queen Cynara looked as though she couldn't believe what she was seeing.

"...Rhalia?" she whispered, and several dozen separate facts clicked into place for Leah. Cynara had mentioned her sister, and somewhere in the back of her mind, Leah had known that her sister was an Elysian Traveler...but *the* Elysian Traveler? The first Incarnation of Elysia, and the one that had almost destroyed Damasca?

Tears welled up in the golden eyes of the legendary Elysian Incarnation, and she staggered toward her sister, wrapping her pale arms around Cynara's red shoulders. "I'm so sorry," Rhalia murmured through her tears. "I always...wanted to tell you..."

They held each other for a while, and then Cynara released her. Rhalia didn't let go.

"Rhalia," the Queen said.

The former Incarnation of Elysia shook her head. Alin shook his head and stepped off the roof, caught by Orange Light, flying away to join Simon.

One roof over, the Helgard Incarnation landed in a crouch. Her one-eyed giant stepped up beside her, raising its fist as if to smash the roof on which Leah stood.

"Rhalia," Cynara said, more urgently.

"I've waited three hundred years for this," Rhalia said, without releasing her sister. "I can take a little longer."

"No, you can't!" Leah yelled. She drew as deeply as she could from her Lirial source, tried to summon the Lightning Spear—it failed; her father must still be holding it—then tried to summon the Titan Shield, but that failed as well. Her father still had a grip on everything useful.

As the giant's blue fist fell, she wondered if her crystal would be enough.

Then an orange sun bloomed between her and the descending fist. The giant's hand rose into the sky, pulling its enormous body along with it. At any second, Leah expected the orange light to vanish, letting the one-eyed titan fall back down to earth. It never happened. It kept drifting up, silently struggling, until Leah lost it among the clouds.

Helgard seemed more stunned than anyone else, her mouth working soundlessly.

Rhalia finally let go of her sister, smiling proudly. "I *am* sorry," she said at last.

"Yes, well, I spent the last three and a half centuries sealed inside a blood-sucking tree," Queen Cynara said dryly. "For the first hundred years, I kept planning out how to escape and make you suffer."

Rhalia's face crumpled, and she looked as though she were about to cry again.

"…stop that. You're almost four hundred years old, act your age. It's been a long time since I blamed you for this. I paid my price, and I reaped the reward. Bitter as it may have been."

Ignoring the Helgard Incarnation, who looked curious rather than confused, Queen Cynara gestured to Leah.

"Leah, daughter of Zakareth, this is my older sister Rhalia."

Rhalia beamed and drifted over to Leah, spinning circles around her in midair. "This is Leah, huh? She wears the Eye well. Much better than that old man."

Cynara's expression hardened. "Anything was better than the old man."

At first, Leah was inclined to correct them about her name—she was the daughter of Kelia, not Zakareth. But Cynara had never met her mother, so she let that slide. Then she thought they were talking about her father as the 'old man,' but the context made that unlikely. Rhalia would have never met Zakareth the Sixth. Someone from their own time, then?

A shrill alarm from one of Leah's scout crystals shrieked in her ear, and she spun around to find a dozen White Razors—sharpened snowflakes the size of wagon wheels—spinning straight at her, out of the snow.

She blocked the first one with crystal, but Cynara shattered the rest with a fistful of crimson darts. They shot out of midair and pierced each snowflake straight through the middle.

Leah was forcibly reminded, then, exactly how much she had left to learn about the Crimson Vault.

"We can handle this, Leah," Queen Cynara said, launching a red wooden javelin at Helgard.

"Could you go see to the Elysia Gate, if you don't mind?" Rhalia asked. "There's a golem that cut his way inside."

That's right, I almost forgot. Ornheim had been using his gatecrawler to slice his way into Elysia, and the rest of them had been too distracted by the other Incarnations to pay him any attention. Without another word, Leah started climbing down from the roof.

"Too slow!" Rhalia called, and then Leah felt herself lifted up by the shoulders and carried down to the street below.

…it wasn't the most dignified way to travel, but at least it was fast.

Alin fought side-by-side with Simon, and it was the most fulfilling thing he had done in years.

He blasted King Zakareth with Gold Light, sending the Incarnation staggering, but when he turned to launch his spear in Alin's direction, Simon was all over him, swinging that gold-and-silver blade of his so fast that Zakareth had to summon his shield. He used both that and his spear to keep Simon at bay. Meanwhile, Alin had the space to summon a coil of Blue Light underneath Zakareth's foot, snagging his grip and draining a bit of his armor's power away.

The Ragnarus Incarnation broke the Blue binding, but it still made him stagger a bit, took a little energy away from his weapons. He would fall to the two of them, and soon.

And there was something…right about it. Alin and Simon, standing side-by-side, fighting the evil Incarnation. Alin was even fighting like a Traveler; he couldn't call much more power without endangering Simon as well, so for a moment he could pretend that all was as it should be, and he and Simon were about to vanquish the evil king together.

If you hadn't made so many stupid decisions, the Violet Light said, *perhaps you could have fought this way in truth, and not just in your mind.*

Simon finally landed a good blow, knocking Zakareth's shield aside and slashing across his breastplate with the tip of his blade.

While the Ragnarus Incarnation staggered backwards, Alin called Gold.

The hammer of Gold Light blasted King Zakareth off the roof, sending him flying down and toward the original building, where a hastily torn Elysian Gate waited.

"Thanks," Simon said, panting.

"You didn't do too bad yourself," Alin said. "You know, for someone who's not a real Traveler."

Simon stared at him from behind the mask for a second before he snorted a laugh. "You know, I—"

Something caught his attention, as if he was listening to someone else talk, and then his whole body tensed. He leaped off the roof after Zakareth, his blade held in both hands.

Obviously he had thought of something that Alin hadn't noticed with his Silver Light, so Alin flew after him on wings of Orange Light.

Leah was there, crouched at the edge of the Elysian Gate with her hands raised, as if she were about to summon some power. Her father had one leg raised to enter the portal himself, shield in one hand and spear in the other. His gold-and-ruby-patterned face caught the light. Simon landed, his knees bent, blade drawn back for a strike, his mask turned up toward Zakareth.

As had happened once before, in Malachi's mansion, the moment froze.

Alin stepped away from his own body, turning to look at himself. His rainbow eyes had frozen with orange prominent, so the slices of orange glowed most brightly. His hair had turned from blond to something that looked like strands of actual gold—he wondered for a second if the hair on his head had turned to metal, or if it was just his appearance that had changed. His armor was practically in ruins again, and after all the effort he'd gone through to have it repaired the first time.

But it was his expression that bothered him the most. He stared forward, looking completely blank. He showed less emotion than a statue, as if nothing had ever happened that he cared about, and nothing ever would.

In his featureless confidence, he looked just like King Zakareth.

Rhalia walked up beside him, casually strolling along, glancing into everyone's eyes one at a time as if to memorize the scene.

"How did you do this?" he asked.

"Oh, you should know that by now," she said. "And now your brain won't sizzle quite so fast, so we can take our time."

When Alin bothered to think about it, with all the knowledge of Elysia, it seemed obvious. "It's a Silver artifact, combined with Red Light to enhance the mind."

Rhalia clapped three times. "You win the prize! My body's over there." She motioned to a building across the street, where her white-robed form fought next to her red-clad sister. "So let's see if the wisdom of the Silver Light is all it's supposed to be. What do I have to tell you?"

"Something about the King," Alin said. "Does he have a weapon I don't know about?"

She shrugged. "Probably. But no, that's not why I'm here."

Rhalia hopped over to Simon and pointed at his collar.

To Alin's surprise, Simon was *still moving*. Everything else looked perfectly still, but Simon actually crept forward, his legs springing up, his sword drifting around in a strike that would take days to land.

"How is he not frozen?" Alin asked.

"No one's frozen," Rhalia corrected. "We're experiencing time very, very quickly…and separate from our bodies, of course. The fact that we can perceive him move at all is a reflection of how fast he's managed to go. But that's not what I'm here to point out."

She gestured under his cloak again, and Alin leaned in for a closer look.

Those black marks, the chains that crawled up Simon's arms, had reached all the way around his neck.

The final link was gray, like the fuzzy edge of a shadow, but when it turned black, the chain would have covered Simon's body completely.

"What does that mean?" Alin asked, quietly.

She shook her head. "I'm not familiar with Valinhall, but even I can sense it. He's too far in debt to his Territory. When that chain is completed, he will either Incarnate or die."

Simon had warned him about this, about what would happen if he wore the mask. The chain must be his time limit.

"There was another Valinhall Incarnation only days ago," Alin said. "He told us."

"Then, when this chain is completed, Simon will die." Rhalia waved a hand. "Or he may fuse with his Territory or the current Incarnation. In those cases, he will wish for death."

That would be a tragedy, the Rose Light whispered. *Simon has never tried to do anything but good.*

You owe him, the Orange Light said.

There's nothing you can do about it, the Silver pointed out.

You don't need to worry about him, the Gold said proudly. *He's a warrior, dying in battle. He's lived a full life, short though it was. Everyone should be as lucky as he, dying like this.*

"He has lived a good life," Alin said out loud. "He will die with honor."

Rhalia swept a strand of hair out of her golden eyes. Alin knew they weren't really in their bodies, but it all sure *looked* real.

"Wouldn't it be better if he could live with honor, instead?" Rhalia asked.

She knows a way, the Violet Light said.

"What do you want me to do?"

Rhalia turned and looked at the Elysian Gate. "There is one door you have yet to open."

The White District. Whenever he asked Rhalia for advice, it always came down to the White.

"...in the City," he said.

"Yes. The White Light can only be used on another's behalf. It can empower Simon with all the might of Elysia, giving him the strength he needs to win this battle. But it would mean staying here, with me."

You have to save him, if you can, the Blue Light said.

Going through that Gate would be like dying, the Red argued. *Worse: it would be like giving up!*

Alin took a moment to think of the problem from every angle. "I wish I could go," he said at last, "but I can't. I would be trapped there, and the people need an Elysian Traveler to lead the way into the light. It would be selfish of me to save this one man and deprive the world of the City of Light." He wanted to save Simon, but it wasn't practical.

He had to admit a certain measure of relief, though. The thought of staying trapped in one Territory forever chilled him; he almost thought dying in battle would be the better fate.

"That's...not exactly right." Rhalia smiled a little. It was the kind of smile that said, *I have a surprise, and I'm not sure you're going to like it.*

Then she walked around the King, standing in front of the Elysian Gate. She stood, waiting expectantly, clearly indicating that he should follow.

With an unexplainable sense of dread, Alin walked after her. And he looked into Elysia.

The field of grass and flowers outside the walls was all but torn up. Four people stood engaged against the towering Ornheim Incarnation and a small army of golems. One was the blond girl, Andra, her black-spotted sword clenched in both hands. She had driven her sword through a golem's neck joint, popping its head off. The gem-spotted boulder still hung in the air, wearing a comical expression of surprise.

The second person was also a Valinhall Traveler, but much older. Kathrin was in the middle of swinging a giant mirror-bright hammer at Ornheim's stone kneecap. A mask of blood covered her forehead, and her snarl made her look as though she wished she could bite the Incarnation in half.

The other two people were his sisters.

Ilana, five years older than he was, stood ten paces away with a bow in both hands. She had hardly touched a bow in years, but this one was made of some golden wood, and she was fitting a gleaming arrow to the string. One small, dog-shaped golem had been impaled through its gemstone eye by a shining arrow that matched the one Ilana held in her bow.

That brought him to his little sister, Shai. She had the same bored expression she always wore when she was intensely interested in something.

And she was wielding a strip of Violet Light in each hand, like a pair of whips. Piles of rubble sat at the end of the light, as though she had reduced a group of golems to inanimate gravel.

"She's…alive," Alin said, his voice unsteady.

Practically glowing with pride, Rhalia drifted over to watch his sister. "Back in Myria, when you opened the Gates to Elysia, I was able to bring her inside. She needed a lot of attention in the Rose District, but I kept her in the City. Safe from Naraka, and from you."

Indignant anger welled up in him for a moment—*I would never hurt her! She's my sister!*—before he crushed the feeling down. All things considered, Rhalia had made the right call.

"Thank you," Alin said. "You probably saved her life." Another thought occurred to him, and he almost dared to hope. "What about Tamara? Did you save her?" He had seen his oldest sister die, but if Rhalia had managed to heal Shai…

Rhalia shook her head, but she said nothing else.

Alin's hopes fell, but Green patience saved him from grieving anew. Instead, he focused on the sister in front of him, the family that had been miraculously restored from death. "Is she a Traveler?"

"It wasn't uncommon, back in my time, for there to be two natural Elysian Travelers from the same family." Rhalia kept her words quiet, studying Alin as if to gauge his reaction.

"What about the prophecy?" he asked.

Rhalia sighed. "That was after my time, but I can make a good guess. The fact that there was a prophecy at all suggests that Avernus was involved. Strigaia-tribe owls can see the future, but only in vague, specific pieces. I have no doubt that you were the boy some Grandmaster Avernus once predicted would free the Incarnations. And so you did. You even killed King Zakareth, which may or may not have been part of the same prediction."

But that doesn't mean those things were good, the Silver Light pointed out. *Nor does it mean you're the only one.*

"Call Violet," Rhalia suggested. "Tell me the truth. What does this make you feel?"

"Relieved, that my sisters are alive," Alin said, through a haze of Violet honesty. "Confused. And...disappointed, because I thought I was the only one. I wanted to be the hero."

Rhalia looked back at Simon, who was still inching forward through the frozen moment. "You can be."

You're out of time, Caela said.

Simon slammed Mithra into King Zakareth's back, knocking him through the gold-edged Gate and into the City of Light.

I know, Simon sent.

Something else blasted past him into the portal, something orange and gold and glowing, but he didn't get a good look. All his attention was focused on his enemy, as he threw himself through the Gate and after the King. There was even a battle going on around him—he vaguely noticed Kathrin fighting a huge, white golem—but he ignored it.

If he was about to die, he wanted to do it while taking Zakareth's head from his shoulders.

I wanted to tell you... He hesitated. He'd never been good at saying the right thing, but he had to try. When would he get another chance? *Of all the swords I could have gotten, I'm glad it was Azura.*

So were we, Caela whispered. It was hard to tell, with her shifting, windy voice, but she sounded on the verge of tears. *You were so much better than Kai.*

Alin hurtled through the streets of the City of Light, blasting past shops and homes and towers. In seconds, he reached the heart of the city.

Please don't be too late, he said to himself. He would have hated to do all this for nothing. *Please don't be too late, not too late...*

Relax, the Green Light told him.

He spun around, surrounded by colored doors. He saw the violet, the red, the orange...and there. So small and shabby that it looked like it belonged on a garden gate.

The White Door.

He twisted the handle and pulled, flooding the room with White Light. For a moment, he panicked: this hadn't happened when he opened any of the other doors! The power washed his mind clean, swallowing him whole.

For what felt like an eternity, he drifted on an endless sea of white. All his concerns melted away, and for the first time since he gave up his humanity, Alin finally relaxed.

After a time, the White Light asked him a question. *What do you want me to do?*

From deep within him, the other virtues of Elysia responded.

Defeat the enemy, the Gold Light said.

Protect our allies, said the Orange.

Give us peace, said the Green.

Finish the battle, said the Red.

Help us save the day, said the Violet.

The White Light was quiet for a long time, though Alin himself floated in complete peace.

Those are all wonderful goals, the White Light said gently, *but it's not about you.*

And everything was silent.

Finally, the Gold Light spoke up. It sounded almost reluctant. *Simon has proven his valor,* it said.

He needs help, said the rose.

I'd like to have your power myself... the Violet began.

...but you should give it to him instead, the Blue finished.

Help Simon, said the Silver Light. *Give him whatever he needs.*

And, floating on White Light, Alin agreed.

That, I can do. The White flowed out of him, draining his strength, carrying it away...to Simon.

Helgard was coming after her, but Leah sealed the Incarnation's legs in a quick layer of crystal before tumbling through the Gate.

It was all chaos and madness inside. The Ornheim Incarnation had summoned a bunch of golems to fight Kathrin and Andra and what looked like Alin's *sisters,* one of whom was laying everything around her to waste with a couple of glowing violet whips.

Setting aside her shock at seeing the two sisters both alive and in Elysia, Leah stared at the most horrifying thing she could see.

The huge, dark chain stretching away from Simon's neck, leading into the distance.

To her Eye of Ages, each link in the chain was as wide around as a wagon, binding Simon closer and closer to his Territory. That chain was almost complete, and she knew with instinctive certainty that as soon as it snapped shut, terrible things would happen. Certainly terrible for Simon, and possibly for all of them.

He was facing her father, so Leah summoned the Lightning Spear. To her shock, it came spinning through the air toward her—King Zakareth must have been even more surprised by Simon than she was.

She snatched the Spear out of the air, preparing to throw...

...and then the chain turned white.

Not just the spectral chain that she saw through her crimson eye, either. All the black chains on Simon's skin glowed a pure, bright white, and white light blazed from the eye sockets of his mask. Was he Incarnating?

The dark chain stretching out from his neck dispersed and blew away like the memory of smoke. Meanwhile, Simon glowed white.

Leah heard a cry, and she looked down to see the doll in the blue dress and bonnet sitting on the grass next to her. Caela.

What's happening? the doll asked, in her mind. *We thought he was going to die, so he left me here. What's going on? Did he call too much?*

"I don't know," Leah said, studying the scene through her Eye. "I don't see the chains of Valinhall on him anymore. Wherever he's calling that power from, it's not the House."

As she spoke, something faded into existence behind him. She could barely see it with her Eye of Ages, but it was becoming clearer every second: a winged sword, point-down, on a field of white.

Elysia.

If this was how death or Incarnation felt, Simon liked it.

Before, he'd felt as though the powers of Valinhall were flowing through him with the strength of a river. Now, it felt like a placid ocean. He could draw as much as he wanted, for as long as he wanted, and it would never run dry.

He never wanted the feeling to go away.

With Mithra's dull edge, he knocked the Lightning Spear out of Zakareth's hand. Immediately it spun away, hopefully over to Leah. The King struck out with his shield, intending to knock Simon backwards, but he caught the rim of the shield in one hand and tore it away, tossing it to the grass.

Andra shouted behind him, and it occurred to him that he should be back there.

His body moved as soon as he had the thought, and he was standing in front of Andra and Kathrin. They had already knocked the Ornheim Incarnation over onto his back, but he was still flailing around with a rocky hammer.

Simon brought Mithra forward, idly noting as he did so that the line of gold in her center had turned a bright, vivid white. He slid the Dragon's Fang in and out of Ornheim's head, as simply as slipping it into a pool of water.

The Incarnation fell apart.

Then Simon was moving again, over to Helgard, who still stood in the border of Elysia and the outside world. He struck at her, but his blow was turned by a staff of black ice. His blade sent a chip spinning off into the distance, and he attacked even faster than the bar could react, slashing at Helgard from the other side.

Then a *second* shaft of dark ice flew out of nowhere, blocking his other strike.

The two bars worked in unison, spinning with impossible speed and turning his every attack. No matter how fast he moved, it didn't matter; there was always one in the way. Helgard stood with both her blue-skinned hands out, her frozen eyes narrowed in concentration as she bent all her power to warding him off.

A red blade emerged from her stomach.

The two bars of ice quivered in the air for a moment, then fell to the ground. Helgard put two fingers to the blood on her stomach, then raised the fingers to her eyes.

"Fascinating," she murmured. Then she fell over.

Erastes pulled the crimson Ragnarus blade from the Incarnation's body and wiped it on the grass. "I knew I'd find a use for this," he said.

Simon laughed and ran out the Gate, chasing the final Incarnation.

Lirial was floating away as fast as she could, which wasn't nearly fast enough. He caught up with her in a handful of seconds, but she spun toward him and flared with white light.

His eyes felt like someone had stabbed them with steel picks, and he was flash-blinded, but that hardly made a difference.

Caela, he called.

I still want to know why you're not dead, she said. *Above you, and a little to the left.*

Simon leaped, Mithra spinning in his hands.

When he landed, the Lirial Incarnation followed him a second later. She hit the cobblestones in three pieces, each of which shattered like thin glass.

Those white chains look good on you, Caela observed. *You should keep them.*

I will if I can, Simon said. He'd found that power like this never lasted, but it would be nice if this was the exception.

When Simon returned to Elysia, King Zakareth was holding the crimson Ragnarus blade in both hands. Erastes had the good grace to look ashamed.

For someone facing down a growing half-circle of opponents, the King didn't look afraid. Andra, Kathrin, Erastes, Shai—wait a minute, was she an Elysian Traveler now? It looked like she was using one of Alin's powers—Ilana, and Leah stood facing the Ragnarus Incarnation, each of them brandishing their weapons.

Simon stepped out, Mithra held loosely in one hand.

"Seal yourself in the Vault," Simon said. There was no sense in making it any more complicated than it had to be. "If you do, I'll let you go."

Zakareth looked over to Leah. "Remember this, Leah. This is exactly why you save up power for emergencies."

With his spare hand, he reached up and grabbed the huge ruby at the center of his breastplate.

Then he crushed it in his fist.

Crimson light flowed like blood from the center of the breastplate, highlighting each plate in the armor. All of the rubies he wore started to glow like stars, and even the fire in his left eye socket flared. He lifted the Ragnarus blade.

Erastes! Caela cried. *Simon, he's going for Erastes!*

With all the speed he could draw, Simon hurled himself toward Erastes, even though he didn't see how the King could possibly get there before him.

One instant, King Zakareth was standing on the ground ten paces away, and then he was lunging straight at Erastes' chest. Simon got there in time, turning the red blade with Mithra's edge.

Alin's sister!

Which one? Simon screamed in his mind, but Caela didn't know their names, so he dashed toward Shai. This time, he'd guessed right. He managed to catch this blow on Mithra, but it took both hands. Zakareth struck with so much force that Simon felt his feet being driven down into the soil.

"This is the power that the blood of thousands will buy you," King Zakareth remarked.

Then the King was gone again, and Simon had to follow, desperately hoping his increased power would last longer than the Ragnarus Incarnation's.

Leah almost threw the Lightning Spear, but Murin screamed in her ear. Her mental projection—that throwing the Spear would be a bad idea—seemed unnecessary considering the bird's sheer volume.

Mentally, Leah ran down a list of her options, which was depressingly short.

Until she got to the final item on her list: her last resort. Which now seemed much more appealing than it had before.

Leah hurried out of the Elysian Gate, pulling the Seed out of her pocket as she ran.

Bare patches of earth were easy to find, considering the way the street had been torn up in the battle. Even the layer of frost created by the Helgard Incarnation had been shattered in most places.

Strangely, she was having trouble finding a blade. She would need to spill blood for this to work, and—though she bled from a thousand tiny cuts—she had to make sure that she gave it enough.

It took her a moment to think of a blade from Ragnarus that wouldn't do something horrible to her with a simple cut. At last, it occurred to her: the Whispering Blade. It was a long dagger made to cut through manifestations of Traveler powers that were normally insubstantial, but it was still a dagger. It would cut her hand well enough.

Leah hurriedly scooped dirt away in a shallow hold, shoving the seed down inside. Then she drew the Whispering Blade across her left palm.

True to its name, the weapon seemed to murmur in her ear as it cut. Then she bled freely down onto the soil.

How long will this take? she thought, as she banished the Blade.

Then a red tendril burst from the soil and wrapped around her bleeding hand.

She could feel the blood leaving her, which was an even stranger and more nauseating sensation than the pain. Her hand grew cold, then her arm, and she managed to pull away before she lost too much blood.

With the newborn Hanging Tree snatching at her heels—and still growing at an alarming rate, pushing soil aside to make room for its roots—she stumbled back into Elysia. The crimson branches waved at the

Gate, unable to cross the portal.

Good. She had thought, staring at the Seed with her Eye of Ages, that it had to be planted in the Unnamed World. It was nice to see she had guessed correctly.

Now all they had to do was get her father outside.

Simon had the advantage of reach, and he was still stronger and faster, even considering the King's enhanced armor. He should have been able to cut Zakareth down.

But every time he got an inch of space, the Ragnarus Incarnation struck at someone else. They were all doing their best to resist—Ilana and Kathrin fired supernatural arrows at the King, and the others tried to hold him off with their blades—but Simon and Zakareth were operating on a level beyond them, now. When the King changed direction to attack Andra or Shai or any of the others, Simon had no choice but to turn aside and stop him.

Which meant, essentially, that he was letting his opponent dictate the fight. Chaka would have killed him.

Worse yet, he could feel the White Light leaking out of him. It had lasted much longer than he thought it would, doing more for him than he could believe, but he could feel that he was reaching the end of his new-found strength and speed. When he did, he suspected the mask would take its toll.

And at that point, one way or another, he would die.

"I'll give you Indirial's job," Zakareth said conversationally, as he ducked under a sweep of Mithra and drove his red-bladed sword at Ilana's ribs. Simon summoned a second blade from Valinhall in time to parry, knocking the crimson point away from Ilana.

"We could pull down Elysia," the King continued. "We don't need them to rule over us, especially not with Valinhall to deal with the Incarnations."

"Stop...talking!" Simon shouted, kicking the King in his breastplate and knocking him three paces backwards. Maker, but he *hated* it when people tried to talk to him instead of fighting.

The King stood with his back to the Elysian Gate…which, Simon noticed for the first time, was filled with thousands of waving, flailing branches.

Leah.

The Lightning Spear blasted toward King Zakareth from the side, intended to knock the Ragnarus Incarnation out of the Gate at an angle.

For a brief, frozen instant, Simon thought it was going to work.

Then Zakareth snatched the Spear out of the air, turning it as if to examine the blade. "I have a lot to teach you, Leah," he said. "Using my own weapons against—"

Simon dashed forward and kicked the former King of Damasca in the chest. The Incarnation staggered backwards, his elbow peeking out of the Territory. The Hanging Tree took advantage of the gap, swarming over him and grabbing his arm, yanking him backwards and devouring him in a flurry of crimson branches.

Maybe that would teach him not to talk in the middle of a fight.

Zakareth thrashed and fought for a few seconds, then the bright red light of his armor faded. His struggles weakened, and the Tree raised him into the air, preparing to swallow him.

Even now, the King didn't look surprised or defeated. He stared Simon down with utter confidence plain on his fate. "Maybe it will take three hundred years," he announced. "Maybe a thousand. But I will return. What about you, Simon, son of Kalman? You've used great power today. What price will you have to pay, Valinhall Traveler?"

Leah stepped up beside Simon, watching King Zakareth with her father's eye.

"I've been told it's a fate worse than death, for a Ragnarus Incarnation to be sealed beneath a Hanging Tree," Leah said quietly. She was holding Caela, for some reason, and the doll looked upon the King with a smug expression.

"Perhaps we should show mercy," Leah said.

Simon looked at the Queen of Damasca. "Is that an order?" he asked.

"A favor," she said quietly.

The Tree had begun to swallow King Zakareth into the earth, but Simon stepped forward, Mithra flashing in his hand as he cut down every single branch in his way.

"So," Zakareth said. "She gets you to do—"

Simon cut his head off.

Chapter 28
REWARDS

359TH Year of the Damascan Calendar
1ST Year in the Reign of Queen Leah I
15 Days Since Spring's Birth

"I've heard reports that you were present at the Battle of Enosh," Leah said, leaning back in her chair. "They say you rallied the troops and led the victory, once we had taken care of the Incarnations."

Overlord Feiora Torannus sat across the desk, her arms folded and her jaw set. "I don't think I had to take a single Damascan life. They were more than ready to surrender once the Ragnarus Incarnation left. Besides, I'd been looking for you for days, so as soon as I found out you were in Enosh, I naturally headed straight there. It's not *my* fault I ended up in the middle of a battle."

Implying that it *was* Leah's fault. There was no complimenting this woman.

"Be that as it may, the fact remains that you have given excellent service to the throne this past few weeks. I am inclined to grant you a favor."

Feiora scratched her chin. "Well, I could use a little more land…"

An awkward pause stretched the seconds between them.

"That's an…unconventional request," Leah said at last.

The Overlord cleared her throat. "It was a joke."

"Ah."

Silence.

After a few seconds, both of their ravens each gave a loud *caw*.

Leah decided to move on. "Your brother tried to kill me," she said. "But given that it was an incompetent attempt, and considering the service you have rendered me personally and the Damascan cause as a whole, I have decided to remand him to your guardianship. Please, keep him out of trouble."

Feiora sighed. "I'll try."

"If he does anything else remotely traitorous, I'll have him executed on the spot."

"He's an idiot," the Overlord said. "I understand. I'll keep him in Avernus, for the time being. Maybe he'll learn some patience…or at least some better assassination techniques."

This time, Leah gave a little laugh. "He literally *threw birds* at me. I've felt more threatened by an unruly horse."

The Overlord hesitated, shifting in her chair. That caught Leah's attention. Any display of discomfort was unlike Feiora, who usually walked around as if she intended to march straight through anything in her way. If she had something that distressing on her mind, Leah only hoped it didn't have apocalyptic consequences.

"I…used to be…working against you," she admitted at last. "I was staying at your camp, trying to follow you around so that I could find a chink in your armor. I wanted to rally the other Overlords against you, so that I could bring you down and force you to release Lysander."

Leah wanted to be shocked by what was, essentially, an admission of treason by one of the Kingdom's highest officials. But she simply wasn't surprised.

"Why didn't you?" she asked.

"Given the way things went…" Feiora shrugged. "There was too much at stake. I couldn't risk the nation to get back at you."

If Leah had been blessed with a brother or a sister who had understood that, she would never have been Queen. "You'd be surprised how many people wouldn't even think it through that far," Leah said dryly.

"I deserve exile," Feiora said. "But, given my service, if you could find it in your heart to simply demote me instead…"

Leah sighed. "Did you actually talk with any of the other Overlords about a rebellion?"

She shook her head. "Just a mocking remark every now and again."

"I can live with that. At this time, I don't find that any disciplinary action is necessary." Leah stared across the desk, taking advantage of her bright red eye to make the Overlord uncomfortable. "But, Feiora? Don't do it again."

Feiora nodded sharply, and even leaned forward in the suggestion of a seated bow. "Thank you, Your Highness." Then she whispered something to her raven, Eugan. The bird let out a *mewl* in response. "There is something else," Feiora admitted. "Without him, I would never have been able to rally the Enosh Travelers. He managed to get an entire squad of Damascan Tartarus Travelers to surrender without killing any of them, which was the single most impressive achievement I've ever personally witnessed. If it weren't for him, I might have had to kill a lot of Damascans."

Some of the reports had mentioned a young Traveler from Enosh who had helped Overlord Feiora win his people over. Whoever it was, Leah looked forward to meeting him.

"Send him in," she said.

"Come on in, Gilad," Feiora called. A young man shuffled in, perhaps as old as twenty. He held his hand down and his hands in his pockets—not at all the confident strut she normally associated with genius Travelers. At first, she wondered if this was the right person.

"Gilad, let me introduce Queen Leah the First, of Damasca."

He went clumsily to one knee, but his eyes widened as he looked up and saw Leah. "I know you! Er, at least, I thought I did. I didn't know you were the Queen, I'm sorry."

Leah's mind was completely blank. "I apologize. Have we met before?"

Gilad frowned. "I *think* so, but you weren't the Queen then. Or I didn't know it. You were coming from the village of Myria, right? You stayed in Enosh for a while. I think Eliadel rescued you, or something."

That was her, but she wouldn't remember this boy if he had offered her another crown. "I'm sorry, perhaps I simply don't recall. In any case, I've heard you did a great service for both my people and your own. Is there anything I can offer you in return?"

This time, Gilad met her eyes more boldly. "Don't burn my city down, ma'am."

Leah gave him what she hoped was a reassuring smile. "I'll see what I can do."

Simon had never attended an official Damascan awards ceremony before. He desperately hoped he never had to do so again.

The first hour wasn't so bad. Leah stood next to the entire Agnos family, Erastes, and Denner—Kathrin had disappeared after the battle in Elysia, and no one knew how to contact her. Leah had provided them matching uniforms: crisp black trimmed with silver thread. A silver badge over the heart showed the emblem of Valinhall, which she claimed to have designed herself: a Dragon's Fang, point-up, wrapped in chains.

Standing there in his clean new clothes, standing next to others in the same uniform, Simon felt like a real, official Traveler for the first time.

Then the second hour crawled on. Each of the Overlords made speeches. Indirial's wife emerged from Valinhall to deliver one on behalf of the Overlord of Cana, who couldn't make it due to 'binding personal issues,' which was apparently court-speak for being sealed in his own Territory.

By the time the third hour began, Simon was *still* standing. Andra had fallen asleep on her feet, snoring quietly, and Lycus shifted from foot to foot, clearly longing to sit down, and just as clearly determined to remain upright.

But that wasn't the worst part. The worst came when all the Overlords had finished speaking, and Leah called on him to make his speech.

She looked regal, as well she might considering that she was sitting there on a throne. The ruby-and-gold seat had been hauled out of the ruins of the main palace and relocated here, a separate building on palace grounds that had miraculously escaped destruction.

Leah rested on the throne, looking perfectly comfortable on top of a block of solid ruby. Her dress was long, red, and pristine, trimmed in thread-of-gold. She wore the same silver chain and white stone on her left wrist, and in her right hand she held the Lightning Spear like a scepter. The silver circlet on her head gleamed a strange red, as though it were always reflecting a red light, but her most commanding features were by far her eyes. Her right eye was the bright blue of the Damascan royal family. Her left, a blazing crimson stone.

When she turned that gaze on him and told him it was time for him to speak, a sick feeling grew in his stomach. Though, to be perfectly honest, that might not have had anything to do with her Ragnarus eye.

Simon made his way up to the podium next to the throne, where everyone else had made their speeches. They had practiced this. He would be fine.

Woodenly, he recited his speech.

"I, Simon, son of Kalman, accept the burden of Valinhall's leader. On behalf of all Valinhall Travelers present and future, I commit my Territory to the service of Damasca, and pledge my sword in defense of the ruling monarch and the nation." As if he were about to take a plunge into icy water, he took a deep breath and forged ahead. "As the primary duty of Valinhall, I hereby agree to supervise the Incarnations of all eleven Territories, taking action when and if my Queen decrees them an issue of the nation's safety."

That created a buzz. He'd heard from Leah that no one knew how she was planning on handling the Incarnations now that the Hanging Trees were destroyed, and it had been a source of much speculation. Handing the job over to a new, mysterious Territory must have created quite an impression.

"On behalf of the Damascan crown, I accept your service," Leah said. Then she departed from the script. "As a token of which service, I ask you to receive these symbolic cloaks representing your new office."

A train of servants appeared from behind the throne, each carrying a folded black cloak. Simon had wondered why she insisted that he wear his cloak over the uniform; he had assumed she wanted him to look more like Indirial. Now it made sense.

The Eldest is going to kill us all for this, Simon thought, but he had to accept. The Nye were going to think these 'fake' cloaks were mocking them, since most of the people wearing them wouldn't actually have access to the Nye essence. Maybe they could get away with only wearing them outside the House.

"And on a more personal note, I'd like to address the absence of Overlord Indirial," Leah said, still ignoring the lines they'd practiced. "Due to his…binding personal responsibilities…he will be away from the capital for the foreseeable future. He will still be able to oversee the day-to-day management of his realm from within Valinhall, but he has left another vacancy that must be filled."

She smiled straight at Simon, and he had a moment of panic. "I need a bodyguard."

Simon had fallen off cliffs and walked away feeling less stunned. "I… you…I have many other responsibilities, uh, Your Highness."

Leah adopted a regretful look. "That's too bad, since I expect my safety will be seriously threatened over the next few years. I already have guards for my day-to-day activities, but who else would you recommend to oversee my security on missions involving great personal risk?"

Simon struggled with that for a moment, glad for once that he didn't have a doll with him. Finally, he snapped his heels together and swept a bow that would have done Indirial proud.

"I would be honored to accept the position of your personal protector, Your Highness."

Leah's smile widened, and she nodded graciously. The room burst into spontaneous applause, and Andra looked like she would choke herself laughing.

"Stand behind me," Leah whispered, so softly that only he could hear it over the applause. He took up a position behind the throne as if it was his idea, and tried to look intimidating instead of bored.

"I realize not all of you here today are Travelers," Leah went on. "However, I trust the impact of my next announcement will not escape you."

Simon perked up. They had practiced this, but he was still looking forward to it.

Leah nodded to a teenage girl sitting on a nearby bench. "The City of Light, Elysia, is now accepting students."

Shai stood, in her own white-and-gold uniform. She executed a bow that was much better than most of what Simon could manage, and stepped forward. Then, in the full view of the whole room, she tore open a Gate to Elysia.

She had angled the Gate so that Leah could see inside, for which Simon was grateful, because otherwise he would have been staring at the featureless back of a portal.

Alin stood inside on the Elysian fields, and Rhalia drifted next to him. His golden armor had been repaired, and he already looked much less like an Incarnation. His skin was still a little pale, and his eyes still looked like rainbows, but at least they didn't glow.

And he was smiling.

"Lords and ladies of Damasca," Alin said, "welcome to the City of Light."

He got a much warmer round of applause than Simon had.

"In the past, I have been your enemy," Alin confessed. "I have hated you, and set myself against you, and even tried to destroy you. I tell you all that to show you that I am now as sincere as I have ever been in my life. We in Elysia are now taking students. We will train students from Damasca, from Enosh, from the villages, from the Western Isles…anyone, of any age, may be tested. For we seek to build a force of Travelers that benefits not only Damasca, but all of mankind."

He sketched a bow—*How does everyone get so good at bowing? Do they practice?*—and turned to Rhalia.

She smiled at everyone before she began to speak. "There were a few bloodlines that produced natural Elysian Travelers, but in the old days, most Travelers of Elysia were trained. With the permission of the Damascan throne, we would like you to send volunteers for testing. In the City of Light, all are welcome."

Leah applauded, and everyone else followed suit, if with a great deal of whispering among themselves. They'd do it eventually, though. Elysia had a reputation as the most powerful Territory, and the opportunity to get involved with the founding of a new Territory—or the re-founding of an old one—was too tempting for most people.

Looking at Leah's smile, Simon couldn't help but think, *I doubt she cares much for all of mankind, but she definitely sees some benefit for Damasca.*

Not that he blamed her. He wasn't sure how he felt about more potential Elysian Incarnations running around.

It was another two hours before Simon was allowed to go home.

As he placed Mithra on her rack in the entry hall, Simon realized that there was a girl he didn't know standing in the hall, looking up at Vasha. She had pale skin and short blond hair, and she looked eighteen or nineteen, at most. She turned, slightly, and Simon realized where he'd seen her before.

"You're…Indirial's daughter, right?"

She got the rest of her coloring from her mother, but she had her father's eyes.

"Elaina," she said. Then she pointed up to Vasha. "My father has the strength to swing this with one hand."

"He does," Simon said warily.

"That's a power he earned in Valinhall."

"Yes…"

She turned a confident smile on him. "So when do I learn that?"

Simon begged off for the moment, pleading exhaustion, but he had to promise tutoring later. She didn't seem interested in any explanation that the Fang itself would have to approve of her, and that it would probably take months of training before she could lift a blade of Vasha's size.

At last, he made it back to his bedroom.

The thirteenth bedroom, the room Valin had built for himself, was certainly…big. The bed was twice the size of Kai's, and all the furnishings were trimmed in gold. It even had a little door that stepped into a private outhouse, though Simon found himself wondering if the hole simply emptied into an infinite abyss.

But there were no shelves. No dolls. No one whispering at all hours of the night, keeping him awake.

He couldn't stand it.

Today, though, he was tired enough that he didn't let it bother him. Simon tossed himself on to the bed, lying fully clothed on the blankets while staring up at the ceiling. It wasn't long before he fell asleep.

He woke to something tickling his face, and he swatted his own nose out of reflex before it occurred to him to open his eyes.

Curly blond hair and a blue bonnet filled his vision, along with a painted wooden frown. Caela stood over him, her hands on her hips, expression disapproving.

It's your first day of three *new jobs, and you decide to sleep?*

Caela, he sent. *I didn't think…*

She waved a hand through the air, which was the most motion he'd seen from a doll since Kai's death. *Advising the bearer of Azura is more of a career than a necessity. I can speak with whomever I wish, and there are plenty of my sisters around. I think I'll allow you to carry me a little while longer.*

Simon's spirits lifted, and he couldn't stop a smile. *I'd like that,* he said.

She scowled at him again and kicked his shoulder. *Then you'd better get to work!*

The Eldest materialized out of shadow next to the bed, which was a much less pleasant surprise. His voice scraped out of an unseen throat. "She's right," he said. "You foolishly accepted the positions of royal protector and custodian of the Incarnations, when you already must see to your responsibilities as Founder of Valinhall."

"I will begin my search for the lost Fangs tomorrow," Simon promised. "It's the first thing I'll do."

The Nye shook his hood. "No," he said. "I have another job for you. You recently met the last soldier of the Dragon Army, the one who has all but abandoned her Territory. She did not aid us when the Incarnation was freed, nor when the House was attacked by foreign forces. Yet she still holds her Dragon's Fang. If she does not return to her duties as a Traveler, then she should relinquish her blade to someone else who can use it."

"Why does it matter?" Simon asked. "Kai barely did anything when he was here. Kathrin's still a Valinhall Traveler, so she can do what she wants."

The Eldest chuckled. "You understand nothing. A bond to this Territory works both ways. If she wishes to enjoy Valinhall's powers, then she must pay her debts."

"Who says?"

The Nye bowed. "You, Master."

He tried to think of a way out, but the Eldest had a point. If he was going to act like the Founder of Valinhall, he might as well start now.

Simon sighed and rolled out of bed. "I'll get my cloak."

THE END OF THE TRAVELER'S GATE TRILOGY

COMING THIS FALL

A NEW SERIES!

BOOK ONE OF SOME NEW SERIES

Available Autumn 2014

Also, check out Will's website for book updates, news,
occasional fiction, and the Antidote.

www.WillWight.com

Twitter.com/WillWight

DON'T WORRY:

The Traveler's Gate Universe will return!

... Eventually.

WILL WIGHT is the author of the Traveler's Gate Trilogy, and he has dominion over all sea creatures. He began the Traveler's Gate Trilogy when he was 23 years old, and plans on living to at least 200. Under the light of a full moon, he is revealed as a sentient penguin.

Will graduated from the University of Central Florida with his Master's of Fine Arts in Creative Writing. He still lives in Orlando, and he can smell fear.

Visit his website at *www.WillWight.com* for dark secrets the world was not meant to know.

If you'd like to contact him, send him an email at *will@willwight.com*, or else just turn around. He's behind you.

(All books guaranteed 100% asbestos-free!)

Printed in Great Britain
by Amazon.co.uk, Ltd.,
Marston Gate.